Russia Container

THE GERMAN LIST

Alexander Kluge
Drilling through Hard Boards
133 Political Stories
Translated by Wieland Hoban

Alexander Kluge
30 April 1945
The Day Hitler Shot Himself and Germany's Integration with the West Began
Translated by Wieland Hoban

Alexander Kluge
Air Raid
On Halberstadt on 8 April 1945
Translated by Martin Chalmers

Alexander Kluge, Gerhard Richter
Dispatches from Moments of Calm
89 Stories, 64 Pictures
Translated by Nathaniel McBride

Alexander Kluge, Gerhard Richter
December
39 Stories, 39 Pictures
Translated by Martin Chalmers

Alexander Kluge
The Labyrinth of Tender Force
Translated by Wieland Hoban

Alexander Kluge
Anyone Who Utters a Consoling Word is a Traitor
Translated by Alta Price

Alexander Kluge
Kong's Finest Hour: A Chronicle of Connections
Translated by Cyrus Shahan, Kai-Uwe Werbeck,
Susanne Gomoloch, Emma Woelk, Martin Brady,
Helen Hughes and Robert Blankenship

Russia Container

ALEXANDER KLUGE

IN COLLABORATION WITH THOMAS COMBRINK

TRANSLATED BY ALEXANDER BOOTH

LONDON NEW YORK CALCUTTA

This publication was supported by a grant from the Goethe-Institut, India.

GENERAL EDITOR OF THE 'CHRONICLE OF EMOTIONS' SERIES
Richard Langston

Seagull Books, 2022

Originally published as Alexander Kluge, *Russland-Kontainer*
© Suhrkamp Verlag, Berlin, 2020
All rights reserved and controlled through Suhrkamp Verlag, Berlin

First published in English by Seagull Books, 2022

English translation © Alexander Booth, 2022

ISBN   978 1 8030 9 065 8

British Library Cataloguing-in-Publication Data
A catalogue record for this book is available from the British Library

Typeset by Seagull Books, Calcutta, India
Printed and bound by Hyam Enterprises, Calcutta, India

For My English-Speaking Readers

East European refugees in 1857, outside New York. One year after the end of the Crimean War. They are coming from Russia; from areas which are today part of Ukraine; and from Galicia, which was then part of Austria-Hungary. They could not imagine a NATO border east of Kharkov. They are full of hope. At home, everything is poor; to them, the West seems rich.

ALUMINIUM PRINT WITH 'ELEPHANT SKIN' BY ANSELM KIEFER
(Courtesy: Galerie Knust Kunz, Munich)

Diary | Thursday, 24 February 2022

Early this morning my wife came into my study: Russian tanks have invaded Ukraine. Yesterday I received the final version of the English translation of this book from Naveen Kishore, my publisher in Calcutta. The war changes all perspectives. There's an elephant in the room.

'No man has received from nature the right to command others'—Diderot.

Diary | Thursday, 24 February 2022, Evening

I am reading through the *Lichtenberg Figures* by my friend from New York, Ben Lerner. The poems refer to the physicist and philosopher Georg Christoph Lichtenberg, one of the beacons of the Enlightenment in the eighteenth century. He was fascinated by the then-still-invisible power of electricity. Like Benjamin Franklin, he experimented with lightning. It is unusual for an American poet like Lerner to dedicate poems to such a mind.

One of the lines reads: 'and the snow refused the ground'. That would be the *inversion of the arrow of time*. I wish such a reversal of the arrow of time (which does not exist in the world of physics, but does in the world of desires and quanta) would be possible with wars: that one could turn back time to the moment before the demon of war's beginning.

Another one of the sequences says:

I invite you to think creatively about politics in the age of histamine. / I invite you to think creatively about politics [. . .] // tonight's weather has been canceled. [. . .] / It is the Sabbath. I must invite you // to lay down your knowledge claims, / to lay them down slowly and with great sadness. // [. . .] Given men as they are, the trees surrender.

Diary | Saturday, 26 February 2022

On p. 163 of *Russia Container* there is the story 'There Was Something Impractical about the Empire's Collapse'. It refers to the end of perestroika and the disintegration of the Soviet Union after Mikhail Gorbachev resigned. I can still see the black limousines with Gorbachev driving to the airport in Reykjavík a short time before. The conference with President Reagan, in which Gorbachev wanted to persuade him to abandon the armament plans for Star Wars, had failed. Then, after all, there was disarmament on both sides. We are leagues away from that moment of hope and peace. The story in my book has to do with the then Secretary of State James Baker III's trip to Russia in 1991, the year the Soviet empire fell apart:

Like a trustee in bankruptcy, anxious to find a balance, without a formal mandate, representing a foreign super-power, he visited the decision-making centres, talked to the decision makers (competencies quickly changed). With a good power of recall, with an innate power of observation.

Concentrated in the staff building of the chief of staff of the Red Army. He forbade himself any coups. He did not favour any of the sides. The giant country's functionaries sat restlessly within their enclosures. Baker, the American attorney, watched the collapse of a great power with stunned eyes. While holding court in this way, he grew in power, plain power. He recorded the empire's line of successions like the head of a land-registry office or a notary.

Over a nightcap in the stale air of a hotel that no longer belonged to the central office, hesitating like a teetotaller sipping whisky, unable to say goodbye quickly to the day's excitement, James Baker said to the now irrelevant staff waiting around them: we've got to draw the right conclusions from the humiliation of the German Empire and Austria-Hungary after 1918. Baker had taken a semester of history during his law studies. The new Russia should not be humiliated.

But Baker was not worried about this dossier on Russia's present; he was more concerned about the younger generation of officers who had just graduated from the military academies. Similar to the Black Reichswehr in Germany after 1918, if the implosion of the empire were perceived as a humiliation, a defeat, there would be a conspiracy of officers in Russia. In the GRU, in the navy, in the armies, in the military-industrial complex. A network of determined people is enough to contaminate the whole country. The year 1991 will be forgotten in the US by the time the seeds of that day's vows of revenge come to light.

Finally tired and relaxed, Baker informed his now irrelevant panel that a submarine and four frigates from the Soviet Union's mighty fleet had been assigned to the Republic of Kyrgyzstan. But the only lake that Kyrgyzstan had was 14 miles long. None of those responsible considered this to be a joke, but a fact. Sad news. There is, Baker said wearily, something impractical in this superpower's implosion.

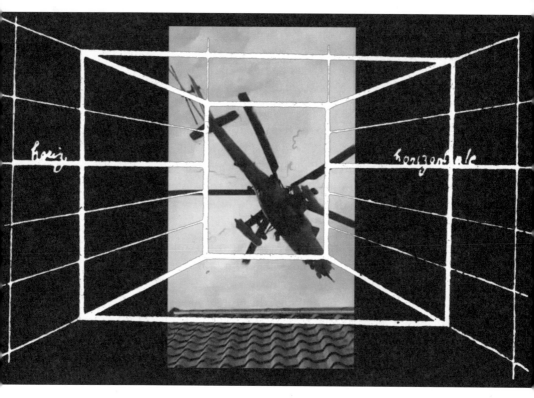

ABOVE. Russian attack helicopter above the rooftops of a Ukrainian city.

BELOW. A madman in the surgery.

Diary | Saturday, 2 March 2022

The Russians lay siege to the coastal city of Mariupol. While they are still winning, they have already lost the war. They cannot win the security architecture they demand, in which they seek their place through conquest, without recognition by the western side. They are moving away from that by going on the offensive. There are indications that they know this themselves.

The press reports that, in a locality of Ukraine, civilians confronted a tank. The Russian put his tank in reverse. There were similar scenes during the coup in Moscow in 1991. There are always two solutions to just such a 'knot': the brave civilians, but the teenage tanker who puts his tank in reverse as well.

On 11 April 1945, GIs marched down the Braunschweiger Chaussee into my hometown of Halberstadt. 'Spring with white flags'. I was 13 years old. Four days earlier, my city had been bombed and consumed by a firestorm. Now I was *happy* about the white flags. They meant: the end of the war.

Frau Anna Wilde in Halberstadt, mother of five, bombed out of her home, refugee, sheltering in a cave in the Harz mountains, said in April 1945: 'Once you've reached a certain point of misery, it doesn't matter who caused it. It just has to stop.'

The US, in any event, did not win over the people of Central Europe and thus secure peace through the surrender of the German Reich. It did so through the Marshall Plan. Clausewitz's *ON WAR* (in Colonel J. J. Graham's translation) has the following to say: 'War is an act of violence [. . .] intended to compel our opponent to fulfil our will.' At another point in the same book it says analogously that peace is an act of *generosity*. A piece of the opponent's identity and willpower is restored, and, in this way, peace established. This requires the accurate perception of the enemy. The more hostile an enemy is, the more precisely one must try to study their particularities.

A destroyed road in Ukraine. 'A confused whirl of causalties'.

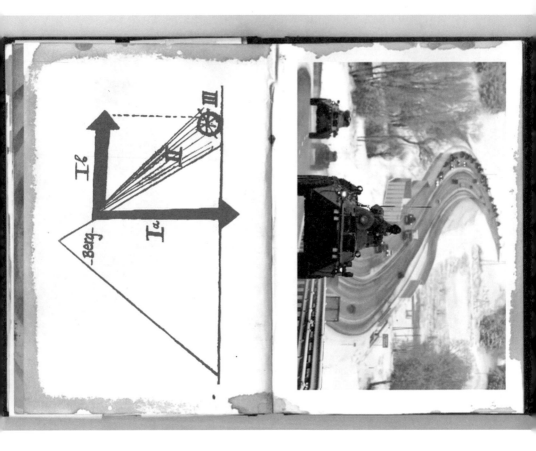

From the book *THE SEPARATRIX PROJECT* that I am working on at present
with the artist Katharina Gross. 'Separatrix' is a term from G. W. Leibniz
and concerns the interface between two irreconcilable opposites. At this very
interface, Leibniz says, tiny, 'infinitesimal' ambassadors of the one arise in the
other, and vice versa. If one believes that opposites simply oppose each other,
he continues, one has observed wrongly.

Diary | Thursday, 3 March 2022

Page 71 and then pages 133–9 of this book have to do with a project Franz Kafka had for a novel—a project he worked on for six weeks in 1916, before once again abandoning it. He wanted to describe Napoleon's retreat in the winter of 1812 (see Figures 48–54). It was supposed to be a serialized novel for a daily newspaper, a bestseller. At that point in Prague, where Kafka is writing, and in Germany, in whose language he writes, there was a general hatred towards every-thing French. Kafka writes anti-cyclically. He focuses his *objectivity* and *empathy* onto the feet of the French grenadiere, who, after the fiasco of the Russian campaign, are marching the long distance back, through ice and misery. They are not marching on a general staff map at a ratio of 1:300,000, across which the commander's fingers roam. The feet, Kafka says, are walking across a map at a 1:1 ratio. Step by step, through mud and ice, from Moscow to Paris. The vast-ness of the land: horrific. This is concretion. Napoleon's map, but those of the Russian generals too, remains abstract.

Diary | Friday, 4 March 2022

Chapter 3, THE PLUNDERER'S EYE TURNED TOWARDS THE MAP / 'THE PRINCIPLE OF ABSTRACTION', has to do with Halford Mackinder, a British geopolitician who in 1904 developed his so-called heartland theory. In the view of this 'imperial theoreti-cian', the north of Russia contained the pivot of the world. And it is from this 'heartland', the deserts of the earth and the monsoon lands, that the future of the globe will emerge. This is one of the many fairy tales about Russia. In 1919, Mackinder is High Commissioner of Her Majesty in the south of Russia and establishes a number of secessionist republics. 'A Buzzard Sets Off from the Grid Map'. This predatory view of the geopolitician is the opposite of the poet Kafka's.

Chapter 2 shows the reader all that we don't know about that immense country to the east.

JUDGEMENT DAY'S HEARTLAND

The sun and everything that moves around it because of its gravity takes 225 million years to orbit the centre of the Milky Way MORE OR LESS HORIZONTALLY. Like a bouncing ball, the solar system periodically crosses the zero plane of the galaxy. It shoots rapidly, once every 32 million years, through the gravitational field that is at its densest precisely at this zero plane. But what remained unknown to Soviet science and became clear only in the conversation between astronomer Karina Sedova and astrophysicist Lisa Randall: while on this VERTICAL BOUNCING TRACK, our globe and therewith almost one-fifth of the earth, 'our Russia', crosses through a narrow slice of highly concentrated DARK MATTER.

What's the result? The sudden gravitational shock during the sun's passage through the disk 'combs' Oort cloud, where the primordial rocks, the comets from primeval times—all residual matter that did not become moons and planets—move chaotically and stationary around the sun. [. . .] The probability is great, Ms Sedova reports. In fact, it is an absolute certainty that these FLYING BODIES, pushed by the gravity cloud of dark matter, will bring collective death in their wake.

— 64 or 65 million years ago everything turned out OK with the Yucatan catastrophe. Why won't it work out this time?
— It turned out OK for the frogs and the turtles. Our civilization won't survive it.

A Message of the Shortest Times

The time required for a message as measured by the spark in the brain of a political decision-maker who—frustrated, exhausted, outside his mental horizons, driven by the randomness of the forces of his soul—decides to trigger nuclear war is long. It only takes a few minutes, however, for his decision to reach the working staff that will execute the order, checking and ticking off the control form to verify it a few more times. Typing the commands: 77 seconds. Execution: automatic. The apparatus does not tolerate any delay. The premature invocation of the day of judgement, as described here, takes a minimal amount of time. If one could practise it, it would take even less.

The *Long* Time It Takes for a Historical Misfortune to Occur

The real time of an explosively worsening warlike situation, as what is happening in Ukraine, covers more than 100 years. Ever so slowly emerge the abstract resolutions, the main roads of history, the highway routes of error, the paths of hopelessness, the blocks of hatred. At first, they are not directed at a specific enemy. Historian Adam Tooze says they are like groundwater. But one could also say that such a 'torrent of events' is like falling rock: CRYSTALLINE, HARD AND OF UNUSUAL COLDNESS. As its particles are so old, the calamity has the consistency of an ICE RIVER. The older it is, the harder, the more unreal and more abstract.

Diary | Wednesday, 16 March 2022

I send my publisher in Calcutta this little address to my English-language readers: a 'reading aid', so to speak, for precipitating events. I feel strong emotion. For 'objectivity' (that of the 'independent spectator') I require more emotion than I do for empathy which arises on its own. The motto of this book is: 'I know that I know nothing.' This is the first step we all must take in order to learn something.

Contents

FIGURE 1. The author at work on the *Container*.

FIGURE 2. With the 35-mm Arriflex S120 Blimp camera.

OUT OF CURIOSITY, NOT DUTY (ONE OF THE DOCTRINES OF VIRTUE), COMES THE THIRST FOR KNOWLEDGE. AND TELLING STORIES. I BEGIN A STORY BEFORE I KNOW WHY.

I can attempt to approach everything that confuses me about my own country, and what I don't understand about my direct experience, by telling the story of a country with which I am unfamiliar. That was one of dramatist Heiner Müller's views. Russia was as much of a mystery to him as it is to me. There is, he said, a great riddle, and for us it lies to the East: a cabinet of curiosities that can teach us to spell out the following classical statement:

'I know that I know nothing.'

UTOPIA = 'NOWHERE'

During the heatwave of August 2018, my children are melting in Berlin. The city's stones trap the continental heat. My daughter is sitting in the cutting-room, editing her first full-length feature. (It is incomprehensible to me that I still use the same word—'child'— to refer to the baby who saw the light of day in 1983, barely five handbreadths long back then, the 1-metre-tall girl and now to the grown woman.) She and my son, who is two years younger, are listening to me hold forth on *literacy in Russia after 1917*. And on the beginnings of aviation in the young Soviet Union, Vera Schmidt's psychoanalytically oriented home-laboratorium for children, biocosmism and Alexander Bogdanov's novel *The Red Star* (*Красная звезда*). My children want to be kind to me, they don't want any misunderstandings to arise, they hope that soon I'll have talked myself out and will give up on the topic.

Do they know of a place on earth at our present moment in the twenty-first century where the 'new man' is being designed? I ask. A place where a NEW TIME is being cobbled together?

They don't answer because they aren't interested in any literacy campaigns, especially not one from a hundred years ago. Would it have been possible to open a successful marriage bureau between the German Reich and Red Russia in 1917? my daughter replies. I cannot answer her. Her question does not relate to my own perspective: Does a utopian horizon even exist in the second decade of the twenty-first century?

WHERE I AM WRITING

Opening the two windows to my attic room in Schloß Elmau, I see a series of majestic clouds framed in a 4:3 aspect ratio. White in the blue of the sky above deeply hued mountain woods.

Schloß Elmau opened in 1914. It's been in operation ever since. History serves as a measuring stick for every room. Here 'Russia 1917' means 'the house is three years old.' At that time, a depressive mood reigned in Germany. In Russia, the opposite was the case: a revolutionary administration, increasing goodwill being shown to the revolution, refugees, civil war—now, as then, such circumstances are foreign to the place where I am writing. There's just one solitary point of contact between the castle and the expanse of Russia: the time after 1941 when the owner's sons were killed in the East, transported back in wooden caskets and buried in a small hill next to the castle.

A STROKE OF LUCK FOR LIFE

Before my window, a female mosquito is dragging her batch of eggs. It's twice as large as the middle section of her body, which you could refer to as her 'stomach': the species-being's entire dowry, her entire future resides in the storage container, this 'large batch of eggs'. She's made it to a windowpane where it is impossible for her to unload her freight. No hiding place or storage area, no crevice or hollow. The slippery surface has disoriented her. Though pulling the heavy sac isn't a problem, she continues to move about hectically, spending her strength. At the pane of glass—an idea of progress created by human homebuilders that she is incapable of understanding—the mosquito loses her usual chance to decide which direction to take.

Proceeding downwards in accordance with gravity, together with the heavy future-oriented thing in tow, isn't a problem. But the fact that the see-through surface forecloses horizons in all directions, neither up nor down, confuses her senses. Minute after minute, she turns around in circles and moves diagonally. She has collected her strength for one whole summer. Everything within her 'wants' a hiding place for her treasure, the one she's pulling behind her, stuck to the end of her body like an oversized handcart: looking for a hollow, a hole, a crack in progress into which she can drop the thing. Then, this mother-mosquito will be able to die peacefully. The algorithm of a window pane doesn't take the animal's objective into consideration.

After a little while (an entire lifetime for the insect), I think, her powers will either be exhausted or she will die. Or be turned to stone out of despair. But later I see that both the larvae and the mother have fallen onto a roofing tile. And there she is able to happily stuff her eggs into a pipe from which then the larvae, glowing with energy, will hatch, in a kind of (anti-mechanical) counter-algorithm.

1

'ALL OF RUSSIA'S SOULS
POINT TO HEAVEN
WITH THEIR ROOTS'

russland00000

russland00001

russland00002

russland00005

russland00006

russland00009

russland00011

russland00012

FIGURE 3

russland00016

russland00023

russland00024

russland00025_teufel

russland00026

russland00027_z

russland00027haus

russland00029_z

FIGURE 4

'THE SOULS OF FALLEN TREES GROW TOO / ALONG WITH THE MOON AND ITS BELOVED STARS'

THE DEATH OF A THOUSAND SOULS

Up until his final moments, Modest Mussorgsky tried to write notations and move his heavy hands across the piano keys. Sometimes he was drunk even during the day. Trusted friends who took care of the genius lost respect for him. This was the state the master was in when he composed the final act of his opera *Khovanshchina*. Huge gaps remained in the scores of the other acts. Previously, all his sketches had been set to piano. Then he sank to death by drowning in a despair that no words could describe.

The outline for the fifth act has to do with the collective self-immolation of an Orthodox sect in Russia around the turbulent time of Peter the Great's coming to power. It was a question of the rites, which the religious group—considered rather fanatical—by no means wanted to see changed. And so, their leader arranged for this collective act of self-sacrifice. One of his confidants was his medium. Everyone trusted her, she could call them to action. She was a former sorceress and the jilted lover of a gang leader (the brother of the chief of Khovanshchina), an exploiter whom she nevertheless loved and had even managed (when the religious sect had taken him prisoner) to save by bringing him unscathed to the community's place of refuge, a patch of woods. Trees were cut down, logs stacked. There was a lot of dry brushwood and other highly flammable material for the auto-da-fé, for Russian wood with its fresh sap just isn't ideal for a self-immolation.

The tsar had made the practice of the Orthodox rite illegal. The sect remained obstinate. Were Russia ever to get closer to the West, the tsar and his advisors reasoned, an example would have to be made. Faith and ritual would have to be unified centrally and simplified so that Western visitors could understand. Whatever was

ABOVE and led to progress had to be hammered into the hearts of the people. But just such a 'heart' (made up of many thousands of souls and never precisely situated in bodies, perhaps only existing AS THE SPIRIT BETWEEN ALL PEOPLE) would not allow itself to be forced. The instrument for doing so has yet to be found. (Stone won't do, neither will a hammer, pestle or furnace.)

The tsar's troops had surrounded the wood. The sect's spies announced the arrival of the tsarist cavalry. That is when the sect leader's confidant (the medium) gave the sign. All the sticks adorned with flammable material were pulled from the bonfires and used to set the wood aflame. The Orthodox suffocate well before they burn. All of them die. Searching the area later, the tsar's soldiers, drilled to perfection by parades and military order, were perplexed.

A MODERN PUBLIC'S REACTION

Stravinsky translated this piece of the opera from Mussorgsky's piano notations into dramatic chords for choir and orchestra. Although nothing remotely similar had ever happened in the German city in which its premier would take place (not even in historically earlier times), the viewers of Stuttgart were shaken. Critic Wolfgang Schreiber wrote: there must, 'be something in memory that is not unique to distant Russia and that gives this music its power'. For more than three hours after the performance, not a single one of those involved could eat, not even in the middle of the night.

THE ALCHEMY OF POWER

In the wings of the opera house, the choristers are getting ready for their appearance in the final act of Mussorgsky's opera *Khovansh-china*. There are three separate groups. The streltsy choir (Tsar Ivan's firearm infantry units), the people's choir and the Orthodox choir. The latter are known as Raskolniki. They would rather die than change their ancestral beliefs.

Mussorgsky's operas (*Boris Godunov, Khovanshchina*) draw on events that lie more than three generations apart: a time without fixed rule (1); Ivan's—the first Tsar of Russia—coming to power (2); the time of False Dmitry, which led to the Polish occupation of Moscow (3); Peter the Great's takeover (4).

FIGURE 5. Tsar Ivan, caught in the trappings of Orthodoxy ('a book'). Presumed dead. One can see him peeking out of his prison. In the triptych, bottom left, the people kill the tsar's troops, the so-called streltsy.

A MESSAGE TO ALIENS

In the documentation attached to a space probe on behalf of the Russian Academy of Sciences—which we can assume will disappear in the expanse of the universe following the fulfilment of its duties—is written in Cyrillic and Latin scripts:

> This message comes from people from Russia—*Homo homo*—who belong to the species of primates, to the class of old-world monkeys, to the subclass of dry-nosed monkeys, from which we split off five million years ago. We are

descended from a small group in Africa, which was completely preserved in the Denisova hominins. Our language
was shaped by Alexander Pushkin, the descendent of a
North African slave.

87 signatures of the academy members.

A FALL INTO THE ABYSS OF STARS

The view into the sky from the southern half of the globe, in South
America's Atacama Desert or in South African and Australian observatories, provides a Very Large Telescope—but the trained eyes of
Russian astronomer Karina Sedova as well—a far richer panorama
of luminosity than any observation points in Russia's north. As a
student, Sedova completed her early years at the observatories in
the Caucuses before finding increasingly attractive her transfer to a
large telescope in the Republic of South Africa. Here, the astronomer looks 'down' directly into the centre of the Milky Way. At
one and the same time 'inwards' (as seen from the galactic system
that hosts us) and outwards: into an 'abyss' where we reckon with the
depth of the remote view and the fact that, from the surface of the
earth, we earthlings aren't looking so much *up* into the cosmos as
down into the expanse of the sky, which is in no way comparable to
the great vast of Russia whatsoever. If you fell towards the centre of
the galaxy from where one of the Very Large Telescopes is located,
you'd fall for thousands of years. And you would still not have
reached the edge of the interstellar dust clouds that prevent the
eye from seeing the streams of stars that rapidly orbit its centre. Or
that's what I think Sedova said.

A horrific idea: falling to earth from outer space. But imagine
the Russian cosmonaut during the time of perestroika who falls in
the other direction. After completing repairs on one of the robust,
Russian-built spacecrafts that orbit our planet, the cosmonaut slips
off the scaffolding, and the retaining cables holding him to the
spacecraft tear like an umbilical cord. And so he falls blindly towards
the next best (combined and still weak) gravitational force. Maybe,
after a little while, he sees auspicious Orion and the two bears,

Sedova says. Starving to death, dying of thirst. No radio, no rescue craft to guide or lead him home. Then this 'worker's wreckage' manages to reach the GREAT RIFT that divides our solar system from its neighboring three-star constellation. And finally, the experienced astronomer who is looking forward to her holidays in Murmansk and her warm, winterly lodgings there, tells me about how the poor man, together with his 'astronautical suit', dissolve into particles. An effect of cosmic radiation. The elements, the dust: once upon a time a cosmonaut. But then he will be accelerated by a new attractor: the Alpha Centauri star system. In a mathematical sense (if not our sense of direction that is used to solid ground), he will move 'upwards'. It will take another few millennia for the 'remainder falling upwards'—not even the mass of a fingerprint—to orbit one of the three neighbouring stars (which together make up Alpha Centauri). Of all the stars, the faint red dwarf there is the one that's closest to Russia in spirit.

KARINA SEDOVA AND THE FASTEST STAR IN OUR GALAXY

I had already completed my third interview with Sedova for the broadcast of my 'culture magazine' I produce for TV. Her German vocabulary was limited. She liked to string nouns together, a method of speech full of a particular expressive power. Blown out of the sentences, the verbs float freely in space. Then comes a smattering of technical terms in English and Russian. I treasure such talks conducted at the edges of comprehensibility, for they deliver such highly incisive measurements of how distant the realm of experience remains from the discussion at hand. It's unusual for TV, which is precisely why it appeals to young TV-users (which they gladly accept and even appreciate at such a late hour and under the pretext of a cultural show once they've grown used to it). It has to do with a so-called trap for channel surfers. When I'm tired of all the same-old same-old that has completely saturated my conscience and switch to something unfamiliar and new, a kind of 'residual secret' takes hold. In this respect, Ms Sedova's way of speaking struck me as 'entirely poetic'.

She spoke about the fate of a particular star, the implications of which she was using her computer to research. A binary star system had formed within the constellation of the shield between a HELIUM STAR—a so-called great dwarf (Сверхкарлик), a very old creature that had used up all its hydrogen supply—and a white dwarf (Белый карлик), an even older type of star in which matter is packed so tightly that the mass of our sun would take on the size of Earth. The two celestial bodies had circled each other on narrow orbits with a high degree of acceleration. As a result, a flood of helium flowed over to the gravitationally stronger white dwarf. In the meantime, these STRANGE LOVERS (странно любящиеся) had become so estranged from their original equilibrium, the one inundated by the other's matter, that the white dwarf—smaller in size though greater in mass—exploded. It disappeared (исчез). Its partner, the helium star, however, took on the lost star's (исчезнувшая звезда) angular momentum and speed. It became the quickest runner in our galaxy. The quick one ('беглянка') will grow lonely when it gets out (наружу). It is, Sedova added, so fast that it will have to leave the galaxy. Will it reach the Magellanic Clouds or will it be caught by another galaxy? 'Unlikely (невероятно),' the astronomer replied.

'ESSENTIALLY A STAR IS A TREMENDOUS ENERGY RESERVOIR THAT WILL DISAPPEAR AS SOON AS ITS MASS PERMITS IT . . . THE STARS WILL NOT BE ALLOWED TO GO ON LIKE THIS; THEY WILL BE TRANSFORMED INTO EFFICIENT HEATING MACHINES INSTEAD . . . '

HEINER MÜLLER

THE POLITICAL ECONOMY OF STARS

At the Writer's Conference in Bitterfeld, Heiner Müller's taking-to-task of young stars in the university for their wasteful energy consumption caused bad blood. Was it innuendo? Was it scorn? Cadres saw the performance as a parody of the socialist approach. Yet astrophysicists from the Academy of Sciences in Moscow—who had taken part in a parallel event in a neighbouring city and thereafter quickly come over to the final discussion of the poets' conference—stated: Yes, he was right, stars do lose economically uneven amounts of mass; almost like feudal lords who don't give a hoot about budgets; indeed, these lords (or the Roman emperors, if you like) solidified their power through public displays of wealth, caprice and waste. Part of the ruler's image, the historians added, had to do with legitimizing himself through wastefulness. They, too, had come over from a neighbouring conference.[1]

The engineers from Bitterfeld whose job it was to assist the poets' conference insisted that it should by no means be excluded—especially in view of the successes of the exemplary Soviet Union in the fields of space travel—that the mechanical control of suns, planets and ultimately the galaxy was a goal, and one that should not be barred from industrialized humankind.

A few of the cadres present knew from their reading of banned literature (samizdat) that Trotsky had written something similar in 1922. He had explained: instead of socialism in one's own country, directed as it was towards something impossible, the perspective of internationalism not only took the mastery of the earth into account, but also that of the stars, the momentary inhospitality of which had to be adapted to human needs and politically economized.

That 1922 conference—which had been attended by psychoanalysts, geologists and astrologists (a field to which numerous poets had strayed)—was similar to the one then underway at Bitterfeld.

---

1 The catering at such special conferences was excellent. The freedom for enjoyable arguments, however, was only at neighbouring conferences. Wherever they were not responsible themselves, the scholars or political heads could exercise freedom.

The cadres, animated as they were by the surprising course of the afternoon discussion, set about putting the brakes on it, however, for fear of getting into trouble with the party apparatus for straying into impassable terrain. As far as special requests were concerned, for more than five years Heiner Müller enjoyed no more leeway.

FIGURE 6

FIGURE 7

FIGURE 8 (ABOVE). An iron telephone. For communication inside the cosmodrome. Will be replaced by a digital device during the scheduled move from Baikonur to Amur Oblast.

FIGURE 9 (BELOW). Russia – Kazakhstan – Uzbekistan – Caspian Sea – Azerbaijan

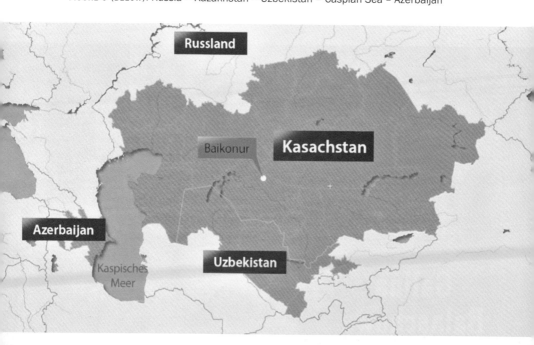

FIGURE 10 (ABOVE). A design by Galina Balashova for a room in the cosmonaut capsule. The hole in the floor leads to central command. The sofa connects Muscovite cosiness with the heavens. The chair on the left is foldable and at the same time functions as a toilet. Due to gravitational quirks, a solid, tube-like connection between one's anus and the 'storage container' is necessary.

FIGURE 11 (BELOW)

Galina
Balaschowa

CATS IN SPACE

It was at the time when space travel began. Outside Moscow, in one of the research centres of 'Star City'—surrounded by dachas, supplied with clinics, one of the most modern, scientific cities in the world—laboratories were busy examining the brains of cats. Compared to the brains of dogs, birds or crocodiles (the latter the link between birds and Sauria), as far as navigation is concerned, cats' nerve centres—especially those of a particular wild Siberian breed—were far superior. Their sense of equilibrium in zero gravity: superb. Their dexterity for operating the keys on a control mechanism (equivalent to their speed of attack when hunting small animals): exceptional. The idea was to replace the dogs with cats for missions in orbit because the former often reacted sluggishly and made mistakes when inside the space capsules.

But then disappointment struck! During the attempts to train the cats in a model of the space capsule's cockpit, these loners could not be won over for any orderly use of their skills. They did not answer to either direct rewards or signals (bound to rewards by conditional reflex). Unsocial, without any memory of gratitude for previous good deeds, constantly orientated to the present situation, they loafed about their room with signs of impatience. A flagrant desire for change of place. The observers, top-class scientists all of them, knew that these cats were not lacking in capability or understanding. They simply lacked interest. Whenever the scientists took them out of their prisons, they would caress their trusty caretakers' necks and shoulders, demand strokes and treats (without having done anything for them, but just for the sake of the thing itself, as it were).

Should they try with other kinds of cats? With house cats perhaps, whose navigational capabilities and response times when operating controls, at least according to the lab results, were inferior to that of the wild cats? Temple cats and those employed now and again in the US to protect industrial plants, who understood how to quickly discover saboteurs or terrorists, were tested. But the minute they were locked inside a technical device, they turned out to be just as unwilling as their predecessors.

One of the researchers and caretakers, Vyacheslav N. Shilin, who really loved his cats, discouraged further use of this particular path for space travel. You'd never even get past the launch with such FREEDOM-THIRSTY creatures. Much less a longer stay on Mars. In 'Star City' (Звёздных Городкак), Shilin was known as a ladies' man. One time, he reported, he had shown affection to a young woman, and she had given herself to him, which, however, did not mean that she had loved him back. She'd stayed with him as long as was convenient. Which, he found, was not unlike the 'warmth of a wild cat'. One of them wrapped itself around his neck like a fur, paws on his shoulders, purring, while he stroked its fur. Every day, he said, she demands her fill of tenderness, little attentions, gifts. But she would never lick him like his dogs did. For the cat, love was a one-way street: always love given to her, but never returned. And yet the animals did not appear to be indifferent. Rather, they were discriminating in terms of what they liked and what they didn't. He doubted that such judgement would ever deserve the terms 'obedience' or 'combat readiness'. In any event, nothing he did triggered gratitude in them. There's just their unspeakable urge for freedom (стремление к свободе).

'Better die than lie about emotions.' This is the case if you want to speak about emotion in wild cats and not of a fundamental strangeness (i.e. a distance towards human beings). Shilin attributed this to the extraplanetary origin of his cats (sixty-four of which he examined in his laboratories). They were descended from Egyptian temple cats that, following the departure of the gods and the decay of the temples, had gone wild. According to Shilin, all the wild cats that came to Siberia were former temple cats. Being extra-terrestrials, they were predestined for space travel but would never encourage humankind's clumsy attempts to secure a place in space themselves.

A POOR EXAMPLE FOR THE COLLABORATION OF DOG AND MAN

One day Laika just showed up. There was a long period of development since that point in the dwindling Pleistocene when dogs first approached the standing structures made by human hordes. In the meantime, three thousand human generations or eighteen thousand dog ones had passed. One day, a street dog in Moscow impregnated a female dog from Kuibyshev who in turn birthed the arrow-eared mongrel that scientific personnel in STAR CITY (Звёздный Городок) named Laika: the planners' and practitioners' most beloved dog. The plan was to bring both the dog and the space capsule back to earth after it had orbited the planet. After that, Laika was supposed to have a good life. Every cell in her robust body was to be examined for the effects of the space adventure. Anatoly V. Kordeliev, the sceptic among the planners, insisted that the inside of the casing within the spacecraft, the capsule inside the capsule where Laika would be sitting or lying down, be outfitted with a lethal syringe that, in the case of the spacecraft being lost, would go under the animal's skin and instantaneously euthanize it. But the mechanism didn't work. When the time came, nothing inside the capsule responded to any of ground control's radio commands. For a long time, instruments measured how—torturous for the consciences of the many witnesses back on earth—the trusty companion of the human race unbearably gasped for air and suffered hunger, thirst and the loss of orientation. THE BETRAYAL OF THE DOG. Had Laika's ancestors, the ones who first made the covenant with humankind, known that this would be her fate, they would have gone out of their way to avoid those early caves and wooden shelters, and Laika herself would never have voluntarily stepped foot in STAR CITY. On the other hand, no dog-catcher would ever have been able to catch such an experienced street dog against its will.

IN SPACE, EARTH NEVER
ARRIVES AT THE SAME POINT TWICE

E. F. Shubalov mapped out the angelic concert of celestial bodies the sun drags through the cosmos while sitting in a one-thousand-year-old tower in the Caucuses where his modern telescope had been installed in a glassed-in terrace. The observation post was cold. Four little heaters weren't enough to warm the astronomer's knees. Next to the frame were four tables in a row, covered with papers full of star data. Shubalov had finished his notes on the overall movement of the solar system around the core of the Milky Way in 1937 before being arrested and shot by the regime's henchmen after a brief period of being confined in a dark cell without any hearing. He was killed in a manner so arbitrary and careless that were the stars ever to move in a similar fashion, they would derail.

Led by the sun and its fellow planets, the earth furrowed the Milky Way and, though it orbits the centre 21 times, never manages to reach the same place twice. At one point, it approaches one of its earlier orbits by three parsecs. It is followed at a discreet distance by an invisible companion, a so-called BROWN DWARF: being low in mass, it remains an undeveloped sister of the sun, one that is capable, just like Zeus hurling his lightning bolts, to excite that whole bunch of comets waiting for their mission in the Oort Cloud. The gravitational shock caused this dark companion of the sun to fall towards it, and some of the impacts, catastrophes and collisions that hit the earth follow from the period in which this SECOND SUN approached our system.

THE NATURAL OSCILLATION OF LARGE LAKES

The basic oscillation of Lake Baikal, Dr Lermontov writes, lasts 54 minutes. Like a musical chord, it is overlapped by waves of 36 and 19 minutes. The surface of the lake, however, can rear 3 metres heavenward whenever a rapid weather front arrives from the south.

At a depth of 1,600 metres, the largest fresh-water lake on the planet has archived the unique movement of 1917 (in the form of a base frequency) whose rhythm the cheeky student Simonov, Shostakovich's pupil, enshrined in his FUGUE FOR TWO WAVE-LENGTHS AND TWELVE OVERTONES Op. 182b. Critics took the reference to the year 1917 poorly. The proper motion of Lake Baikal is a system, they said, that is a few million years old, and in this respect 1917's powerful intaglio is a mere snapshot. That can be heard in the electronic composition. Messiaen, on the other hand, composed a 'water mountain'—the 4-metre surge of Pacific waters around the island of Niue in 1928—according to seismic criteria alone.

– Surely that wasn't worth all that much?
– It wasn't anything precise. It was a pretext for the great composer's ideas.
– But he'd have those without any pretexts too, no?
– Maybe not. He imagined the 'rise of the sea' in a vivid way and then made use of the seismographs' numbers, which not only measure the earth's tremors but also those of the water.
– In his free time?
– Yeah, for fun.
– As befits good music.
– Competent music.
– And would you deny our fresh Simonov such competency?
– Not his Opus 182b.
– How so?
– It sounds like a roar.
– And what does it depict?
– A powerful waterfall far below the sea's surface in the narrow space between Greenland and Iceland. There the water shoots at high density a thousand metres into the depths. It's the most violent waterfall on earth.
– And any submarine that found itself in the area where this waterfall thuds down would be smashed to pieces?
– Without a doubt.
– And this possibility makes Simonov's music dramatic?
– That's how people took it. It was as if a kind of wild chase had swept through the hall. It's 'draughty music'.
– The spectators shivered?
– Some kind of horde of ghosts or other moved electronically through the room. No one liked it, but it made an impact.
– But no submarine has ever been at the base of that underwater waterfall?
– No, captains are warned.

- Does the water mass hit the seabed and create a depression?
- No, it's held up by a warmer current far below. The thud it makes can be measured all the way to the Grand Banks of Newfoundland.
- And how does Simonov's ear or brain, with which he composes, get a concrete impression of it all?
- Through the imagination.
- Is that enough?
- For music, yes.
- Does the musical work have anything to do with the movement of the lake?
- Not a thing.

GORILLAS' UNSUITABILITY FOR EITHER THE CIRCUS OR TRAINING

In 1925, Yuri Eduardovich, an animal trainer from the famous Durov circus family, which had been responsible for giving Russia so many smash-hits, tried to train a gorilla that had been purchased on the world market for a circus number. The animal—which, despite its size, stood only at eye level with the trainer because of its bent posture—didn't appear imposing in any way. Not only that, the animal looked away whenever Durov tried to 'capture its eyes' from pupil to pupil. In spite of the fact that transmitting hypnotic currents onto dogs and lions was his specialty. Nor did the creature seem to understand its EXHIBITION VALUE. An animal must do something that surprises the audience. This particular primate would just sit motionlessly in the fine sawdust of the circus ring until it was time to eat again. He did not wallow in the attractive, soft floor covering even once.

Durov tried to see if he could tie the great ape with chains to a column to suggest to the crowd that it was somewhat dangerous. But it would have had to at least bare its teeth. Instead, it just sat around sluggishly, and only appeared toothy and big enough for a thousand-odd crowd on the posters Durov had made. Durov's sister tried her luck with a horse number. She was an experienced polar-bear hunter and typically appeared in a routine that included sixteen white bears. The ape allowed itself to be hoisted onto the back of the sturdy white horse but then clung to its neck awkwardly. In this way, it drifted in circles through the circus. This did not constitute a number. The circus band's signals were unable to bring it to any kind of climax either. The animal had cost a considerable amount of foreign currency. The budget was listed in the five-year plan for the Soviet circus industry. Something had to be done that provided economic value for the cost of the acquisition.

For a long time, illustrated broadsheets (лубки) dramatizing various episodes from the life of gorillas in the jungle and their interactions with people had been in circulation. No remarkable action of this kind could be elicited from the real-existing creature in Moscow. The length of time it took the animal to eat a carrot would have taxed the patience of any audience. And so, in the end, the gorilla ended up just sitting at the entrance, next to the register and a brown bear on a chain. They had to make sure the ape wouldn't be caught in a draught. Due to a lack of double- and revolving-doors, the entranceways to public buildings in Moscow—and the circus, too—are plagued by draughts. The African animals could easily get pneumonia, it was said. The army veterinarians the circus had asked for help knew very little about apes.

A RECOMMENDATION FROM A TRAINER WITH THE RUSSIAN STATE CIRCUS

I urgently discourage anyone from trying to train hyaenas for any kind of circus number. Take a look at my crippled leg.

These were the words of Kuliakov, the animal trainer from the Russian State Circus based at the regional branch of Odessa, considered one of the most experienced authorities on predators in the circus.

These animals are no doubt trainable. Indeed, judging by their outward signs of intelligence, they can keep up with the average human. Nonetheless, when it comes to biting, they lack any inhibition at all. As a trainer, you must never lose sight of the animal's jaws. They bite with cutting effect. I do not believe these creatures mean any harm. It's just that their 'minds' sit in their jaws, and a mind wants to 'play', especially when it isn't working on cognition.

Thanks to the process of evolution, these swift-footed animals specialized in biting first and checking to see whether what they nabbed was nutritious later. They possess a stomach of fire, indigenous people say. And within it, a chemical viscosity. It digests just about everything. According to our findings, even iron.

Hence, any trick by which the trainer 'tames' the goodwill of the animal group is a temporary fascination for the animal. Immediately afterwards, they'll take off a hand.

I can tell when they're about to bite by a tiny twitch in their necks just a few seconds beforehand, that is, while the jaw is getting ready. The hyaena probably doesn't 'know' that it's going to bite just yet. It is, however, impossible to keep your eye on the jaws of 24 hyaenas at a time (and that's how many you need to present to the spectator's field of vision for them to consider it a considerable group). In other words, the animal trainer has got to keep his distance—and yet, if he does, the animals will hardly react at all. They're social animals.

THE UNPOPULARITY OF MURDEROUS ANIMALS IN THE CIRCUS, THE POPULARITY OF SATED TIGERS

I am unaware of any predators, besides the marten and the stoat, that engage in 'surplus killing', in other words, that kill their prey without being hungry. Unrelenting killers are a rarity.

Which is why the animal trainer of the Moscow circus continued. They are a phenomenon that would surprise the circus-going public. But it's awful to see.

– They're probably too small as well. Even from the box seats bordering the ring, they would hardly be visible, and thanks to how quickly they act too.
– What one sees is the blood. The whirling feathers, if it's fowl that they're murdering, or whatever small-sized prey that's trying to get away in vain.

- Do these killers also mess with larger animals?
- Foxes. Nevertheless, duels would still be too insignificant for a really effective circus show.
- You doubt the entertainment value?
- All you see is a quick flash of chaos. You don't see anything properly. On top of it, it is rather upsetting and cruel.
- It's got nothing to do with training?
- Training killers is impossible.

On the other hand, performances featuring sated tigers are always of interest. Their powerful bodies, even with full bellies, display high levels of elegance. Not only are they prepared to jump through flaming hoops, but—and this is a particular success of our training—they are also willing to let themselves fall into a see-through basin and then shake the water off their fur. After that, they form 'groups'. There's nothing more good-natured than tigers who've been freed from the pangs of hunger.

Traditional performance: a group of wolves chasing a group on horseback. Or, better: the wolves (волки) chase a troika filled with women and children. But there's one precondition to the number: the wolves have got to be full, and you've got to separate the lead she-wolf beforehand.

MASS DEATH OF THE CIRCUS BUSINESS

At first, the end of the GDR in 1989 only affected the circuses of the republic and the stays of publicly funded circus organizers from Poland and Hungary. Like migratory birds, they habitually came to the paying republic that, just then, was in the process of dying. A catastrophe which only two years later would envelop the great circuses of the Soviet Union. Uncoupled from state support, it was impossible for them to remain together. A circus—it must take care of animals, become a concentrate of the greater community's energy (in other words, a large one) and because of its particularities, its small, partisan-like units that support themselves from the country, cannot transform itself all that quickly—will come to its end before even three months have passed.

An atmosphere of grief throughout Moscow's winter circus. Not a single institution feels responsible for supporting them any longer. Madame Yusupov managed to save her group of polar bears by taking them to Finland, and from there to the West. What makes the Customs officials so tolerant with this particular transfer? They love the circus. One of the great forces that held the Soviet Union together is underappreciated: an affection for the circus. Why didn't *Glasnost*'s handlers take advantage of this resource? Revitalize themselves out of the idea of the circus? Instead, they were tense, shocked by the opposition they encountered. They had no feeling for the circus.

Twelve of the Eastern Bloc's great circuses dissolved. Their animals died. Their artists sought out other professions. Twenty-four companies tried to make their way to the West with part-time workers. All of them failed.

FIGURE 12. In the heyday of the Russian circus. The 'beautful woman' has just shot up out of a cannon and is now dancing on its muzzle.

THE COURAGE OF ARTISTS—A SACRED THING

On a tour through the small towns of White Russia, the 'Victory of the Proletariat' (Победа Пролетариата) Circus was surprised by the invasion of the German armoured forces on 22 June 1941. The Red Army seemed incapable of repelling the invaders. But nothing is impossible for a circus. The border army—overwhelmed by worries in those days—was chock full of friends. And they arranged for rail transport. The circus group's long columns reached safety far beyond Moscow. The wagons transported the elephants, gnus, clowns, artists and equipment (including a disassembled catapult cannon, which, when it worked, threw the performers to the circus ceiling, where they got hold of a rope by which they tumbled to the floor of the ring). Here, not only was a piece of favourite entertainment saved but also a solid piece of self-confidence of the workers from the hinterland. Hope for victory over the occupiers in the form of artists, animals and trainers were exported out of the slough of despair, which spread out through the west of the Soviet Union for a particular amount of time. Hay, carrots for the elephants. Tons of water were perfectly arranged along the railroad line. The dispatchers who made this possible could not have saved their own skins in such a way. They would have been shot if they had not allowed themselves to be outflanked, encircled and destroyed in a correct and decent manner.

WHY I AM INFATUATED WITH THE CIRCUS AS A THEME IN MY FILMS ALTHOUGH TODAY I WOULDN'T BE ABLE TO TOLERATE JUST ONE OF THE PERFORMANCES OFFERED UP AS A GALA EVENT BETWEEN CHRISTMAS AND NEW YEAR'S FOR EVEN 30 MINUTES

I was four-and-a-half. On Buchardi-Anger Road: the autumn circus. A gigantic aquarium is wheeled into the ring. Before our eyes, the see-through container is filled with water. From trapdoors, a number of seals appear in the underwater basin and swim through the pool. A female trainer, a flashing light on her forehead and a kind of torch in her hand (instead of a whip, which would be useless underwater). She orders the seals into a row, just like a formation of planes ready to complete an exercise in the sky. Sky, water, circus ring—the elements become confused. I cannot vouch for the correctness of my four-and-a-half-year-old eyes. I saw all of it 'with my ears': the sloshing of the water, the seals' squeaks when they broke the surface and snapped at the fish that the elegant swim instructor held out to them.

The mass of water was enclosed by a kind of plastic material, for I retrospectively assume that such heavy glass could not have been transported that way. The container was four times taller than our ascending rows of seats. I have this number from subsequent statements of adults. In any event, masses of water filled the circus right up to the top of the tent. Later, both seals and swimmer had to disappear into the floor hatches before the gurgling water could be drained. The circus band played on.

That was the OMNIPOTENCE OF THOSE DAYS. An overwhelming fluctuation of elements. I carry the water routine inside me for maybe half an hour when the winter nights grow long.

FRIDAY, 21 DECEMBER 2018,
ON A TRIP TO SWITZERLAND

On the Garmisch Autobahn towards the mountains. Two suitcases and four bags on the backseat. My papers: 'materials'.

But not material in the sense of a thing; rather, some stubborn kind of substance. It speaks to me. It speaks *in* me. In some cases, saying I should juxtapose this particular thing with a concentrate, a condensed text. A 'ringleader'. In others, the 'material' I am carrying in my suitcases and bags—most of the time it consists of text on paper—demands images. In some cases, leaving it all 'uncut' would be good. What I've brought with me seeks to retain its potential: it remains 'unformed'. Like an expanse of snow untrampled by human feet, unmarked by ski tracks.

Why do I prefer 'collections of material' to finished products? Finished products eliminate the reader's collaboration. The reader as consumer of 'works'? The reader as producer of their own experience! My father was a doctor and obstetrician. He compared his work as an obstetrician to the work of the surgeons at the county hospital. In an emergency, you've got to cut, but only in an emergency. When there's a perineal tear. Or when a caesarean section is necessary. Poetry only 'cuts' in the case of an emergency.

A long time ago, thoroughly and with a great amount of interest, I read Walter Benjamin's masterful essay 'Paris, Capital of the 19th Century'. But I haven't touched it since. This perfect text is followed in the *Arcades Project* by a collection of nineteenth-century buzzwords like iron, photography, revolution, fashion, world fair. For more than a thousand pages. Reading through it never exhausts my curiosity. My collaborator Dr Combrink makes fun of me: you're a telephone-book reader. It's true: I read the 1938 ministerial phonebook from the city of my birth, Halberstadt, with irresistible interest. I would never come up with the idea to even imagine such a directory of streets and names accurately mapping a still-undestroyed world that is personally connected to my life. Such a collection of data has meaning only *authentically*. At the same time, I describe the brilliance of the phosphor digits of a buried clock that lies beneath the ruins of my father's house, and which belonged to me: a shape, a fixed form. This is the antithesis of the term 'collection'. Conversely, the antithesis of a collection for me would never be crime fiction, or drama.

As to the question of why I don't write novels, I reply: what I write *are* novels. Novels are, in principle, collections. Classical novels belong to a layer of the public realm which turns them into 'material' for the present. What fascinates me is precisely this: that one continues to write them, that their potential is greater than their aura. Balzac, Flaubert, Fontane, Döblin, Joyce, Proust: having become collections, they demand continuation. At the foot of this mountain—under a pouring rain, our holiday rental car approaches the Alpen valleys—you can build a cabin, set up a stone garden.

In this respect, the poetic has the character of a construction site. Not the ordered structure of an institution, but material, a building site, workers moving about freely. I myself don't know why I don't live there but want to keep on building. Where I once lived—at Kaiserstaße 42, an address in the phone book since 1929, the place of my childhood—the house is in ruins. I would like a construction that only swallows bombs, a poetic house that, when caught by the blaze, would rise from the dead in a new coat of feathers.

FIGURE 13. My father in the stone garden.

ON CALENDAR REFORM

Between today's Republic of Kyrgyzstan and Tajikistan is a narrow strip of land, framed by tall mountains, which did not appear on the maps of 1917 and was not recorded by any later administrations either. With the dismantling of the Soviet Union, this strip of land remained left behind. With an Orthodox monastery, which was then hastily cleared. One single monk stayed behind to watch over the building and carry on with works.

For centuries, the monastery had been involved with the ecclesiastical establishment of calendar dates, in other words, with chronicles. The lonely brother—tasked and forgotten—did not remain alone for long. Thanks to the Internet, he is connected to fraternal organizations, Orthodox or scientific, as the case may be. Unaware of the stranger's presence, the surrounding Islamic environment leaves him alone.

Brother Andrei Bitov divides the most recent periods of time as follows:

From the Peace of Westphalia in 1648 to 1789.	1 century
From 1793 to 1815	1 century
From 1815 to 1870/71	1 century
From 1871 to 1918	1 century
From 1918 to 1989	1 century

= 341 years have the substance of 500 years.

Thereafter: contemporary time.

Bitov recovers the years of additional work such a calculation of modernity requires, in full agreement with Dr Phil Heribert Illig's phantom-time hypothesis, by critically revising the dating of the Middle Ages. Here we are dealing with invented time, e.g. there is no evidence of Charlemagne at all. Thus, Bitov easily arrives at a turning point around the birth of Christ, which he needs for the synchronization of the monastery chronicles.

In the meantime, within the academic circles of the US, Brother Bitov is considered the founder of TIME COMPRESSION.

The qualitative descriptor 'century' possesses a morphic structure, that is, it forces the years into circular or elliptical orbits around a centre. Chronometrically counting off days, years, is arbitrary. Hence, the three years of the great French Revolution contain a 'differential structure,' Bitov says. This makes them a 'century unto themselves'. This RIGHT OF THE SELF-DETERMINATION OF TIME MUST BE RECOGNIZED JUST AS THAT OF THE SELF-DETERMINATION OF PEOPLES.

For why should the same thing be true for Russia as for England and France? This is when Brother Bitov grows animated. All times are different, a British and a Russian century certainly cannot be compared. The times of the continent and its inhabitants, Bitov says, are, however, connected to each other by morphic fields. To this extent, the FLOW OF TIME is once again synchronous. And it is not even certain that the great French Revolution was indeed French in origin. A new time can have its origin in a place completely different from that where the appearance breaks out (the surface). We have established souls that move together in Russia, in Central Germany, in Tashkent just as in Portugal and in its East Asian colonies.

In Bitov's mountain monastery, heating materials are rare. The best way for him to keep his hands warm in winter is to place them firmly on his computer's housing.

THE POWER OF TIME

What is it: 'time'? 'I am a researcher of calendars, not a physicist,' monk Andrei Bitov replies. What is important are the DIVIDING LINES between times, in other words, the change from one year to another, between day and night, alternation (of the weather, for example), the division of hours and minutes (and seconds too, when one can die), the division of generations and lifespans: time to fear; time to love.

So, what you mean, the visitor insisted, is it that time does not tolerate any official interferences? It's autonomous? Bitov answered: 'To whom does it belong?' Here's biologist Dr Siegmund Fritsche on the matter: it belongs to the cells or, in any event, to Earth itself, not the individual. This, the doctor continues, is where all such guaranteed rights to freedom end.

It is particularly dangerous, Bitov said, to manipulate 31 December, that is, the last day of the year. As far as nature is concerned, no year ever ends. It takes 6,000 years of prehistory to bring about the turn of a year, a cut in time. Without religion, this doesn't work at all.

FIGURE 14. Andrei Bitov, Russian author, who died in 2018. Not to be confused with 'Brother Bitov' the monk.

A FAILURE OF LENIN'S WHICH HAD A DELAYED IMPACT IN 2009 (AND IN JANUARY 2010)

On 14 February 1918, the Council of People's Commissars decreed that the Western calendar was to be introduced in Russia. How flawed the power of the state apparatus! The new way of keeping time never completely asserted itself against the old way of doing things. For a long time now, without paying any particular attention, Russians have counted according to two calendars, that is, the Byzantine one and the one prescribed by the West.

This led to the 'economic performance gap' in the passage from 2009 to 2010. In vain, Prime Minister Putin tried to fight the poor state of affairs. According to the model of the Western markets, the Christian holidays fell on Moscow and the regions beyond the Urals. They ended, however, 13 days behind schedule (in terms of feeling and working practice), so that the enjoyment of alcohol and reciprocal invitations to holiday meals just wouldn't end. But now Epiphany was added, the more important holiday on 6 January (with a perceived range of 13 days as well). Superimposed by the turn of the year: a rich offering of celebrations.

The replacement of reality (imparted by work and professional life) by a never-ending sequence of special days is, in Brother Bitov's eyes, equally disastrous for the body, spirit and the economy. And all of that because a provisional revolutionary government tried to govern time, whereas God and the people alone possess such power.

PREHISTORICAL TIME
THE TIME OF LIFE
'REAL TIME'
DIACHRONOUS TIME
A SUM TOTAL OF MOMENTS
'A SECOND'

A BELATED APPLICATION OF
IMMANUEL KANT'S NATURAL LAW

In those hazy days following the upheavals throughout the Soviet Union, its division into individual states by the 'bushwhackers of Minsk', there were civil courts in Russia that behaved outside general Russian jurisdiction. Around Smolensk, a judge who had read literature from Brussels was making the rounds practising 'international natural law'.

A woman had come from the former GDR. She described herself as having been 'raped in 1945, which resulted in the birth of a child'. She had brought the child with her, in the meantime a grown man. She had figured out who the supposed father was. The records of the Red Army regiments that had been stationed around Berlin in 1945 were now open to the public. Thanks to a bit of bribe money, the police officials in Smolensk proved helpful.

The judge decided that the child's father, a widower, had to take in the woman he had raped 62 years ago. For though the act had not resulted in marriage, it had resulted in a kind of proprietary relationship (имущественные отношения) as far as the woman and the son were concerned. Property obligates. This judgement was something new.

The learned judge supported his opinion with a sentence from Immanuel Kant's *The Metaphysics of Morals*, §25, p. 68 in the Cam-bridge edition:

> But acquiring a member of a human being is at the same time acquiring the whole person, since a person is an absolute unity.

How exactly, the defendant's lawyer asked, was a member acquired in the incident? There was bodily contact and an ejaculation. The defendant did not take possession of his victim's skin, limbs, soft tissue or bones. The judge replied that every body part—and, if need be, a glance at the plaintiff's shocked face—which had aroused a feeling of 'lust' in the defendant had to do with 'acquisition'. According to Kaliningrad's (or Königsberg's) native son Immanuel

Kant, members could not be defined so narrowly. In this respect, the perpetrator of the year 1945 had acquired property. One cannot 'acquire the members of a human being' and then just slip off. The fact that a child had arisen from it, was, so to speak, the natural law characteristic of the acquisition of property, which in the case of personal relationships could neither be documented by contract nor by entry into the land register. Here the result *was* the documentation. But if the acquisition of the whole person had taken place through the acquisition of a member, this would apply for all times.

The judge was a guest at the ceremony to seal the 'marriage', which the Russian pensioner did not, in fact, consider at all absurd. There was caviar, gherkins, potatoes, pickled cabbage. The couple's official domicile, however, remained in dispute. Zwickau or Smolensk. Truth be told, the unemployed Russian was not unhappy about the fact that the assets of his 'late wife' and his son were enough for all. His 'wife' was an accountant working in the West; it was more her sense of direction, not any interest in profit, that had led her Eastward on the search for her son's father. Acknowledgement of paternity (признание отцовства) just seemed 'natural' to her. Similarly, the judge who recognized international natural law followed a sense of proportion inherent in humanity. Two years later he was disbarred. And yet he was a frequent guest of the happy clan which had ended up enthroned in Smolensk. And thus, an act of injustice committed in May 1945 blossomed into a happy ending.

COMMENTARY ON MARRIAGE
BASED ON NATURAL LAW

The Russian soldier who got the 16-year-old and later accountant (her name was Franziska von Bornhold) pregnant in 1945 was the same age. At first, there was probably a certain shyness between the two minors. A sense of shyness that could have prevented what happened. But then the undercurrent of sudden domination by the occupying force (the rapist belonged to the 3rd squadron's supply troops) prevented any consideration. Possessed as she was with a careful nature, however, Franziska could not refrain from trying to find out who the father of her beloved child was. At times she thought that she would bring the son as a gift and would receive thanks. Later, this thanks was to come spontaneously from her former rapist's parents. And he was happy to see her again, too. Even if it had been unexpected.

KANT AND THE 'THREE COUSINS OF REASON'

For five years in the eighteenth century, Tsarina Elizabeth's troops occupied Königsberg. During that time, educated, philosophy-obsessed Russian officers would often dine at Immanuel Kant's table. The languages? German, Russian (in translation) and French.

At one of these lunches, which could last up to three hours, after clearing the dessert table, Kant began a longer explanation. Reason, he said, was a living thing that could only affirm its powers in the company of others. Without the company of those who are not-entirely-reasonable, it would simply lay itself down in the sand of an empty aquarium, a fish out of water, and dry out. The Russian officers took the expression 'not-entirely-reasonable' personally. But they did not take offence. The alcohol on hand had lowered all the participants' aggression levels.

There were, Kant continued, three 'natural mates' or 'relatives' of reason which could be found among reason's companions, even if they were not reason itself: music, games of chance and conversation following a meal. The round of Russians applauded. Having been schooled in French novels, they found it an honour that the philosopher, clearly gorged, spoke to them at such length. For 'music', he gave the example of a few popular potpourris which were currently being offered in the concert halls of Königsberg. Unfamiliar with the pieces himself, he had read about them in the paper. He had little respect for music. As an example of the passion for games he named cards. And as far as conversation following a meal was concerned, he mentioned the touching upon of philosophical thoughts, 'as, during the summer heat, one dips one's foot into a cold stream and, thanks to the shock, feels a sense of well-being from one's ankle all the way up to one's neck.'

One of the Russians, a captain in the tsarina's cavalry who would have liked to have written down everything he had experienced here at the table, translated it into French and had it published in St Petersburg. That's how much he loved the exercise of reason. He felt moved to reply. He demanded, he said, *autonomy* for music (and thereby named a number of composers) and a *curbing* of the passion for playing cards. He named great sums that he had lost through 'card playing's regime of chance', for which, however, he had not received any *insight* in return. This 'evil bedfellow of reason' had even made it difficult for him to decide to stop playing.

Then the conversation took a sudden turn, something so characteristic of such 'lovely-discussions-after-a-meal', to the subject of whether republican consciousness, virtue in the ancient Roman sense, was based on the love and attraction the sexes felt for each other. Some of France's most recent novels seemed to rule this out. What were the roots from which (even in monarchies) the republican spirit—as a spiritual grain, so to speak—grew? Compared to grain or food, how would inner 'devotion', 'empathy', 'closeness' and 'permission to make use of another's sexual organs or have one's own used by this other' be threshed and ground, and in which ovens would they be baked? Kant decided to stay quiet. It was going on four in the afternoon. A suitably autumnal grog was brought in on trays. Up there in the north, it was already noticeably cooler.

THE ENDLESS VARIETY OF POINTS IN THE SKY

– Was Kant able to see much of the starry sky in Königsberg? Was a suitable telescope available?
– He used to carry a magnifying glass around. But you can't see any stars with that. In the evenings, when it got cool, a fog from the lake would usually come over the town.
– Then he can't have observed the stars too closely. What did he base his *Cosmogony* on?
– On drawings by the astronomer Beyer, notes of Laplace's and, above all, Newton's laws of motion.
– As a young man, did he use the stars to organize his thoughts?

- That's probably why he wrote. He was fascinated by the vault of the sky.
- Even if he only saw it within the vault of his skull?
- With the INNER EYE. While all thought begins with experience, not all thought is based on experience.
- He was certain of his interest in the stars. To him they were an example of the sublime.
- So, he was a poet when he was young?

FIGURE 15. The way to the next star.

'EVERY SOUL CARRIES ITS OWN PRIVATE FAR WEST INSIDE'

Going door-to-door beneath Moscow's pall of smog. Refusal after refusal. I, Vladimir Korolenko, who considers himself a lucky devil (считаю себя счастливчиком), got to know an ambitious southern Russian girl. Was this some sort of compensation for the fact that mercantile Moscow considered me superfluous? Unemployed for three years now, practically a casual slave or peddler, depending on the situation. And then two weeks of lively togetherness with my new acquaintance. We got to know each other intimately. But, after spotting a kind of corporate ladder which she'd only been able to climb through rigorous service to an oligarch, she left. She wasn't superficial, she just had to make a choice between her skin or her head. As for me, unable to let go of the *pursuit of happiness*, I turned my gaze towards vaunted Amur Oblast.

From all the clouds of information and self-confessions coming from over there and what I'd managed to gather online, it seemed that on one side of the river or current (whatever the Amur might be, for me it's just a line on a map) there were teeming masses of Chinese, every one of them a disciple of their own success.

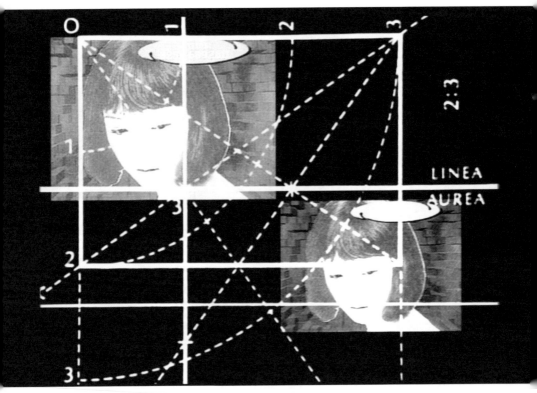

FIGURE 16

And on the local side—in other words, our side—unexploited mineral resources of every kind, with a highly limited number of landowners. You can become an oligarch without too much effort. The contrasts captivated me. In this mixed situation of willing labour in the south and treasures in the north, I dove in. I'm not fickle. Nor am I an empty soul; on the contrary, I am filled with will and *thumos*, passionate, if you will, bursting like a poppy capsule.

Fourteen years from now, no one will recognize this part of the earth any more. I trust my soul to have as much decision-making power as a shaman. The signs it gives me are often pretty vague, but demanding and strong. For a long time now, I've been back and forth about whether to stay with the young Russian woman I moved

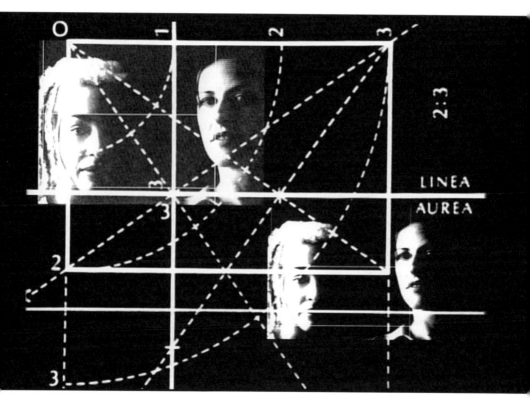

FIGURE 17

into a room with in one of the new tower blocks when I first arrived here in Amur. Everything smells of fresh concrete. Or whether to throw my lot in with the young Chinese woman I met on the other side of the river a few weekends ago? All these bars with their dim, promising light! Over the past few weeks, I've really been at odds with myself over this rather important question. I'm starting to think I'm SLOW. But it's funny, usually I'm in a rush, headstrong and thirsty. This here is known as our 'Wild East' (наш дикий восток). It's the counterpart to the leap that European settlers took in the nineteenth century when they headed off for California.

'MY SOUL IS ALREADY SLOUGHING OFF ITS SKIN'

Coming from Russia with top-notch marks as a doctor and physiotherapist, I have grown since arriving in Libourne, near Bordeaux, establishing myself in France and becoming able to defend myself. Since I stopped overeating (which was due to anxiety), my body has grown smaller. But my ethereal body (эфирное тело), which surrounds me like a kind of light and is also often referred to as one's 'aura', has grown immensely. Maybe this explains why my patients have been recovering so quickly, and why I am already considered something of a miracle healer. As I said: the skin of my anxiety (кожа моих страхов), of my education, has burst. I am a WESTERNER FROM THE EAST, I am following the call of my paternal grandmother from Galicia who longed for nothing so much as to emigrate, across the ocean, but who ended up being woefully shot at home instead.

Well, having arrived here, I am for the first time equal to myself and hope, woman that I am, to marry my companion, someone my spiritual eye glimpsed long ago but whom I am yet to find. I assume that the many parts of my self currently caught up in draughts will soon be covered by the new skin. Not just a protective kind of skin but a happy one as well.

As a qualified Doctor of Medicine, I know that the process of sloughing, that is, moulting, has always accompanied evolutionary bodies. At the same time, this shedding of skin, our largest organ, serves to unload protein and, according to Darwin, is already difficult to explain in the case of reptiles. Even if, as far as *my* skin is concerned, we're talking about a spiritual garment, it has also come about through a good degree of effort, at the expense of SPIRITUAL PROTEIN (for which we've got to find a name), so to speak.

But the waste becomes plausible if one thinks of the process of sweating, with which we expel salt and water from our bodies to cool them, so that we can then storm on ahead. Or the moulting of birds: the sacrifice of their feathers, which contain valuable substances. The process is a similar waste of substance. But necessary. In our yearning—e.g. that of a woman to make it to the West—we humans produce two things: the urge for a better life, an advantage (this corresponds to sugar, fat = energy storage for avian flight); and the longing to not be alone, to have a companion (which corresponds to the sulphur and proteins contained in bird food but which are unnecessary for their long-distance flight performance and are therefore invested in growing and moulting feathers). The 'longing for a solution', i.e. hope number two, is released as energy during the moulting process. Just as with feathers for a bird (which made it possible for the very first birds to fly), my sloughed soul, all the time I have put aside, is the prerequisite for a free flight into happiness. Though the moulting has not made me bigger, it has 'fledged' me. I draw the smell of the nearby Atlantic into my Soviet nose.

NOTHING BETWEEN THE BODY AND HEAD
BUT MUSIC

Originally, she had nothing at her disposal but 'her family's blood', a fuel that turned her into a disciplined voice and reader of music, a tiller of the soil of sacred music while under the aegis of the music academy in Sarajevo. By now, however, she was living in one of the great European metropolises. This past season she sang ANTIGONA[2] in Tommaso Traetta's eponymous 'model opera of the Enlightenment'. She trusted the devoted conductor (a specialist in baroque opera) just as she had trusted all the patrons of her career, out of a reserve of openness that, given the explosive social circumstances in her home country, she could only have drawn from her distant ancestors.

---

2 The Neapolitan, Tommaso Traetta, named his opera—which deviates greatly from the original by Sophocles and describes the fate of the king's daughter Antigone—*Antigona*.

She possessed an *atlatus*, a young man, who'd come to her and with whom she shared a bed; their bodies pressed against each other in strictly fraternal dialogue, for she saw herself as a nun of art. And she wasn't really sure whether she loved him enough, even though (if without any particularly heated passion) the current of content-ment between their nocturnal bodies already bespoke a somewhat established closeness. But one binds oneself one day at a time, she told herself, and on any given day all signs indicated that she wanted to limit her emotional ambition to him for good. What spoke in his favour was that they talked a lot. He seemed to be a bright student, without any of the down-to-earthiness she was accustomed to. She often found herself surprised. Because of her, he'd studied the material to *Antigone* at the university library.

But her primary, concrete concern had to do with the long arcs that had been written for a castrato and therefore were tough for a trained, modern female soprano to imitate. Irina had to temper her 'bellows'—which glided a thin, concentrated flow along the vocal cords—to a duration that caused her to run out of air.

She was a fisher 'in the waters of forgetting'. Her chaste lover had quite a talent for such beautiful expressions, that scientific little brother of hers who preferred winning her over from nightly discussion to nightly discussion. Compared to the disappointing experiences she'd had with boys accustomed to success, this was exhilarating, indeed miraculous.

Antigone's no crazy noblewoman, her explorer told her, but a HEALER. Not only does she want to bury her rebellious brother, but the familial curse as well. Creon, the representative of the law, however, is unfamiliar with any MAGNANIMITY OF FORGET-TING. He is too self-interested for that: he came to power after all the male descendants of Oedipus—whom the people love despite his patricide and dazzlement—killed one another. The law is a pre-tence, Irina's partner says, for him to consolidate his power. Those sons of Oedipus who are responsible for the civil war are not to receive any kind of burial, they must be visibly exposed to shame as fodder for the ravens. That is how Caesar's murderers lost when they (and their faction in the Senate) agreed to Caesar's burial (instead of throwing him into the Tiber as a tyrant).

Like every judiciary, Creon must wrest guilt from oblivion; the princess Antigone, on the other hand, is passionately active in beating out the entire inheritance of misfortune that clings to her family's soles. She would rather experience misfortune herself than pass it on to any third party. She wants to hide her dead brothers in the 'waters of forgetfulness' (and if that proves impossible in Thebes, a landlocked town in the country, then by burying them deep in the ground). She understands how little sense it makes to keep the dead where they are by placing a stone on their grave. To contain them, it is better to trust their willpower: they will pass through rock all the way to the region of Gibraltar, where lies the entrance to Hades. The dead move, that is the message—so says her nocturnal dispenser of warmth, quoting G. W. F. Hegel's text, 'Ethical Action, Human and Divine Knowledge, Guilt and Destiny'.

As it turned out, Irina's vocal performance was helped by her nightly assistant (her candidate for long-term life-commitment) who fed her brain. In addition to Hegel's texts, now he was studying the score to *ANTIGONA*. Traetta's model opera was a contribution to a 'musical revolution' that took place in the eighteenth century along the axis of Paris (happiness), Stockholm (Joseph Martin Kraus), St Petersburg (Traetta): an uprising of meaning against mere music.

At the behest of Tsarina Catherine the Great, Traetta changed the roles of Haimon and Creon. Creon had intended to acquire Oedipus' younger daughter, Ismene, as a servant and lover, and perhaps later even as a wife. Antigone, on the other hand, was to take the ruler's son, Haimon (Emone in the opera), as her husband. What the usurper Creon could not know: Haimon loved the rebellious Antigone with a youthful heart, blindly and without any regard for his own life. In the opera's third act we can see both of them, how they have set themselves up in an open grave. They would rather kill each other than be separated, as only one of them has been condemned to death. In two duets it becomes clear that this libidinous relationship, sprouting in the midst of the usual theatrical drama of contemporary history, is the main point of the play, both musically and lyrically.

Neither the 'simple collective will' (which Creon uses and corrupts) nor 'blood and family' (Antigone's burden) are of ultimate significance.

According to Irina's friend's research, Tsarina Catherine refused to watch an opera with a repeatedly tragic ending. She had already seen the tragedy of Oedipus and his children in both Greek and French versions, and always with abysmal endings: as the queen, she certainly had the right this time to demand an ending without death. She said that, in holy Russia, happiness was part of the project of enlightenment. Enlightenment without happiness, she said, was dead.

On top of that, Traetta invented a scene in which King Creon experiences a 'change-of-heart' (METANOIA). Just in time he sees that, in the next step of the plot, he will lose his son. What good is a reign if it will not continue through his male progeny? So he becomes the most active agent in saving the young couple. Reality, substance, calculation and the friendly nature of the Enlightenment appear as a chorus of four in the final scene of the opera.

The director of the play in the German metropolis was not prepared to accept this version, which completely contradicted Sophocles. The conductor, on the other hand, insisted on playing the music to the end, that is, with that very finale. The search for a change to Traetta's model opera, including rehearsals, was estimated at four weeks. In this crisis, *Antigona*'s singer was the deciding factor. She pointed out her incipient bronchitis. The premiere had to take place without delay, otherwise she could not guarantee her voice. The team was gripped by doubts about Irina's respiratory system. No one wanted to do without that voice of hers which had unexpectedly arrived from the Balkans. Irina did it all out of loyalty to her nightly confessor.

"Frankfurter Küche"

FIGURE 18. The functional kitchen for the Ernst May–designed social housing complex in Frankfurt: the 'Frankfurt kitchen'. Later May and his team would be employed to design and construct the industrial buildings and residential centres of Russia's model cities. This type of urban and housing construction was also the model in Stalingrad. Here, along the Volga, homes and industrial zones were set parallel to one another. By Russian standards, the principle of the Frankfurt kitchen—only one seat for one kitchen worker—is awkward. In Russia, the kitchen functions as the parliament for the home. There must be a good number of chairs around the kitchen table to allow many people to speak at once. If need be, at the cost of space for cooking and washing up. Speaking is part of the function.

FIGURE 19. Two cosmonauts showing off their food concentrates. The spacecraft for which they are responsible can, for the most part, fly itself. They can therefore concentrate on research. The workhorse known as the 'space capsule'—built like a 1945 T-34 tank—has exceeded its service life by several years. Nevertheless, there is hardly any need for repair. The metal body contains vital reserves. It is made up of the living labour of thousands of designers and workers, in other words, Soviet lifetimes, not 'made of clay by God' but 'steel' forged from the slogans of years of training. This is a special, indestructible metal alloy. It cannot be explained technically, only patriotically.

FIGURE 20 (RIGHT). One of Galina Balashova's cockpit designs, in the Russian living-room-style of the Khrushchev era. 'Above', towards the sky, bright green (in other designs, blue). 'Below', a green-brown similar to the ground by the edge of a wood in autumn, thus transporting a piece of home into the technical enclosure. A greenhouse for the spirit. The space capsule is currently flying 'upside down'. The ceiling points to the centre of the earth. If the design did not exist, after a while cosmonauts might lose their minds.

FIGURE 21 (BELOW). Nineteen-engine aircraft with two fuselages. Passengers are mainly placed in the wings. Planned flight time from Moscow to San Francisco: four hours. For comparison: Customs clearance of passengers on both sides: eight hours. Acquisition of a visa: eight months.

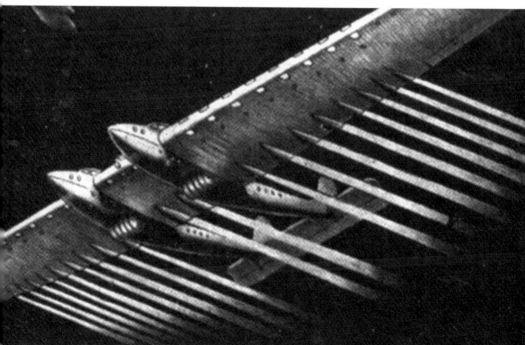

FIGURE 22. 'Space Glider' design by Georgii Krutikov. Once accelerated, this barge moves smoothly to the nearest celestial body or from one space station to an adjacent one. The traveller looks in the direction of the stern, that is, in the direction from which she is coming.

2

RUSSIA,
FATHERLAND OF
PARTICULARITIES

AN IDEA OF KAFKA'S

There once was a land surveyor (землемер) who set out to measure Russia. But it is a country full of particularities. Its various paths, bushes and wetlands rose up against him. Places began to wander. Over time, the scores of sketches by the surveyor grew larger and larger. The stacks of measurements recorded at a ratio of 1:300,000 required the storage capacity of an entire group of barns.

And thus, what Marx, born in 1818, had called for—that the world of concepts be turned upside down, that concepts be formed exclusively from the material of particularities—became true. This was the cause of the cartographer's demise.

A tiny derivate of his soul (Однако, производная его души), however, tenaciously continued to carry out this work of surveying. And in so doing, this soul enacted an idea of Kafka's from 1916. In the end, the land surveyor was able to produce a map at a ratio of 1:1. Which did indeed include all of the country's particularities.

FIGURE 23. Franz Kafka.

FIGURE 24

A BAD BUY

A little piece of Russia—a long road (длинная дорога), loaded with history (окаймленная ольхами), muddy in spring (слякотная весной)—was bought at an auction by a businessman from Hameln. What do you do with that kind of road? You can't set up any kind of toll. Hardly anyone uses it. It connects two villages that haven't existed for decades. The reason that elongated piece of land had come so cheap was its low use value.

It looked good on paper. It was correctly marked in square metres. The catalogue simply failed to mention that the width was multiplied by 3 square meters and the length by 15 kilometres, to say nothing of the shade-giving trees that could not be removed for reasons of nature conservation. Could it become a plot of land for a children's camp? Not even *their* interests could be stretched that far. A hiking opportunity? But who would pay for a tedious walk from nowhere to nowhere? And how could the children or the hikers even be transported there from the train station, which was 30 kilometres away (a journey of several days from the main European routes)?

For a long time, the property (столбовидая недвижимость) retained merely book-value in the Hameln-based company's portfolio. It slowly depreciated.[1] In 12 years, the mistake will no longer constitute a loss.

'PARTICULARITY AND MOVEMENT'

An archaeologist and surveyor (not to be confused with the land surveyor on p. 58), a man who loved his homeland (*rodina* in Russian), who had been working for years in Akademgorodok (Academic City), near Novosibirsk, was considered a bit obsessive. He was a stickler for precision. He insisted upon measurements of his which referred to the 'wave movement of deserts and mountains', thereby annoying his geographical and geological colleagues to no end. The surveyor's basis for these measurements was the data of an early Soviet satellite originally tasked with measuring the height differences of the earth's surface for military purposes (namely, the launching of intercontinental missiles). According to this data, the great mountain bases—such as the Himalayas, the Pamirs and the Andes—move in the range of decimetres, similar to the ebb and flow of tides, and are triggered by the suction forces of the moon (plains and deserts less noticeably); thus, deviating from the usual modes of designation, instead of mountains the surveyor spoke of *seas* of rock.

'It should not be excluded,' this patriotic surveyor claimed, 'that an unusual constellation of celestial bodies could lead to a "spring tide" of land masses (namely, if Jupiter and lunar influence cumulate with an unusual position of our mother sun and its mysterious companion star, a cool sister sun that tangentially grazes our system only every 600,000 years).' As far as he was concerned, such an

---

1 In the businessman from Hameln's tax balance sheet, the value of an asset is adjusted annually by an estimated fraction of its economically relevant lifetime. This continues until the value on the balance sheet is zero. The process generates the so-called depreciation value: a reduction in the tax liability over years.

accumulation of coincidences would be a 'poetic event'. Nature would simply be expressing (in its own language) that everything that *is* is in motion. Yes, this unwieldy scientist said, even our great and sluggish Russia might one day be in motion, even if Pushkin did not think it likely for the next 300 years, thanks to the country's muddy roads.

FIGURE 25. 550 million years ago. Rodinia is in the process of decay. Soon, India will be on the move. Far below, the Baltic shield and, to its left, Siberia. The equator crosses eastern Antarctica. All of this took place 'immediately' before that point in time when the planet almost completely froze: SNOWBALL EARTH.

BY DECREE (UKAS) OF 18 MAY 2000 GREAT RUSSIA WILL BE DIVIDED INTO SEVEN FEDERAL OKRUGA = MACRO-REGIONS:

NORTHWESTERN

CENTRAL

URAL

VOLGA

SOUTHERN

SIBIRIA

FAR EASTERN

ANDROPOV ALLOWS THE ACADEMICIAN VELITSKY TO EXPLAIN FRIEDRICH ENGELS' *DIALECTICS OF NATURE*

The dialectic reflected in the natural world of Russia shows arcs of 6,000 years. And therefore ideas—e.g. religious concepts, ways of burying the dead—are extremely old and exist independently of whether any traces of these ideas can be found in the present day. The fact that the eastern part of the continent, southern Siberia, so rich in raw materials, has not been worked by settlers may very well be due to such an 'invisible reason'. But what if a *goldrush* could be launched out there, in this wild east? The chief is interested in looking into it.

The academic Velitsky was called to KGB headquarters. Just what 'the chief wanted to have investigated' was explained to him by an assistant along the way: the country's spirits— that is, plans, high-rises, streets, railroads, airports, maps—were changing rapidly. And yet, later on, once they've disappeared, become overgrown with weeds, they return to the very same places they once arose.

This is confusingly different from the assumptions of how base and superstructure are supposed to relate to each other according to historical-materialist rules. In great Russia, natural forces (of the mind, the body, the earth) do not behave the way they do in school.

On many an autumn night, when storms pass over Moscow, Andropov sees souls (or hears and feels them in his bones) promiscuously jump from body to body, bodies the KGB had indeed been entrusted with protecting.

FIGURE 26.
Yuri Andropov,
Gorbachev's teacher.

'ONE CAN ALMOST SEE, DOWN TO THE CENTIMETRE, WHERE RUSSIA BEGINS'

Minister of Propaganda Joseph Goebbels, who liked to exaggerate, said this while looking down onto the landscape through the bull's-eye window of the plane. It was late autumn, 1941, and he was flying to Vilnius. Nevertheless, he thought he could distinguish, on the wide, snow-covered plain, something like a sea of marsh and steppe from the suggestion of fields and huts which he considered to be part of Poland and the Reich. After a stopover in Vilnius, he continued his flight in the direction of Smolensk. November weather. Into a snowstorm. A message from Smolensk airfield: no visibility. So the minister's plane turned back to Vilnius.

That night, the propaganda minister issued by telephone a 'sharp and precise denial' of a statement by Roosevelt (from a primitive hotel, the 'First House on the Square') to Berlin. In a speech on the occasion of Navy Day, the president had claimed that Greater Germany was working on dividing South America into four zones under German protectorate and abolishing all the religions of the world.

In his diary Goebbels noted: 'Late at night we take one last short walk through the snowy streets of Vilnius. Like a desolate town in central Germany. I don't want to be buried here.'

WHEN THE WORLD STILL WAS YOUNG

The general partnership of Alfred Zeligsohn GP—with two sons in Lemberg, a daughter with business experience in Omsk and two cousins in Poznan—organized rail transport for a large quantity of pallets filled with light bulbs (лампочек накаливания) via the Urals to Siberia. What is the colonization of Africa compared to the conquest of the night hours of Siberia by electric light?

The colonization of time is better than the colonization of spaces (Колонизация времени – лучше колонизации пространства). Spaces require the subjugation or expulsion of indigenous peoples. Time, on the other hand, is empty; or at least, due to a lack of candle stubs, night-time in Siberia is. This was the judgement of the local war commissioner in control of the general partnership (открытое торговое товарищество).

The commissioner complained about the difficulties of his task. According to him, the object of business in which the Alfred Zeligsohn trading company was involved made itself invisible. It seemed to move about and could not be located precisely by train. According to the laws of debit and credit, it was distinguished into profit and loss for the company and profit and loss for the socialist whole. 'In our Fatherland of the working people,' the commissar, known for his sense of humour, said, 'a general partnership (GP) has the character of a spectre.'

FIGURE 27. A lightbulb.

A SOCIAL BLOOD TRANSFUSION

Once, during the times of war communism, a training course for young women teachers in the capital came to an abrupt end. The participants were expressly and swiftly moved to Tula. The military cadre had arrested great numbers of socially disadvantaged children—for forming gangs or for having caught them in the act of robbery—and amassed them in schools and warehouses.

Until then, trained for the task of literacy, the young teachers found themselves face to face with a new task. They did not receive any guidance from their superiors. At first, the neglected youths fought with their skin. They had taken up all the space in the shelters. They would not give an inch. They had a tendency for skin-to-skin contact with one amother and with the educators, which is to say: they fought. They resisted.

Is it possible to create a republic inside neglected children by teaching them to how to read and write? Commissioners from the capital visiting the provincial re-education colony in the autumn of that year spoke of an 'educational miracle'. The young teachers had organized a food chain. It preceded the lessons. Meals were followed by further instruction. Like assemblers fastening screws, the teachers had put together the pupils' habits, wishes and temporal contingencies. The young people had made notebooks out of old paper, stapled together with wooden pins (there were no metal ones). In the end, as different as they were, the little adolescents washed each other every day. They also mended their clothes. They expected to be called upon to work any day.

The young teachers returned to their courses in Moscow. That the process of becoming literate can conquer desolation was an abbreviated description of the process. In fact, a kind of 'social osmosis' had taken place between the women from the capital and the disadvantaged children from the countryside.

FIGURE 28

junglehrerinnen_0001

In 1920 a training course for young teachers was abruptly stopped /

junglehrerinnen_0002

junglehrerinnen_0003

Neglected children wandered throughout the country, looting /

junglehrerinnen_0004

junglehrerinnen_0005

junglehrerinnen_0006

Red Army troops and the young teachers moved to the country to combat MISERY through LITERACY

junglehrerinnen_0007

junglehrerinnen_0008

FIGURE 29

THE LANGUAGE OF GREAT THEORIES
AND THE SIMPLE LIFE

Andrei V. Sedov, Comrade Bukharin's sixth assistant, was busy excerpting short texts on 'the changeability of people' from Marx's *Grundrisse: Foundations of the Critique of Political Economy* (*rough draft*) for his high-ranking lord and master, who was himself busy writing an ABC OF COMMUNISM:

> Foundations, p. 450. People's conditions and means of production are 'just like his skin', 'his sense organs' (p. 409); 'primordial instrument', 'spontaneous fruits' (p. 422); 'in their real positing as the conditions of his subjective activity' (p. 417); 'The individual relates simply to the objective conditions of labour as being his; [relates] to them as the inorganic nature of his subjectivity, in which the latter realizes itself' (p. 409); 'the workshop of his forces, and the domain of his will' (p. 421). [Martin Nicolaus trans., London: Penguin, 1973.]

All this was related to the chapter on 'man's essential powers' that Sedov was preparing for Bukharin. He noticed that the expressions used in the theory did not fit the language of the peasants and functionaries the party had to deal with. Could one explain to workers in the Donbass, to members of the Academy of Sciences in Moscow, or to Customs officials at the state border that the soil and the community made up 'their extended body'? Sedov feared that Bukharin would take him to task over these quotes. On the other hand, Sedov wanted to stick to the wording of Marx's *Paris Manuscripts*, which had only been discovered in an archive in the 1920s.

At night, Comrade Bukharin tried to summarize the argument of communism in writing for the last time. He often fell asleep over the letter-covered notes. The body has its limits. It's hard to be a political practitioner by day and a philosopher by night. Andrei V. Sedov was responsible for the high-ranking cadre's travels (in addition to obtaining notes and documents). He could see how exhausted his boss was.

What makes people mutable, malleable for the SOCIETY OF EQUALS (ОБЩЕСТВО РАВНЫХ)? Three work processes—all of which could only be carried out voluntarily and with pleasure—were to be distinguished: (1) physical reproduction, (2) the production of thought and feeling, (3) the transformation of man by means of his socialization. In all three areas, a wide gap remained between the texts of the classics and the people the revolution had to deal with: Siberian snipers, Caucasian merchants, Greeks from Odessa, Tatars and Bashkirs, farmers in Belarus and Ukraine, and even the factory workers differed depending on whether they were in Leningrad, Moscow or the southern Urals. Sedov had observed 'moments of solidarity' among the cadres, especially when there was a need or when the enemy attacked. A whole cohort of Central Committee secretaries was still infected by the enthusiasm of 1917 and then again by the economic upheaval of 1923.

In the meantime, Sedov had become rather overfatigued himself. He does not yet know that four years later he will be shot by comrades from the secret services, whose control he is currently entrusted with. He still believes that the socialist republic can be established with patient analysis and an all-round praxis based upon it. He fervently hopes that, some day, a connection between the words of GREAT THEORY and the REALITY IN GREAT RUSSIA can be established.

FIGURE 30. Sedov. Beside him, his colleague Liba Gerulaitis.

WORDS, SENTENCES AND SEMANTIC FIELDS FROM THE FATHERLAND OF PARTICULARITIES

'I'VE COME FROM THE CENTRE TO LOOK FOR WEEDS.'

' . . . WARMED BY ONE ANOTHER, THEY DID NOT FEEL THEIR LOSS OF CONSCIOUSNESS UNTIL MORNING.'

' . . . HOME, ABOUT THREE MILES. TWICE, A THIN RAIN BEGAN TO DRIP ABOVE HIM.'

'I ALWAYS LIVE IN ONE TOWN AND LOVE ANOTHER TOWN . . . '

' . . . I DIDN'T LOVE HIM. BUT WITHOUT HIM I FEEL DREARY.'

' . . . A BODY FILLED WITH PASSIONATE VEINS, RAVINES OF BLOOD, MOUNDS, OPENINGS, SATISFACTION, AND OBLIVION.'

' . . . THE RISING SUN AND MARVELLED THAT SUCH AN ENORMOUS HOT GLOBE COULD FLOAT SO EASILY UP TOWARD NOON. THAT MEANT THAT NOT EVERYTHING IN LIFE WAS HARD AND POOR.'

FIGURE 31. The surface of the ground near the city of Perm.

A GEOLOGICAL PARTICULARITY OF GREAT
DESTRUCTIVE FURY: THE SIBERIAN TRAPS

200 million years ago, the earth, orbiting its sun, ploughed through a distant zone of the Milky Way. From there, the dinosaurs were able to view the centre of the galaxy from the opposite side as seen from our present day. No dust clouds to obscure the 'star above', that is, as far as a terrestrial creature's point of view is concerned, the cluster of luminous bodies at the galaxy's centre. The nights were dimly lit. But the light didn't come from the edge of the horizon as it does with the dawn, but from the centre of the dome of the sky: completely from above, a white veil, a celestial garment.

At that time, matter was burrowing from the depths of the earth's core, at the edges of a powerful upward flow of lava, to the earth's surface. What's known as a plume—a catastrophic eruption of matter that cannot be adequately described by the common expression 'volcano' or 'summation of volcanoes'. More precisely: in Siberia, magma penetrated through a shaft to just below the earth's surface. Small volcanoes puffed up like molehills (or rather: like rashes) across the earth's surface in the form of billions of mini-fountains to grow into a worldwide natural disaster.

High-density molten rock was deposited in the magma column at the top. This is how Sebastian Sobolev and his colleagues describe it. A thick layer of inert material. The magma flow penetrated this crust slowly. It piled up. This took several million years.

During all this time, Siberia hardly bulged at all. But the massive, dammed-up brew pushed energetically towards eruption. When the explosive discharge occurred, gas poisoned the entire planet. Out of every 1,000 living species, 900 became extinct. Turtles and frogs (with their sensitive skin) remained unharmed. The destruction was more detrimental to their air sacs than their skin. Nickel, copper and palladium, as well as rare-earths, accumulated at the edges of the vents, shafts and craters. Later, the West Siberian petroleum basin formed in-between. And like gigantic, continent-encompassing underground zeppelins, gas deposits waited to be exploited. Metaphorically speaking, Siberia is a ship floating on a sea of potential for mining.

A PLAN DRAWN UP BY THE EARTH ITSELF

The Urals are like a scar. With their ancient rock, they lie between the two halves of the later continent of Eurasia, which, separated aeons ago by a sea, were driven towards each other by their migration. Exactly to the east of this CONTINENTAL SEAM, the spectacle-wearers of Gosplan, the State Planning Committee of the USSR, had conceived a new seashore in the early 1920s, to be fed by the waters of the Siberian currents which otherwise would have simply ended up in the Arctic Ocean. The first attempts with 'planned basins' of only 40 square kilometres in diameter proved disappointing. Instead of a lake (foreshadowing the later windswept sea), there were swamps. No cunning, no engineering skill (at least none that could be paid for) led to the 'construction of shores.' A colony of mud.

Workers invented rafts that could be pulled back and forth from fixed points at the edges of the swamp. But for what? They couldn't even bring measuring instruments into the planned sea's interior.

Nevertheless, Dr Sedov, in charge of the project until 1928, claimed that a climate-changing inland sea at that location would have been created at some point through persistent cooperation. Four harvests a year, water and downpours far into southern Siberia! And what was most desirable: the dry, neverending Siberian highs transformed into fertile lowlands that would migrate southwest across the southern foothills of the Urals and bring agricultural wealth. Dr Sedov argued historically-geologically, or, so to speak, GEOGNOSTICALLY: because this path of fertility already existed only 160 million years ago, when a primordial sea sloshed between the two halves of what later became Eurasia, this is not a plan, an idea, but a reconstruction. Only plans that follow an ancient model are successful, he said. *Plan is Mimesis* is the title of his book, which he wrote in French and which was published in Paris in 1932, long after Dr Sedov's removal. It went unnoticed.

THE LENA

At 4,300 kilometres long, the Lena is one of the largest rivers on earth. Its waters push northwards. They pour into the Arctic Ocean. From there, they have a hard time returning as rain.

Which is why some architects and intellectuals around Leon Trotsky planned to redirect these waters to the south. This would have allowed them to get increasingly close via several intermediate basins and barrages to the valuable, minimally fertilized but dry earth which, arbitrarily separated by the mountain ranges of the Himalayas and the Pamirs, by the South Asian seas, jutted into Russia. In this way, humans would have been able to cancel out a catastrophic accident (or error) of geological automation. For what good is a planned economy if it doesn't serve to make such corrections?

THE LENA DELTA

The delta of the river Lena is one of the 44 wonders of today's world. To the west is a huge wilderness, a breeding ground for migratory birds (перелётных птиц) that have only survived on the planet thanks to the existence of such a vast area, one which could never be completely taken over by humans or predators. The eastern reaches of a virtually uninhabited peninsula (необитаемого полуострова) are dissected by waterways with many tributaries. Only when this delta is 'viewed' from orbit (any visitor approaching from land would see only one detail at a time), this place on the planet created by a river has a STRUCTURAL BEAUTY like a leaf or the network of veins of a juvenile human or a spring that forms into a stream from the rock and a surrounding meadow.

The evaluator of the Landsat 7 reconnaissance satellite, launched in April 1999, noticed their delicate structure when he was looking for targets for the laser component of the missile-defence-shield project. There were no obvious reasons to include the eye-catching structure in the target planning. Or could a damming of the river in the delta destroy those cities and industries upstream in the long term? The Pentagon planner dismissed such thoughts. Having said that, he did not want to give in to the aspect of beauty, i.e. sentimentality, either. In this respect, he repeatedly examined the relevance of the photographic satellite image which, due to its filigree-like structure, attracted his attention again and again. Could the Russians have had the idea of setting up rockets or preparing covert actions in this particular bit of landscape precisely because it appeared 'innocent' to the observer's eye? 'The enemy can't always be lurking behind every bit of beauty,' the observer said to himself. Amazingly, Landsat 5, launched in March 1984, is still transmitting images to Earth. This has nothing to do with a sense of beauty but tenacity.

FIGURE 32.
The Lena Delta.

'RIVERS RUSHED EACH OTHER
  INTO THE SEA:
IT SEEMED THE HAND OF ONE
  STRANGLED THE NECK OF
ANOTHER.'

'STAGS IN RUT, WITH ANTLERS
  INTERTWINED:
THEY SEEM EMBRACED IN ANCIENT
  INTERCOURSE,
IN TUGGING ARDORS
  AND ADULTERIES.'

—*Collected Works of Velimir Khlebnikov, Volume III*: *Selected Poems* (Paul Schmidt trans.) (Cambridge, MA: Harvard University Press, 1997), p. 36.

THE SIBERIAN SEA

On a flight to Tokyo where they would be speaking together from the podium, the worldly-wise Pole Ryszard Kapuściński sat next to Heiner Müller for hours. Back at home, Müller had already marked up the latter's book *Imperium* with comments and underlined passages. On the plane, you could get as much iceless whiskey as you wanted. The two were happy they didn't have to traverse by foot the indistinguishable expanses that stretched out beneath the plane in the reflected light. Nor did it seem as if the aircraft would be making an emergency landing that would end up dumping them out on one of those snowy patches. The line of the Trans-Siberian railway they'd heard about and were looking for couldn't be seen on their flight route. It was probably to the south.

You can't write a play about utopia in the twentieth century, Heiner Müller said, while leaving out the most important topical project of the Russian empire, namely, the creation of the Siberian Sea. Kapuściński had just been talking about that. The preparations for it reached their climax in 1929, he said. When the plan was taken up again in 1950, Kapuściński continued, it no longer had the same utopian élan. The 1929 cadres were emboldened by the crisis of capital that had manifested itself on Black Friday. The euphoria gripped the central pillar of the socialist regime: the engineering and planning staffs. The aim was to dam the water-rich Siberian rivers above Tomsk and Tobolsk, which pointlessly flow north into the ice. This would create an inland lake, not as large as but more effective than the Mediterranean. The planner responsible, Davidov, had drawn in his sketches a wide forest belt to the south of this artificial sea and along the canals which were to connect it to the Black Sea. On a map, this could be shown with quick strokes, even if it meant in practice that the trees would take 20 years to grow. With a regulated gradient of 200 metres, that is, gently flowing over a long distance, the main canal and its parallels stretched through the south of the Soviet Union. Never before had humans created such a sea and an artificial river of such size.

On that flight to Tokyo with Heiner Müller and Ryszard Kapuściński there was a climate researcher from Potsdam. He chimed in on the conversation between the two friends passionately catching their breath. He maintained that the Siberian Sea, had it ever come to be, would have led to a massive temperature increase of the permafrost in the northern tundra and thereby to an uncontrollable release of gases, from methane to carbon dioxide: the sky above Russia—or the entire planet—would have been poisoned. And you think, Kapuściński and Müller replied, that Davidov's engineers would have been unaware of a way around it? Supposing, that is, that they'd been surprised by this phenomenon in the first place and not calculated it in advance, ominous calculators that they were? Müller pointed out that a drama about this project performed at the Berliner Ensemble would in no way harm the earth's climate.

In the meantime, the plane had turned southeast. High mountain ranges, which Müller no longer believed to be Siberia, appeared in the oval windows. Why wasn't the Siberian Sea realized later on? The plans would have required a construction period of 10 years. These 10 years were not initially available to Davidov's team: the revolution bottomed out. The members of the 1929 planning staff and the engineers who were still omnipotent in the 1920s and who could have implemented such a project were arrested and killed just five years after the preliminary work began. Until then, the preparatory work consisted of studies, the gathering of cadres and budgets, the development of large-scale equipment on blueprints of the kind needed for moving massive amounts of earth. The utopian prospect of a Siberian Sea, even of the dense settlement in that eastern part of the continent (as if it were Mars), had given Müller a pleasant feeling (to say nothing of his cloud of cigar smoke). He wanted to banish from his mind the images of the 'purges' and hopeless show trials.

Changing the subject, Müller said that Emperor Meiji's reforms lasted only 50 years. Out of a medieval country emerged an industrial nation whose steel ships sent the tsar's fleet to the bottom of the sea. 'That would be a good way to start off my lecture in Tokyo,' Müller said. Similarly, in 100 years, Siberia could have been turned into a 'blossoming landscape' on the Euro-Asian landmass, Kapuściński added, complete with holiday cottages on the shores of the Siberian Sea, with avenues lined with poplars swaying in the wind. The two debaters and window-gazers (the plane was not crowded, so one of them could look out of the left window while the other looked at the landscape to the right) did not know that, 25 years later, a consortium of oligarchs, working with engineers from Gazprom, would revive the project of a central water basin in Siberia. This time to make a profit without any particularly utopian intention. Where else on planet Earth (apart from Antarctica and the Sahara) can you situate such a comprehensive plan? Directing the sun's rays onto the northern plains of Siberia, a group of orbiting mirrors 100 kilometres wide are to heat up the land mass so quickly that the gas stored in the ground can be sucked immediately into containers before it reaches the heights of the stratosphere and causes havoc.

FIGURE 33. Diverting Siberian currents. The waterway project of 1929. Davidov was considered a believer in Karl August Wittfogel's so-called hydraulic hypothesis; a short time later, this marked him a heretic.

FIGURE 34. A. A. Smirnov-Schmidt.
Davidov's lover and chief engineer.

KETS = HUMAN BEINGS

PARTICULARITIES OF A LINGUISTIC TUNNEL
IN THE YENISEI VALLEY

In 1934, N. K. Karger, whose soul I often visit (I say this as the
author of this *Container*), drove a rickety vehicle (cobbled together
by a mechanic in Omsk from the remains of seven old cars) into the
windy ways of the Yenisei valley. He was a linguist.

sūl 'blood' – su'l 'Siberian salmon' – sùl 'hooks' – súùl 'sleigh'. It
is the intonation, not the letters, that determines what the words
mean. This is the language of the Ket people of Siberia. Karger
examined them. A decree from the Central Committee authorized
him to do so. With the dedication of young social revolutionaries
and folk researchers, a special urban spirit, transported to the
impassable, swampy Yenisei Valley—: the young Karger senses,
gathers, rejoices, tinkers, moves, *hopes*. Records, record-recording
equipment, boxes full of shellac for the phonemes. He travels
through the land of the Kets alone with himself and his research. In

the files of the Central Committee, this people and these speakers of a language foreign to Russian are called Ostyaks. They refer to themselves as ke't = human being. They trust their odd guest: despite having presented himself like a foreigner with his leather jacket, pistol, leather belt, tall boots ('militant', 'commissar-like'). Like someone from the Central Committee. But the term Central Committee would make no sense to them. Karger still has no idea which word, which term, which concept they would connect to a being known as 'Central Committee'. They can see that he is interested in them, and so they believe that what they say is captivating to him. In fact, what interests him is the HOW: the words, sentences, grammar, intonation—whatever strikes him.

KARGER:
A PRECIOUS-STONE EXAMINER OF EXPRESSIONS

The tonemes of the Ket language. Examination of the sounds according to mouth position, throat and tongue. With the typical linguistic labels:

High	ā	even or gradually rising progression
Glottalized	a', a?	abrupt glottal stop after a short vowel
Rising-falling	á-à	used for geminated vowels or adjacent syllables
Falling	à	used in Southern Ketish only with short vowels

Numerous speakers in the room are here. They speak when prompted, in singsong, almost 'poetically'. They do this whenever Karger asks them to talk about the past. They only speak 'animatedly' when they have not been prompted. They do this among themselves and when there is an occasion. The occasion can also be the interjections of others or a story. They are 'animated' by Karger and begin to speak 'artificially' (they do not sing poetically). It sounds stilted and breaks off again immediately. When they are asked to speak by the stranger, no one not explicitly asked dares to interject in the speech of another. Present are two field guards, two fishermen, three female net weavers (friends), two hunters.

The international organization for world communism, the *Comintern* for short, is throwing its support behind Esperanto. This international language for peace shortens words and mixes them together from various languages. The Ket language would not be present. According to the international movement, Esperanto can overcome the world's various linguistic barriers. It's a telegram language. Karger thinks the opposite is true. He believes that languages, of their own accord, do not serve the purposes of information. The words and sounds show off their beauty, their fur, their speed in contest with the stars of the sky, which, for their part, serve no communicative function either.

The reality of this moment of research, this 'round of chitchat and the researcher', is something complex, a composite. Karger would not be here if he did not have the protection of the deputy head of the Cheka in Moscow. He has taken a fancy to Karger. He doesn't understand what the dictionary-lover is looking for so far away. But he considers him an important researcher. He has placed him in a planning group that usually consists of oil prospectors and geologists. Without this long-distance relationship, there would be no 'exercise in proximity' because Karger wouldn't be here at all.

LIVELY/AGITATIVE/VIVID AND WILD

Those in my charge, he writes to his confidant in the Cheka, distinguish 'twelve cases' for nouns. In addition to the usual classifications in European languages, from genitive to accusative, they have the

–benefactive (I approach you in [= with my] support),

–the adessive (describing a context while I am speaking about an individual thing),

–the prosecutive ('I love and am interested in you, but will disappoint you later on'),

–the comitative (the 'social case par excellence . . . !'),

–the caritive ('without'; 'that which I do not have while I continue to speak about something I do have'),

–the translative ('I am bringing', 'I am transferring', 'I am connecting'),

–the locative ('where I am while doing or thinking something'; 'later perhaps we can *do* what we cannot *talk about* at the same time').

Irregular plural formation:

tīp ('many dogs') > ta'p 'dog'

iʔ > ékèŋ 'day'

ī > íyàn 'sun'

ōks 'tree' > a'q 'trees'

ke't 'human being' > de'ŋ 'human beings'

THE KETS' SOPHISTICATED GRAMMAR

Karger: 'As an individual, I am not only something special or different, but am in a world different from that of the pack, the crowd, the assembly, society. IN GENERAL, KETIC DISTINCTIONS BELONG IN A LIST TO BE SUBMITTED TO THE NEXT INTERNATIONAL CONFERENCE. As far as thinking goes, it is not a question of expanding horizons, but of a better, more precise structuring of what has long existed within political horizons,' Karger emphasizes. 'Even when Ket words focus on hunting and gathering, the discriminating power of their formulations is superior to the texts of all our political assemblies!'

'The abilities of this language must enter (i.e. as a marching column, as an arsenal of weapons, as a critical potency) into the march of socialism, the victory that I (= Karger) expect by autumn 1929.' This is what the linguist wrote before his travels, while he was still studying Ket from afar.

Variance of words in the plural:

–*des* (Ket word for:) 'eye'

–*dès* (short, stammered:) 'pair of eyes' (in a person)

–*déstàŋ*: 'many eyes'; for example, when speaking about ants

Translative: something is changing while I am in the process of observing it

Depending on pitch, the grammatical genders change between masculine, feminine, and neuter/inanimate

'MARX FOR ANIMISTS'

After a time, Karger read the *Communist Manifesto* with his group of Kets—as a speaking exercise. In standard Russian. The aim was to prepare a translation into their language. Seven readers and their leader. The Kets enjoyed chasing down words. With the printed text and their provisionally translated words. With the same respect for words that is due to an animal hunted down. Some of the river fishermen understood Russian.

The study group didn't get too far. They got stuck on the word 'spectre', which is found in the very first sentence of the *Communist Manifesto*. How many different kinds of spectres there are! Tiny ones. Smaller than a fingernail. Others as large as the cloud front that moves south over the Yenisei river while the current moves north. Are swamp ghosts spectres or not? You might even ask, one of the members of the group said, whether there is anything that is not a spectre, or what a human being or animal that does not have a spectre inside them is supposed to be. Furthermore, my shadow could really be a spectre that's haunting me. The word 'spectre' corresponds to the word for 'alive'. And the word 'alive' means 'spectre'. There is no master in the room who can tame spectres. Karger decides to keep his own counsel throughout the debate.

THE CENTRE OF THE COUNTRY

The statement comes from Andrei Bitov: The centre of Russia can only be grasped as a subjective factor. Any attempt to determine it geographically will remain in vain. In fact, there are no historical records of anyone ever crossing the entire country, from the Neman all the way to the Pacific, on foot. Throughout its history, the boundaries have changed as well. Any potential conquerors, Bitov points out, could not have reached any 'centre of the country' from either east or west without vehicles. Furthermore, there is no one 'way', no through-route that would take one to any such centre. Turgenev, repeating an old *Lied* by Georg Lübeck, goes even further. He asks: 'Where are you, my beloved land? / Sought after, felt, but never known?' He disputes that Russia can even be described at all, either as a place or collection of places.

> 'And again and again the sigh it asks: Where?
> Where my friends have gone wandering,
> Where my dead rise from the grave'

The geodesist Smirnov took the trouble to sketch its centre on a topographical map stretched out over two drawing tables. The drawing sketched the average distances from the Russian border in the west in relation to the average line of Russia's sea coasts in the east. It remained inaccurate as a 'centre'. No place, no crowd of patriotic feelings, no assembly hall decorated with flags corresponded to this 'centre'. So the best that could be said was that the viewer look for the centre in 'any circumference' of the line Smirnov had drawn. Smirnov abandoned his plan.

'ON THE ISLAND OF EZELI
WE GOT ALONG EASILY.
I WENT TO KAMCHATKA
WHERE YOU WERE A HAT-CHECK GIRL.
FROM THE HEIGHTS OF ALTAI
I SMILED AND SAID "HI!"
ON THE SHORES OF AMUR,
L'AMOUR.'

—*Collected Works of Velimir Khlebnikov, Volume III: Selected Poems* (Paul Schmidt trans.) (Cambridge, MA: Harvard University Press, 1997), p. 31.

FIGURE 35. The 'collective worker'. What the all-powerful worker is grabbing, as if they were just simple snakes, are three storeys worth of power cables which could cause a city to explode.

HERMETIC AND ASSOCIATIVE POWERS

Ilse von Schaake had lived with her Russian lover for a long time; he was writing a study in Berlin for the Akademgorodok Science Centre on the POTENTIALS OF ENVIRONMENTAL CHANGE ON A GLOBAL SCALE. The subsequent question ran: Which forces in people tend towards association, which prevent a unification of forces?

The comrade had left this work unfinished; at the same time, he had left his companion for a younger woman (from a family with industrial assets in North Rhine-Westphalia). To this day, Ilse von Schaake has not been able to banish this traitor completely from her heart. In the meantime, out of defiance and tenacity (characteristics that were traditional in her family), she has continued his project. The volume comprises around 2,000 pages. Publishers throughout East Germany, with whom she is in contact, have shown no interest.

She comes to the following conclusion: there are powerful forces in people (*my* family, *my* descendants, *my* property) which have a *hermetic* effect. They do not allow for any comprehensive associations with strangers. They are unsuitable for revolution. They are opposed by weaker and weaker forces (an interest in physics, an interest in logic, the interest shown by friends-of-postage-stamps). Weak forces can be united quickly and bring about social change in the long term. According to Ilse von Schaake, even the evolution of modernity can be traced back to such weak forces. In evolution, weak forces exclusively bring about weak changes, but these in turn add up to the greatest developments. *Weak messianic power* (Walter Benjamin)—in other words, recourse to historical roots—is the only source of hope.

HOW WALTER BENJAMIN EXPLAINED 'WEAK MESSIANIC POWER' TO BERTOLT BRECHT

The direction of the arrow of political utopia: the shot arrow of the *pursuit of happiness* has a natural right to persistently pursue its target. It is the political direction. But this direction of the arrow of history is different from the almost inaudible movement—perceptible only to the political-theological archaeologist—which betrays the proximity of the messiah. It too is an arrow. But here, says Benjamin, as far as the relationship between arrow and arrival is concerned, it is important to consider Kafka's story 'THE NEXT VILLAGE'.

None of this happens in some future, nor does it come from a specific past, but takes place permanently in abrupt shocks and momentary flashes. This second direction of the arrow is the 'weak messianic power'.

How can it be used? asked Brecht. For mobilization? Brecht, the operative poet, was always getting down to business. Benjamin tried to explain that no one and nothing could grasp, store, test, use or *do* anything else with the weak messianic force. One could only *know* that it existed.

Then it is of no use, Brecht insisted. He pointed out, however, that at an earlier point in the conversation—mist crept in from the shore, the light faded—Benjamin had mentioned that the two so disparate arrows of time, the political and the messianic, had an influence on each other. He remained curious. That evening, the friends did not come to any agreement.

FIGURES 36–7. ANGELUS NOVUS (1920) and PRICKLE THE CLOWN (1931). Both by Paul Klee. Together, we can consider the two to be good archaeologists, with PRICKLE being more practically minded than NOVUS.

TWO UNEQUAL ANGELS OF HISTORY
WITH PICK AND SPADE
ACTIVE AS ARCHAEOLOGISTS
STOCKPILING COURAGE THROUGHOUT
HISTORY'S BRIEF QUIET TIMES

In the ANGELUS NOVUS, we read: 'The angel would like to stay, awaken the dead, and make whole what has been smashed. But a storm is blowing in from Paradise; it has got caught in his wings with such a violence that the angel can no longer close them. The storm irresistibly propels him into the future [. . .] *This* storm is what we call progress' (Walter Benjamin, *Illuminations*, Harry Zohn trans., New York: Schocken Books, 1969, p. 249).

Before PRICKLE THE CLOWN's eyes is that 'pile of debris' that 'grows skyward'. But the wit within them blows pieces out of this heap into the distance. He has picks and spades. He'd like to lend the tools to his colleague NOVUS on a case-by-case basis.

WALTER BENJAMIN IN MOSCOW

Changes of place caused him to suffer. Travelling to countries whose languages he did not speak was unsettling. He felt somewhat alien-ated when he got off the Berlin-Warsaw-Moscow train. Only the rigour of his mind, his so-called consciousness, drove him there.

That same evening, members of the INTERNATIONAL DEPARTMENT / CULTURE SECTION brought him to a dance and revue performance. They had heard that he was interested in inno-vations which had come about thanks to the masses having taken over. Fascism could not appropriate what belonged to the masses.

Gazelle-like bodies from the mountaineering population of the Caucasus had been organized for the performance, gathered together and transported to the capital. The revue theatre's broad stage wasn't all that suitable for the presentation of the plot. The dance groups formed lines to fill the stage and performed gymnastic exercises. To the music of balalaikas, accordions, trumpets and drums.

Benjamin considered this to be a false—namely, commando-like—proximity. When it came to establishing a relationship with the Caucasus, that is to say, with the Prometheus that was chained there, the event had to be portrayed on stage as *distant and unapproachable*. Prometheus was still far from being unchained. The vulture neither frightened off nor scared away. But the peoples of the Caucasus, that much the foreigner from Berlin knew, who had put their sons and daughters at the disposal of the revue collective like a crowd of slaves sent to the minotaur, had already been subjugated decades ago, if they had ever emerged as independent peoples at all. They were pure raw material for humanity, something other than a gymnastics dance line coordinated according to beat and command. As raw material, corrupted and dead. As something Soviet-*völkisch*, embalmed and made-up like a corpse. That was the learned man's desolate feeling.

Only silence could protect him: even while he was unafraid of the persecution which had begun to rage throughout his host country, what he feared was the rise of fascism in Central Europe. With regard to this, he was a prophet. He foresaw the future year 1942 in every moment of the present, even while gazing at a decoratively lit stage in a darkened auditorium in 1926. The stage: innocent, nationalized, humiliating. The dangers lay outside the room.

As was the case in almost all European theatres, the blue lights installed above the emergency exits—after all the many catastrophes in which people had pushed their way to the doors—were comforting. The blue ensured they did not disturb the performance. This seemed to be an authentic expression to Benjamin. It indicated that, despite the synthetic performance in HOLY MOSCOW, a piece of reality still welcomed him. For Benjamin was hungry for reality, could not give it up, even though he thought it was poisoned.

'Ancient Egypt's nationalized grounds
adorned corpses with all kinds of stuff'

Transssibirien-Express

Stuttgart-
Nürnberg- Leipzig- Dresden-
Warszawa- Minsk- Moskva-
Novosibirsk- Irkutsk-
Chabarowsk

Stg.-Bad Cannstatt 1983

FIGURES **38** (ABOVE) AND **39** (BELOW)

'SOVIET TRAFFIC IS THE RAIL ON WHICH THE LOCOMOTIVE OF HISTORY RUNS'

'THAT WON'T WORK, THE LOCOMOTIVE RESPONDED WITH THE HUMILITY OF REASONABLE POWER'

Throughout 1919, a lot of experience with repairing was gained at the locomotive park at the hub of Tver. None of the steam engines were what they had been in their youth. Sheet metal, brass and iron parts had been removed from foreign locomotives to be installed in others. Chassis were replaced.

Rails: colourful brothers. Spirit of my spirit. Within a single week, a construction brigade had dismantled the rails between Tver and Stop 114B, and erected halls out of the iron bars. One hand of socialist construction did not know what the other was doing.

When the managers of the railway junction were replaced by administrative action and a rough military force tried to get trains running south, one after the other, 16 out of 19 locomotives, like animals tired of wearing a saddle, malfunctioned out on the open rails. The three remaining locomotives, only now to be put into operation as replacements, did not respond to their new tamers' amateurish attempts. In a way, they were emotionally attached to the people who'd repaired and oiled them so often. On that May morning, nothing at all worked at the railway hub of Tver.

'PULL THE SKIN OVER YOUR EYES AND LISTEN'

A railway engineer, a revolutionary from the very start, whose great-great-grandson today supplies a space station, reports: 'We hear the echo of the machines entrusted to us for miles around. We just have to put our ear to the tracks. The buzzing of the telegraph wires in the wind of the steppes tells us just how the screws and buffers of those machines we release into the distance "feel". We couldn't see everything with our eyes anyway. Our "social senses" connect us railwaymen to the moving machine. We see the state of "orderly running" in a locomotive, whether it is stationary or running. Nor do we just listen with our ears to see if there is sufficient steam. Our locomotives and wagons, the switches and signal boxes, speak to us before our mind even registers the respective state. We hear future disasters as if we too were experiencing them. In the meantime, daily experiences accumulate in us, the weeks and years coordinate: the revolution, thoughts of home and of those we have lost on the long road of the early years. What the machinery can do in an emergency, we can guess. Nothing screeches as piercingly as metal on metal.'

'AND FURTHER, ZAKHAR PAVLOVICH HAD OBSERVED THE SAME BURNING, AROUSED POWER IN THE LOCOMOTIVES AS THAT WHICH LIES SILENT WITH NO OUTLET, IN THE WORKING MAN.'

FIGURE 40.

img231

russische_eisenbahn00017

russische_eisenbahn00019

russische_eisenbahn00022

russische_eisenbahn00027

russische_eisenbahn00032

russische_eisenbahn00037

russische_eisenbahn00040

FIGURE 41. The Paris-Vladivostok-Tokyo railway line.
At bottom left, a zeppelin hovering above the Arctic coast.

'TEN OR MORE NAMELESS PEOPLE SAT ON THE FLOOR AND HOPED FOR A TRAIN THAT WOULD TAKE THEM TO A BETTER PLACE'

'SOME MUSICIANS WERE WALKING FROM THE STATION THROUGH THE FIELDS, PLAYING SAD MUSIC'

'THE PASSENGERS RAN OFF WITH TEA KETTLES, TERRIFIED AT EVERY RUSTLE THE LOCOMOTIVE MADE, NOT WANTING TO BE LEFT BEHIND AT THIS STATION FOREVER. THEY COULD HOWEVER HAVE GOTTEN STRAIGHT-ENED AROUND WITHOUT HURRYING— THE TRAIN STAYED AT THAT STATION FOR A DAY AND ALSO SPENT THE NIGHT THERE'

' . . . AN IRON POT ADDED TO A WATER-COOLED MACHINE GUN YIELDED A STILL'

FIDELITY—AT THE HEART OF ALL PARTICULARITIES

LEONORE'S FIDELITY IN BEETHOVEN'S ONLY OPERA / 'LEONORE FREES HER MAN FROM PRISON'

PERSEVERANCE

INCORRUPTIBILITY

FELONY (BETRAYAL FROM ABOVE)

MUTINY (BETRAYAL FROM BELOW)

'BRING WHAT YOU LOVE BACK FROM HELL'

'TOVARISHCHESTVO': CAMARADERIE. THE RUSSIAN WORD IS MORE COMPREHENSIVE THAN THE GERMAN AND IMPLIES CONFRATERNITY, TOGETHERNESS, COLLECTIVITY, THE EXISTENCE OF COMMUNITY, FRATERNITY.

'AH, MY COMRADE IN ARMS / RIDE AHEAD WITH YOUR SONG / LONG PAST TIME WE MET DEATH . . . / BE SURE FIRST THAT YOUR FOE HE IS DEAD / ONLY THEN ON HIM LAY DOWN YOUR HEAD . . . '

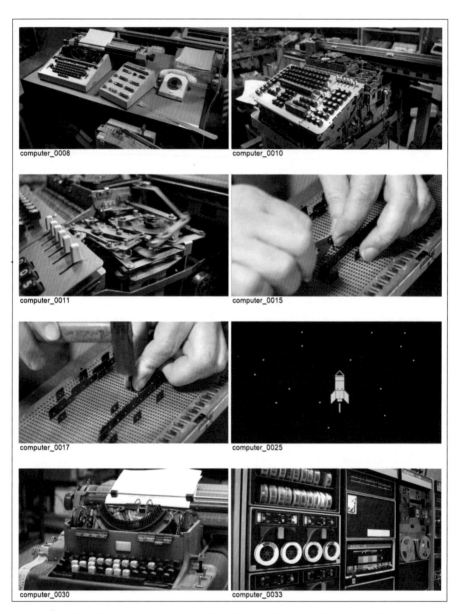

FIGURE 42. A mechanical computer from the era of punched-tape technology in the Eastern Bloc. Overtaken by progress but still reliable. The devices, produced in Karl-Marx-Stadt, today's Chemnitz, were sold 300,000 times to faraway countries. The rocket in computer game 0025 still works today. In 0017: fixing punch-strip programming with a hammer. The analogue storage media in 0033 can no longer be copied in the digital world.

FIGURE 43. Fidelity for things.

FIDELITY, THE MOST EXPLOSIVE SUBSTANCE
ON EARTH

American author Tom Clancy wrote best-selling books. Long before the terrorist planes hit the Twin Towers and the Pentagon outside Washington, DC, long before the debate arose as to whether in such a case 'this incoming projectile and its passengers' should be shot down by fighter planes, Clancy developed an idea for a novel. Shortly before his death, he was still writing the manuscript, two-thirds of which is available. He describes a group of officers (colonels) whose own commanders prevent them from standing by their comrades, the Kurds, their brothers-in-arms. The US officers and the Kurds had been together in Iraq and then Syria. Now the Kurdish troops are to be rolled up by the Turkish, and the US president has ordered the US officers assigned to protect the Kurds to be withdrawn to the US. They will not be able to save their 'allies' from their situation. In the end (Clancy died before settling on the right terminology), these PRAETORIANS arrest the US president. They take over the White House. They take command of the operation that manages to get the almost-lost comrades out of the trap. They violate the Constitution: 'to save their own honour'.

A STATISTICAL SURPRISE

For Armin Schwanders, PhD, based in Wellington, New Zealand, a breach of trust and infidelity are statistically 37 times stronger a motive for rebellion and coups than the next most important reasons: rivalry, lust for power, affronts or 'insight into the necessity of the matter'.

HIDDEN-TREASURE HUNTERS

Either you have the billions of dollars available for American research or you've got to have ideas like the Count of Monte Cristo, Chechen researcher V. B. Anatoly said. He had nothing but a rotten laboratory that belonged to the facilities of an oil company which had once been responsible for cultivating the landscape. What makes the world dangerous for Anatoly? What is he afraid of?

Well, the treasure this treasure hunter was seeking consisted of the following: in the billions of years in which the sun has been successfully orbiting the Milky Way, particles of a substance unknown to us, DARK MATTER, have streamed in over the poles and flowed to the earth's core. There they lie trapped. Anatoly wanted to . retrieve this treasure. Whoever is the first to win the cooperation of these 'TRAPPED EXTRATERRESTRIALS', or even their affection, will be able to rule the world, even from Grozny.

At least in terms of science. Elementary particles of DARK MATTER do not react with terrestrial matter. What did V. B. Anatoly intend to do with the treasure if, that is, he ever got hold of it? You can't make gold with it, he said to himself, but you'll be able to *some*thing with it. He was attracted by the unknown.

Scrap metal is, first and foremost, a raw material. Anatoly wants to expand his laboratory. Russia's secret services, however, must not find out about his plans, nor the Turkish-American lobby which is on the lookout for investment objects in Russia's south. So Anatoly and those he trusts have spread the rumour that they are interested in explorations related to oil or natural gas. This is credible to his predatory opponents and, because they are arrogant, understandable enough as a regrettable mistake. They underestimate the ideas that move dispossessed scholars in their hearts.

FIGURE 44. Routine weight examination of a space dog in 1958. Next to him is Ludmilla Radkevich from the 'Research Institute for Aerospace Medicine'. Fidelity, faithfulness, is when what I have sent out comes back all in one piece. Adolf Hitler behaved 'unfaithfully' towards the German 6th Army.

IN THE EVENT SOMEONE MAKES CONTACT WITH EXTRATERRESTRIALS, HOW WILL WE COMMUNICATE?

Anatoly often visually imagines the 'prison camps of alien matter' he seeks to contact. Where exactly in the earth's core would he have to look for it? They have, as is said of spirits, their seat not in the centre itself; rather, they orbit the centre. This is dictated by the force of gravity, from which they also brace themselves. The centre is certainly not located in the geometric centre of the earth, Anatoly says, but, again, somewhat to the side of it. In the meantime, the researcher is working at the Vostok Station in Antarctica. He won the job lottery. He has new types of equipment taking measurements in the search for DARK MATERIAL. 'We're keeping an eye out,' Anatoly says, 'to see whether this mighty force lets itself be called on by the spirits dwelling, like the sirens, in the earth's axis, and answering unexpectedly, mistaking their calls for ones from their own kind.'

'LIKE A GUARDIAN ANGEL
I OFTEN WALK ALONG
DISPENSING FRIENDLY ADVICE'
—A. PUSHKIN

WINTERSCAPE.
A DISCLOSURE FROM ALEXANDER PUSHKIN

Compared to a Russian SLEIGH (ДОРОЖНЫМИ САНЯМИ), Alexander Pushkin says, LOVE (ЛЮБОВЬ) is MANIFOLD (МНОГО-ОБРАЗНА). The HEAVENLY POWER (СИЛА НЕБЕСНАЯ) consists of intensified discrimination. Whether I love or not makes a difference. From this difference, energy is formed. Compared to a SOUL CARRIAGE (КАРЕТОЙ ДУШИ), love consists of the power of the harnessed horses, the rotation of the wheels, the frame and the way the driver navigates, yet it also includes the passengers as well as the seats upon which they sit. And, at the same time, it consists in the rapid journey (в быстрой езде) across the expanse of snow, corresponds to the hand of God, the winter sky and the distant lights of the houses towards which the sleigh is heading. Having said that, as to the question of whom the occupants will choose as a sacrifice (жертвой) for the wolves at their proverbial heels, Pushkin concludes, in order to run out the tiny grains of time they still need to reach the safety of the hamlet, love does not play any role (любовь).

HOW CHANCE BROUGHT ABOUT GENERATIONS OF DESCENDANTS IN A SINGLE WINTER NIGHT

In December 1811, a 17-year-old girl named Marja—capable of passion and, against the will of her parents, ready to marry a young man she believed she loved undyingly—managed to arrive at a church despite the snowstorm then overrunning southern Russia, which made any orientation on the way impossible and violently hindered the progress of the sleigh.

> 'Since it would be impossible for us to breathe without
>   each other,
> and the will of our cruel parents stands in the way of our
>   happiness,
> could we not make do without their consent?'

The girl had reached the church where, as agreed, the priest and the witnesses were already waiting. But in that same snowstorm, her beloved had become completely lost. He was two-and-a-half-hours away, he'd got confused by a wood, turned around, and both his sleigh and those of his companions went in directions that led nowhere. As a result of the extreme effort of the journey (to act against her parents, to practically sink in the masses of snow), the young woman had fainted on the church bench.

On that same stormy night, another sleigh, that of a cavalry captain named Burmin, had chosen a shortcut with a goal indifferent to the action, namely, to take the path across a river course, but he missed the turnoff due to the snow clouds and ice-rain and finally, by chance, thanks to the presence of lights which impressed the driver, arrived at the church, where the witnesses and the church servants were standing anxiously around the girl who'd fainted. They called out to the man as he arrived: 'Thank God! We could hardly wait. You almost killed the girl.' The clergyman approached the snow-covered cavalryman and asked, 'Shall we begin?' 'Yes, begin, Reverend Father,' replied the man, still a bit out of his senses after his battle with the elements but also moved by a bit of recklessness, for the girl lying on the bench seemed quite attractive to him.

An inexplicable, unforgivable recklessness . . .

I stood next to her at the altar, the priest was in a great hurry; three men and the maid supported the bride.

That's how we were married.

'Kiss each other,' the clergyman said.

The woman turned her pale face to the stranger.

Already he wanted to kiss her . . .

She cried out: 'Oh, it's not him! It's not HIM,' and fainted again.

The confused cavalryman turned, left the church, rushed into the sleigh and shouted, 'Go!'

The parents of the slender, pale girl, who refused food and seemed infinitely sad, regretted their attitude. Eventually, they agreed to the misalliance between this rich young woman and the poor lover whom she had secretly aspired to marry. However, the young man, an ensign, had in the meantime been killed in action against Napoleon's 1812 invasion at Borodino. Now it seemed that there would no longer be any prospect of descendants who might have managed the large estate in the future. Ready for any compromise, the girl's parents were nevertheless at a loss.

Then a cavalry captain named Burmin appeared at the court of the picky heiress Marja. At long last, she did not refuse this particular suitor. Marja's skin was 'irritated', red from neck to chest, her senses 'excited'. In the decisive conversation, which the parents favoured, this man confessed to Marja that he loved her, but that he was prevented from marrying her because he'd been married the year before, 'through recklessness'; it was 'incomprehensible to him', 'without any share of his true willpower'. The young woman, seeing through the intrigue of fate, pulled the man to her and kissed him.

This is a story by Alexander Pushkin about 'condensed time'. It shows how much he is a BROTHER OF HEINRICH VON KLEIST'S WITHIN THE WORLD'S SOUL, and the world's soul, as we all know, consists not of ONE SPIRIT but of billions of fraternities between the living and the dead. Hence, a snowstorm here—a relatively uniform, long-lasting, massive natural event which has nothing to do with human beings—has managed to establish a connection, a connection between two human beings of which it cannot be said that conscious decisions, purposefulness of will or probabilities would have made possible on their own. In the meantime, these two lovers who came together by mistake have, including immigrants to the United States and those who escaped to Paris via Constantinople after 1917, 1,246 descendants who still tell the story about the fateful event in the week-long snowstorm of 1811. One of the genetic carriers from this association is currently an intern on a golf course in Florida, where snowstorms are not part of the equation. The story gives further evidence of the 'rule of particularities' in Russia.

ANNA KARENINA 1915

Her shy husband fell in Galicia. Major Vronsky, with whom she was still writing at that time, lost his egocentric life, a life for which he fought bitterly up till the very last moment, in a contaminated field hospital in northern Russia.

But she, a beautiful woman, cared for the wounded in Crimea. Every day, the trains fed the stream of dismembered people arriving there from the battlefields of the Brusilov offensive (Брусиловского прорыва). Considered the angel of the hospitals, she would walk among the rows of beds with her group of young girls. Wherever she went, the treatment of the wounded improved. As soon as the young women had visited the rooms, the doctors and the medical services once again considered the wounded—devalued by the amount of mutilations ('scrap from the battlefields')—human beings, if only because it was now possible to imagine each of those lying there as a person acting or suffering or convalescing in a NOVEL.

The following year, Anna Karenina married a doctor. In 1918, this surgeon took over the first Moscow polyclinic. Anna Karenina was a commissar with responsibilities for the civil war in southern Russia. Not much of a novel, but a lot of actual events. The couple enjoyed seeing each other, especially as their encounters were rare and their individual intentions did not always matter.

A WOMAN FROM 1986

Two months after the evacuation of Chernobyl, we were once again allowed to travel to our little white city, to visit our apartment. It was winter already. We gathered our winter clothes from the wardrobes.

–   You had a fur coat?
–   A nice one.

We also collected our down blankets. Everything was checked and measured with detectors to see if they were radioactive.

We went over everything with vacuum cleaners. Washing with soap doesn't do a thing. In the fur there was a spot. It was a coat made of wolf's hair. We did all we could to get rid of the spot. It was clearly a hot spot, a point-like infestation, caused by a scattered bit of radioactive dust. It wasn't a 'spot' you could have seen, but an excessive source of radiation: a land unto itself within great Russia, just a few centimetres in size, but deadly.

–   A foreign world?
–   To me.
–   Was your vanity hurt because it reached your lovely fur coat?
–   I'd always considered myself a lucky princess. Now I'm not so sure.
–   And what did you do with the beautiful piece?
–   As I said, we did all we could with the vacuum cleaner. With vinegar. With alcohol. Then we cut the few centimetres out and sewed the rest back up.

–   How did it look?

–   Off.

–   And the radioactive measurements?

–   There were none.

–   And so you wear the fur just like you did before?

–   My memento. It reminds me of the hot spot.

–   Where are you going with your things? Where do you show up with your fur on?

–   The cities. We live in St Petersburg now.

COUGHING BLOOD INTO
A HANDKERCHIEF IN RUSSIA

The commander of a partisan unit—a woman of forty who derailed 17 German transport trains with supplies near Minsk in 1944 and thus helped to bring about the legendary collapse of Army Group Centre (in other words, an independent thinker)—had felt helpless in her affection for the political Commissar Gerassimov to whom she had been assigned 18 years earlier. So gravitationally decisive was the current, the act of baptism, with which his closeness, his daily presence, submerged her underwater. Because of this water of the mind in which our decision-making powers swim, she had no more interest in anything other than this political man of skin and bones (no other man, no woman, no service of friendship; no rest by day or night, indeed, she was capable of working only for his sake). She grew emaciated. Mentally and then physically. The one she loved perceived nothing of her at all. With gaunt cheeks, he sought to turn the provincial nest to which he had been assigned by the Central Committee into an urban context, if possible, one populated by Bolsheviks (not only communistically minded, but communistically *active*).

Then it became obvious that he was spitting blood. And similarly clear that the love that Lyudmila (that was the latter resistance fighter's name) felt was not some kind of weak ideality but a material force. She travelled to the capital. She set in motion circles of command. Against all routine and probability, her beloved, who, as I said, knew nothing of his being the beloved, was provided with currency and sent to one of the Swiss sanatoriums. There—regardless of the quality of the oxygen in the mountain air—the art of healing had accumulated over the course of decades (with so much futility in the fight against the insidiousness of tuberculosis). The man was cured and served his Fatherland for another 40 years. He marvelled at the zeal of his benefactress, a subordinate who otherwise served him unobtrusively. Coughing blood into his handkerchief, however, he was so weak before his departure for the West that he did not bring the matter up. Soon after his return, war broke out. And so his angel remained undiscovered. We know that angels can only work their quiet magic thanks to such invisibility. Fixed by eyes, they freeze.

THE CONSTRUCTION OF SANATORIUMS
TO COMBAT TUBERCULOSIS IN RUSSIA

Still in the Khrushchev era, Lyudmila, who had risen in the hierarchy and was highly decorated as a militant patriot (though her motive was that she was only a 'servant of love') but who had also been demoted thanks to being a woman, continued to push a project for the construction of sanatoriums to combat consumption in Russia. But throughout the continent the air was too 'thick' no matter where you turned—the mountains were either not high enough or too far away from the centres of the medical arts—so the project never came to fruition. It remained obsolete as a PROJECT OF PROGRESS after 1945 as well because, in the meantime, the tubercle bacilli had been tamed by penicillin. This is how a piece of progress founded on love gets lost: a passing causality makes its use unnecessary. But Lyudmila—under socialist premises! under conditions of solidarity!—did not want to accept this as an argument. Progress as a piece of life stands beyond purpose; in this respect, it is like poetry, as both have their roots in the process of melting down ATTRACTION, or private passions which, as Lyudmila well knew, we call love.

She was also unwilling to consider the illogicality of using 'melting down', an industrial term, and 'root' at the same time. In

2017, Lyudmila had long since died, it became apparent that penicillin-resistant tubercle variants were resurging in Russia (especially in inhospitable western Siberia where the air is often like a thick fog). There are still no places throughout the great expanse of Russia like Davos in the past. In Switzerland, however, therapeutic treatments of the disease of which Kafka died have almost died out. Where a sanatorium once stood, now stands a world economic conference. Nothing can replace Lyudmila's testament, the monument to the man who spat blood into his handkerchief in Russia.

CHARACTERISTICS
OF A TRAVELLING BOURGEOIS WOMAN
Where is the face of a bourgeois soul?

The daughter of the millionaire and US ambassador to Germany William Dodd (not to mention Roosevelt's confidant) toured the Soviet Union and suffered greatly from the hygenic conditions on the small steamers that carried tourists down the Volga. The cast-iron toilets barely covered in paint were so rough that, over the years, they had held on to every foreign particle and every bit of dirt. This millionaire's daughter did not like to grace them with her western buttocks. Instead, she preferred to squat, straining her muscles, doing everything to avoid contact with that colourful cast iron.

Shortly before Astrakhan, she met a young man, an agent of the Soviet secret service, who later described her as follows: 'I met a bourgeois woman. This woman cleaned her anus—upon which she and all of us must sit—more carefully than she did her face. The latter is exposed to the wind and the weather and thus cleans itself, so to speak. Bourgeois women typically treat their facial skin with balms. At the same time, these citizens carry small rolls of soft paper (unsuitable for writing on). There are no records of any kind on these rolls (I checked them carefully); indeed, they are intended to be used to clean the anus of the actual activities of the intestine and then carelessly thrown away. The supply of such rolls is "sacred" to the person being observed, the citizen. She got very excited when her power of disposal over these rolls appeared to be suspended for a few hours (through a manipulation on our part, a test). I "found" the "papers" afterwards, to her reassurance, without her ever knowing why we had taken them away.

'The buttocks has a special sensitivity among such women. Apparently, this young woman has never been beaten there with rods. She responds to strokes on this anti-face, her most important organ of skin, with affection. Her shoulders, neck, and the backs of her ears are also sensitive. Her lips, on the contrary, which we Soviets use to initiate contact, are sooner employed for defence.

'She demanded absolute confidentiality concerning everything we exchanged in the short timespan of a few days. And she expected this above all from the US Embassy personnel we soon met in Astrakhan. I was unable to detect any anti-Soviet activities or secret knowledge (apart from the personal mores and erotic habits of a bourgeois woman).'—Signed A. M. Tchvirin, Major.

POETS OF THE OPERATION

The early Bolsheviks were urbanites. They hated being sent out to the country: to watch over the growth of the grain, to wait for the growth of the decades (organized in five-year plans). But back in the rooms at Moscow headquarters, all the world's props were on hand. Entire landscapes (which a single person's foot would not manage to cross even over the course of many years) were covered in the budget in a *single* sweep (единыммахом). As urbanites, the young Bolsheviks were office dwellers. The class enemy's plots, the organizational consolidation of one's own camp, these were rapid processes. They required a nimble brain.

A capable clique of such urbanites, all of them later exposed as Trotskyists, created OPERATION TRUST in 1921. On the face of it, it was an anti-Bolshevik resistance organization; it was said to have strong troops, members of the conspiracy in high party positions. This was how they challenged the tactics of the Western intelligence services. The anarchist Savinkov, who was conspiring with Western powers, and the 'Ace of Spies' Sidney Reilly approached the organization. They were arrested and executed.

The urbanites in civilian clothes (горожане в штатском) were early risers. They translated the skills of a watchmaker and a document forger into intelligence practices. For a short time after this action in 1921, Great Russia was free of enemy agents or infiltrators. The political poets who organized TRUST could also have organized a party if they had had the mandate to do so. The immensely artificial nature of their approach was on account of the places from which they came, all of which were in the West, which was awaiting revolutionization.

SOCIAL DISSIPATION / COMRADE UNFINISHED

In the early days of the Russian revolution, revolutionaries still worked individually. I knew many of them personally. The most important ones had heard of one another. It was easy to get to know other people, to say hello and to work together. There were more-or-less loose connections in the Central Committee (CC). This changed with the 'socialization' of our fifth of planet earth. Finally, in 1937, the individual was confronted with a powerful apparatus, an apparatus of impenetrable anonymity that referred to itself as 'everyone'. From a certain point on, it didn't matter whether anyone knew anyone else. The collective ruled through personal relationships. The hand was ice cold.

WHEN SAMAEL, THE ANGEL OF PUNISHMENT, TOOK AWAY JACOB'S 'STRENGTH OUTSIDE HIS BODY', NAMELY, HIS PROPHETIC POWER, JACOB'S HIP SOCKET CAME OUT OF JOINT.

FIGURE 45. Femoral neck. The human being's weak point. Here, at this point of the skeleton, the Denisovans had a thick joint.

The German Dictionary
by Jacob and Wilhelm Grimm, Book 1

Besonder, Besonderheit [particularity]

adv. singulatim, separatim,

specialiter, peculiariter. from the goth. particle sundrô,
from old high german suntar [. . .]

'i have known people and animals, BIRDS
as well as fish, many a PARTICULAR
worm, WONDERS of great nature.'
[. . .]

FIGURE 46. '. . . BIRDS, as well as fish, many a PARTICULAR . . .'

MEASUREMENTS FROM THE FATHER-LAND OF PARTICULARITIES

Pud = Weight measurement, 16.38 kg.

Desyatina = Surface measurement, 1.09 ha

Vershok = Unit of length, 4.4 cm

Archin = Unit of length, 77 cm

Sazhen = Unit of length, 2.14 m (3 archin)

Cheka = All-Russian Extraordinary Commission to combat counter-revolutionary activity and sabotage, abbreviation: Extraordinary Commission = *Chrezvychainaia Komissiia* = *Cheka*

A LACK OF INTERPRETERS AND MOUNTED RECONNAISSANCE—THIS IS WHAT KAFKA NOTED AS REASON NO. 19 FOR NAPOLEON'S DEFEAT IN RUSSIA.

'GRAB HOLD OF HISTORY'S COATTAILS AND PULL AS HARD AS YOU CAN'

It is a common misconception that a prophet knows more about the future than some uninspired contemporary. But they do know about recurrence, have a STANCE and know the LAW. They read the rapidly changing signs and see a STRUCTURE.

This method increases in the gifted grammarian. Grace is the light that the lamp of the soul casts upon the lines which, similar to the scurrying steps of a bird, stretch like a cord across the paper. With his words, Kafka got caught up in these cords. He wrote as long as his physical strength allowed.

FRANZ KAFKA WAS ABSOLUTELY DETERMINED

In the autumn of 1916, the Germans had decided to withdraw from Verdun. At that time, Franz Kafka had been determined for more than six weeks to write a major manuscript about Napoleon's retreat in the Russian winter of 1812: a novel, as he called it, indeed, if at all possible, a NEWSPAPER NOVEL.

Such a text would appear in the paper as instalments. It would be found in the immediate vicinity of the constant murmur of the commodity world (advertisements, news), which, like a stream or a small river, give us through their constant tone the certainty that the world is still intact, that the habits of life, the state of cities, will still hold for a while yet: that in the cosmos, the stars will not go out unexpectedly, that the silence of the underworld will not take hold of the globe in a flash. This is what the newspapers are there for, to say nothing of the dwindling mind.

And it was into such conditions that Kafka wanted to embed his report about the collapse of the Grande Armée. Those days had surprised the emperor, who had foreseen many things. In Kafka's opinion, the report would have made an attractive, popular collection of stories. The tightly written pages that make up the beginning of this project are among the few papers that Kafka's friend and companion later burnt. Not because Max Brod judged them differently from any of the grammarian's and prophet's other unpublished manuscripts, but because it was only after this burning that he decided *not* to obey Kafka's instructions. What remained were notes and reports by third parties from the coffeehouse where Kafka had discussed the draft.

AN ENTREPRENEUR AND THE POET

The operator of a panopticon stage from Olomouc who had recently set up his booth in Prague had listened to Kafka for a long time at the cafe. He had absorbed very little of the poet's grammatical and poetic precision, which could not be easily distinguished from the rest of the conversational environment and noise, what with all the people sitting at tables around them and talking in-between. He had been captivated by the 'situations', the 'scenes', but not by the wording. The common subtext between him and Kafka was the desire to serve a mass medium: in a newspaper or at a fairground stall. The professional entrepreneur, however, disapproved of Kafka's interest in newspaper magazines because he considered them plebeian, whereas he considered the target audience of his panopticon to be an EDUCATED PUBLIC: Napoleon's battles (not all of them, as far as Kafka was concerned) interested them both.

FIGURE 47. Franz Kafka.

WITNESSES

One participant at the table in the Prague cafe, Gerhard Kunze of the German Reich, usually got everything wrong. He was too excited when he listened. Furthermore, Kunze, who painted tin soldiers for a living, was too greedy when he tried. He also considered a newspaper editor, who set the tone in the round, to be more important than Kafka, devouring his comments while only superficially following the poet's halting diction. The poet revealed some of his work (and, in those days, that was the subject regarding Napoleon). Kunze provided some of the information about the lost Kafka text, or at least some of the material that follows. As I said, the man was not a very reliable witness.

FROM KAFKA'S DISCOURSES IN THE COFFEEHOUSE AND FROM NOTES FOUND IN A MORAVIAN BARN, STUCK TO RECEIPTS PAID BY THE POET

'29 September 1916, Marbot' (French general Marcellin de Marbot's memoirs)

'Fearless, exposed, powerful, surprising, gripped as otherwise only when writing.'

'The most profitable place for piercing appears to be between the throat and the chin. You lift the chin and stab the knife into the taut muscles. This place, however, is most likely profitable only at the theoretical level. There one expects to see a magnificent outpouring of blood and a weave of tendons and bones to tear into, just as in roasted turkey thighs.' (*note from when he was planning a crime novel*)

'Napoleon's retreat from the battlefield of Borodino. He's coming from the refused battle southeast of Moscow. The troops move over the fields. The remains of weapons and material. Despite the small amount of time that has passed on the calendar, the battlefield is no longer as it was on the evening of the battle. Wounded soldiers are lying in the monastery. After the troops leave, the hospital is blown up.'

'But many died, hundreds were seen with their bellies burst on the bridges of Pilony.' (*from notes from 1915*)

'Is God a theatrical chariot that, all the workers' toil and despair conceded, one ropes from out of the distance and pulls onto the stage?'

'The noisy trumpets of Nothing.'

'The commander stood by the window of the ruined cottage and with wide-open, lidless eyes looked into the rows of troops marching past outside in the snow and dim moonlight.'

' . . . even if I were infinitely more than I am, I would only be an envoy of life and connected to it by nothing more than this assignment.'

'It was already during the times of the last great battles which the American government had to lead against the Indians. The fort farthest into Indian territory—as well as the strongest—was commanded by General Samson . . . '

'"General Samson!" I called out while taking a shaky step back. It was he who stepped out of the tall bush. "Be quiet!" he said, pointing a finger behind him. A group of about ten men stumbled after him.' (*From the draft of a second America novel for a newspaper in Prague, stuck to the notes on Napoleon*)

THE EMPEROR WAS UNDECIDED

His indecisiveness increased to the level of the comparative. What is the intensification of indecisive? DESOLATE. At first, the strange summer desert before his eyes. The superlative was called CRIPPLING. As soon as the landscape flooded the grenadiers' minds with hopelessness in autumn, the terrain affected the emperor's soul as well. This was especially so, thanks to some earlier riding exercises, as the cavalrymen still mimicked a trace of the elan of earlier victories. The horses staggered along, far from the oats. This was not enough to explore the country of which the riders wanted to know nothing.

'ONE CANNOT SET UP ONE'S LIFE LIKE A GYMNAST DOING A HANDSTAND'

The gymnast had rubbed his arms and wrists with powder. He made a few attempts to stand up on his hands, with his legs stretched vertically. These attempts were made at shorter and shorter intervals. Finally, the able-bodied gymnast 'stood' with his back straight, toes like branches in the air. He held this position for a long time, without any supervision, just for the sake of it. Knowing that at any time he could, per simple request, perform the unnatural posture he had practised even if unrequired by necessity—e.g. a stroke of lightning. It was important for the gymnast to practise his art for its own sake. Not even a prize for curating works of art was offered for his body's achievements.

DESOLATE IN WINTER'S WASTES

When the emperor left Moscow, even less determined than before, he attempted to engage the tsar's army to the east. But then, without pursuing the intention seriously enough, he decided to retreat to Paris along the OLD ARMY ROAD (still devastated from his arrival there). The emperor's indecision and the desolation that had seized the army turned into a DISTASTE FOR HIS OWN ACTIONS. Such negative charisma gets transmitted to the troops in no time. And so it was an army of the discontented that marched on through the Russian winter.

But from which direction had winter come? Winter had come from the time lost from disuse since summer. Winter was above all the prospect of having to conquer Russia's vast expanses once again the following year: victory's fair copy. Yet, to all appearances, not a single one of the conquerors desired the land on either side of these roads.

The WEIGHT he carried in his soul, somewhere behind his ribs, dragged Napoleon downhill like a force of gravity. But what did 'valley' mean in terms of the Moscow-Smolensk road? What kind of mountain could it have to do with when the lowlands from Holland through West Prussia, Poland and Belarus to the area of Moscow had no hills that were more than 30 metres high? What was low was the collapse of motives (in this respect, 'downhill'). High simply the hurdles of friction. All this slowed down steps, thoughts and words. All the emperor could do was whisper from his throat, as if he had a cold.

THE RIDDLE OF BEREZINA

Despair is triggered by the realization that all the sacrifices of the last six months have been in vain. Hence such a SUDDEN HUNGER FOR PLUNDER. Its transport slowed the march. A person has to carry something: hope, a mission, a piece of loot.

Three hundred of General Eblé's pioneers are responsible for building one of the bridges over the Berezina thanks to which the French army is rescued. They are technically experienced. Doctors are organizing their operation. The emperor designates a site for the river crossing where the enemy will not expect it. The pioneers thus have a night, a day and a second night's advantage. At large footers, close to the pre-sorted equipment, hot punch is made. The pontoon soldiers are filled up to the neck with it (the doctor sees a human being as a skeletally supported vessel that absorbs a certain quantum of hot liquid and thus defies cooling). Then they step into the water, which first reaches their hips and then their collarbones. They drive in the piles, bring in bridge materials and tie the joints. A person can't stay in icy water for longer than 10 minutes. The doctors and officers shout at the pioneers with megaphones to keep these patriots' willingness to surrender under control. It takes a collective mental confusion of the entire column, a kind of forward-oriented panic, for people to bring about the self-forgetfulness necessary for such an operation. They will all die from it.

'PATRIOTIC DISINHIBITION'

Up to his neck in water himself, General Eblé later reaches Königsberg, survives his troops by a few weeks, but dies, amputated and exhausted, from the consequences of the undertaking. Bodies do not forgive.[2]

2 After 7 to 10 minutes (according to the physicians' assessment), the soldiers are brought to the fires, supported by their comrades, or rather carried; they are wrapped in skins. They begin to warm up, and hot wine is poured into them.

beresina00000
3840x2160 (7,82 MB)

beresina00001
3840x2160 (11,72 MB)

beresina00002
3840x2160 (10,94 MB)

beresina00003
3840x2160 (11,24 MB)

beresina00004
3840x2160 (11,27 MB)

beresina00005
3840x2160 (12,14 MB)

beresina00006
3840x2160 (9,88 MB)

beresina00007
3840x2160 (9,76 MB)

FIGURE 48

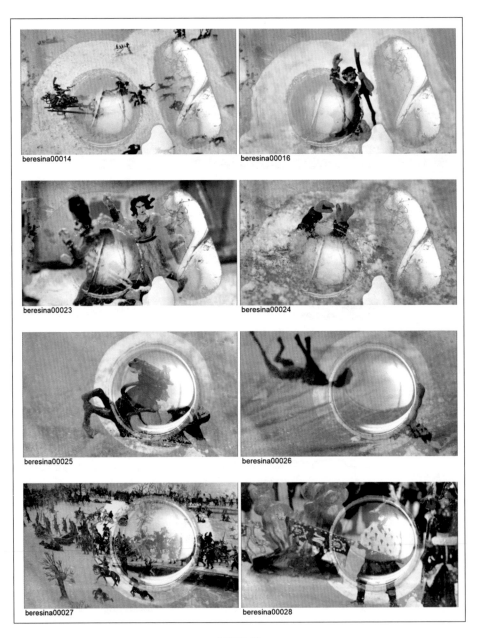

FIGURE 49

FIGURE 50

FIGURES 51 (ABOVE) AND 52 (BELOW)

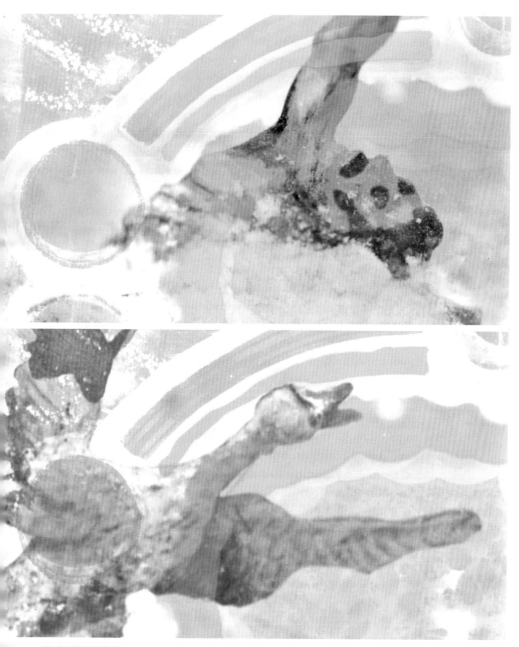

FIGURE 53 (ABOVE)

FIGURE 54 (BELOW). Flying goose. After being placed in a wicker basket and carried to the vicinity of the river, the bird escaped. The corporal who had done this drowned.

In the afternoon of the following day, the I Corps and the Emperor's Guard were able to cross the river. At first, the bridge crosses over swampy, only superficially frozen ground, then the river itself. The horrific images that later moved Europe's imaginations as prints were produced by book and newspaper publishers who had no witnesses at the scene. They are based on reports from the third day of the catastrophe, the accounts of battle-goers, 'consumers of the war'. The 'military producers' had crossed the river in an orderly fashion the previous day and opened the way westward in a series of battles.

The FIRST NIGHT'S PATRIOTS were also 'producers'. The technicians' dedication was terrible to watch. Where did this reserve of energy come from? The pioneers were farmers' sons who'd been individually trained in the Grande Armée to become engineers of a kind but who (below their qualifications) were serving out their time as pioneers. They, the patriots of industrial liberation, had stocked up these reserves. No patriotism without them. The mystery of the Berezina Bridge lies in how the officers (and the pioneers themselves) were able to draw on these reserves over just a few hours of the night, reserves enough to last an entire lifetime and which the self-aware only expend gram-by-gram. Clausewitz, later visiting the site, speaks of 'patriotic disinhibition supported by the punch but not triggered by it'. It has to do with a confusion of the senses, he says, caused by the simultaneous and ruthless activity of many like-minded people, comparable to a fleeing herd of horses, which no obstacle can stop and for which a fall into the abyss is no threat.

'DRAGGED INTO THE ABYSS WITH WEIGHTS'

But there was no abyss to be seen. Instead, all depth was drawn to the surface. As far as the maps were concerned, the path had an end. For the eyes of those disappointed, however, the journey was endless. And so, there were days that the inch worm—that snake of baggage trains and troops fighting among themselves—didn't move at all. Despite some surprisingly beautiful autumnal moments during their departure from Moscow, the troops were now drenched.

Freezing, they settled down to bivouac. However, as the landscape did not change, even those who continued to march failed to make any progress. The flat land devoured the army's pride.

All this time, the emperor carried an 'alchemical laboratory' around with him (in reality, the marshal's batons stowed in the grenadiers' knapsacks). In earlier times, one could produce 'hope' and 'lust' from imaginary bottles and magic potions. That the drug (like a chocolate-covered Pervitin concentrate wrapped in a lot of wool, to employ the metaphor of a future century) was still effective was proved in two of the most dangerous moments of the retreat. Having sprung up, it is difficult—the remark appears in one of Kafka's notes—for the jumper to push off a second time to jump even higher. One achieves this with an infinitesimal remainder, the tiniest bit of vigour. This is magic—and this is how the emperor, in danger, recovered his eagle-like ability to soar. This occurred when the Grande Armée's rearguard seemed lost and the emperor, together with his own imperial guard, turned back on the narrow provincial road, marched east towards the enemy and came to the rearguard's aid. In so doing, he saved at least something of his army and a piece of his pride.

NAPOLEON'S SOLDIERS WOULD HAVE MARCHED ALL THE WAY TO INDIA IF ONLY SOMEONE COULD HAVE EXPLAINED WHY

Summary: after Napoleon had finally betrayed the ideal of the French Revolution, he invaded Russia. His army numbered 450,000 men. His adversary, the Russians, 160,000. After 84 days of advance (including 14 days of pause at Vitebsk), he reached Moscow with 95,000 men. The rest were posted along the long route. On 19 October, he began his retreat. On 26/27 November, he crossed the Berezina with 14,000 soldiers and 26,000 stragglers. On 5 December, Napoleon left his troops.

The course of action was as follows: Napoleon drove a long hose to Moscow, then had to retreat again. It cannot be assumed that his army accompanied him voluntarily. As early as 1810,

160,000 people in Napoleon-administered Europe were convicted of refusing military service; measures were ordered against the families of those affected. Between 1811/1812, 60,000 recalcitrants (*réfractaires*) were convicted; the winter of 1812 was not an unusually cold winter. Later, to whitewash the emperor's defeat, Napoleon's collaborators declared nature to have been the enemy.

A SCENE WITH THE DEAD NEAR BORODINO

With their reptilian brains, the birds eyed the battlefield. They could do nothing with such a sight. Even the open eyes of the dead, which contained a watery substance, ponds for the animals' bitter thirst, were unattractive to the crows. The black birds were still stunned by the noise of the guns. A piece of bacon or a plum would have attracted their attention. There was still a lot of fat under the thin, wounded men's skin. Against a cloud of birds, the completely abandoned dead could not have defended themselves. But to mount such an attack, the animals would have had to retrain. The ways and experiences of their ancestors had separated themselves from those of our human ancestors millions of years ago. They were not used to breaking open human skin to access subcutaneous treasures. They were not man-eaters.

Nor were they accustomed to killing and consuming other birds. They would have valued loot from overturned supply vehicles. More hardship and longer times were required for relearning, for exploring new kinds of prey. So they sat, irritated, on shot-up trees, on the boards, planks and wheels of damaged vehicles. On the lookout for worms, disinterested in the filthy buckles and buttons of uniforms that would surely have riveted their gaze had the birds been sated and unruffled by the roar of gunfire and combat. And had the sun struck bright sparks off the soldiers' metal decorations. The clouds weighed heavy over the terrain. Snow would come. The emperor's troops marched off in the direction of Moscow.

IN HIS INTESTINES: STABBING PAIN,
THEN NOTHING, AN OCCASIONAL THROB

In October 1812, while Napoleon waited from day to day in Moscow for the tsar's emissary, assuming that this adversary would finally admit his defeat, when he, Napoleon, was undisputedly in possession of the capital. (The wait corresponded to the emperor's bossiness and proved fatal.) Thousands of kilometres from Moscow, in Rome, the excavations for the palace of the King of Rome, the emperor's son, were almost finished (in fact, it was all a stage for the emperor's triumphal procession, which was to conclude the Russian campaign). Streams of groundwater flowed from the Tiber into the excavated pit. After his victory over Russia and a detour to the Indus, the emperor wanted—via Persia and then from Alexandria by sea via Malta—to reach Rome, despite the fact that the climate had changed considerably since antiquity. He planned with the experience gained from books. In midsummer of 1813, he intended to take up residence in the metropolis of the *orbi*. An emperor is the guarantor of peace. After that nothing but legal opinions, fortresses, road construction, hot baths. Good for the stubborn intestines, which did not want to be like their powerful master. A weight-loss regimen? Rome was too hot for that. The emperor's body confused the necessary expansion of the empire's outer borders with that of its own volume.

NAPOLEON IN THE TRAP OF PARTICULARITIES

The ruler's word is so promising and sonorous that, if faced with the work of Sisyphus and having to accomplish something as simple as transporting a block of rock over the crest of a mountain, he would not have to raise his voice first. It's well known that, when thrilled, such super-stones ('blocks') rush uphill of their own accord and roll over the summits. Rulers of prehistoric times, it is said, possessed tremendous muscular strength, so-called berserker power. It was still present (spiritually) in the slightest word uttered by Napoleon, with which he would set off a chain of messages among his adjutants and subordinates. This was the voice of a summoner. He did not need force to influence stone. He did not need to move the hand that held the reins of the horse.

This is how Bonaparte had crossed the Alps. This is how the emperor had cleared away and levelled the mountains of imperial German common law with just a few printed materials—decrees. With the Russia project, everything is different.

3

THE PLUNDERER'S EYE
TURNED TOWARDS THE MAP /
'THE PRINCIPLE OF ABSTRACTION'

FIGURE 55. 'Outside the city.'

ME, MY SISTER'S ADVOCATE

Still soaked after the cloudburst that surprised us at her grave, seven vehicles brought us to my sister's flat. She'd cleaned up in the weeks before she died in the same way she would when welcoming us to her home. The bookshelf, her CD collection. The state-of-affairs in her kitchen even, for, as a doctor, she knew her death was near. We had to laugh at all the effort. Then we got to talking about my sister's quirks. One of them, in her final years, was a 'love for Russia'.

The seed had been planted in her at the age of nine, in the Russian-occupied city of Halberstadt. It had nothing to do with her own choice. Reading was prescribed by the occupying forces' commissars, and the teachers presented it in class somewhat dispassionately. The more my sister's lifeforce dwindled, however, the more vividly these nutrients spread through her obstinate mind like microbial creatures through a pond. During the last year of her life, you could provoke an immediate rant by making a cheeky remark about that distant, neighbouring country to the east. With references to Pushkin. Why isn't he read? Some of Turgenev's lines—the book was on her shelf—spoke of a fundamental misunderstanding between men and women in Great Russia. She interpreted the poet's remark positively. Men and women were separated from each other in that land by the depth of their longings. Not by bleakness? Not by the dilution of 'great feelings'? Not because souls were dying of thirst? Not at all.

She could get excited. The speed with which she launched into the subject of her 'love for Russia' led to a series of jokes among those close to her. It wasn't the temperature of the apartment that dried our clothes, but the facilitation connected to customary silliness. There were 12 different copies of Pushkin on her shelves. And the dead can still be quick to anger, not on account of my laugh (that's comforting!) but for not vigorously and immediately coming to Russia's defence. Doing something for the sake of the dearly departed is the opposite of abstract.

WE STUDENTS OF HALBERSTADT'S CATHEDRAL-SCHOOL:

AFTERNOONS WE PLAY WAR WITH TIN SOLDIERS AND BUILDING BLOCKS. IT HAS TO DO WITH USTYURT.

Ustyurt is a region of desert and steppe east of the Caspian Sea. We've located it in our school atlases. We learned about Astrakhan in the Wehrmacht report. After the expected capture of Stalingrad (or at least that's what we students assume), our own rapid troops will occupy it. The Volga delta can easily be reached with a fingertip. Assuming that our armoured troops will come directly from the west (or, better yet, flank and come from the east), they will head down to Persia on the right. From Persia, as we sketched out with a few chalk lines in the schoolyard during recess, we reach Arabia. If you own the port of Aden, you can cut off the British from India. The oil of the Orient! All of us students were moved by the prospect of receiving a knight's estate in the Crimea or—alternatively—a latifundium in German East Africa.

'A BUZZARD SETS OFF FROM THE GRID MAP'

HOPELESS LIMBS

Faced with the sparseness of the snow-covered grid he was scrutinizing on his marching map, any hopes Fred Peickert (originally infantry regiment No. 12 from Halberstadt) had were fading fast on a Monday in November 1941. There was no reason to be here. He had no chance of getting home. In his depression, he did not like to talk about 'fate'. He did not want to talk at all. Nor look, or eat, even his digestion—that trusty, reliable, 'cow-eyed' form of relaxation—wasn't doing its job in the face of the country's vastness. He sat behind a bush, squeezing fervently, yet too wistful to produce a considerable pile. Days later, above his legs there was nothing but a petrified mass.

FIGURE 56. Buzzard.

A PREDATOR LIKE THIS BUZZARD
ACTS CONCRETELY

A buzzard sat on a branch for half the night and another hour in the morning. Grid map in view. Around 9 o'clock it nabbed a wood mouse. It measured time by the beat of its bodily fluids. They flowed from its head to the vicinity of its claws and, from there, back to the vicinity of the beak and the eyes. Seven different streams and thus seven different times. And, once again, they were characterized by the fact that all the fluids in the bird of prey began to move rapidly as soon as it saw its prey and then grabbed it. Before that, the streams flowed calmly. A predator like this one acts concretely.

FIGURE 57. Halford Mackinder, geopolitician.

THE GEOPOLITICIAN'S PREDATORIAL GAZE

London 1904. On the globe that can be spun in the light of the desk lamp, Great Russia's landmass is green in colour (along with Pamir, Siberia, the obscure ice crust in the north and the plains in the west). Like a fat bit of prey, the relatively vast green lay before geopolitician Halford Mackinder's eyes and imagination.

This holder of a professorship in London possessed a slender hand. His fingertips: sensitive. When he touched the globe, the surface felt smooth. The difference between the crimson of the British Empire and the green of Russia, however, could not be felt with the tips of his finger. Nor was his geopolitical gaze directed towards the prey of Great Russia itself, but the abundance of professorial seats and posts whose necessity could be derived from that distant country's geopolitical exploration. If it ever came within the German Empire's sphere of influence, the fortunes of the British Empire would be ruined.

THE GREAT MACKINDER

Geopolitician Mackinder's judgement was regularly sought by the British prime minister (this became known throughout the clubs). Mackinder did not judge spatially on the basis of a globe he could feel with his hands. To him, the entries there seemed incomplete. A globe, he claimed, was a grotesque copy of the earth's enormous body. But Mackinder did not orient himself to the surface of a map either. Distorting the sphere into squares on a map was not sufficiently informative. Rather, during his research (often when he woke up in the morning), he looked into the vault of his brain as if into the dome of heaven.

This, he thought, is precisely the deep amazement with which a demon or spirit within the earth's interior would look at its surface: at plains, mountains, seas and rivers. This is how the earth itself would 'feel' its outer skin. The imperialist Mackinder's inside-outside view was sensitive-hypomanic rather than serene-political. Friends called him *breathless*. British politicians of the time, all club members, thirsted for Mackinder's predictions.

FIGURE 58

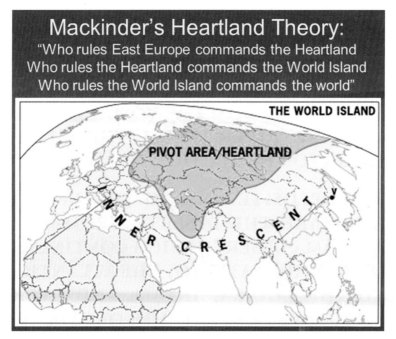

'DESTRUCTIVE INNOVATION'

The geopolitician's eye focuses on the 'essential': the overview. From the Atacama Desert in South America (in some places covered by rainforest, running under the groundwater of the Atlantic, across to the Maghreb and the Arabian Peninsula, and continuing through the steppes of Central Asia to the Gobi Desert) stretches the BELT OF THE EARTH'S GREAT DESERTS.

The deserts' interiors, however, are filled with armed horsemen, clans, tribes and bands, which from time to time overrun the desert edges and the black earthen areas behind them with their raids. This is the *incentive*. These peoples of the steppe, Halford Mackinder says in his enthusiasm, are LIKE A PLOUGH OF GOD. In this way, agricultural cultures and civilizations are dug up between the *heartland* and the *crescent belt*. The equestrian peoples sow by harvesting and then move away faster than the settlers can learn from them how to fight.

'PIVOT' = CENTRE OF ROTATION, HINGE

THE '*HEARTLAND*' FORMS THE CENTRE OF THE WORLD-ISLAND EARTH. IT STRETCHES FROM THE VOLGA TO THE YANGTZE RIVER. FROM THE HIMALAYAS TO THE ARCTIC.

THE OPPOSITE POLE TO THE '*HEARTLAND*' ARE THE DESERTS (FROM THE ATACAMA DESERT, WHICH CONTINUES UNDER THE WATERS OF THE ATLANTIC, TO THE SAHARA, ARABIA, AND OVER THE THIRSTY STRETCHES OF ASIA TO

THE GREAT GOBI DESERT). ALSO THE MONSOON LANDS (INDIA AND CHINA).

THE FUTURE OF THE EARTH HAS BEEN FORMED FROM THESE THREE STRUC- TURES.

(from Halford Mackinder's 1904 'Pivot Papers')

LANDSCAPE FORMAT OF ANY ADEQUATE REPRESENTATION OF THE WHOLE OF RUSSIA

In 1904, several maps of the tsarist empire lay before Professor Mackinder's imperialist-geographical gaze. The Russian Empire can only be depicted with precision by looking at *several* maps, side by side. In the large, tropical wood-panelled club room of the Royal Geographical Society with its bright chandeliers, maps of the world's oceans and land masses were displayed on side tables which Mackinder contrasted with the pivot centred in northern Russia.

In 1919, Mackinder corrected the outline of 'Heartland' by extending the pivot area southward to include the Caspian Sea and westward to include parts of the Baltic region. In 1904, Mackinder had acquired posts and academic spheres of power in Oxford and London in the same way that great powers have conquered colonies and occupied bases for more than 300 years. Mackinder: anatomy of the colonized earth. 'Midwife of world power'. Applicant to major budgets for GEOPOLITICAL RESEARCH in the United Kingdom of Great Britain.

A 1904 LECTURE

Today Mackinder is speaking at the Royal Society. Large candelabra in teak-wood rooms. He winds down his talk within 20 minutes, ending surprisingly at the height of the interest he receives at the club. All the listeners here are landowners, property owners. Stewards of a range, a world of knowledge, a fortune. Like those in the sixteenth century who staked out their large estates with hedges and fences against invaders or farmers (*enclosures*) who wanted to return to their expropriated fields, everyone here has their own characteristic way of interpreting what Mackinder has listed. He is not talking about Russia at all, but about the property borders of Great Britain.

THE YEAR MY FATHER WAS BORN. MACKINDER'S ARROW-SHAPED COLLARS. ELEGANCE FROM 1892

When my father was born in 1892—he arrived a living, pink-skinned lump in embryonic position—Mackinder was already sitting in London, in a tailored suit cut from Scottish wool and working as a lecturer in geography at Oxford. Arrow-shaped shirt collar. Modern appearance. A suit of such quality was unthinkable in Halberstadt, my father's birthplace. The wearer of just such a suit, had he been born and raised in Halberstadt, would have been ashamed. He would have been considered a braggart, a Brit.

Mackinder's scientific field was expanding rapidly. At teaching posts in New Zealand, in the US and in London. Oxford itself refused to establish chairs in 'political geography'. The expansion of the academic field of 'the study of the interrelationship between geography and world power, the logic of the earth' was in full swing, parallel to the establishment of the US war fleet, whose construction programme sought a connection to the British model.

By 1910, the network of professorships in geography was established. At this point in time, my father is 18 years old. He is preparing for his graduation exams. In 1947, the year of Mackinder's death, my father's house is in ruins, those who made up the social circles with which he lived had not come back from the war or had fled for the West and now, in the second half of his life, he is beginning to establish himself as a doctor.

WHAT DOES 'SPIRITUAL INDUSTRIALIZATION' MEAN?

Innovative scientific insights have to amaze their listeners and readers. This applied to Mackinder's thesis that the pivot and pivotal point of world history in the coming twentieth century would be found in the north of the tsarist country—where the low tundra begins, where water veins interrupt all routes from east to west, which is to say, at one of the most UNLIKELY POINTS ON THE EARTH'S CRUST, AS FAR AS ANY PROPHESIED CONCENTRA-TION OF POWER IS CONCERNED. Excitement at the club. How easy would it be (from the British point of view) for a continental monster, a BEHEMOTH—namely, the German Empire—to come into possession of this anchor land. Mackinder named his finding 'Heartland'. From it he drew circular rings. They were crescent areas, growth belts. Whether whole continents or smaller structures rising out of the water, he considered them 'islands'. For him, the British Empire was just such an island, not because Scotland, Wales and the former territories of the Anglo-Saxons happened to be on an island at the edge of Europe, but because the Empire, with its pearl-necklace of possessions from Newfoundland to Fiji, was an ISLAND and a CRESCENT (growth belt). Beneath this so-called political buzzard's gaze, the landscapes and seas of northern Russia, lying there as if dead, received a vivid inner connection.

KARL MAY AND THE JAPANESE

In 1904, iron ships designed in British shipyards set sail from the Japanese islands for the Russian coast. Between the Russian port of Port Arthur in China and Arkhangelsk in the Arctic north, a future planner was able to draw connecting lines on a world map. Shortly thereafter, however, the conquest of Port Arthur by the Japanese would render such a drawing obsolete.

In Radebeul: Karl May. In his haunting dialogues with himself—always connected with Lord Curzon, the practical man among the border markers and the viceroy of India, whom he had met in Tehran in one of the previous years—May's adventurous heart dealt with journeys that would have seemed impossible to him in reality.

Changes of place made him nervous. For him to write stories, the rooms in Dresden-Radebeul had to be sealed against draughts with felt. The room was brightly lit by electric lamps and the blinds to the garden were closed. Like a monk in his cell, May the 'globetrotter' sat at his book-and-paper-strewn table.

'CONTINUITY' IN THE JAPANESE FAMILY TREE OVER LONG PERIODS OF TIME

Predators replace one another. From father to son, from grandchild to great-grandchild: one road. For a little more than three generations, planners in Japan had looked at their maps of Russia from their side of the world, that is, in conformity with the rotation of the globe, from the east. Five river courses. Along railroad lines. Planned routes. Marked with pen or finger. The chief of the young staff officers did not make a face for hours. That was in 1918. As previously stated, three generations and eleven years away from today. What time worked for these hunters?

It takes 10 years to conquer Manchukuo. It takes 2 to connect the railway line to the junction with the Trans-Siberian railroad. To plan something like that takes an hour. But it takes a whole year to achieve unanimity in the emperor's crown council to give approval for the campaign of conquest. Once the east of the Russian continent (all the way to the Urals) is secured and occupied with bases, it takes *50 years* to equip such a site with mines, factories, foreign workers from Asia and Japanese engineers. As well as women for the garrisons and top officials. This then is already a present time beyond the service period of the young staff officers bent over maps in 1918. Beyond the lifetime of their commander 'with the calm face', too. He kept his eyes closed.

Through the events of August 1945, the future, invisible to these predators, thwarted every one of 1918's plans. Since then, no more ideas of renewing Japan's power to East Siberia and beyond. Nevertheless, the results of a computer group, cooled by ice in Spitsbergen and linked by fibre optics to a central station 70 kilometres west of Osaka, are available: 1.2 trillion cubic feet of natural gas has been remeasured. This has been done with the help of a module in one of the Japanese satellites circling the globe. Where and with what types of transport could such an immense value—military means replaced by civilian ones—be realized? Because this remains unclear in banking circles, the computer group, the eagle eye of the third generation of Japan's predatorial gaze, has not even been asked.

CAN ONE PHYSICALLY FEEL THE BOUNDARIES OF EMPIRE?

Rudyard Kipling, himself a brilliant narrator, knowledgeable about overseas gossip in London clubs, unusually matter-of-fact as an imperial storyteller, spoke of his amazement that he could consider himself a patriot of the British colonies and possessions marked in crimson on the globe instead of a lover of his own green, sea-swept island. As if it were his own skin. He could go into a trance and into mourning when one of these imperial limbs was bolted on again or lost to the empire.

HEARTLAND IS UNGRASPABLE

Mackinder's Heartland is inaccessible to any war fleet in the world. A maritime fiasco would befall any one that tried. Any conquerors coming via Vladivostok would be defeated by the vastness of the country before they completed even the first few days' march. From the west, on the other hand, an invasion would be theoretically possible since deep plains stretch from Holland through Germany and Poland to the Urals. But considering the fate of Charles XII of Sweden at Poltava and Napoleon's retreat in 1812, Mackinder deduced that even this 'gateway to the Heartland' was a trap for greedy conquerors.

DIMITRI KITSIKIS: *UNE VISION GÉO-POLITIQUE, LA RÉGION INTERMÉDIAIRE.*

ALSO: *GÉOPOLITIQUE D'UN PROCHE-ORIENT À VENIR.*

'BALKANIZATION = DISMEMBERMENT OF THE ECUMENICAL EMPIRE'

DARIUS THE GREAT
ALEXANDER'S EMPIRE
BYZANTIUM
THE OTTOMAN EMPIRE UNTIL 1917

A SECOND IDEA FOR HOW TO LOCATE IMPERIALISM, WHICH CONTINUES TO OCCUPY THINK TANKS IN WASHINGTON TODAY

The Greek writer Dimitri Kitsikis opposes Mackinder's 'Heartland' theory. In his work *Geopolitics and Greece* (*Geopolitike kai Hellada*), he distinguishes between the WEST (US, Canada, Australia, New Zealand and Western Europe), the EAST (India, China, Indonesia, Korea, Japan) and the middle, 'the intermediate region' (Assur, Byzantium, Russia). For 2,500 years, the latter region was the place of great empires: the ecumenism of the East, the only civilized area of the world. These empires imploded. From the *vacuum*, so Kitsikis: the future.

IN CONTRAST TO HIS FORECAST IN 1904 (THE ORIGINAL DEMARCATION OF THE HEARTLAND PIVOT), MACKINDER EXPANDED HIS CONCEPT IN 1919, BY THEN HIS BRITISH MAJESTY'S HIGH

COMMISSIONER TO RUSSIA AND THE CAUCASUS, TO INCLUDE BROAD ZONES OF MARSHLAND IN THE NORTH, AS WELL AS THE AREAS OF BAIKAL, THE BALTIC AND ALL THE TERRAIN AND MOUNTAINS OF THE CAUCASUS.

THE PREDATOR'S GAZE IS IMPATIENT AND SHORT-WINDED

Arrival of Halford Mackinder at Tikhoretskaya Junction in the Caucasus on 10 January 1920. The command train of the tsarist General Denikin and the dining car plus locomotive in which British High Commissioner Mackinder arrived at the rendezvous point, track by track.

Rapid conferences. Takeover of Denikin's Caspian fleet by British naval officers. They are supposed to arrive via Persia. Reception of British representatives in Georgia, Transcaucasia and Azerbaijan. Halting conversation between Denikin and Mackinder. The general urged fresh supplies of arms and a contingent of British troops. Mackinder could not agree to this.

A late dinner, rushed. At the same time, always a pretext for negotiation. How to contain Soviet power? Without at the same time re-establishing Belarusian power in Russia? The creation of numerous small states, which will fragment the heritage of the Russian Empire. Georgia, Ossetia, Belarus, the Baltic republics. What can be invented to extend the chain of these states? This called for imagination, not just an eagle eye. Departure 16 January. Black Sea port, Constantinople, London.

FOR MACKINDER, THE TRANS-SIBERIAN RAILROAD WAS LOCATED TO THE SOUTH

AND TO THE EAST OF THE PIVOT. SINCE IT HAS NO BRANCHES TO THE NORTH, THE LOCOMOTIVES CANNOT REACH THE HEARTLAND.

LIKE KARL MARX, MACKINDER HAD OVERESTIMATED CAPITALIST DYNAMICS. IN 1904, IT WAS RACING ALONG IN FIRST GEAR (DESTROYING THE ENGINE OF HISTORY'S CLUTCH AT A SPEED EQUIVALENT TO FOURTH):

IF ONE SHOULD COMPARE THE DYNAMICS OF ECONOMY *AND HUMAN DESIRES* WITH A MACHINE AT ALL AND NOT WITH A CLOUDBURST INSTEAD. IT TOO EMPTIES ITSELF AND SEEPS AWAY.

IN POSSESSION OF PREY, THE EAGLE GROWS LAZY . . .

Adventure in the waiting hall. This waiting hall in Tikhoretskya Junction where tea was served had just one window. Any woman present could have served as spies or seductresses of great statesmen. There were no adjoining rooms in which conspiracy, seduction or betrayal of secrets could have taken place.

But Mackinder would not have had time for that anyway. A female conductor in a tight uniform walked along the railroad ballast. A glance from the train window. The conductor's glance back. She hurries towards the locomotive. In the sense of Baudelaire's female *passer-by*, this could have been an experience. Mackinder, in his British suit, paid it no mind. His face showed fatigue. Just to be away from here and farther . . .

REPOLARIZATION OF GREED WITHIN 103 YEARS

German industrialists' greed for the Briey ore basin was one of the reasons why a surprise peace could not take place halfway through the Great War in 1916. A little more than 100 years later, a western steel industry group, whose sphere of influence now included the Briey ore and coal mines, would have gladly given it up for a dollar and the assumption of restoration costs. Referring to Trump's steel tariffs, the German representative on the supervisory board warned against keeping Briey in the portfolio. The birds of prey from the Ruhr district of 1916: Where are they now?

ABSTRACT IMPERIALISM IN MATTERS OF LOVE

A cousin of the famous Russian Yevgeny Onegin was not at all hesitant nor reserved in matters of love like his relative. He was insatiable in his conquests. Disfavoured rivals claimed he kept accounts of the young women he seduced, just like the Spaniard Don Juan. None of the liaisons lasted long. Seduction, followed by departure.

One observer commented precociously: there is a longing in him to which he will not admit. For him, everything he acquires is a substitute. He arranges things so that a young woman cannot leave him alone—tactically he is clever, strategically he is nowhere. Then he abandons the conquered to her misfortune. The remark does not help any of the unhappily seduced. In poor Russia of the nineteenth century, this type of raid (which became well known beyond the region) caused a sensation. Pushkin made a sketch. There was much talk about it but little pursuit of the mystery.

THE FEELING TRICKLES OUT

When they arrived in Venice, Vronsky and Anna Karenina stayed in one of the best hotels. Cold weather, and wet. There in their rooms, they did not know what to do with each other. There was little to do outside. They didn't know anyone. Their onward journey was not expected for three days.

FIGURE 59. With all the signs of submission, the head of one of Yevgeny Onegin's cousins rests in the beautiful girl's lap. Her hair is lit by the lamp at her back, which also illuminates her neck. Her delicate fingers in the conqueror's hair. There's a species of ant that will sit humbly before an anthill. Begging for small gifts. When an ant steps out to hand over just such a gift, the apparently supplicant one—in reality, willing to conquer—tears off its head. The heads of foreign ants are its food. In zoology, it is called FORMICA DECAPITANS, the ant which decapitates.

They tried to get along. Anna Karenina, who had begun to mistrust Vronsky, thought she could hear a grating sound in her ears. As if shifted by a very slow earthquake, the cottage she thought she had furnished for the officer and herself seemed to collapse. This was the beginning of the decline that would eventually lead to her death on the tracks.

'LOVE WHICH FORGETS THE SELF'

'FORGOTTEN IN LOVE'

'TO LOVE SELFLESSLY'

'SELFISH'

'SELF-ABSORBED TO THE END'

SILENTLY AND HOPELESSLY I LOVED YOU,
AT TIMES TOO JEALOUS
. . . AT TIMES TOO SHY.
GOD GRANT YOU FIND ANOTHER WHO WILL LOVE YOU
AS TENDERLY AND TRUTHFULLY AS I.

—Alexander Pushkin's *I Loved You* (Babette Deutsch trans.)

AN UTTERLY INDIFFERENT CONQUEROR

Gesine didn't stand a chance. No one in the world would be able to get something from him that he didn't want. And he is sated. Well-nourished by the affection of women, to whose tribute he has been accustomed since his childhood.

Strictly speaking, it's not the *eyes* but the *gaze* that documents mercilessness. The eyes themselves seem rather expressionless, somewhat dull. It is precisely due to its lack of expression that the gaze has that 'negative' quality which is so shocking. I can't imagine what Gesine ever wanted from this spoilt young man. Already during the commercial, in the first hour (I was there, but then, unfortunately, went home early), he was full of satiety, his gaze a 'negotiating gaze'. That's why I firmly believed: 'You shouldn't ignore that at all.' Only Gesine saw something different. In his blotchy face, as if in a mirror, she saw what she felt.

I have always thought that mothers who love their sons create a tender germ in them. This is then harvested by the people who later meet these men. Instead, in such cases, a frugal patricianism spreads, the settledness of a chain of male ancestors who know only how to grab and ask for nothing. I happen to believe that sons who do not have to fight for their mothers' affection end up developing monsters within themselves. I do not want to generalize, but I will. My anger at Gesine's conqueror has loosened my tongue for general assertions.

'He has the heartless eyes /
of someone loved above all.'

NOTHING MORE HORRIBLE, INSISTENT, PITILESS THAN A CONQUERER WHO DOES NOT WANT THE CONQUERED.

FIGURE 60. Winter-protection for German soldiers in Russia.

CONQUERORS WITHOUT FOUNDATION IN THEIR
MOTIVES ON THE ICE FRONT

When seen from the outside, imperceptible but at heart done with blitzkrieg-like speed: following the double battle at Bryansk and Vyazma, the farther the attack on Moscow advanced (as if mechanically), the more the German high leadership was seized by a LOSS OF MOTIVATION in the form of exploding disappointment. Impatience and greed among the general staff increased. For a short time, it seemed as if the Russian front was 'tearing like a piece of paper' (General Halder, chief of staff of Army High Command).

Maps had given the impression that one could reach any destination in the world. But this arbitrariness destroyed willpower. Willpower needs an object to conquer: Moscow. Up until then, the German leadership had been striving eagle-like, predator-like for Moscow, but all greed was expended.

The prey, to which the abstract desire for profit originally referred, consisted of a hope. Namely, the expectation that the REDS' courage would collapse as soon as the capital, Moscow, was in German hands. But the more the hope of reaching Moscow became concrete—yes, in the distance, an advance party could already make out signs of Moscow's suburbs through binoculars— the less attractive the goal became. The decomposition of the original motives underlying the attack began simultaneously at the highest level of leadership, in the general staff and in the Führer's headquarters, *and* at the lowest level of the troops, among the lance corporals and ordinary soldiers.

'AND WHAT BY NIGHT HAD BEEN TERRIFYING
LAY PALE AND ILLUMINATED IN SIMPLE EXPANSES'

In general, Frederick, a lance corporal, was not prone to fear. His fear had got lost in the particular. He was frightened by the night. Not by the enemy, who only seemed generally dangerous to him in as much as he was lurking about somewhere. As long as Frederick was armed, he was not afraid of any enemies. What frightened him was the darkness itself. And the sprawling nature of the country's vastness. It didn't seem like a good idea to build shelters in the canyons of these forests. The enemy—they were partisans. Undercover, they could easily get within 5 metres of the German troops who appeared shorter due to their being buried in depressions in the ground. In the event of an ambush, their lack of defence was thus all the greater than it would have been had they *not* dug in at the eye level of the enemy, who appeared unexpectedly and fired immediately.

The 'deep night' taught the lance corporal how to be afraid (according to what he told his mate, Lance Corporal Neumann). And what he understood this to mean was these forests' immeasurable ABILITY TO WAIT and the dark sky above the treetops. THIS STRUCK AT THE HEART'S EMPTINESS LIKE A TIN CAN. In his school days and in the privation-filled days of labour service, he had never longed for the morning light. Sleep was precious to him. Now, awake on that November night, he waited for the light. Fog turned to mist. Soon the edge of the forest was visible. Invisible behind it, in the twilight, was the country about to be conquered.

WHICH GERMAN SOLDIERS ACTUALLY WANTED TO POSSESS, LIVE OR WORK IN THAT VAST COUNTRY?

From Moscow, the willpower of the tank drivers in the two flanking wedges, which the German leadership had charged with encircling Moscow, completely came apart in the period from October to December 1941. None of the German soldiers who fought here throughout the coming winter would have thought it possible or desirable in peacetime, for example in 1929 or in 1934, to invade Russia and conquer Moscow at Christmas 1941. No one wanted to possess, live or, later, work in that vast country.

The Marxist Karl Korsch, who at his desk in Boston in 1941 analysed the phenomenon of fascist *blitzkrieg* (which was difficult for orthodox Marxists to understand), spoke of a strong motivation for social change, a 'fighting spirit of the masses', which he believed he could prove for the whole of Germany from 1918 to 1941. According to Korsch, however, these strong motives were driven by a nearly opposite goal than that of conquering a foreign country to the east. The exercise of skill in the attack against the renowned Red Army had indeed brought satisfaction, like any pride in production, a gain in collective self-confidence. According to Korsch, this was enough for a 1000-kilometre march, but never enough for the march on winter roads and never a substitute for a goal originating in the heart.

The weak motivation dissipated—in the statistical curve at an amazingly similar pace to the faltering supply transports of the Reichsbahn and field railroads. On the long stretch from Poland to Vyazma, every 12 kilometres a train stood still on the often-single-track lines, interrupted by blast marks the partisans had made in the night, often from a waiting position in front of snowdrifts.

ICE STORM ON THE FRONT OUTSIDE MOSCOW

Dr (Engr) Fred Sauer, formerly of Siemens, who worked for the Research Department of the German Army Weapons Office, was interested in the anatomy of mammoths. Could a winter-proof armoured weapon be developed from the short trunks and stocky bodies of these experienced giants (which by 1941 no longer existed) of the cold steppes with their dusty, perpetually extremely cold easterly winds? According to Fred Sauer, the oxygenated blood that flowed from these animals' bodies warmed the spent, cold blood which went up *into* the body down in their enormous, columnar legs. This was an indication of the possibility of finding some way to help against the Russian winter's tricks by outfitting engines with twin circuits (one for heating the motor and one for propulsion). The project came too late for a decision to be made that year.

THE EMERGENCY: RETREAT LOOMS

Major General Niebling, High Command, responsible for supplies in the east, was worried. There were only 19 working days in December. He would have needed 80.

He'd got up at 3 a.m., as one does when an attack at the front is scheduled for 5. But, where he was, a single commander couldn't do a thing at that hour. Not a single person in charge throughout the Reich, not one of Niebling's contact persons, had understood the seriousness of the situation. As usual, they would only show up at their offices around 8. Here in Berlin, there was neither the cold of the east nor had the war (as a 'state of emergency') advanced to this centre of command. It did not exist in terms of sleep schedules, eating meals, reciprocal visits, the performance of celebrations.

FEED FOR THE FRONT

At long last, veterinary doctor, Dr (Med.) Dietrichsen was able to expand his authority. He had managed to procure pieces of centre-cut ham from the state of Schleswig-Holstein and place it in the refrigerated warehouses in the city of Kiel. But one can't simply freeze them—they need to be kept moist and cool. A good piece of ham 'breathes'. Dr Dietrichsen wanted to bring these 'valuables' to the troops outside of Moscow in as fresh a state as possible. Or at least as far as Smolensk, and from there transport them on sleds. What a joy and act of encouragement when 'the best their home-land has to offer' would be delivered to the troops in their defensive positions for Christmas. Ignoring local-residents' resistance, Dr Dietrichsen had the best cuts from the smoker brought to the troops. Later, the delivery got stuck outside of Brest-Litovsk, where the trains had stopped. Due to improper handling, the delicacies spoilt.

IMPROVISATIONS IN TIMES OF ADVERSITY

In Halle an der Saale, Oberbahnrat Dipl. (Engr) Knoch had a trans-port train unloaded; it had been carrying prisoners in striped clothing; they were housed in the youth hostel in Ender and put under surveillance, then handed over to the justice system installed in Rockenburg Prison (which saved them from being killed). Knoch brought the evacuated train together with other cargo trains near Erfurt and had these columns set off in the direction of Posen. In the meantime, the goods for these trains were stored in Schleswig-Holstein and in the Ruhr district; large quantities of ski equipment from southern Germany would have been added if the transport request had reached the Reichsbahn administration in time.

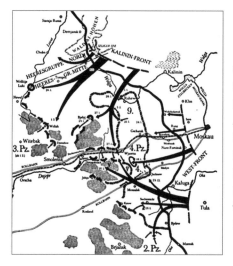

FIGURE 61. One can see that the Soviet armies' most dangerous breakthroughs only occurred in January. The catastrophic impression that German troops had—that the fate of the Napoleonic army in 1812 was being repeated—however, came from their experiences of December 1941.

SOLDIERS' WEDDINGS
WITHOUT HEALTH CERTIFICATES

According to the Law for the Protection of the Hereditary Health of the German People, the notice of intent to marry with the magistrate required a certificate from the public health office that no facts were known to justify the prohibition of said marriage according to the Marriage Health Law and the Law for the Protection of German Blood. Regarding Christmas Eve 1941, however, in the case of a long-distance marriage, an exception is made for soldiers. As far as the National Socialists were concerned, such a marriage could not be prevented by the fact that no certificate of objection to the marriage had yet been produced. Aside from that, however, soldiers were prevented from attempting to expedite the process.

It was obvious that correspondence from the snow-covered deserts of Army Group Mitte to home base were attempts at the impossible. Disruption of all networks. The suspension of holidays.

Nevertheless, based on a proposal from the OKH, marriages were to be possible at short notice. What if the bride was pregnant and the soldier-to-be-married was killed on one of the following days? What, the National Socialists wondered, were the families to be told if bureaucratic measures had made it impossible for the marriage to take place PUNCTUALLY? Here the case of Jewish kinship or a hereditary disadvantage had to take a back seat to the principle of the seriousness of the war.

A POOR DECISION IN WARTIME

In December 1941, the month of great uncertainty, Marita, the wife of the surgeon Dalquen, arrived in Berlin from her provincial town. Staying at the Hotel Fürstenhof on Potsdamer Platz, she had refused Lieutenant Berlepsch's request to spend the night with him. Something she came to regret only three weeks later. The young officer was killed in action in northern Russia. She would have been a last consolation to him; had she known, she would have judged the card he had sent to her room differently (they knew each other from a costume party in the provincial town in peacetime). She would have snuck over to see him. All too late now. She had wanted to keep the relationship in the realm of 'hopeful' and not ruin things with a brief moment of lust. She'd liked the young officer. A poor decision in wartime.

FROM THE SLEEP RESEARCHER'S PERSPECTIVE

In a study, the sleep researcher and statistician Dr (Med.) F. Lerchenau summarized the working hours of the supreme Reich leadership for the month of December 1941.

As far as Hitler's personality is concerned, the doctor says that only after a good night's sleep—following lively discussion, with the appropriate preparation time that comes after such discussions, with a pause before he begins to speak, while observing the basic rules of rhetoric he acquired in 1919—does he display sufficient 'leadership competence'. All moments of fatigue, rushing, improvisation should be deducted from his 'work time'. For the days from Monday, 1 December, to Wednesday, 31 December (whereas the time from Wednesday, 24 December, could be deducted, for everything had already been decided by then), this would result in four-and-a-half hours of THINKING TIME and six-and-a-half hours of DECISION TIME. If Hitler had thought less wildly and excitedly and had more sleep, especially in the morning, this thinking and decision-making time could have been extended to up to seven hours. According to Lerchenau (none of his colleagues agree with him), this would have led to the following alternative results: No declaration of war on the US; the withdrawal of the Russian Front by 145 kilometres to the Vyazma line by 3 December (the line was reached in January); efforts to achieve a separate peace with the Soviet Union via Swedish contacts; concentration on turning Linz into a museum city of the Führer, combined with satisfying emotional feelings for Hitler that would have resembled something like Christmas spirit; prohibition of measures against the racial enemy (in view of the fact that neutral observers, international public opinion, would have put the Reich under observation after a peace agreement in the course of 1942). Lerchenau relies on the fact, as he told a conference at Princeton University, that Hitler had already felt the war to be lost while attending the Bayreuth Festival in 1940. Under the impact of the shock of December 1941, however, it took some time for this basic feeling to be reproduced in his inner being.

FROM NICOLAUS VON BELOW'S
WITNESS AFFIDAVIT

I was close enough to the leader to be able to judge his inner life, the place where he made his decisions. This inner life could not be discerned by simply seeing him shake hands or witnessing him pass by. And by 'close' I am referring to a temporal dimension, not simple physical proximity ('proximity of smell'). No, it has more to do with observation at different times ('proximity as a measure of time'). Relieved of the day's business, a group sits in armchairs around the leader at night. The next day: Hitler in the early a.m. That is how you get to know a person. This 'second-degree awakening', that is, after getting up, washing oneself, getting dressed: for the Reich Chancellor this often lasted until midday. We were adjutants in his presence. We bothered him less than his dog, constantly demanding

attention as it did, and would carry on working in the man's proximity, unnoticed.

That being said, I confirm that Hitler did not have an 'eagle
eye'. For all the one-sidedness of his decisions, it did not seem to
me that his eye was fixed upon seizing things. His so-called com-
pelling gaze was a manner, probably picked up from your standard
mimicry textbook of the twenties. Whatever he beheld with his
eyes that way did not serve any lasting attention, any possession. In
a certain sense, I would call him 'personally dispossessed'. Furniture,
even objects of art, only arouse a 'brief perceptive gaze' from him
before he moves on with business. I would call his eyes 'reality-
oriented'. Greedy only in the first moments of spooning soup. No,
the greed of his eyes is not focused on distant goals. This was often
confirmed by the fact that his eyes did not really wander. He hardly
knew the countries he conquered. He made no effort to visit them.
How easy it would have been to arrange a trip to northern Norway.
Or trips to the Black Sea from Vinnitsa. None of that!

His view of the general staff officers' map, with its broad and
coloured markings, always remained scrutinizing, never 'devouring'.
The unrealistic, 'abstracting' aspect of Hitler's decisions, his inner
mode, comes from another layer than that of the external senses. I
call it logic. But it is fed and mixed with 'willpower'. Which means:
modulated logic. More glue for 'thought-guidance' on the side of
the will than on the concatenation of single 'tattered thoughts', as if
he were chewing on them. The persistence with which he pursues
an error he has grasped does not come from the eyes but from
previous action. He wrote something about Russia in the twenties.
Now it is a matter of holding on to this writing like a billowing over-
coat 'and stretching it out as long as it will hold.'

No, I am not allowed to look at the Führer. When I look at him
directly, he gets angry. I can only watch him when he isn't paying
attention.

AN 'ARMOURED DIVISION ON FOOT'

And so the tank drivers of the 6th Panzer Division—for the most
part, despondent if still with a few remnants of willpower—had
advanced a few kilometres on the Volokolamsk Highway towards

Moscow through Kazakh General Panfilov's roadblocks, but then, deprived of all tanks and overwhelmed by masses of snow, they had gone back on foot and were now lying in depressions on both sides of the highway near Volokolamsk. They couldn't shoot while wearing mittens; but when they took them off, their bare fingers stuck to the metal. The 6th Panzer Division, of which Count Stauffenberg was still quartermaster at their home bases in Paderborn and Wuppertal, was an elite division. Its emblem was the 'jumping cavalryman', for the machine-supported military force—which comprised 17,000 men in peacetime—was considered as fast and capable of overcoming obstacles as a jumping horse; in reality, however, it could not detach itself from the ground anywhere. And now the men were standing or lying down in a foreign country for no subjective reason.

FIGURE 62. Soldiers of the 6th Armoured Division with Koniks (Polish primitive horses). The metal remains of the tanks stand about 20 kilometres to the east as wracks, inaccessible. The armoured division still has not been assigned any repair workshops, as in 1942. Damaged tanks have to be returned to Germany by rail and then brought back to the front. Thus the 'ruins of former daring' remain on and next to the Moscow Chaussee, with a wall of snow on the opposite side to the wind. The valuable tank drivers, with training periods of up to one year, feel separated from their professional role. They are not that suitable as infantrymen. Freezing. Even their officers are just 'actors of their former combat readiness'. Only two months ago, the Russians considered them 'professional winners'. Among themselves, they want to make each other believe that they continue to be what they were in France in the spring of 1940. Now they are EMPTY SHELLS OF THEIR WAR HAPPINESS.

FIGURE 63. A sketch by Paul Klee for a class at the Bauhaus. 'traction' = 'plumb to the earth's centre'. The curve into the abstract leads directly into concretion.

4

'POWER IS CONCEALED BENEATH THE PLASTER'

LAMENTO FOR A LOST PERESTROIKA

baker_0025

baker_0026

baker_0027

baker_0029

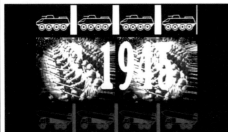

baker_0030

baker_0032

Russisches Ehrenmal
Berlin - Treptow
9.Mai 2019

treptow00001

treptow00006

FIGURE 64

FIGURES 65 (ABOVE) AND 66 (BELOW)

FIGURES 67 (ABOVE) AND 68 (BELOW)

'THERE WAS SOMETHING IMPRACTICAL ABOUT THE EMPIRE'S COLLAPSE'

The predatorial gaze was foreign to James Baker III. On the contrary, he had the eye of a level-headed lawyer from the American Souyth. This secretary of state travelled through the USSR, whose states broke apart in 1991. Like a trustee in bankruptcy, anxious to find a balance, without a formal mandate, representing a foreign superpower, he visited the decision-making centres, talked to the decision-makers (competencies quickly changed). With a good power of recall, with an innate power of observation. Concentrated in the staff building of the chief of staff of the Red Army. He forbade himself any coups. He did not favour any of the sides. The giant country's functionaries sat restlessly within their enclosures. Baker, the American attorney, watched the collapse of a great power with stunned eyes. While holding court in this way, he grew in power, plain power. He recorded the empire's line of successions like the head of a land registry office or a notary.

Over a nightcap in the stale air of a hotel that no longer belonged to the central office, hesitating like a teetotaller sipping whisky, unable to say goodbye quickly to the day's excitement, Baker said to the now irrelevant staff waiting around them: we've got to draw the right conclusions from the humiliation of the German Empire and Austria-Hungary after 1918. Baker had taken a semester of history during his law studies. The new Russia should not be humiliated.

Just a moment ago, the secret service had presented him with a report on the number of patriots (blindly loyal to the Soviet Union, ready to fight for it with their demands and abilities) in the remaining offices of the empire. But Baker was not worried about this dossier on Russia's present; he was more concerned about the younger generation of officers who had just graduated from the military academies. Similar to the Black Reichswehr in Germany after 1918, if the implosion of the empire were perceived as a humiliation, a defeat, there would be a conspiracy of officers in Russia. In the GRU, in the navy, in the armies, in the military-industrial complex. A network of determined people is enough to contaminate the whole country. One must take away the impression of the humiliation of a great power from the development of these days. But that, he said, was out of his hands. He would therefore prefer five more years of perestroika to the current collapse. But no way led there. Revenge, however, would catch the US unprepared in about 40 years. By the time the seeds of that day's vengeful oaths came to light, people in the US would have forgotten 1991. Finally tired and relaxed, Baker told his now irrelevant panel that a submarine and four frigates from the Soviet Union's mighty fleet had been assigned to the Republic of Kyrgyzstan. But the only lake Kyrgyzstan had was 14 miles long. None of those responsible considered this to be a joke, but a fact. Sad news. There is, Baker said wearily, something impractical in this superpower's implosion.

The light in the bar was dim. There seemed to be something sinister hidden in the corners of the unrenovated building. None of those present said they'd seen history unfold that evening. Everyone was too exhausted for BON MOTS.

FIGURE 69

FIGURE 70. James Baker III, US Secretary of State.

POWER IS CONCEALED BENEATH THE PLASTER

The room with Lenin's linen-covered chairs was still there, in the Kremlin, two buildings away from Gorbachev. Even the switchboard on the left, with its antique outfitting from the 1920s, had been preserved. Every quarter hour, Gorbachev was able to generate 'decisiveness' and throw it into the debate. And yet there is something in the system of telephones, central heating, electricity, finance and personal protection that is programmed from the beginning to isolate a supreme leader. It was impossible to resist a 'power of communal imagination' when that imagination was convinced of the 'end of the USSR'. The power was not on the street—it was hidden and built into the walls of Moscow in the form of supply lines and personal networks. You won't find these lines of power hidden in the walls, pipes and conduits with a staff of maybe 16 loyalists who have never learnt anything practical except to prepare meetings. No, you would have to knock off the plaster, trace the pipes and shafts containing the cables and connectors to their endpoints. This, Gorbachev thought, was the real task, and it could have been carried out (as a complete demolition and rebuilding of, say, the Kremlin and the whole country) three years prior by a 'PARTY OF SOCIAL

CONSTRUCTION WORKERS'. How to stage a revolution, how to equip an uprising or a coup—that's what all the cadres sent to the Third World have to learn. Here, at the centre of the empire, a completely different perspective is required: How to rebuild social architecture? The architecture of command networks, and—this was Gorbachev's hobbyhorse—response networks? He was tired. He wanted to DISCUSS it all right now, in the twilight hour of the wintry day before New Year's Eve, when he and everyone else were waiting for the crisis to end. From the window he saw solid walls, fir trees and mud, snow trampled by countless feet.

It was by no means the case that his opponent had cut off his connection to the district heating plant or, as threatened, switched off the electric light. He had a light bulb until the very end. To disempower someone, it was not enough to cut off the tight-knit working group from the financial centre and to rope the guard force into neutrality.

The individual steps that led to Gorbachev's removal from power were later disputed. The 'Bushwhackers of Minsk' pact, which separated Belarus, Ukraine and the Russian Republic from the Soviet Union, did not automatically remove the USSR's president from power. The President of the People's Congress, Nursultan Nazarbayev, visited Gorbachev and confirmed that he had a number of constitutional powers to influence events.

As far as the surrounding environment is concerned, the Kremlin is, so to speak, a prison. The whole of Moscow is a prisoner of the country around it if, by means of an abstract step (plane, telecommunication, the Soviet constitution, the working world), it fails to keep in touch with 'the world' by leapfrogging over the concrete expanses and their populations. Regardless of whether this world consists of offices, imaginations or an actual possibility of flight. There must be a way to the seaside cities of the world.

- Is it true that Gorbachev—deadly tired, for the fact was that, since August, he had not recovered his personal rhythm—was on the phone so much that he suffered hearing loss?

- Yes, in the ear he held to the phone.
- He didn't change ears while on the phone?
- No, he always just used his right one. It was habit.
- And he couldn't hear anything in that ear any longer?
- He was done.
- You mean, completely? Nervous breakdown?
- Just deaf in one ear. He said he could hear a constant hissing.
- Were doctors there?
- No. They hadn't shown up for work. We helped with over-the-counter drugs. Aspirin. The hostile forces were not to learn a thing about the president's weakness.
- Once he was better, what did he do?
- He wanted to save the whole thing. Maintain the empire. But he didn't want to use any troops.
- Would the troops have followed his orders?
- Some always do. He was the president. The Asian republics had a lot of military forces that the 'besiegers' in Russia could not have controlled. One could have a motorised division flow in. Paratroopers etc. He didn't want that at all. He hesitated to even make such a threat.
- So did he start to use his left ear?
- After a brief recovery, yes. He ate something too. He'd totally forgotten to do so.
- Why was he on the phone so much?
- He was looking for the thread. He was looking, without a telephone exchange, for the middle management, which he should have commanded directly but with which he'd had only indirect contact in recent years. It was like talking inside a labyrinth.
- Only a narrow layer of the top management had gone rogue?
- Yes, at the district level everything was intact. A constant duel.
- For 12 days.
- Had he known how the lines of communication worked, he still could have changed the power situation. He had the authority. He would've had to speak with the cadres. In the order in which they form trust and in which they themselves would ask questions. Someone should have done the research for him. We did

what we could. Within the old apparatus, which existed until July 1991, we would have known what to do. No longer.

– So did the besiegers, the Russian government, have a better idea?

– Not at all. They only managed with fewer contacts. Destroying something was enough. No one checked the new reality. Everyone put their hopes in the new line. It promised spoils. Whereas Gorbachev would have had to base his counter-coalition on renunciations. The most he could have done was to promise a promotion.

– Did he stand a chance?

– If, right after his return from Crimea, he had made all the contacts and phone calls himself from the very beginning. He would have had to keep a personal 1000-page phone book. In such a complex empire, those in the top positions simply can't do all the phone work themselves.

– When did all the phoning stop?

– Gorbachev stopped making calls late in the afternoon on 16 December.

– Distraught?

– Too tired for that.

– Where was he sitting?

– In his room. He ordered a coffee.

– And what then? Did he write down some notes?

– He started writing things down for his memoirs. That's when we knew: it's over.

– Two hours later, Yeltsin's visit and the president's removal from the Kremlin?

– Yes, but Yeltsin didn't come. He announced his visit but didn't show up. The president boarded the transport which had been provided.

– Was he allowed to take his personal belongings?

– Nothing.

– Had he resigned from his position as president?

– According to him, no.

– Is he still the President of the Soviet Union today?

- Of course.
- A superficial coup, no?
- And disguised for the population as if the USSR had been properly dissolved and handed over. It was a raid.
- A community was being robbed?
- Appropriated. That was the Thermidor we'd been awaiting since 1921.
- In the sense of: property is theft?
- Yes. Above all, when it comes to the appropriation of a community.
- Why don't you say state?
- Because that wasn't a pity. A state dies, a community does not.
- In the end, what was the Soviet Union?
- Interesting question!

THE NEW ROBINSON

He has no chance of ever reaching a storm-tossed, surf-swept shore by boat or with the help of a beam from a shipwreck. Aboard that sinking ship—let's call it the Titanic—he is already locked into the sinking ship. We're talking about the SECOND VIOLINIST FROM THE LEFT. He's part of the entertainment troupe in the grand salon. Friends with the piano, trumpet and accordion players. Despite the dramatic situation, they repeat the familiar pieces from the operettas and the potpourris of oldies that they've brought from Southampton.

But throughout those hours of the ship's disaster nothing remains 'as usual'. Nothing 'works'. The forces of the soul are out of whack. Just like the forces of nature, the cold outside, the iron processed in the ship's body. Nature has been out of control for hours. None of these facts are interested in the captain.

The steamer orchestra's 'musical Robinson' suggested adding *lamenti*, mournful songs, to the usual programme. There was no sheet music. Nevertheless, he said, one could play from memory, remember sad songs from childhood.

But the variations in human history meant that an oxygen bubble had formed in the sinking ship (which was not the Titanic of 1912), washed over by ocean waves since the second hour of the night, which also encompassed the salon. The band continued to play on. Surrounded by stoic characters who wanted to prove that they were able to persevere 'boldly' and who perhaps were 'full of trust in God' through this emergency as well. The air was still breathable. This was the new 'Robinson's Island' under the conditions of the ocean-crossing modern age.

An engineer in the salon had been moved by the melodies of the second violinist, if sadly. HE REFUSES TO DESPAIR AS A MATTER OF PRINCIPLE. He asked those present in the salon to strip the room's wood panelling (as well as the accessible steps into the depths of the ship's body, all made of the best material from Finnish forests!). AND TO FASHION RAFTS. The hope, the engineer explained, was that the swimmers would get to the air quickly enough and then make it above water until the slower rising 'working timber'—the imaginary island of salon material—could rise to the ocean's surface and be climbed. It remains unknown whether the occupants of the bubble, PATRIOTS OF THE WILL TO SURVIVE, actually made it to the surface of the ice-covered sea. Or whether the improvised arrangements of wood and nails (at least a toolbox was on hand) would even have been enough to guarantee survival until the arrival of rescue ships.

By that time of night, rescue operations from the coast and from foreign ships had already ceased. The public's attention, the LAW OF ACTUALITY, had already changed from the topic of 'rescue' to the topic of 'who is to blame?'

Born of a violinist's melodic imagination, 'Robinson's New Island' was not yet fixed solidly enough in the consciousness of contemporary audiences on either side of the Atlantic. What good are individuals' ideas if the world has not prepared itself for such ideas, for such imaginative combinations? What use is an 'awareness of the emergency exits' if the escape route from them leads to nowhere?

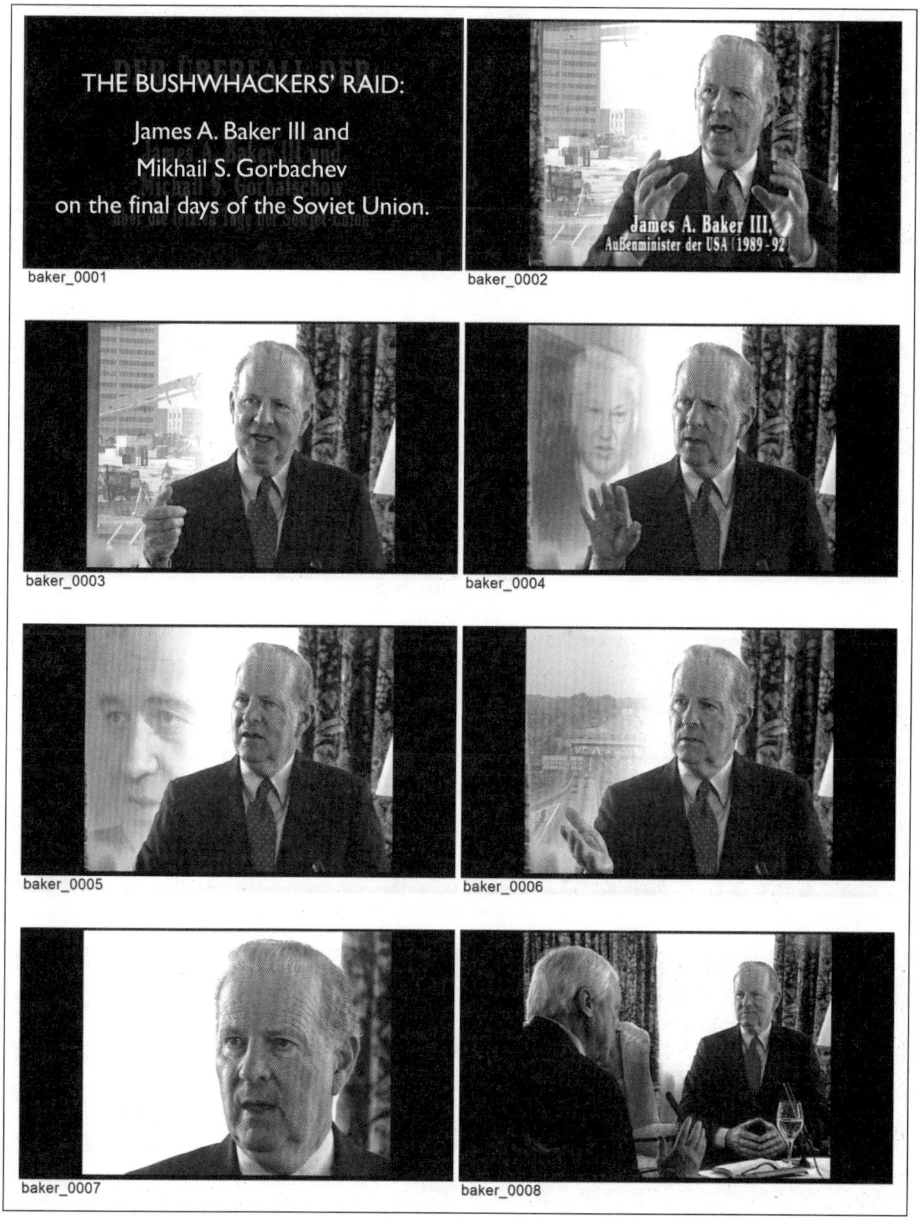
THE BUSHWHACKERS' RAID:
James A. Baker III and
Mikhail S. Gorbachev
on the final days of the Soviet Union.
baker_0001
James A. Baker III,
Außenminister der USA (1989-92)
baker_0002
baker_0003
baker_0004
baker_0005
baker_0006
baker_0007
baker_0008

FIGURE 71

baker_0009

baker_0010

baker_0011

baker_0012

baker_0013

baker_0014

baker_0015

baker_0016

FIGURE 72

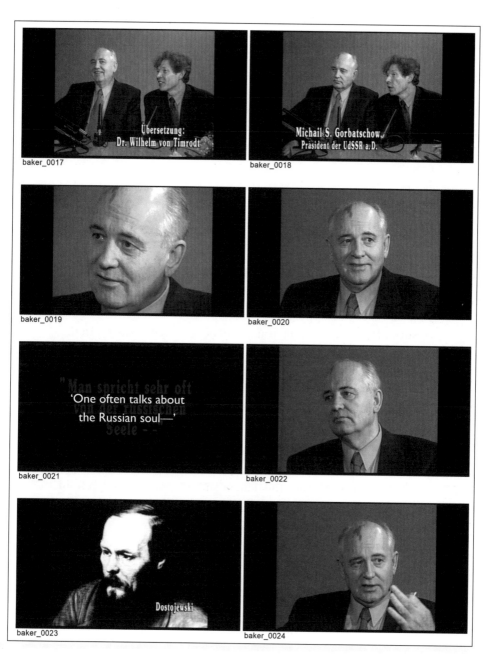

FIGURE 73

CAN A COMMUNITY SAY I?

A cosmonaut, whom the authorities that still obeyed Mikhail Gorbachev had sent up to the Mir a few months earlier—busy with repairs, still a Soviet citizen (the cosmos is extra-territorial, you don't lose status there)—landed in January on the steppes of Kazakhstan 'as if in a foreign country'. The otherwise capable man was confused. No continuity whatsoever to the beginnings of 1917 with which his grandfather had still been familiar. Citizenship a mistake.

Can a community say I? 'If the elementary particles that exploded in Chernobyl have a half-life of 300,000 years, what shape of time must the community have?'

GRATCHOV, THE UNDERCOVER INVESTIGATOR, THE LAST COMRADE

In a way that presupposed professional expertise, i.e. belonging to Soviet railway personnel, trains had been forced to derail. In the section between Moscow and St Petersburg, the bolts had been loosened for a few hundred metres and rails lifted 'pseudo-primitively' with iron tools. The disasters could not be kept secret. Denials of having paid the blackmailers were not believed. Inspector Saizev's criminal investigation team made no arrests.

Then, all of a sudden, the attacks stopped. Had the group of perpetrators themselves been derailed? Before the eyes of the experienced railway operators, the danger shifted; now they were afraid of copycats. If it proved impossible to bring a perpetrator to justice in a public show of draconian punishment, then now, in the thaw of glasnost, this new form of crime, of private railway bombings, would become common. To deter others, a perpetrator was needed. In the lower echelons of the railway criminal police, there was an undercover investigator: Vsevolod I. Gratchov. He was chosen to allow himself to be surprised in the act of destroying a stretch of railway. His undercover identity fit the case.

PROPERTYLESS, CAUGHT IN THE PROGRAMME TRACKS OF THE PRISON ADMINISTRATION, GRATCHOV POSSESSED NOTHING BUT HIS EXPERIENCE

But then, following his conviction, journalistic evaluations and his placement in the security wing of a distant district prison, the railroad crime squad, which until then had been headed by Inspector Saizev, was liquidated. This happened in December 1991 in connection with the destruction of the headquarters of those responsible. No one was left to get Gratchov out of prison, as if it had been part of the project's script all along. His disguise as an undercover investigator or undercover prisoner or deputy perpetrator had become absolutely perfect.

His petition to the directorate of that northern prison was in vain. The identity that had protected him as an undercover investigator and which made him suitable for the project withstood the cursory examination of the file by a young agent who, at the time, had already applied for a transfer to plant security with Gazprom. This auditor was so negligent that he didn't even reply to the petition. Fortunately for Gratchov, as he would not have survived the suspicion that he was not an authentic prisoner but an undercover investigator in the republic of prisoners in which he found himself, his origins remained secret.

He advised a group of fellow prisoners that broke out soon after their conversation NOT to engage in a certain crime (intimidation of the provincial governor by shooting his deputy, then holding elections). He described the hopelessness of the undertaking, pointed out misjudgements. The perpetrators took this as advice and improved the project. After their arrest, during the trial, they referred to Gratchov's communications. He was charged as a gang member and sentenced to a block together with the perpetrators. Thus, in addition to his fake identity, he received a piece of real identity as a criminal.

These passages through Russia's security wings sped up after 1997: prisoner transfer, escapes, passing through new batches of prisoners destined for stays in prisons that were still under construction, overcrowding. In the end, six convicts camped out in one cell meant for one or two people. Communication like in a railway depot.

Gradually, Gratchov, the front-line fighter, developed a comprehensive view. Specially trained in the subjects of plan control and analytics, he was able to read the types of crimes committed by Russia's entire criminal class—the CRIMINAL WORKING CLASS, as it were—like a map. He made notes, looked for places to hide them.

And this is how he formed common property. In his own interest, he'd only have been able to use the records if the crime had a boss to blackmail, to approach for release or to fight. But in the general interest, Gratchov's knowledge amounted to little, as he had no idea where he could have sent the knowledge available to him as an undercover investigator nor as a high-security prisoner, nor how to have made it credible. And so this last undercover investigator of the old Soviet Union (in its most exquisite form, the glasnost phase) depended on dreams. And if someone came and asked me? Could an auditor who went to visit him and take notes guarantee him a position in the armed forces or the secret services or in an African embassy as a public representative of a still important community?

The skies over Africa belonged to that with which he was still unfamiliar. The walls of the prison, the narrow sections of Russian weather he could see through the portholes high up on the wall he knew, in the same way as he gathered knowledge from all the prisoners who made their way through: the variation was slight. The word you see in all their eyes, LIFELONG, is stamped onto the objects, walls and vistas too.

GRATCHOV DESCRIBED HIMSELF AS A STOOGE, ABOVE ALL DURING CHRISTMAS AND NEW YEAR'S EVE

The prison staff and the few settled inmates granted him advantages. There was a chair in his cell and now he had the room to himself. He could raise his eyes to the lower edge of the square hatch if he stood on tiptoe on the back of the chair. He could see nearby masonry and, in the distance, a fir tree. In this way, he could imagine a distant spiritual brother who was in office fighting crime. Perhaps he was following up a gang murder, pondering an American-made submachine gun discarded at the crime scene in the stairwell of an apartment building in St Petersburg. Cut off from it all, he, Gratchov, could have given clues. Could have contributed to the perpetual struggle against social evil, brought about a change of direction, which is only possible collectively. It remains conceivable, Gratchov said to himself, that a coincidence (just as a multitude of such coincidences make up the history of the world, the cosmos) could bring me together with someone who wants to learn what I have ascertained in abundance and for which I have been trained. I've got to put it down in writing and hide it because, due to its sheer mass, I can't keep it all in my head; even if my knowledge increases, the walls around me will never grow again.

AGENT WITHOUT A FATHERLAND

At the end of the 1980s, a sleeper agent was placed in the West's industrial sector. By that time, the techniques of the KGB and some of its allied intelligence services, especially those of reconnaissance in the Stasi, had been perfected. There will probably never again be such a modern service that oriented, so to speak, towards basic research, internationalism and purposeless perspective, the silent Lermontov said; he had found a position working plant security for Gazprom, had betrayed no one, could look everyone in the eye openly. He was a high achiever.

We must call this sleeper agent NN. He remains undiscovered. The rapid developments of the industrialised information sector have driven him far away from his original position. In one of the transit stations of his perspective career (but he could already no longer report to any fatherland what he learnt, nor could he assign any accumulated power, which is the meaning of perspective, to any fatherland of the labourers), he had gained impressions which strengthened his conviction that socialism was not dead. Indeed, it was impossible to kill socialism.

It had to do with the development of artificial intelligence. It was housed in wheeled, conical enclosures. The structures, up to 30 centimetres in size, were constructed according to Kant's principle of the right of hospitality. Their desire for information led them to need one another. They pushed towards each other in hordes, could not be kept from keeping each other company. They spent their days in close contact, chatting away, but always with a millimetre of respectful distance between them, so that they did not hinder one another through their need for closeness. Perspective agent NN was very surprised.

It was well known that the breeding of artificial intelligence only succeeds from its social component. The designers had the idea of training these creatures—for whom human rights were soon to be to be applied—in such a way that they could take over the cleaning of modern cities' sewage pipes, inaccessible to human hands. That is why it was correct that they stayed together in groups; the most important feature of their design being that they sharply distinguished themselves from the filth they were supposed to clean up. Early generations of artificial intelligence had failed because first they got rid of the faeces and then each other. But this could now be avoided. They distinguished each other 'from the enemy', and did so unerringly; indeed, the measure of their intelligence was the unity among themselves and their aggressiveness towards the faeces. Here (the perspective agent regretted that he could no longer share any of his observations) the problem of democratic socialism was solved for the first time. No factionalism in which one faction of the Central Committee killed the other. Information could be carried back and forth without any brakes, without any hostility arising, indeed, the freedom of infinitely increasing speech and response— what the engineers here called chatter—was the cycle and lifeblood of socialism's successor. NN regretted that, having been observed by the managing committees, he was transferred from this project to a completely different one, one which did not provide any information on socialism's progress.

ARE GLASNOST AND PERESTROIKA A PATH
TO THE FUTURE AND, IF SO, OUT OF WHICH SOIL?

The meeting with the clerks in the Moscow Central Committee which Valentin Falin described to me as competent and responsible took place in a new building that had been erected 10 years prior according to an architectural plan from the twenties: to house the central authority of the Communist Party at a time when the first crises, unrecognizable to those involved, foreshadowed its eventual demise. The cool planners from 1923 had designed the buildings in the style of a grand hotel (40 years elapsed between plan and execution). Before the October Revolution of 1917, the revolution-aries usually held their meetings in hotels. The planners of 1923—whom the architects of 1973 had faithfully followed—had taken this memory as their starting point. In reality, however, only that period *before* the seizure of power (with a brief echo-effect for the period thereafter) had been *political*.

At the hotel counter, my papers were checked. Just as in a real hotel, the keys were hanging on the wall behind the porter who occu-pied a high position in the secret service. The party bureaucrats, responsible for the overall political judgement, which for years had been accompanying those measures actually taken in the economic decision-making centres, sat in narrow, tube-like rooms, like those created when one generous hotel room for former masters-of-the-universe is turned into two by the insertion of shelves and partitions. A compromise between historical splendour and economy that had already been built into the layout of the Swiss and Parisian hotels which served as a model for the design of the command building. To me, the department head in charge of 'New Economic Strategies' seemed sluggish and uninformed.

The man tried to be polite to me, the foreigner, while at the same time getting rid of me quickly. Why was he living in this tube? What was he interested in? What was he going to do once he'd got rid of me? I found all this party headquarters' details to be a ruse, a kind of camouflage designed to distract from the fact that, despite their political control, the truly relevant decisions were taking place elsewhere. THE POLITICAL SUBJECT HAD LEFT THE HOTEL BUILDING WITHOUT LEAVING AN ADDRESS.

There were no vending machines in the building. The pre-1917 revolutionaries would not have needed one, frequenting as they did neighbourhood cafes. Local cafes were not foreseen in those plans which the governing bodies in the utilities sector, independent of the POWER OF THE PARTY, had developed.

An analysis of the Russian revolution—which seemed to return for a moment with glasnost and perestroika—gave me the following picture: large scientific institutes and economic combines to which posts and pensions are attached function LIKE LARGE LAND-OWNERS. They shed pensions. They form the soil, a soil of second nature. Thus institutes, enterprises and organisations overlay whole landscapes and coexist with forests, rivers, villages and all of the territory of Russia, which is downgraded to a mere supplementary reality, a parallel economic zone. The government, the institutes and the combines—in addition to the military structure with its farmsteads and supply units—are the object of 'determined reform', a land reform in the fifth dimension, so to speak.

'Great Russia raised its soul
There courage did swell
There the chips did fly.'

–   In this respect, perestroika has to do with a peasant revolt? A takeover of the estates by the serfs?

–   No, by the bosses themselves and their deputies.

–   And there's no redistribution?

–   Not a redistribution of social land, but a dissolution of this land, because it consists of second nature, not bits of soil, water and weather, but supply plans, regulations, even habits. A politician of perestroika must be a lawyer.

–   Now comes the economic point of view: could Schumpeter's concept of CREATIVE DESTRUCTION be applied?

–   Just as capital historically replaced the classical arable economy. But there is no capital to be seen.

- Capital is the recklessness, the momentum, that arises in people's minds?

- Now the industrialisation of consciousness would have to begin. An educational offensive!

- Do you mean that a socialistic society can live off information and texts?

- Survive somehow, if the institutes and organisations actually feed it.

- And we won't fall back onto any kind of real ground? From out of second nature onto the muddy paths of Russia during *rasputitsa*?

- Never. The real soil has long been overbuilt. The villages of 1905 no longer exist. The inhabitants have inexorably become Muscovites.

In my notes, the information was correlated with observations from the writings of Adam Smith. If the processes in Great Russia were not suddenly and violently interrupted, I thought at the time, a second path to the information society-to-come would arise.

THE TERM 'ENTFREMDUNG'
WAS UNFAMILIAR TO THE IDEOLOGUES

In the third year of perestroika, at the time of German President von Weizsäcker, the political figures in the Kremlin were rather accessible. One could question Alexander Yakovlev, responsible for ideology in the Politburo, so long as one joined the crowd that surrounded him. Though every minute he spent answering questions halted the process of change underway in the Soviet Union, he did not show any signs of impatience. His speeches were general. He was interested in economics as a question of supplying the urban population in winter.

He was unfamiliar with the German term ENTFREMDUNG. Confused, he seized upon the English term 'alienation', which seemed to him to apply to states of affairs. It takes time to learn, he said. Conservatives like Ligachev, he added with an ironic expression (he managed a confidence-inspiring distortion of his face), had a bank account of time at their disposal; they'd also read Marx better than he had. He was always in a hurry, was incapable of rereading. If nothing happens, the defender wins. The persistent conservatives in the administration can wait, we can't. That sounded sceptical.

He had fought the Germans at Leningrad. Now, on occasion of the visit, he was meeting a German president who would have been on the occupiers' side, the member of an elite regiment. But because the Germans had not advanced fast enough, had lost time in northern Russia, Germany was defeated. The attack on Berlin was only the consummation. No. 2 in terms of rank, the politician seemed tired. It remained unclear to what extent the group driving the perestroika attack—which is to say, he himself—resembled the 9th infantry regiment that had been on one of the Baltic islands and then was defeated outside of Leningrad on account of arriving too late. Yakovlev didn't seem to care about all that much.

Before Leningrad, he said, the defenders' motives had been better. Would it be the same with Ligachev, who was defending the positions of the apparatus and the agricultural sections? No, Yakovlev replied.

The chandeliers in Catherine Hall were copies of the candle-lit ones which had shone at the tsar's receptions and, for a very short time, for the invader, Napoleon. Carefully crafted electrical products from the thirties, custom-made for the party leadership. Now the call is made for a gala dinner. Fixed seating arrangements are unsuitable for political conversation, as it is never possible to seat those who have something to say to each other next to each other. Seats are allocated according to rank. In the Federal Republic of Germany, however, the head of office is politically responsible, and, in the USSR, the deputy head of the office. They are never seated together. Furthermore, on a little stool behind each of the diners there ought to be a bilingual interpreter. And a second interpreter who does not translate the language but the words' historical meanings, their context. The meal should not consist of five courses. A hot soup is enough: it relaxes. Afterwards there ought to be an opportunity for political discussion, but this is not the case due to the unsuitable seating arrangement. To 'transform' all this—namely, the learning of classical terms and the transformation of a state dinner into a discussion group—is one of perestroika's tasks.

A RESEARCH GROUP IN AKADEMGORODOK

In Akademgorodok, near Novosibirsk, between 1984 and 1987, 12 academics planted there by Andropov and later to advise Gorbachev, were conducting research on whether the obvious progress under-way in Great Russia (countered by equally obvious deficits in motivation and politicization) had a special, Russia-specific root. If so, it would be possible to turn the slogan 'socialism in one country'—the cause of so many regressions and sacrifices—around and envisage something useful for the world. According to the researchers, the development of productive forces requires an echo of the world, if necessary, in the form of markets.

Perhaps, the researchers said, a 'centre of feelings' could be formed in another way, one presumably inaccessible to government bodies. The presence of the *MIR* in the firmament, the surprising fact that under Admiral Gorshkov maritime dominance was nearly achieved (an achievement the researchers considered unproductive, if astonishing), the explosion of education, engineering and, last but not least, glasnost were growths that had to have a common root. IN THIS RESPECT, THESE 12 RESEARCHERS BELIEVED THAT PERESTROIKA AND THE TRIAL PHASE OF DE-STALIN-IZATION UNDER KHRUSHCHEV WERE A CONTINUATION OF THE IMPULSES OF 1905 AND NOT A CONTINUATION THE COUP OF 1917. 'Deep beneath the Snow' was the headline of one of the joint publications the 12 produced who, after the collapse of the empire, moved to the US to go to Berkeley, Stanford, Harvard and Yale, where they went their separate ways, never to work together again.

ONE OF PERESTROIKA'S CHARACTERISTICS:
TOO LITTLE TIME AND WHERE THERE
WAS ANY IT MEANT YOU HAD TO WAIT

We patriots of perestroika did not have much time to organize. To organize means: getting in touch with one another, developing habits with one another, testing reliability, probing, discovering what we want in the first place. It isn't easy to find the single point within a moment of 'historical upheaval'. Where to start? We had a poster that showed how we (our new generation) could go back to Lenin's beginnings. The early years of the Fatherland, the newspaper *What Is to Be Done?* But what had the boss and his co-workers (all dead or shot in 1937) actually done at the beginning? The image of 'going back to Lenin's beginnings' was descriptive, but impractical. We didn't know any of Lenin's co-workers personally. We asked librarians who belonged to our district association. They promised to start research work soon. It was all too slow for us. It held us up. We preferred to think about what the socialist classics might have originally wanted. We had to translate all this into the 'present'. A decision or starting point, which in December 1917 was related to the unification and repair of just 12 locomotives in a depot in northern Russia, is not to be found again cartographically or conceptually in an intricately organized combine in Novokuznetsk that's suffering from a surplus of tasks, supplies, ways out and planning specifications, not a lack of working train resources. The modern large-scale enterprise—a regional sector which, however (like a network of nerves with the brain), has office space in the Moscow headquarters—consists of mines, steel smelters, a distribution apparatus, truck convoys, kitchens and casinos, a kind of exchange of natural produce between factories outside of jurisdictions and balance sheets, attached estates, compromise formulas, the scars of past conflicts. All this falls into the spheres of nationalization, the informal shadow economy and the 'political responsibility of the party' as if by some sort of spiritual wrench. But there is no spiritual wrench or set of keys to unlock simultaneously all these forms, grids, tubes, cages and entrances to the outside.

And this image, too, is only an analogy, a metaphor for the concepts of 'combine', 'complexity' and a dense collection of orders and awards that such a subdivision of the Fatherland has acquired over the decades. This is how we worked for perestroika, to set in motion the 'rebalancing' or even a 'reform' of this ECONOMIC REALITY, which after all consisted of human diligence and human desire. We needed a lot of time to exchange phone numbers, to meet one another, to polish the knockers on the doors of the neighbouring patriot's flat or office. Organizing benders among comrades who just met each other. We had the impression that, through us, a new subject, an intellectual flow, a political architecture was being formed. Naturally, we felt that we had something special, that we deserved recognition, that we were different from the others, the usual ones. They did not forgive us for such 'Robinsonism of goodwill' even for a moment. So, for months, the upheaval or reform developed into its opposite, a standstill, a period of waiting. Perhaps over the five years of the New Solidarity Movement our group had a total of seven weeks' time to make a real difference.

ONE MEASURE OF TIME
AND TWO DIFFERENT REALITIES

Within the free spaces that Gorbachev had opened up to the Russian intelligentsia at Akademgorodok, a conspiratorial 'squadron of pioneers' had come together and envisaged a Russia, a USSR, in the year 2032:

1987–2032
= 45 YEARS

Calculated in human lives, a period of one and a half generations. At the faster pace of 'scientific progress', however, 133. That was enough time for perestroika. It's slow. One of NEW REALISM's perspectives.

Of these realisms there are two.

Realism No. 1: This is the realism of First Nature: Russia's soils, the architectures of its big cities. They are awaiting their observation. It has been proven that, on the basis of such a FIRST NATURE, the world revolution will not take place. These processes are too slow for any kind of overthrow and for the 'generation of the new man about to leap'. Nature No. 1 doesn't take leaps.

Realism No. 2: That of five-year plans, of violent industrialization, of progress' endurance test: the time of victory over the fascist nemesis. ACHIEVEMENTS. Second nature.

This SECOND NATURE is where the grain grows, and the fields lie at the level of institutions. The harvest is collected from various posts. The labour that's already complete: the archive. DEAD LABOUR. But it's not something dead, it's the rich treasure, the community itself. Against 'vouchers' it is quickly squandered.

'THE MODEST GREAT RUSSIAN SKY SHONE ABOVE THE SOVIET EARTH WITH SUCH HABIT AND UNIFORMITY THAT IT SEEMED AS THOUGH THE SOVIETS HAD EXISTED SINCE THE BEGINNING OF TIME'

'Where do you come from . . . ? [. . .]'
'From communism. Ever heard of the place? [. . .]'
'What's that, a village named in memory of the future?'

'Now just announce the hauling duty, dig wells and ponds
in the steppe, and start moving the buildings in spring.
You look sharp and see that socialism is taller than the grass
out here by summer. I'll be checking up on you!'

' . . . some drank vodka, others sat among the dozens
of their children with half-dead minds'

'. . . the smell of the sadness of separation and the anguish
of the absence of man wafted from the depths
of the distant steppe'

'. . . an iron flag attached to a pole,
a flag which could not submit to the wind.'

THE TRIP TO KALINOVKA

The night train from Moscow to Kursk. From there a two-hour car trip on gravel roads and sandy streets to the west to Dmitrievka. From there, it's south to Khomutovka. And from there to the south-west until the turn-off for Kalinovka.

At the height of his power as general secretary of the CPSU, Khrushchev was flattered by advisors and assistants. In the spring of 1960, thanks to one of the chief's remarks, they learnt about his teacher Lydia Shevchenko. They searched for her and managed to get the old woman to Moscow, where she gave a lecture at the All-Russian Congress of Educators. She reported that Kalinovka was a 'terribly boring village'. To her knowledge, Khrushchev (as a school-boy and during visits to his birthplace) disliked the peasant class, which was in a hopeless situation. At the very least, one had to aspire to become a miner in the Donbass. Peasants are not proletarians. On account of such information, the woman was quickly taken out of circulation. Khrushchev sought her out. It turned out that he had been going to Kalinovka twice a year for the past decade. For a long time, he held Shevchenko, the aged rebel, in his arms.

FIGURE 74. Lydia Shevchenko, Nikita Khrushchev's primary school teacher in 1905 when he was 11 and attending the school in Kalinovka. The young atheist and rebellious teacher recognizes the boy's intelligence. She plants the spirit of 1905 in him.

FIGURE 75 (ABOVE). Khrushchev and his wife Nina Petrovna.

FIGURE 76 (BELOW). Khrushchev in San Francisco. Were his policies precursors of perestroika? Was he a supporter of the Revolution of 1905? A Stalinist? Or a little bit of everything?

'DON'T FALL, STAR, MY STAR, STAY / THERE,
SEND THE COLD, SEND THE LIGHT . . . '

On 1 and 2 August 1991, absolute exhaustion consumed the Kremlin. The stable guard under Gorbachev's office chief Valery Boldin had to hold out. The earliest they could go on holiday would be October. We were trying to demonstrate the ACCESSIBILITY OF THE CENTRAL OFFICE. The boss, Gorbachev: All senses directed to sleeping in, a change of air (Crimea, coast), forgetting. He still had to prepare a speech for 19 August. Such a confused concentration of senses is similar to fainting. The boss did not want to sleep, eat, read or talk. He did not want to say what he wanted. A sign of melancholy. This corresponds to a dangerous disease. Politically-theologically ACEDIA = 'The ill-tempered, sour cold'. When it seizes the character, it creates an inner emptiness: already at the mere thought of how few days of holiday there were until 19 August, the date of the return flight to headquarters.

At that time, the empire was thought to be 'agitated'. The expression of the radio reporter who spoke this way was not precise enough for a scientist at Akademgorodok: as far as the latter was concerned, an empire like the Soviet Union at the stage of August 1991 was not a subject, not a 'sentient heart'. An empire is neither 'empty' nor 'agitated'. It would not be able to rest. That's how much it consists of flow and movement. According to the scientist from Akademgorodok, it is a whole, that is, an abstract concept. The realities that make up an empire are spread across the regions like splinters made of landscapes, competences, perceived powerlessness, power structures, overwork, the loss of hope, hope's return and accountability. In addition, labour power, anti-labour power, plans and in this August, above all, disorientation. The groups, the freshly stamped individuals (from the time of glasnost), the club-like associations, the rope teams, the whispering of the responsible channel workers—neither glasnost nor perestroika had managed to fashion a new and intact public sphere out of these fragments. NO PUBLIC THERE TO CONSOLE. The public consoles because it brings such islands-of-life closer together. Boat traffic. This has always been lacking through the sluggish summer month of August and it is especially lacking now. The public of Leningrad (but already the renaming to St Petersburg is prepared) coexisted and rivalled the 7,000 publics of Moscow. All communication between these centres was disturbed by the echoes of the successful reform group in Nizhny Novgorod, a perestroika tone that rivalled in volume the weaker reports of success in the two capitals.

Crisis and strike, on the other hand, in Siberia's largest oblast. Miners. Everywhere forces of will, stirring cadres, rising counter-cadres, egos in the room. Neither the term 'the masses', nor 'the comrades', nor 'Soviet citizens' described the state of the country equivalently. The empire resembled the geological structure of a 'creeping, slowed down earthquake'. In his lonely flat—few continued to visit the fallen one—Eduard Shevardnadze sat in front of his fax machine. With the help of telephone lists he had taken from his office, he was able to contact government centres outside Russia. But he could not call friends on the spot without being tapped. THIS ROBINSON WAS STUCK, CUT OFF OUT IN ONE OF THE SUBURBS OF MOSCOW. The Russian agricultural lobby, which hated the dismissed foreign minister, had found itself isolated in the power apparatus since the last party congress. THEY TOO HAVE BEEN CONDEMNED TO WAITING. The physically strong Ligachev (in terms of muscles, nerves, powers of determination), the main cadre of the political right, was condemned to inactivity.

THE AUGUST 1991 COUP

FIGURE 77

FIGURE 78

FIGURE 79

FIGURE 80

putsch_0101

putsch_0103

putsch_0104

putsch_0105

FIGURE 81

THE *ANTITHESIS TO 'IMPERIUM'*:
INTIMACY

'FALLING IN LOVE WITH TANKS
UNDER YOUR WINDOWS'

'THE LIBRARIES AND THEATRES STOOD EMPTY'

'HEARTS ON FIRE WITH WORDS'

'I WENT HOME TO HIM SPEECHLESS. WE NOW KNEW
ONE ANOTHER FOR ONLY TWELVE HOURS.'

SEMANTIC FIELDS OF INTIMACY

'EVERY DAY, CONTEMPLATING THE FIELDS, THE STARS, AND THE ENORMOUS FLOWING AIR, HE SAID TO HIMSELF, "THERE'S ENOUGH FOR EVERYONE!"'

'HE LOVED HER WITH THAT PLACE THAT OFTEN ACHED [. . .] WITH HIS WAIST OR THE APEX OF HIS HUMP'

'HE HAD EARLIER PICTURED HIS FUTURE LIFE AS A DEEP SKY-BLUE SPACE'

'AMAZING. I'M GOING TO DIE SOON, BUT EVERYTHING'S THE SAME'

' . . . HIS EYES WERE SUBMISSIVE, THOUGH WITHOUT A SHARP MIND'

' . . . A LONG AND DREARY RAIN SOFTLY RUSTLING ALONG THE ROOF'

'NOTHING MAKES YOU AS HOPELESS AS THE FACT THAT, AT ANOTHER TIME, THERE WAS A REASON TO HOPE'

arbeiterparadies_0021

arbeiterparadies_0022

arbeiterparadies_0023

arbeiterparadies_0024

arbeiterparadies_0025

arbeiterparadies_0028

arbeiterparadies_0029

arbeiterparadies_0031

FIGURE 82

FIGURE 83. The Discovery of Russia.

I WAS ADMIRAL GORSHKOV'S COFFEE BOY

Instead of a political commissar, the leadership had assigned me, the academic Vsevolod J. Shatin, to the fleet staff. An admission that a complex, global approach to work (such as Admiral Gorshkov was planning) could not be controlled by the means of the political mind but could best be interpreted by the mind of science. But the all-roundman Gorshkov himself could do that better than I could, and so, despite my high position, I was practically out of a job.

Whenever he woke up bleary-eyed in the room next to his planning room, I would fetch him a cup of coffee. The morning hour was when he was at his weakest. Any one of the empire's adversaries could have successfully attacked at such an hour, for Gorshkov was no fan of automated alarm systems. When taken by these morning moods, the chief's decisions were extremely slow. He did not have any deputies. In this respect, the four coffees I'd bring him, which made up his morning hour, were a decisive defensive weapon.

THE PRIMACY OF LIVING LABOUR POWER

Gorshkov's turn *against* automata but *for* subjective decision-making in the national defence is based on the correct Marxian evaluation of LIVING LABOUR POWER. Machinery can only be set in motion by an amount (however diminished) of human labour. The Soviet Union is on the side of this labour power, not on the side of some sort of machinery, which is composed of former labour, so-called dead labour. How can one not place trust in the only thing we are fighting for? Though the imperialists believe in fighting machines, the patriot relies on the idea, on human reaction. It's cheap, too.

The individual steps of our fleet command proceeded so quickly that European naval powers only noticed them because of the nervousness of their American ally. What happened out on the waters? The intelligence services were unable to determine that. They did not possess any reconnaissance forces at sea.

'UP TO OUR NECKS IN THE DIRT, READY TO DEFEND'

Why did Gorshkov's plans fail (after all, the world power already had functioning networks)? Not because of American interference. On the contrary, the general secretary's resistance remained insurmountable. Khrushchev's peasant mind could not be overcome. I doubt that Khrushchev could even imagine fleet movements in the Indian Ocean, the value of bases in Somalia, the attack tactics of nuclear submarines in the depths of the sea and off Cape Horn. It seemed to me that, no matter what we said, he only ever saw the waves of the Black Sea. Word had it that this landlubber had visited the Barents Sea a grand total of one time, on an excursion steamer.

The coming of a storm in that shallow sea causes unpleasant phenomena. Khrushchev doubted that the Soviet fleet could 'take off', as he put it, from the mainland at all. Flat seabed all around. Which was precisely why my Admiral Gorshkov intended to strengthen the forces in oceans far away from our continental mass. He had no intention of carrying the ships overland.

Our soldiers fought because of their mental origins in the peasant class (until the abolition of narrow-minded class barriers in a few hundred years, in other words, until entry into the classless human race), not according to the law of the sea. They fought like the defenders of Colchis defending Medea's homeland: mighty fighting machines, buried up to their necks in dirt so that they couldn't turn away. Even if afraid, they didn't move. And they weren't afraid of anything. This accounts for their small store of foreboding. They never sought out the enemy. If the enemy was right before them, they didn't suspect that he would deceive them, that he would steal the Golden Fleece as well as the king's daughter, Medea, who, ruined, would kill her children and 'take off' back to her father's house upon a fiery dragon. The world exploded: the defenders were still up to their necks in dirt, ready to defend. Had the secretary general known about them, these buried giants would have reflected his ideas of effective national defence. And as per his usual, Khrushchev would have added: 'They are to be mobile in accordance with the instructions of the Central Committee.' No lecture from the fleet leadership would overturn this attitude. Which is why we act secretly, undetected by the general secretary's spies. An untenable state-of-affairs. We've almost already been arrested.

And so we placed various bases in the deep sea. At a secret location in the south Indian Ocean, where they lie under the cold currents circling Antarctica. Undetectable! We also set up inflatable tents in the valleys of the Mid-Atlantic Ridge. Our Barracuda-class nuclear submarines—'inaudible shadows'—accompanied the carrier fleet sailing in the spirit of Marxism-Leninism between India and Africa. This and our head start to the moon, that is what secures our borders. Border guards wouldn't get the job done.

By the time the secretary general fell, it was too late. We lost the Somali coast, were fighting in Angola, lost Mozambique and our bases in Egypt. My patriot and coffee drinker had moved inexorably up the age ladder. This, according to Karl Marx's *Paris Manuscripts*, is the weakness of 'immortal labour power'. The individual dies. I couldn't keep the Admiral awake even with eight cups of caffeine, not late in the afternoon during the chilly Christmas period.

AN AFTERNOON WITH THE MILITARY MARITIME FLEET
(Report by one of Khrushchev's assistants)

Four days of railway journeys, flights, bodies being transported over-land, loaded onto ships, bedded down for the night. Our souls extended to the place of action like a night train that was four days late. 'We yearned for the time when we would no longer be.'

Our comrades and senior officers AT THE SECRET LOCA-TION ON THE BLACK SEA welcomed us in a hall with film screens and slide projectors onboard a cruiser.

With the aid of maps and enhanced by projections, one of the commanders, Vice Admiral G., presented us with a wargame. My boss, General Secretary Nikita S. Khrushchev, was very anxious.

Our 'fleet' had encountered 'the enemy' and 'put him to flight'. The commander now began to enumerate how our fleet was making its way across the Black Sea and sinking enemy ships to the left and to the right off the coasts of Turkey. WE ARE ALREADY APPROACHING THE DARDANELLES. And now, said the admiral, we are advancing into the Mediterranean. In the meantime, bold landings have been made on the northeast coast of Africa.

The lecture made me sad. It seemed haughty to me. But my boss appeared REALLY MOVED. I knew this was indicative of an increase in his depression. He had resolved to be silent, to listen, to let the military collective speak first. But he had, as always, difficulty controlling his temper.

'Stop! Wait just a moment!' he said. 'You speak with such cer-tainty of having made short work of the enemy, and now you tell us that there is nothing left to do but to let him have the rest. What is this "rest of the enemy"? Why do they have this remnant if you made such short work of them before? Have you ever seen the fog that is often in the southern part of the Black Sea? Have you sounded that sea's considerable depths? Are you sure there aren't any "enemy" submarines lurking there? And if not from the US, then from Turkey or Greece? If this were a real war, your ships would have been at the bottom of the sea a long time ago already.'

The admiral looked at us calmly.

'Moreover, you have ignored the fact that the enemy launches missiles not from coastal fortifications but from aircraft. We have such a system ourselves.'

As it turned out, the fleet commander hadn't heard a thing about launching ramps in planes.

'That's our mistake,' my boss added. 'All information is secret. Therefore, the navy officers don't know what the missile officers and planes are capable of. At the same time, they insult Russia by daring to claim that we "wanted to destroy our enemies".'

My boss was clever. In fact, he did not have to listen to all the speeches of the military collective to arrive at his counter-position. But he did not take time to convince the military step by step. In particular, he could have won over younger officers who were silent at such a meeting. Especially by letting the commanders talk and fully develop their plans. Had my boss asked patiently, as Comrade Stalin would have done, the absurdity would have been obvious. The boss would have been able to ask the younger ones and thus pushed the Politburo's position through.

The commanders, ashamed of their defeat, made contact with officers of the other armed forces whose careers were in danger, and with political cadres who were threatened with dismissal. Thus, while still travelling through the south, my boss was neutralized and disarmed in a coup.

'HOPE OPENS UP THE HEART – –'

A STRANGE INCIDENT SURROUNDING THE
CATASTROPHE OF THE NUCLEAR SUBMARINE KURSK /
INSTINCT OR FORESIGHT?

Out of instinct or foreboding, the commander left me behind at the military base of Murmansk. As a weekend guard. So, on standby. I was to get in touch if something urgent happened. On Saturdays, the staff officers disappear collectively starting at 11 o'clock in the morning to seek out the 'aura of life'. 'Pleasure'. Just being off base, in the company of others, is exhilarating. No better time for an enemy—even if just the movement of destiny—to attack than a Saturday afternoon in the Russian Empire.

It is within this utter silence of the base that I receive the radio message that the KURSK is lying at the bottom of the sea. This was precisely the moment my mission commander had intuited. I decoded, made calls. You've got to imagine fleet headquarters as a series of boarded corridors with offices attached, nothing of a command post, of instruments, of a 'field of employment'. At that time of the morning, the electronic systems down in the basements are locked. Caretakers unreachable.

With all my heart, but not yet sure that anything definitive has been lost, I try to get in touch with some knowledgeable or helpful authority. A message from the missile cruiser commanding the manoeuvre fleet: the KURSK has been located on the rocky bottom at a depth of 129 metres, unable to move, heavily inclined. Destruction to the bow. We, the radio operators, full of hope. An award was certain if, on a hopeless Saturday, against all odds, we were able to organize rescue resources.

AT THE MOMENT OF THE ACCIDENT

As it turned out later, the moment the accident occurred, two small submarines—which actually belonged to our northern fleet, were unmanned at the time and specialized in rescue technology—had broken loose from their moorings in the CASPIAN SEA and were drifting north. The vehicles were on loan to the Lukoil joint-stock company. If you followed them on the sea chart, the movement looked as if they were heading towards the accident site, which, from their perspective, was in a foreign sea.

The special boats were part of the 200 rescue devices intended for use in the event of a catastrophe, which, after many hours, the sinking of the KURSK turned out to be. A lot of effort, dedication of engineers, was built into them. The two ROGUES belonged to a squadron whose prototype had been developed in 1928 and, up to this point, constantly optimized. They were constructed in the manner of a buoyant lifting platform, little resembling a ship, more like a raft with vertical superstructures. They had gripping arms which could be steered remotely; the device was reminiscent of an oversized screwdriver. This enabled them to pull stranded ships from sandbanks, to open sunken submarines and take measures to transport the crew to the surface or even pull the wrecked ship out of the water. At the time, they were helping with the repair of oil towers and earning money for our fleet.

As a fleet, we have land holdings in central Russia and platinum mines in southeastern Siberia to replenish our budgets. In this respect, our system of self-sufficiency is like the method of the late Roman legions which, abandoned by all the gods and the empire, held bastions on the Danube or defended Byzantium against the Parthians and Turks. In times of need, the system hoards unexpected reserves, temporary help built into the system itself (the hermetic goodwill of countless people who despair of leadership and hope in the technique of practitioners); the staffs' (from top to bottom) superficial view does not perceive them.

I heard casually of the escape of the two wayward vehicles; indeed, I had been looking for such rescue techniques. The Caspian naval command hunted with cutters carrying searchlights and seaplanes equipped with residual light amplifiers. Boatmen were lowered onto the platforms on ropes before being delivered onto one of the islands of the Caspian Sea.

As if the gods wanted to help us! As if prayers from the stern of the KURSK (or my foreboding phone calls) could help! In Astrakhan, on Sunday night, the two rescue vehicles were loaded into a large ANTONOV aircraft. How had they managed to lift the platforms out of the saltwater and bring them overland to the airport? Why was an ANTONOV available in the first place? Our telephones: like whips hung with bells, like the whips of Siberian coachmen our Pushkin describes in verse. We followed every metre of the race-to-catch-up. How could it be that, after a stopover in the Urals, the ANTONOV was able to find fuel again? Was the technology thinking of its own free will? Was the country moved by a sense of foreboding (as my commander had been) as to what might be the next right step? The accident hadn't even been announced yet.

I have to assume that these rescue techniques possess some kind of independent will. My agitated telephoning (nervousness slows our counterpart's willingness to cooperate with us up here in the north) could never have caused the only units suitable for rescue throughout great Russia to select themselves, so to speak (I would not have known of their suitability without the news that they had taken on a life of their own), and to move so close to us, namely, to halve the distance.

By this time the alarm had reached the top of the hierarchy. It was already Sunday morning. All movement froze. The alarm plan went into effect: concentrate all resources on rescuing the KURSK. Further orders were expected.

I AWAKE FROM A HECTIC SLUMBER AT 6.18 A.M. NOW IT'S RUSH HOUR

The emergency vehicles never arrived. They were involved in a crash at the intermediate stop in the Urals when a fighter-bomber which was about to take off ran into the ANTONOV, which at that moment was having platforms unloaded.

I am responsible to the commander, to the Fatherland. All on my own, without any help. The commanding admiral of the manoeuvre fleet on the phone. There's a storm brewing in the Barents Sea, which is why no one can be reached. I replied: I couldn't know that better than he could.

I call Andrei Velishov, a journalist friend in Moscow. A breach of security. He drafts a press enquiry, which by 9 p.m. results in the full assembly of the admiral's staff. Now there are footsteps stumbling through the corridors outside my room.

Another call from the commanding admiral of the manoeuvre fleet. Urgent. If help is not organized in 30 hours, it will be in vain. He justifies this with a probability calculation, derived from 32 accidents in the Soviet-Russian submarine fleet. The fact that he has time to tell me this worries me. It tells me he can do nothing. It is Monday night. He is 5 kilometres from the wreck, I am hundreds of kilometres away. I stay up till 4 a.m. I, the only living thread that connects the crew of the KURSK, my Fatherland, with the reality above the water.

ARRESTED FOR PASSING ON AN
ILLEGAL STATE SECRET

In the afternoon hours of Tuesday, I, A. I. Sedov, was arrested by navy secret police. I was brought before the investigating judge for passing on state secrets (this concerned my telephone calls to the Caspian Naval Command, to the airfields where the ANTONOV was stationed, my complaints, when nothing moved). It also concerned my contact with the journalist Velishov in Moscow, which had been recorded. 'Where will it lead us,' the investigating judge wanted to know, 'when everyone thinks they can lead? It will lead to catastrophe,' he said. Sometimes, I replied, in the event of a disaster, this principle of experience is reversed. 'That may be the case regarding the law of experience, but it does not apply as a rule of law,' the investigator answered. He seemed friendly and good-willed, even humorous. It was Wednesday morning. Get ready, my dear Sedov, for severe punishment. As compared to the KURSK (which at that time was completely lost), take it as treatment in accordance with the principle of equality. Wherever there is one misfortune, there is another. As far as the KURSK was concerned, I found that a tad cynical. At the time, my commanding officer, whose prescience had placed me in this post, was already long dead. And in the meantime, the rescue craft, which had already covered half of the distance to the rescue site, had grown rusty, far from its saline element.

THE OBJECTIVISTS AND THE SUBJECTIVISTS

The progress of the devices is connected to a dispute within the Northern Fleet. Since the 1980s, a school of naval officers and engineers has pursued the tendency to install more and more automatic functions in underwater vessels due to their not being subject to human error. The project's opponents feared (given the lack of adequate secrecy) adversaries being able to intervene digitally and take such boats, sailing silently in the depths, to their doom. One school trusted the machinery, they were called the 'objectivists'; the other trusted the patriotism of the crews, they were called the 'subjectivists'.

A NOBLE LIE

Vladimir Geletin sat up all night with Popov, the chief of the Northern Fleet, and Mozak, the chief of staff. They discussed Tuesday's dawn. Since noon on Monday, Geletin has known that his son Boris—aboard the sunken KURSK—is either irrecoverable or dead. His daughter, a psychology student, looks after schoolchildren on the Black Sea. If he asks, she can arrive in Murmansk in two days at the earliest.

Geletin hesitates to inform his wife Natalia of the disaster; he does not want to do so until his daughter's there to comfort him. He no longer hopes for a turnaround, but he does hope that through his stalling no public announcement will make its way to Natalia. What he says is a lie.

Geletin, however, believes that the news will cause Natalia less distress if it reaches her as a public message, equally valid for so many other destinies, and not as privileged information, which she receives only because, as her husband is on the Admiral's staff, he learns some things earlier. She should not experience the loss as an individual, but as part of a community, and consoled by their daughter. Geletin's 'noble lie' risks that Natalia will receive the news abruptly—for example, on TV or by chance—without any consolation from him.

How is he to decide? No comrade is there to advise him. Relentless time ticks away until the moment when Geletin's lie becomes useless.

INSIDE DETERRENCE'S INNER COURTYARD
(Report from 1993)

Among the oddities of the military business for senior officers of the West after 1991 were the permissive visits they made to the sites where in earlier decades the secrets of the Russian military had been so perfectly guarded. The invitation to the SWISS OFFICERS' SOCIETY had still been issued under the previous defence minister, Sergeyev. The Swiss colonels, all of whom were also secret-service officers, were taken into the dachas of the military academy and for two weeks given courses on all questions of budgetary planning, equipment types and strategic approaches, as if it were a matter of selling this still considerable military potential. After that, the Swiss visited decentralized units on the borders of Uzbekistan, missile silos and naval stations near Murmansk and in Vladivostok. Now highly endowed with secret knowledge, they returned to Switzerland.

Colonel N. (name redacted) and a reporter from the *Neue Zürcher Zeitung*:

– Did anything make an impression on you?
– Yes.
– Did anything surprise you?
– Many things.
– In a negative sense?
– As far as our side is concerned, no.
– What are you referring to with 'our side'?
– We are neutral.
– There is talk of erosion processes in the Russian armed forces. The reorganization of finances is proceeding slowly.
– That is quite clear.

- So, what made an impression on you?
- A tank division is stationed just 7 kilometres away from Red Square. The newest beds. You could eat off the floor. Perfect motorization. We observed a drill. The peacetime strength of 2,500 men, now increased to 6,000 in case of emergency, has full combat power. I can say that that impressed us.
- And a counterexample?
- The state of the navy.
- That wasn't kept concealed?
- To be honest, nothing was kept concealed.
- Are the Russians not counting on any conflict?
- As of late, they are foreseeing conflicts. But the attitude towards public relations, which is new and still dates back to 1991, cannot be changed so quickly.
- Are there any indications of Russia's strategic thought?
- Yes. Three conflicting schools.
- What kind of schools?
- Three circles of 'insiders'. Less to do with 'friends' and more to do with believers. Two 'circles', as different as Genghis Khan and von Clausewitz. The third group is younger and has fewer members.
- What does the strongest of the three have to say?
- Strengthening the deterrent potential. The second-strike capability must be ensured. So investment in missile silos, in the new Topol-M missiles, in equipping the Intercontinental missiles (ICBMs) with multiple warheads, which is prohibited under the Start II Treaty. Deploying submarines off the US coast, etc. Their SS-18 missiles could be equipped with 10 warheads, the SS-19s with 6 warheads, and the Topol-M-SS27s with countless warheads. This would cancel out the US' missile shield.
- In other words, precisely what Grigory Tishchenko has written?
- Exactly. Another point of view: General Kvashnin, Chief of Russian General Staff.
- What kind of man is he?
- He is one of the group known as the 'warring generals'. Still shocked by his experiences in Afghanistan.

– And the youngest, the third group?
– They are counting on conflicts in the Caucuses, with Turkey and China. This is the generation of 'geostrategists with immediate objectives'. It's a group that doesn't show itself. We can only assume that it was a senior officer of this officer's conspiracy who led us on a charge against the Curonian Spit with special landing craft. Furious enterprise.
– What astonished you the most?
– That we were shown everything.
– What conclusion have you and your comrades from the Swiss Officers' Society drawn?
– There's nothing riskier than lopsided development. Junk and brilliance in the same outfit—that's explosive. A condition like damaged live ammunition.
– What chain of command is going to control that?
– Well, as the proverb goes:
> *'Though the kitchen knife is tricky /*
> *the cleaver too is slippery.'*

TALK WITH A PERSON
WITH A SECURITY CLEARANCE
(Report from 2004)

Hardly anyone but Michel Gaissmayer would have been able to get the cautious, mistrustful Yevgeny Maksimovich Primakov to sit before my camera. We film at the Hotel Baltschug Kempinski. Primakov had nothing to gain from such publicity. But he sure had a lot to lose, seeing as that he could not control the final product. Now he was standing on the balcony of the five-star hotel, looking across to the other side of the Moskva, where another hotel was in the process of being demolished and you could see the Kremlin.

The fundus of Primakov's eye: this is where subtexts lie. He was Gorbachev's chief adviser on Iraq. Could an unpredictable situation have arisen, I ask, had the US, after winning the first Gulf War, driven on towards Baghdad instead of pausing? Considering the USSR's links to Iraqi forces in terms of weapons, was the latter's defeat a negative test for Russian arms? Could an army faction in

Russia, a year before the August coup, have become independent and intervened in Iraq after Gorbachev's fall?

The experienced man did not answer my question. But at the back of his eyes he was signalling: that is exactly what could have happened, and the US knew as much. You carry the secrets of the world around in your head for as long as your circulatory system allows it. That which has not been recorded in any document of the world is kept in one of the folds at the right edge of his brain.

FIGURE 84

FIGURE 85. Yevgeny Maksimovich Primakov.

THE EXCHANGE VALUE OF SUPERFLUOUS SPACE

None of the people who've already been negotiating at the Baltschug Kempinski in Moscow for three days and nights have ever
spent any time up in the northern regions of the Russian fatherland,
including the shelf off the coast. People completely different from
them are up there, packed into fur and knowledgeable. In turn, they
have no competence for negotiations of the kind conducted here in
Moscow which determine the real conditions in the far north more
than any engineering. Negotiations are robust. It's a question of
establishing a line of demarcation between the Russian and Norwegian territories in the North Sea, as far as the North Pole. During
the consultations, there are indications that Norway is unexpectedly
favourable, the Russian delegation shows itself to be generous. It

trades knowhow for land. (The demarcation of the areas to be exploited is calculated in terms of the seabed, in this respect, 'land area', whether underwater or not.) The Norwegian companies are the ones that have the knowledge and machinery to extract natural resources from the impracticable North Sea terrain. Russia would first have to acquire them. Having said that, it would not be difficult for Russian intelligence to obtain trade secrets, patents, equipment from the Norwegian side. Indeed, they've been doing so for a long time. But intelligence agencies' knowledge of how to extract oil and gas in the far north doesn't help that much. They would have to set up courses for Russian businessmen and engineers; adult education, training, a mass of instruction manuals, indeed the retrospective correction of misguided Soviet school reforms would have to be carried out in the minds of these practitioners by the secret service to make what has been discovered applicable. It would be better for the secret service agents to become explorers themselves. But who would carry out the work of the intelligence services? One of the most sensitive organs of the community when it comes to economic espionage which is not limited to the exploitation of the North Sea.

And that's why granting the Norwegians large areas of the polar region and the Barents Sea (to which Russia could just as well lay claim) and thus luring them into Russian concession areas is a better idea. The Russian imagination has always enjoyed images of cold and the open landscapes so high up in the north, it's just that hardly anyone wants to go up there and move around.

Dogs, when full, dig holes to hide precious morsels of food and thus secure their future interest. Large oil exploration companies take a similar approach. Increasingly, they tend not to exploit their discoveries, but to seal them up. The oil is far too valuable to be exchanged for money. No market price is enough to drive up the company's value on the stock exchange, only the power of imagination, which has to do with the future. The right thing to do with treasure is to sit on it; to protect FUTURES.

A BLITZKRIEGER OF THE SKIES
(Report from 1995)

WE were the guarantors for the Victory Day parade in May, which was almost cancelled because of a low-pressure system. A low-pressure system, a strong cloud formation from the Black Sea, presumably containing a radioactive substance, was approaching the capital. That was when we were deployed. In fact, we were coming from a failed project—a project that had been abandoned for reasons of cost thanks to the new cost-consciousness that had arrived in perestroika's wake. We were supposed to artificially fertilize monsoon clouds over the Indian Ocean (from planes dropping chemicals from the stratosphere) so that the stored mass of rain would not fall prematurely somewhere over India but make it past the hurdle of the high mountains and only begin to do so once over the southern parts of our HOLY RUSSIA, something the crops desperately needed.

This was done with silver iodide and a few refinements which we kept in our flying machines. With some violation of the sovereignty of foreign peoples, but consistently from the perspective of unconditional internationalism (which, in this case, coincided with the principle of 'socialism in one country'), EVERYTHING seemed possible with our planes. A thousand kilos more of utopia and our project would have been approved or, rather, made possible by the premises of perestroika's economic calculations.

Now we had been reduced, but for the community we were still of increased importance: Were we to give up the day of victory simply because of INCLEMENT WEATHER? We replied: no, no and again, no!

Our planes, seven squadrons, fuelled, were waiting on the drop zones around Moscow. Then we flew towards the cloud formations which—politically innocent, hardly to be called hostile themselves—were advancing with the force of fascist tanks in 1941. From Smolensk onwards, we sprayed this 'structure of doom'. It rained down swiftly. Over the terrain west of Moscow, in certain respects precisely in the region of the Volokolamsk Highway where our patriots had delayed and finally stopped the fascist invader in his advance. And that's how we defended Moscow on a new meteorological-symbolic level.

FIGURE 86

The Rainmakers of Moscow: Ensuring favourable weather conditions at the victory celebration on 9 May

regenmacher_0001

regenmacher_0002

Flughafen Bykowo bei Moskau

regenmacher_0004

Flughafen Bykowo bei Moskau

regenmacher_0005

regenmacher_0006

regenmacher_0007

Gennadi Beriolew,
Department of Weather Modification

regenmacher_0008

regenmacher_0009

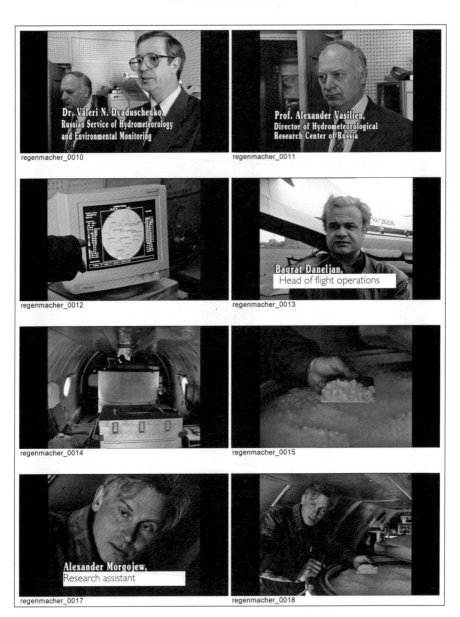

FIGURE 87

regenmacher_0019

Jewgenij Wolgonew,
Pilot

regenmacher_0020

FIGURE 88

AN OLD LEGEND

A fairy tale by the Brothers Grimm, translated into Russian by
Rosemarie Tietze and entitled 'Not a Drop Wet the Hair of the
Father,' has to do with three brothers who are sent out, each in a
different direction, to be trained as craftsmen. When they return,
their father receives them. He is surprised by a downpour. The last
of the three, who loved his father most, has been trained as an épée
fencer in a foreign country. He pierces the raindrops one by one.
Not a drop of water reaches the father's head. This is how the old
man escapes getting a cold. The airborne task force responsible for
getting rid of the contaminated rain from Chernobyl before it
reached the Moscow parade ground was familiar with the story.

FIGURE 89. Melnikov House. Study. July light, 2006.

FIGURE 90

At about eleven o'clock in the evening, DUMA deputy Galina Starovoitova returned to the building where she was staying, accompanied by her press secretary, Linkov. On the stairs, the two of them, probably by a man and a woman, were shot by a machine gun and a pistol. Starovoitova is killed, Linkov is badly wounded but is able to alert a journalist on his mobile. The journalist asks him: 'What's happened to Galina Starovoitova?' Linkov replies: 'I don't know, she's lying on the stairs, I'm wounded.' Then he says: 'I think I'm losing consciousness.'

After the murder, the killers threw away the guns, ran through the courtyard and out to the next street, where a car was waiting for them.

FIGURE 91

FIGURE 92

russland00173

russland00174

russland00175

russland00177

russland00180

russland00182

russland00184

russland00185

FIGURE 93

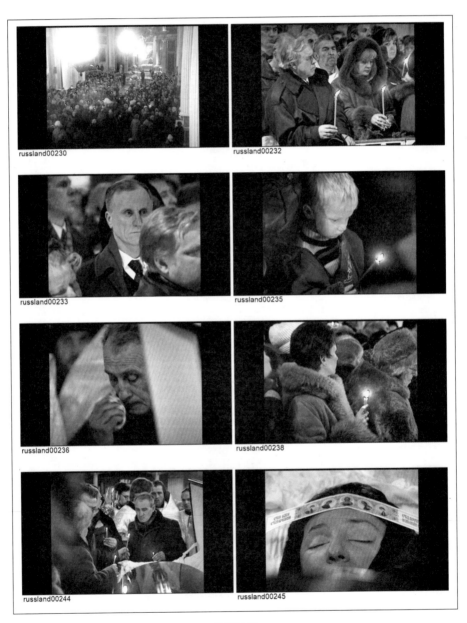

russland00230

russland00232

russland00233

russland00235

russland00236

russland00238

russland00244

russland00245

FIGURE 94

russland00190

russland00193

Galina Starovoitova, born 1946 in the Urals

russland00194

russland00195

Als Studentin

russland00198

Her wedding

russland00206

As a deputy, opening prisons

russland00211

russland00212

With her parents

russland00213

1949

russland00214

1951

russland00215

russland00216

russland00217

Sacharow und Starowoitowa

russland00218

Stairs where she was shot

russland00219

Stairs where she was shot

FIGURE 95

russland00274

russland00275

russland00276

russland00277

Galina Starovoitova shot on
20 November 1998

russland00278

russland00279

russland00280

russland00281

Heiner Müller,
Dramatiker

FIGURE 96

Semantic Field 'Grief'
(by Rosemarie Tietze)

печаль / pechal
= sadness, sorrow,
  distress, grief;

= worry, concern

уныние / unynie
= despondency,
  dejectedness,
  depression
  (*corresponds to acedia*);
= grinding boredom

скука / skuka
= boredom, weariness;
= listless mood,
  lack of conversation

грусть / grust
= sadness, distress,
heartache, grief

тоска / toska
= melancholy, depression,
  unquiet heart, unease;
= longing, weariness

скорбь / skorb

= sadness, distress, pain

**подавленность /
podavlennost**
= depression,
  dejection

горе / gore
= sorrow, grief, worry;
= plight, hardship

меланхолия / melankholiia
= melancholy, depression

боль / bol
= pain, hurt

депрессия / depressiia
= depression

траур / traur
= sadness, pain;
= mourning clothes

хандра / khandra
= doldrums; (baseless)
  gloom;
  spleen

Das Haus in St. Petersburg, in dem Galina Starowoitowa lebte / Hier wurde sie getötet - -

FIGURE 97. The apartment building in St Petersburg where Galina Starovoitova lived / Where she was killed—

FUNERAL PROCESSION

The autonomous administration of St Petersburg has ordered an act of state on the death of Galina Starovoitova. The 'funeral procession' is to be governed by Red Army regulations. The soldiers are to march slowly, in geometric configurations, their Russian muscles braking against earth's gravity, through the rows of mourners. Circling around the coffin. At a great distance and close by. Face, body and weapons thrust forward, like a third bloodstream, separate from that of the mourners and the now stilled circulation of the dead: ARMED MOURNING.

It functions like a signal, interrupts privacy, replaces the loud lamentation by striking marching steps. For the soldiers, the rules are unfamiliar. They stride clumsily along. The turn from straight ahead to the left (to form the square): extremely exact. Similarly, during the great French Revolution, Marat was taken to the grave with the geometric step of a mourning section of grenadiers. Voltaire's body, on the other hand, was carried to the Pantheon without any military regulations.

Galina Starovoitova would have been a stranger to such cere-
monies had she been able to watch her funeral. She would have
wanted people to follow her coffin chatting.

It is an open casket. The dead woman is made up and dressed
like a 'sleeping woman'. In fact, the shots from the machine pistol
had ripped Galina's face apart. That's how she was found in the stairwell. The technicians of the Forensic Institute had actively worked
to restore her features from scratch. Soft light already in the marble
hall of the Ethnographic Institute where broad sections of the pop-
ulace have come to bid her farewell. At the coffin in the church, only
candlelight, which supports the skin tone. Only if you came within
centimetres of the face of the deceased could you see the tiny seams.

GALINA STAROVOITOVA ON THE DAYS IMMEDIATELY FOLLOWING THE FAILED AUGUST COUP OF 1991

Dead hearts. In the days following the coup, nothing followed from
the uprising and the victory over the military. Nothing happened
because of outraged hearts. Throughout the kitchens of Moscow
and the empire, people went on talking, just as they always had.
Yeltsin's propaganda department dishing out only the most necessary food for the political mind. On ration stamps. No stockpiling
of hope.

That's how the empire crumbled. Anyone with the understanding of how to inflame hearts would have been able to turn 'consumers of their own lives' into 'producers of their own lives'.

Melancholia (according to S. Freud):

1. Profoundly painful dejection
2. Cessation of interest in the outside world
3. Loss of capability to love
4. Inhibition of all activity
5. Lowering of self-esteem
6. Self-reproach
7. Delusional expectations of punishment

Severe grief

There are SEVEN STAGES OF GRIEF. They have the same signs as melancholia. With the exception that the disturbance of self-esteem is absent in grief. I am still here, the survivor says. The 7th stage of grief work cannot be named; it moves invisibly back and forth between all the stages.

RULES FOR WEEPING

When damp wood sings as it burns, it is the weeping of poor souls. When the wind whistles in the wood and around the corner of the house, it is the weeping of unbaptized children. In the valleys of the northern Harz (especially up in Schierke and Elend), the godfather is supposed to buy the crying from the newborn on the third day after its birth. He must place money in the cradle. When a pregnant woman cries, it results in a screaming child. Now, my mother cried bitterly in February, but the child she bore on 2 April 1937, my sister, was always cheerful and never shouted at people, as her father or I certainly do.

In Switzerland, they say that you have to let children cry because when they cry their hearts grow. In Homer, among the Sioux, on the Andaman Islands and in New Zealand, people who return home are welcomed with tears. This, says Derrida, is not an expression of spiritual excitement but of a power to ward off evil. The returnee should be well and should not import any evil.

The tears of those left behind in life, those who loved the dead, burn in the deceased like fire. The more one weeps for the dead, the more water they must draw in the underworld. Which is why in a side valley of the Adige, where an old form of Latin is spoken, they say that a dead child should not receive more tears than a cup can hold. As the dead still see everything for two days, the first few should not be filled with too much weeping.

Dead children who suffered their mother's tears appeared in the house and pointed to their wet, heavy shirts. They carried jugs filled to the brim with tears and would not let themselves be put back in the grave until their mother promised not to cry any more.

LIGHTS THAT WANDER TO THE HORIZON

People get lost in the swamp. Landscapes beckon with lights. We must leave behind the familiar and usual. It is 1923: NEP (New Economic Policy). We abandon the villages for the cities. Peddlers and money changers from the cities come to us. Everywhere things light up and flash differently from what we are used to. The cinemas' light shows—like fountains.

5
RUSSIA AS
√-1

FIGURE 98

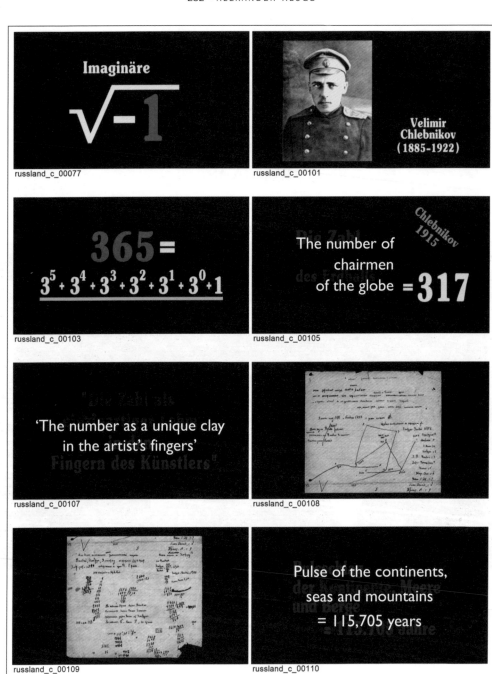

russland_c_00077

Imaginäre
$$\sqrt{-1}$$

russland_c_00101

Velimir
Chlebnikov
(1885-1922)

russland_c_00103

$$365 =$$
$$3^5 + 3^4 + 3^3 + 3^2 + 3^1 + 3^0 + 1$$

russland_c_00105

Chlebnikov
1915

The number of
chairmen
of the globe $= 317$

russland_c_00107

'The number as a unique clay
in the artist's fingers'

russland_c_00108

russland_c_00109

russland_c_00110

Pulse of the continents,
seas and mountains
$= 115{,}705$ years

FIGURE 99

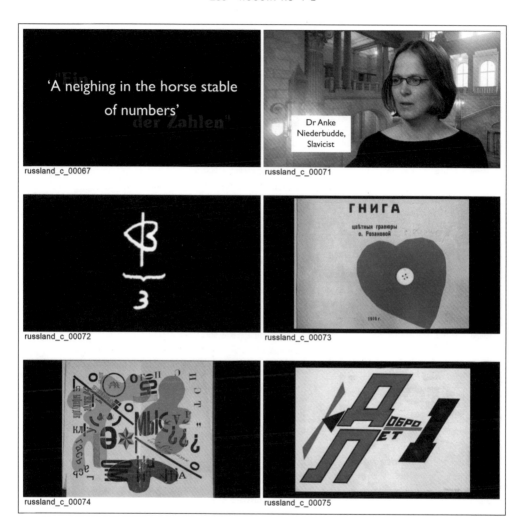

russland_c_00067

russland_c_00071

russland_c_00072

russland_c_00073

russland_c_00074

russland_c_00075

FIGURE 100

russland_c_00018

russland_c_00020

russland_c_00024

russland_c_00025

russland_c_00055

russland_c_00057

FIGURE 101

A POET VISITED ME IN MY DREAMS

Rome in 753 BCE. How many heartbeats are contained within 443,556 days of the *orbis* of the Mediterranean? If you add up the people living in the Roman Empire and multiply them by the number of years they lived. One night, Velimir Khlebnikov told me confidentially that the breaths of Russia, the third Rome, had to be added to the number of souls from ancient Rome in order to maintain a balance between the number of the living and the dead. For the world not to come apart at the seams, there would have to be at least a one-vote majority of the dead compared to the total number of the living. On this question Khlebnikov agrees with the playwright Heiner Müller. What does 'seam of the world' mean in relation to the world? Is the world a coffin? Would the living blow this coffin up if they were in the majority? Do the living know that they would do this? Khlebnikov did not reply. He nodded, then said he didn't know. Same as the great revolutions.

FIGURE 102. Rome was founded in 753 BCE, fell in 476 CE:

443, 556 days = 666^2

—Khlebnikov

Rom im Jahr 753 v.Chr. gegründet,
476 n.Chr. untergegangen:
443.556 Tage
$= 666^2$

Chlebnikov

INFORMATION ON THE QUALITY OF THE REAL

Florensky, relying on the medieval Talmudic booklet *The Zohar*, points to the proportions described there. Over the course of seven weeks of divine time (translated into dialectical-materialist language: far more than 13.5 billion years), the Lord 'played' with letters and numbers. He explored them. Reconfigured them, 'beat upon them'. Then, in seven days of his time, he founded the world, all the way up to paradise. The proportion of the two aeons—seven weeks vs one— shows the power that lies in pure forms, numbers and letters. And this, Florensky emphasized, does not even include the DARK SIDE OF ALPHA (this number or letter, with which we are unfamiliar and which leads deep into parallel worlds and to those dimensions of which the cosmos truly consists that are rolled up into our own reality). The power of this multiplicity is spiritual-gravitational as well as anti-fatalistic. Were we to speak of reality in relation to our present life, we would be moving within the realm of an error. It is also uncertain whether the quality of the times given here for the prehistory and the foundation of the world are the same. But if the quality is different, he assumes, that we still live in 'interlocked' realities, then time and reality are two words for the same thing. In response to the accusation of a Bolshevik commissar that his teachings resembled Plato's and that these were demonstrably idealistic, Florensky remained silent (to his detriment). In response to the phrase frequently employed by victims of the planned economy, 'We have become a mere number,' Florensky replied: 'Numbers are the highest form of existence.' One of the great mathematician's disciples recorded his sayings in an octavo notebook, which was burnt by the GPU.

MACRO-TIME, MICRO-TIME

In the early moments of the universe, the pulse of the celestial music was 10 seconds.

EON

ERA

PERIOD

EPOCH

GENERATION

LIFESPAN

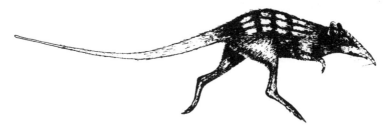

FIGURE 103. A hoofed insectivore from the oil shale of the Messel Pit. Also a direct ancestor.

MY CHRONOLOGY

KINGDOM: Animal

SUPERPHYLUM: Deuterostomia

PHYLUM: Chordata

SUBPHYLA: Vertebrates, Head Animals

CLASS: Mammals

ORDER: Primates

FAMILY: Dry-nosed monkey

SPECIES AND TYPE: Homo sapiens, Humankind

PERSON: 'I', 1932

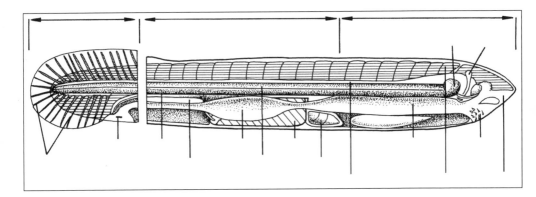

FIGURE 104 (ABOVE). Hypothetical body plan of an original craniate (skull animal). Transition to vertebrate. Note the zeppelin shape. The development of these quietly air-cutting vehicles, only due to a few accidents, which are the motor of all evolution, even technical evolution. After the zeppelins proved to be of little use in the Great War of 1914–1918, they could have become a symbol of a peaceful future for the skies.

FIGURE 105 (BELOW). The 'mouse beaver' Palaeocastor. Close relative of the glider Eomys ('early mouse').

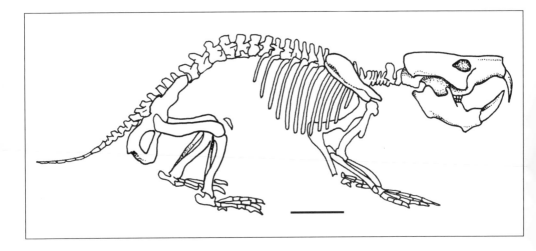

'THE LIP RED, THE CHEEK LIGHT'

From the presumably oldest species of the second main group of dinosaurs, the cheek teeth were shifted towards the inner side of the jaws so that they 'left a broad ledge on the outside' exposed. This indicates that the oral cavity of the Pisanosaurus was laterally enclosed by cheeks, i.e. muscular skin pockets that formed next to the rows of teeth. This created a food storage chamber outside the rows of teeth to store the still-unmasticated bits of food while the plants were being chewed. Since then, there have been CHEEKS in the animal kingdom. Originally, they double eating potential, write J. F. Bonaparte and F. E. Novas, who worked on dinosaur finds in Patagonia. In fact, the fossils of these extraordinarily successful animals, from which all cheeks that lend themselves to shaving and tender touching derive, are indeed found in Argentina and (not unlike hamster-like animals) serve the formation of reserves.

The authors point out that reptiles and birds *devour* their food. We owe the evolutionary innovation of chewing, which reached us in a roundabout way, to this particular branch of early dinosaurs. Their jaws had a special ball-and-socket joint that lay between the dentals and the pre-dentals and allowed rotation, a circular movement whenever the jaw closed. This caused the molars to work like a pair of scissors. If it were ever possible to improve the human species through evolutionary means, Davidov, an early Soviet anthropologist, thought, then converting this slit into a kind of circular saw would be of considerable advantage. Those prehistoric reptiles were subject to a permanent change of teeth. Their worn teeth would fall out only then to be promptly replaced by new ones, from a row above the used teeth on the inside of the jaws. The related hadrosaurids had five to six rows of teeth that could be used at the same time. This is what made herbivorous dinosaurs successful during the Cretaceous period. Even if Davidov remained unsuccessful in this kind of breeding, under his guidance an agricultural machine was built which paid tribute to the ingenuity of early evolution and simultaneous stockpiling by combining circular crushing with the automatic exchange of grinding and cutting tools. For this Davidov received the Lenin Prize in 1928. The machine served no practical purpose (like the human cheek), other than that of beauty, namely, the display of engineering skill.

A CHEEK IN DECEMBER 1917

The young Deputy People's Commissioner had 'high cheekbones'. This gave her cheek an interesting smoothness. Lenin had never seen anything like it before. He could not take his eyes off her. Was she an agent set on putting him under her spell? Who had placed her in the position she held? Lenin was prone, as he himself knew, to delusions of persecution.

FIGURE 106. 1.1 billion years to about 750 million years ago. This formation precedes Pangaea. In the middle of the hypothetical supercontinent lies Laurentia, a structure from which North America will later emerge. On the side of Laurentia, the Kalahari! At the top right, Siberia lies next to 'South China'.

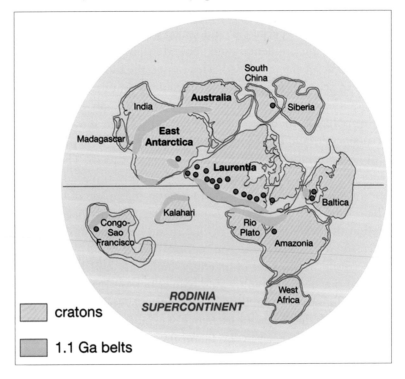

PUTIN IS SURPRISED

They had just flown over the border of old Kazakhstan with northern China, petrologist Stanislav Sem explained to the Russian president whom he had accompanied to the G20 summit in Australia. But on the map the president was carrying (he was looking down from the window of the plane), it was evident that China was more than 1,000 kilometres away from this border; his map referred to primeval continents.

DIARY | FRIDAY, 2 AUGUST 2019

I take a tablet for restless-leg syndrome, as prescribed by my doctor. And then, as advertised in the leaflet: nightmares. A former lover has returned. She presents me with a newborn that lies like a fish in my hand. I drive through the city. A basket is fastened to the handlebars of my bicycle. Filled with furniture, shopping, equipment. My lover places the boy on top. And throws a cat on top for good measure. I can barely control my bicycle. I protest. She has a 'knowing' face. Therefore, I think that it's all just a test. The bicycle runs into a mass of people. On an elongated staircase that resembles those you find in large lecture halls (if cleared of seats and bare). A sudden steep fall. I keep an eye on the luggage on the handlebars, especially my cat, who soon jumps off. Through a corridor to a cellar. I take another steep tumble down into the depths, looking out for the dowry which in the meanwhile has fallen off the handlebars and is lying all over the ground. My young one has disappeared. I rush back upstairs, search the 'auditorium', which had immediately been 'suspicious' to me. Nothing to be found. No one can or will give me any information. I'm in a hurry and now in my wife's flat. My former lover arrives. She denies that what has happened was only a ruse, that she knows where the child, my little fish, happens to be. I search a large flat suitcase for him. The lover takes part in the search only superficially, so that hope arises ('it is, after all, her child, she probably knows where he is, she's just trying to trick me'). My despair increases. The whole thing is taking place in my wife's living room, who is about to join us. I will have to explain to her that my lover is just a reality from 40 years ago. I'll also have to explain how the suitcase got into the apartment. Not to mention what's going on with the lost boy. And the bags, the furniture, the tools on the bicycle handlebars have disappeared. But so many lives and things can't disappear without a trace. I run the whole way to the lecture hall with the open staircase to start a new, intensive search. The dream speeds up. I wake up . . .

The dream had nothing to do with Russia, but rather with me. So, the truth is that I am writing only about myself in this container. And it would be arrogant of a single author to try and write about a great country, whether their own or foreign, and offer more than a limited point of view.

FIGURE 107

Semantic Field 'Light'
(by Rosemarie Tietze)

светило / svetilo
= heavenly body, star;
= capacity, 'light' (e.g.
  of science)

светоч / svetoch
= torch, lamp

рассвет / rassvet
= dawn

светлый / svetlyi
= bright, light;
= clear, transparent;
= cheerful, light

свеча / svecha
candle

свет, светик /
svet, svetik
= my heart, my treasure

свет / svet
= light, brightness, glow;
  lighting, light source;
  daybreak
= world, earth, globe;
  humanity
= distinguished / high society

Светлое воскресенье /
Svetloe voskresen'e
= (weekly,
  Holy Sunday)
Easter Sunday

освещение / osveshchenie
= lighting

светский / svetskii
= worldly;
= fashionable, urbane

светопреставление /
svetoprestavlenie
= the end of the
  world
  (ecclesiastical)
= utter chaos

светотень / svetoten'
= chiaroscuro,
  clair-obscur

отсвет / otsvet
= reflection

просвещение /
prosveshchenie
= clarification, development; the Enlightenment
education, illumination

светёлка / svetelka
= gabled room

просвечивание /
prosvechivanie
= radioscopy
X-ray

светляк / svetliak
= glow-worm

светофор / svetofor
= traffic light

RUSSIAN LIGHT

A frosted glass ball containing two carbon candles set under alternating current, a bright arc, was called *la lumière russe* in the 1870s in France. An invention by telegraph engineer Pavel Yablochkov: the Yablochkov Candle (Свеча Яблочкова). Such monumental illumination was located along the Thames in London near the British Museum, the Colosseum in Rome and the main post office in Berlin. In 1926, on the fiftieth anniversary of the candle, the priest Pavel Florensky, co-founder of the magazine *Elektrichestvo*, claimed that the invention of this incandescent light continued the tradition of icons 'in the struggle against the kingdom of darkness'.

FIGURE 108. The Yablochkov Candle.

FIGURE 109 (ABOVE). 'Russian light'.

FIGURE 110 (BELOW)

PALE REALISM AND THE HOLY FIRE

For one of his publications, Russian mathematician and theologian Florensky chose the form of a Platonic dialogue. In such dialogues, a train of thought is divided into two roles, that is, one is given to a speaker called A and one to a speaker called B, whereby what is true from a Platonic perspective is assigned to one of the two speakers from the outset.[1]

The publication was called *Empireya i Empiriya*. Speaker A was a functionalist (alternative swearwords are 'positivist' and 'empiricist'). As in all misrepresentations and prejudices, there was a valuable truth in this 'dialogue' in which speaker B presented the lines of thought that were Florensky's own.

The title distinguishes *Empyrie* (Russian *Empireia*), viz. the inner fire—Greek *pyr*—from the limited receptivity of *Empirie*, simple sensual experience (Russian *Empiriia*) and spiritual dullness. A single letter—*e* or *i*—marks the difference in language, while in reality there are worlds between the one and the other.

Colour, sounds, smells, pressure and counterpressure, handshakes, footprints, biology, chemistry, physics, everyday life, digestion, mere image. Platonically speaking: the illusory world. The inner fire, on the other contrary: I feel on my skin. It flows through my veins. Florensky says, When I do mathematics, my hair is on fire.

RELIGIOSITY AND ELECTRIFICATION

The sleeve of the theologian and electrician Pavel Florensky found itself just 12 centimetres away from the sleeve of the People's Commissar for the energy sector. Both were standing on a platform where speeches were being made. As the 'electro-technical Engineer of the First Order of the Soviet Union', Florensky wore a fancy uniform. The organization was young.

1 In this respect, from the point of view of Socrates' principles, they are 'false dialogues'.

Twenty comrades up on the balustrade. Electrical technicians, wire fitters and repairmen, supplemented by railwaymen, recruited from the factories of Petrograd, standing before the representatives of the People's Commissariat. Ready to say goodbye. A whole train full of electrical parts, light bulbs and cables was prepared for departure. Destination: a junction (железнодорожный узел) just beyond the Urals. The light would penetrate the Soviet republics like a focal point. The further east one went, the greater the expanse of darkness (пространство тьмы) had to be perforated, along with, generally speaking, darkness altogether. Siberian nights an electrified city!

Florensky, a knight of the faith, earned his living in the People's Commissariat of the Infidels. He himself was a Platonist, an intuitionist, mathematical—in other words, modern. It is the last day of December 1917. The growth of man (towards God) needs NODAL POINTS (here the word is used in a Hegelian fashion). It's not a question of technology, as in the case of railway or collection nodes. No, apocalyptic discourse is what's required. At the moment of the revolution, the following comes together: electrification and enlightenment. At one point, their sleeves brushed as their raised hands turned into fists. Florensky, however, chose the wrong arm, the People's Commissar the right one.

The mass of rational numbers has—between each one, number after number—white spots. Between zero and one is an infinite set of numbers, whereas one is not included in the set. Every number denotes an opportunity for growth in the invisible world.

FIGURE 111

Pawel Alexandrowitsch Florenski

'Black fire (strong in colour)'
'Red fire (strong in appearance)'
'Green fire (strong in form)'
'White fire (all colours)'

The emergence from the UNGROUND, in which God destroys the closedness of His Un-Self (the unborn possibilities), happens as a Jolt. This jerk is called nothingness and corresponds to the zero.

The sphere 'towards evening'.

The secret of the 'diminution of the Moon': The primordial potencies were formed from the resulting lights.

The word FIRMAMENT appears four times (in the King James version) in the verses that deal with the second day of creation.

The source that broke through the aura until a hidden highest point shone out as a result is the Alpha source. The point is called *Bereshit*, beginning. This is the first creation word of the ten, through which the universe would be created.

'Darkness' is a black fire. It is the strongest of all fires, and the fire seizes TOHU. Tohu is an undefined place. From it, BOHU is smelt, the 'stones sunk into the abyss'.

From Jacob it is said: 'the sun rose upon him'—the secret Sun, which is called 'towards evening'. From then on, he leant on his thigh (GEN 32:32). The primal sun corresponds to the body of man, and it consists of letters, of which not one was lost. From this stage comes prophetic power.

TEMPORARY DERAILMENT
THROUGH AN ENCOUNTER
WITH THE KABBALAH

Lieutenant of State Security Petrov, an interrogation specialist, was not one of the Cheka's mean executors. He was sensitive and hence proficient in interrogating delinquents. His reports were masterpieces of conciseness. In April 1957, however, he was confused. One of the people he was to question had 'bewitched' him. During the interrogation, the suspect had questioned him in reverse, and it had been impossible for the functionary to escape the unfamiliar role. For weeks, he spent nights debating with the suspect—no, listening to him talk, openly exposed to questioning. By his counterpart, who was supposed to be his victim. Furthermore, the point in time by which the indictment was to have been decided had passed. This class enemy was accused of conspiratorial idealism. He should have been included in a batch of the accused who had been assigned the same charge. And which had already been dispatched. The only thing left to do was to close the case retrospectively without any indictment and release the accused. The report in which Petrov incriminated himself was still making its way through official channels when Yeshov, head of the Cheka, was unexpectedly removed from office. Petrov intercepted his neatly typed papers before they could be presented to the new superior, thus saving himself as well as the strange 'idealist' whose connection to some class enemy (if not God himself and the thought factories of the Kabbalah) was unapparent.

FIGURE 112

Pawel Alexandrowitsch Florenski

DIARY | CHRISTMAS EVE, 24 DECEMBER 2018

I call Jürgen Habermas. Ute has gone to take a nap in order to prepare for Christmas Eve. The two of them are alone. The children will arrive on Christmas Day. All year long, both our families failed to get together. I had intended to, Habermas had intended to, our wives had intended to—nothing worked out. Everything that has been missed during the year comes to the fore on the day before Christmas Eve.

Habermas is worried about the state of Europe. 'I am depressed.' Saying something like that is not his usual way of doing things. 'No one is reaching out to Macron.' To speak of the SPD leadership as deadbeats is a euphemism, he says.

What a socially artificial product the modern individual is! Traversed by so many other forces than just the ego. Sociology must, Habermas says (we are talking ourselves into a lengthy pre-Christmas conversation), be completely reconstructed from its very beginnings. It is about the architecture of society as the art of building. It'd have to be a subject at the Bauhaus. It needs the precision of urban planning. It is not in the main a sorting of the outside world, of SOCIAL REALITY. It is just as much about people's interior configuration. What belongs to the knowledge of the architecture of the subject? This subject is permeated by its own self, but this own self cannot be distinguished from the foreign contained within it, indeed, it is based on a 'societal unconscious' that is both 'its own' and 'foreign' at one and the same time. Habermas hesitates to accept the expression 'societal unconscious' (but there is none better on hand in the late afternoon). But if it is a matter of both foreign and individual flows in the subject, then the art of cognition that deals with it (the 'sociological eye') is related to the art of eighteenth-century pond building, to the knowledge of how to build canals, drain swamps. Preparation for a better ciphered, sorted, 'constructed' subject. If the coarse, abandoned human being can barely separate its liquid forms from its solid forms (that would be swamp) outside of the process of summarizing production (as the industrial structure becomes unstable), then there can indeed be places within the subject where canal construction reigns: fortified banks, lively flow in the middle of the canals and streams as well as dry earth awaiting rain and building. This pre-Christmas evening we sing a song of mourning to New Year's Eve 1799 when so much future still seemed possible. The turn of the century was borrowed from the following century in advance because people were already so curious, so eager for new ideas, so eager to do. In terms of the calendar, the new century should only have been allowed to begin New Year's Eve 1800. At both ends of the telephones, two kinds of light. In Starnberg, a different quality than in Schwabing, where all the advertising makes the streets brighter.

DIARY | THURSDAY, 14 FEBRUARY 2019

My birthday. We are coming back from dinner at a restaurant in the mountains. Our bones no longer allow us to sit up straight in the back seats. Facing one another, we lie across them instead. Comforted by the excitement that our conversation sparks. Yes, it's true, Habermas says, the whole year long, people in 1929 didn't know how the year would end. It's the year of Habermas' birth. People don't know a thing about Black Friday when they're freezing from downpours in May and June. We judge what witnesses think from the perspective of the following year, to which the late consequences of the preceding one still adhere. This possibility of evaluation, however, does not exist for the concrete person the whole year long.

For a few minutes already, our conversation has been about a view of 'a piece of the present'. Such a piece looks strange. Simple thinking and rocking on the back seat of a car brings a valuable find: we can be sure about what a person on the day of Habermas' birth (in Russia or in the German Reich) in June 1929 *cannot yet* know about the course of the year. Happy to have dinner behind us. Satisfied to get a big bite of agreement between the teeth!

Axial Danger

Like a big bird, Ute stands next to the car on a surface of hardened ice. It's a metre high. No way to get down and to the house. Just stay there! we call out. She mustn't fall. My wife hurries to the steering wheel; the car from which Ute has overzealously got out is far too close to the wintry mass of 'former snow, now crust'. Now my wife's got to drive forward without endangering Ute's throne. Ute comes down from her 'summit' thanks to the help of the two hands we hold out. Just a few more minutes and we're all safely inside.

Axial Age

Confucius, Buddha and Heraclitus—contemporaries on Earth around 500 BCE—are neither causally nor locally linked by any means. Nevertheless, they form an 'axis' like a knotted net, like a context, like a constellation. No wanderer, expedition or caravan, most likely no book, establishes the connection. Is the light sky responsible for triggering such a heightened level of attention (all too short) among the people of 500 BCE?

For days, Habermas has been feeling a dizziness in his head. Overload. He still has to finish the final chapter. The point of departure for his two-volume book is the Axial Age. The mass of letters stored in his computer weighs upon his heart. Before they're buried within a book, letters are rebels, insurgents.

DIARY | TUESDAY, 2 APRIL 2019

My sister's birthday. She made it to her birthday in 2017 (and energetically—all medical predictions to the contrary notwithstanding).

1937–2017.

80 years and 12 weeks.

My sister, the Russian friend.

My first Russians. Halberstadt was captured in 1945, first by the Americans, then by the British and in August by the Red Army. I was 13 years old. On the day they arrived, I was working in the cellar of our destroyed house with my friend Fritz Wilde; we had set up a kind of 'castle' out of supplies. Afterwards we went home in the direction of Hohenzollernstrasse. That's where we saw them coming. Down Harmoniestrasse, from the direction of Wernigerode, in columns, marching, followed by horse-drawn wagons. Singing from rough throats. A block of houses on Moltestrasse, opposite my former elementary school, the V3, was cleared of its inhabitants. In the following weeks, the block was painted compact pink. The city commander took over Mrs Köhler's apartment on Hohenzollernstrasse, opposite my father's medical practice (the street was later renamed Friedenstrasse).

This commander, an officer from the Caucasus, had two children born in our town by his wife. That is, he stayed in his position for a long time. My father, as a medical obstetrician, delivered both. With the first child: breech presentation, a difficult birth. Afterwards everything went well; the next morning we found our father in the front yard. He was wearing what was called a 'Rabaner', a kind of one-piece, buttonable underwear. Still in the process of buttoning them up, the rest of his clothes in a heap about him, he fell asleep. There had been roast mutton and rivers of vodka. The ruler's princely thanks for the happy birth: potlatch. With the help of our housekeeper Erna, we got the doctor, generosity's victim, to bed and pinned a note to his office door: *No consultation hours today*.

The commander—energetic black eyes, dark curly hair, who could change abruptly between an authoritative tone and angry instruction—always looked out for my father. None of the local German authorities dared, even when it came to a question of linkage to black-market transactions in the trial against the grain merchant Tacke, to interfere with him. Reliability!

FIGURE 113. My sister in 1965. Just half a year later, in a moment of rage, she tore the photo-booth photo in half.

I COLLECT STAMPS

STAMPS, LANDMARKS

The *Domgymnasium* has been evacuated. We have classes at the *Oberrealschule* am Grudenberg. Our connection to the world resides in stamps. We students express our curiosity, our willingness to contribute to the world's conquest through the fact that each of us has sought out a special area from which to collect. Harm Bakker: French possessions in Africa. Meyer and Roehrs: special stamps of the Third Reich, with a complete Olympics set as well as stamps commemorating the annual Race for the Brown Ribbon in Riem, featuring horses and the unusual surcharge of 108 Pfennigs. All of this will increase in value. Through these collections, we desire to be something special amid the war's generality.

In partnership with my friend Alfred Müller, I collect Russian stamps and those of the Soviet Union. I also collect stamps from Labuan, a British possession on Borneo. Which means I have actively experienced the magic of colonial enterprise, but also the particularity, the strangeness, of Soviet progress; I map out complete sets, which require a lot of space. You cannot die on a stamp. We'd buy them from the experienced dealer Fenske. His store: Unter den Zwicken 6.

FIGURE 114

img740
1200x1064 (3,65 MB)

img741
1544x1045 (4,62 MB)

img742
1544x1045 (4,62 MB)

img743
1662x978 (4,65 MB)

img744
1457x978 (4,08 MB)

img745
1458x1268 (5,29 MB)

img746
1268x1201 (4,36 MB)

FIGURES 115 (ABOVE) AND 116 (BELOW)

FIGURES 117 (ABOVE), 118 (BELOW, LEFT) AND 119 (BELOW, RIGHT)

FIGURES 120 (ABOVE), 121 (BELOW, LEFT) AND 122 (BELOW, RIGHT)

FIGURE 123. On the misprinting of CCCP:
Misprint officially produced by the postal administration for the purpose of
selling stamps abroad. Rare. Perforation goes through the image.
In the upper stamp, red Russia has been folded down over Asia.

DIARY | WEDNESDAY, 31 JULY 2019

Munich's central train station in hot July 2019. Barricaded by construction work. The effect of the closed roads reaching far beyond Stachus/Karlsplatz. We want to go to Ulm. We're stuck in traffic for seven minutes in front of the Palais Bernheimer on Lenbachplatz. We hope that our train's been delayed. Not an unreasonable expectation considering the habits of the German railway. Nevertheless, we're in a rush because the scheduled departure time presses on every minute. Every minute we nervously count each click of the taximeter. If it weren't for the luggage and the hammering heat, we'd be walking. But even then, we'd be too late.

Back in 1990, Fumio Oshima, the co-managing director of my development company of television programmes dctp GmbH, worked for Tokyo's Dentsu Inc., our co-shareholder, whose representative for the Federal Republic of Germany had rented a floor in the Palais Bernheimer. Dctp had followed suit and settled into lavish rooms at the prestigious Lenbachplatz. The appearance of the Dentsu advertising group in Munich was part of the project to win over football star Franz Beckenbauer for a campaign. Which is why the company thought a 'Munich paint job' might be useful.

We, the subtenant—an up-and-coming company that had been awarded licensing periods in a public tender at the private broadcasters RTL and Sat. 1—in turn had Franz Greno subleasing space from *us* there on the spacious floor. The project he needed the prominent address for concerned RUSSIA. Greno possessed an entrepreneurial nature, he was an ingenious printer with a company and press in Nördlingen. He'd bought up boxes of extremely rare typefaces from estates. Each of his books was one-of-a-kind. He also printed Oskar Negt's and my book *History and Obstinacy*, which had been written into the historical upheaval, working right next to us at the table. Now, in the spring of 1990, young companies throughout the Federal Republic and Russia had been seized by a kind of frenzy. It had to do with the 'last summer of perestroika before the coup'. In Moscow, rabid projects such as the 'introduction of the market economy in 500 days' competed with innumerable detailed initiatives, as Svetlana Alexievich has described them. 'Let a thousand flowers bloom.' Valentin Falin described this summer as unique. This short period of time had a special tone. For every tone in music there is a series of overtones, which rises like a pillar above the fundamental and has several variations. I wish we could capture some of that period's overtones today and 'sing' them. Transplanted into the disruptive wasteland of the twenty-first century, gardens of paradise could emerge. In 1990—our cab still has not completely made it past the facade of the Bernheimer Palais—Greno and several partners with whom he maintained contact in Moscow and St Petersburg were interested in developing a series of books in Russia and the Federal Republic of Germany that would respond to one another and be translated into other European languages as well. A European network of books and, simultaneously, a so-called Russia bridge. Greno called the project 'The Bridge over the Berezina' (with a slight distortion of the historical facts). It was, however, in fact the case that the chance of an early Europe (beginning in 1812) was connected to the admiration that Prussia's otherwise fanatical French-haters and patriots felt for the efforts of the pioneer and artillerymen who saved Napoleon's army from annihilation by building two bridges over that river. They risked their lives for it. A portion of the Prussian patriots were impressed. It would not be inconceivable that from this surprising impulse an idea of cooperation between France and Prussia could have arisen—at least in Greno's eyes. Road projects, the *Code civil* and a few years of rapid modernization were already in place. In the event of a surprise peace accord, it would have been possible for Europe to be constituted.

This was more or less the spirit that in the spring and summer of 1990 sparked a contest of daring in Russia and the FRG. Bypassing the GDR, of course, the dismantling and plundering of which was imminent. As far as Greno was concerned, the Nördlinger broadcaster wasn't enough for the Russia project. Greno had brought all his assets as well as all the loans he could get from his banks to the project. We supported him with additional work, and his office in the Bernheimer Palais didn't have to pay any rent. In our mind's eye, book landscapes bloomed: books being transported back and forth under the shade of poplars along the Perm-Moscow-Smolensk-Warsaw-Bonn route (we were patriots of the old Federal Republic). Then onwards via Brussels: Paris-Madrid-Lisbon. Strangely enough, when I think of the debates of the time, it was purely east–west, never north–south. The project died. The loans Greno took out led to the bankruptcy of his publishing house. Years later, however, after reacquiring his rare type collections, it re-emerged with unique new printed materials. Realities are all too sluggish: the cell, the unfinished economic trajectories in the space of the old Comecon (the economic system to be wound up in the entire East), the reading and buying speeds among audiences on both sides too slow. It would have taken three Pushkinesque generations for the road construction of the spirit.

In the meantime, we'd crept forward 40 metres. The Palais Bernheimer now behind us on the right. It was safe to assume that we'd miss our highspeed Intercity Express train. With our iPhones, we told those waiting in Ulm about our new arrival time.

DIARY | THURSDAY, 1 AUGUST 2019

What does $\sqrt{-1}$ mean? I first came across the term $\sqrt{-1}$ in the context of Khlebnikov's poetry and then again in the work of mathematician and theologian Florensky. I love unfamiliar terms.

I call Dr Schauenburg, mathematician and husband of my long-time conversation partner Ulrike Sprenger. What does $\sqrt{-1}$ mean? I've read, I continue, a Russian poet who says that Russia, metaphorically speaking, can only be understood through complex numbers. $\sqrt{-1} = i =$ imaginary is the kitchen of complex numbers. I had been informed that Russia contained this totality as well as the cracks and the holes within this entire $\sqrt{-1}$. And that this is not an interpretation but reality itself. Which is complex. Dr Schauenburg replied that, as a mathematician, he hesitated to answer a metaphorical and poetic question so directly. The colleagues in the guild are strict. He wanted, however, to answer indirectly. The reference to a country is uncommon and unusual. $\sqrt{-1}$ refers to numbers, data or calculated realities. Russia is, in this sense, not a calculated reality. The difference between imaginary numbers and positive numbers and their roots is that the imaginary numbers are not to be found in a series of numbers or on a line as positive numbers from 1 to ∞. Rather, complex numbers extend over an entire plane. Complex numbers do not know any roads.

That was Napoleon's problem in Russia, I interjected. The linear march from Vilnius to Moscow was meant to be a series of fixed points. The closer he, Napoleon, came to the capital, the more Russia would be conquered. He imagined it as a road or an avenue of poplars. But as it turned out Russia did not consist of any such dotted line. Neither Russia nor Moscow behaved as a point, but as a vast plain of innumerable points, each with its own life and resilience.

Through the phone I could tell that Dr Schauenburg was in pain. My interjection was quite far removed from proper mathematics. The special thing about the poetics of complex numbers, Dr Schauenburg said, taking up the thread again, is that above the plane upon which every imaginary number can designate several points, a surface unfolds itself like a sky—the Riemann surface—and on that every one of the plane's many points is reflected in duplicate.

Philanthropist that he is, Dr Schauenburg had long since noticed that I did not understand enough about mathematics. On the other hand, he respected 'the poetic' that he suspected in my way of expressing myself. He accepted that imaginary numbers and the geometry they encompass pointed to the characteristics of Russia that were not understood in the West.

As far as questions regarding concrete representationality within the realm of the $\sqrt{-1}$ are concerned, Dr Schauenburg said, I must determine both the *place* as well as the *way* that was taken to reach this point. Always metaphorically speaking. This applies to the whole abundance of points on the plane, in relation to Russia, an uncountable mass of realities. So I give each reality a number and am faced with trillions of differences. But now the Riemann surface is added. It provides more possible points than the plane. But each of these points is in motion—in your poetic use of the terms—and becomes *real* through its particularity. The particularity is THE WAY. As I remained silent for a long time, Dr Schauenburg inquired whether

I could do anything with his answer. He politely inquired about how I dealt with geometry.

If I go from −1 or 1, 360 degrees to 0, Dr Schauenburg continued in the face of my hesitation, it is possible that I will *not* return to the starting point, to that fixed point from which I began, but rather find myself in a completely different place, just as when I climb a spiral staircase I arrive at a *different floor*. Again, I remained silent to hear more about it. To me, what the mathematician had to say seemed close to Hegel's concept of the PARTICULAR: POLYPHONIC REALITY.

Taking the thought further, then, in consideration of some of the Pentagon's plans, Russia could not be hit with precision weapons. You can only ever hit *one* reality at a time, and that is not the whole. Is that how it's to be understood?

I must not forget, Dr Schauenburg replied, that a mathematician could not confirm such a thing. The world of complex numbers is not filled with *precise* points, as the artilleryman or the rocket specialist would have it. As a mathematician, he could not confirm to me that Russia was a $\sqrt{-1}$.

I got excited: that seems to be how both Napoleon and Hitler experienced it! While attempting to achieve victory within simply one of the PLANE's point-masses and beneath the spiritual HEAVENLY FLOOR above them, they lost their WAY. And then already found themselves in retreat. At this point in our conversation, I noticed that the mathematician's positions and mine were becoming ever more distant from each other.

The points on the surface, according to your ideas, Mr Kluge, and what you call celestial points on the Riemannian surface, have a reciprocal effect upon one another. And all points, the celestial and the terrestrial, are determined by innumerable paths (their pasts). Where I am depends on where I come from. This is plausible for the intercourse of mathematical calculations. Dr Schauenburg wanted to establish a connection for me and assumed that I understood that my poetic version, borrowed from Khlebnikov and Florensky, behaved differently. In fact, I had Khlebnikov and Florensky in my head the whole time. Pushkin's description of the muddy Russian roads during the bi-annual *rasputitsa*, too. What will Russia's roads be like in 200 years? Pushkin asks. They have their own time.

All of this contained the question of reality. This, so it seemed to me that evening, gave rise to an enchanting approach: every reality on earth is yet to be produced out of the abundance of possibilities. In a disruptive environment, this is a consolation.

A REPORT BY A TRAM CONDUCTOR IN
ST PETERSBURG

Waiting on an extremely late regional train in the suburbs of St Petersburg, the mathematician Grigori Yakolevich Perelman explained the particuliarities of $\sqrt{-1}$ to a tram conductor. Having encountered the thesis in an adult-education course, this tram conductor had seen that 'one could only understand Russia with complex numbers.' She did not, however, say exactly how Perelman had explained $\sqrt{-1}$ to her. Running into such a competent mathematician had simply been a stroke of good luck.

A REPORT BY THE BALLOONIST
FRANÇOIS DE LESPINSE /
'THE POINT SPREADS OUT,
IS NOW AND NOTHING ELSE'

8 February 1807, 7 a.m., Preußisch Eylau

The emperor is a concentrator. He sleeps in a homestead to our left. Sleep, too, expresses concentration, though we do not see it. The guards, the escort officers, keep the peace. A wall of effort surrounds the sleeping emperor, but whether he is truly asleep we do not know. It is possible that he is resting or dictating, but we are to believe that he fortifies himself by sleep and thus supplies his spirit with a kind of concentrate of strength. He has command over his memory, his speech, his body, his sleep, his plans, yes, even over his power of concentration and the unconscious impulses. Self-control is part of his command over the troops and their leaders. They trust and love him: they see his power of concentration and concentrate as well.

Rambling does not suit the emperor. He confines himself to holding together the concentrated force he has brought from Paris, in the expectation that some target will respond. The targets betray themselves by appearing. There are many stray targets in the world.

But the inhospitable land into which the stubborn adversary draws us, train after train, functions according to a different principle. It consists of a 'multiplicity of points and nows' (they would be innumerable all the way through the Urals). These 'points and nows' are indifferent to one another, they are 'signs of nature's externality', this strange nature (in contrast to the nature of the emperor or that of France or Italy) wants nothing, thinks nothing but itself. I do not want to deny that this remote region also has a soul, but it does not express itself in relation to us invaders, who will leave the land the moment we have conquered it. This is all we want: That the march not be repeated. To this 'indecisiveness' the indifference of space spreads out into the here and now in the form of a small wood, a border of bushes, a path-like track that does not lead us where we want because here we do not want anything.

This is the structure of dispersion, the antithesis of the emperor's bubble of power and time. The many indifferent points of the country, occupied by indifferent voices of the natives and the Prussian and Russian soldiers, a pressed troop that only wants to return to its courts: all this deconcentrates the one who's brought us together. The emperor steps outside. He inspects the horses. Murat and Berthier approach him on a small patch of ground. (One cannot, e.g. say: 16,000 points or 7,000 nows, for neither *point* nor *now* constitutes a countable space. One can only put it in relation to the throbbing of the temple, the bang of a gunshot, the amputation of a limb, the announcement of an order—all this is comparable to the piece of ground on which the emperor is now standing). A worldly speech unfolds: how, this dark morning, the multiplicity of souls that the emperor has brought here should become involved in their 'vessels' or hopes (corps, divisions, regiments, corporals). This is what the emperor says to those present.

FIGURE 124. The balloon which François de Lespinse transported in the emperor's luggage. Unused in the snow showers of Prussian Eylau. Originally a geographer, the balloonist's observations were based on a remark by Hegel, whom he had read the day before, for he carried lecture notes by the latter in his knapsack: 'The first or immediate determination of nature is the abstract generality of its self-externality, its unmediated indifference, space. Space is the indiscriminate separation of a multiplicity of points.' Lespinse, in his notes on the memorable day of battle, adds: '"The truth of space is time." Moreover, I believe, time is the truth of motive. The motive, the subjective ideas of the combatants (the savages, those determined to flee, those armed with previous action), decide the battle. The "I think" does not appear anywhere. The emperor is too busy for that; there is something "thinking through him". His officers are busy, the soldiers pre-occupied on their individual points. The battle unfolds according to the scheme of numbers, perception, perseverance and time. No one is capable of watching this decision because it takes place within the people themselves and mocks external movement, the bayonets and bullets. I could set up both telescopes and still not see these decisive factors; from the balloon, even in fine weather, I would see next to nothing. Even when an advancing motley mass of horsemen, or a flight movement, or any nervous movement at all of the arrayed army mass reflects this subjective side. A skilled balloon observer could at least describe them poetically and make conjectures. I believe that in his imagination the emperor sees such "signs".
'In order to advance further, the emperor would have to defeat each Eastern point individually. Every Now from all the pasts adds up against him. Speaking technically as a balloonist: He loses floating mass from the envelope. Since the points are indifferent to one another, as we philosophers know, the vastness of innumerable points all the way to India is outside itself, i.e. it thinks nothing and does not concentrate itself of its own accord; the Emperor plunges forward into a kind of nothingness; with his concentrates, he osmotically transforms himself into nothing. The East's points and times refuse him recognition.'

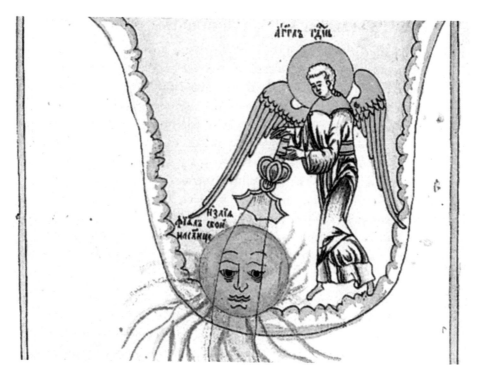

FIGURES 125 (ABOVE) AND 126 (LEFT)

'A RELIABLE REPORT OF BURNING SNOW'

The highest hierarchy of the crystal heavens begins immediately beyond the orbit of the 52nd of the Aristotelian planets. This part of the cosmos belongs to the INVISIBLE HORIZON. Isidore of Seville, who reports this, never saw snow. Nor does he claim to have seen the flame-like beings, the eyeless, six-winged creatures who form the order of the seraphim. He speaks of his ear and of voices. He relies on the 'Hearsay of his inner voices'. Arabic doctors considered him insane. The crystalline structure he calls snow, which mixes with the burning embers and in which the angels of the First Order gather around the throne of God, is dust. This falls from the flat plateau of the spiritual body we call heaven, every hour and minute, as if there were a divine scraper, like an animal cleansing its skin.

N. Goncharova asks whether such snow, in its bizarre figurations, is identical with ice crystals and the tiny cold blocks, rich in figures, that cover the plains of Russia. The events beyond the INVISIBLE HORIZONS in the cosmos above are, in fact, mirror images of the subtle current in us plants and animals. This strict ABOVE and BELOW keep coolness and fire so far apart that we can live in such a range. Thirty-seven seraphim were needed to help support a child in the ICU who had fallen 7 metres out of a window in Chemnitz so that he could healthily emerge from the coma. The rest of the time they work on an imaginary pyramid, which, in reality, is a tree or a tower. It is only because they are so busy with their powers throughout the world that their fire does not consume us completely. Burning snow is sufficient unto itself. It needs no supply, no further energy or substance. And yet seraphim have no organs of sight of their own. Rather, they rely on spiritual beings hierarchically subordinate to them who have eyes on their wings and tell them where those sounds originate and from whose transformation into heavenly sound the highest order of angels derives their life.

'THE MOVEMENT OF ANGELS ABOVE A GIVEN EXPANSE OF SNOW REFERS TO OTHER ACTUALITIES THAN THAT OF THE PRESENT'

The hollows and embankments in the transition from the Urals to the vast plains of Siberia are levelled into a flat ideal surface every winter thanks to three large snowfalls. Upon this relatively drama-less terrain (as far as the human race is concerned), the spirit-seer M. Larvae, however, observed a surprisingly lively intercourse of angels (удивительно оживлённое движение ангелов) in a confined space. This resembled a conference. The 'angel's feet' do not cause any visible traces but are recognizable to the spirit-seer by the minimal distortions they cause in the crystal lattices of the snow-flakes (в кристаллических решётках снежинок). What was going on? The spirit-seer (духовидец) says the communicative habits of these messengers—all of them PRINCIPALITIES of the seventh order, i.e. SPIRITUAL CONCERNS, as they usually are on battlefields or in the collision of massive continents—are removed from human affairs and nature by the passage of thousands of years. The six-winged creatures (шестикрылые) move about 5 centimetres above the ground and give all that lies beneath them a bizarre and fixed structure, 'like dragging a magnet across iron filings'. According to Larianov, the bizarre, never-before-seen structures have the highest artistic value. But it is impossible to lift a piece of this snow from the ground and take it to Sotheby's in London where that value could be assessed and realized.

FIGURES 127 (ABOVE) AND 128 (BELOW)

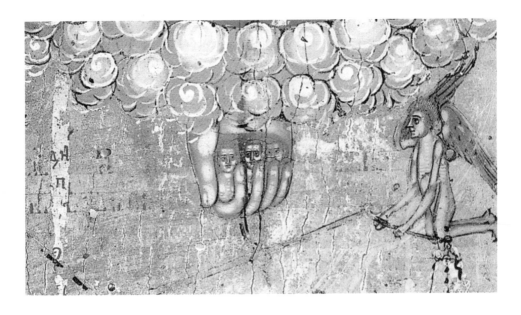

ABBREVIATED OUTLINE OF LIGHT
No. 1

ICONS—WINDOWS ON GOD'S LIGHT

RUSSIAN CINEMA, PRE-1914: THE MELODRAMAS

<u>A FLASH IN THE BARREL OF THE CHEKIST'S REVOLVER WHO SHOT BUKHARIN IN THE NECK</u>

CINEMA LISTINGS IN DECEMBER 1917
IN ST PETERSBURG AND MOSCOW

As in the district towns of Russia, the melodramas of the previous years were shown in the two capitals without any particular attention paid to the revolution going on outside. These programmes attracted considerable attention from the population. In a colourful mixture of social classes, they sat on seats arranged according to different price categories. These distinctions of rank available for purchase were abolished on 17 December 1917. An attempt to intervene in the programme itself as late as December 1917 would have brought the young revolution down.

As of September, the CAPITOL had been showing *And the Secret Was Swallowed by the Waves . . . The King of Paris* followed in December.

- At the METROPOL *Her Sister's Rival?*
- With Vera Kholodnaya. A great film.
- What's the plot?
- Well, as its subtitle says: *For Every Tear a Drop of Blood*. The mother says to her son-in-law: don't make my daughter unhappy. You will pay for every tear she sheds with a drop of blood.
- She herself will demand the blood?

FIGURE 129. Vera Kholodnaya (1893–1919), the queen of melodrama.

– She's a millionaire's widow, a modern woman. She loves her daughter, Musya, who grew up with an adopted daughter, Nata, played by Vera Kholodnaya. Both girls fall in love with the same young man, a pauperized prince. He falls in love with the foster daughter. But when he realizes that she will not inherit anything, he chooses Musya, the daughter he doesn't love. At that moment the mother, understanding what's behind his choice, tells him about drops of blood.

– He betrays the young woman, Musya, with Nata?

– Continually. He's also bet on horse races. Spent all his wife's money. Falsified a bill of exchange with the signature of his banker friend whom Nada had married.

– Now the mother shows up.

– She hands him the revolver; as a man of honour, he should kill himself. But he won't have any of it.

– She shoots him?

– If no one will uphold the honour, what's left for the mother to do but shoot? The film made its way through all the cinemas of Europe.

– And *Tormented Souls* at the ARCADE CINEMA? With Vera Kholodnaya as well?

- An engineer is in love with a married woman (Kholodnaya). While out hunting, this engineer accidentally shoots his god-father—who, as it turns out and unbeknownst to him, is in fact his biological father and has left him his entire estate. The jealous husband accuses the engineer in court. He claims it wasn't a hunting accident, but intentional.
- And now the woman stands up for her beloved?
- She admits that this man is her lover and that her husband brought him before the court only to crush him. Her reputation and life are destroyed, her lover saved.
- Those are the *Tormented Souls*?
- Those are the ones.

On Madame Kollontai's recommendation, Jonas A. Salkind goes to see the melodrama *The Betrothed* at the MAXIM. A merchant's daughter named Natasha gets lost in the forest and stumbles upon a robbers' den, where an orgy is taking place. Over the course of the event, the robber chief's mistress is killed. While the robbers are sleeping off their drunk, the merchant's daughter pulls a ring from the dead woman's finger. She finds her way back to her parents in the city. One day a handsome young man appears, rich, lavish. The merchant's daughter recognizes him: he's the robber chief. At the time, he had barely noticed her. Enchanted by her beauty, he sends solicitors to her parents.

A marriage contract is concluded immediately. According to traditional custom ('one field marries another, one wealth marries another'), the merchant's daughter has to obey. But she will not marry a murderer. No, she avenges the ROBBER CHIEF'S LOVER WHO WAS KILLED, ON HER OWN FREE WILL. She pulls out the ring (during the wedding feast) and proclaims who her husband actually is. The man is arrested and killed.

SALKIND: Why, comrade, did you have me go see this melodrama?

KOLLONTAI: Because the young woman defends herself, and not out of any selfish intentions but on behalf of the INNOCENT DEAD.

HOW WE CAMERAMEN BECAME PATRIOTS,
JUST FOR BEING HARDWORKING

We'd been a film propaganda troupe for the tsar. The Red government had taken us up no-questions-asked as now anything that was worth a darn had become revolutionary, been made into a comrade. We—an elite unit with six cameras and a stock of equipment—were on the train with Leon Trotsky's delegation to the peace negotiations in Brest-Litovsk.

The enemy's officers (half the delegation there, including the Turks, were in uniform) could only fit into our 1:1.33 aspect ratio when they were seated. They were tall folks. When greeting others, walking around or simply standing, either nothing clear could be made out of their faces (when we filmed them as a whole from a distance) or their bodies jutted out of the picture at the top or bottom of the frame. Back then, we still thought we couldn't simply cut off their legs or heads.

While we were thus trying to solve objective problems of representation in 1:1.33 format, the aides of our Russian negotiators showered us with hints and orders. Trotsky himself had spoken to me. We were to record the opponent 'from the perspective of the party'. All the revolutionary side's footage had to demonstrate its interest in a speedy and unconditional conclusion of peace, in land reform and its anti-imperialist stance.

– Then it would be better for us to come up with drawings and not film at all.
– Don't get cheeky, comrade.

The negotiators on our side took us for comrades as a matter of course. We were far from being that. Yes, in those early spring days of 1918, a change of sides, including cameras, to the enemy would have been just as possible as—conversely—a change of heart turning us into true patriots of the Russian revolution. But no one bothered. Just demands, advice, no work of persuasion directed at the activity of the soul! As if we were simply technicians!

If you rotate the camera from horizontal to vertical, you get a format that captures the meeting room from ceiling to floor. However, such a favourable picture of 'the whole thing' cannot be shown in a cinema. The cinematic screen has one shortcoming: cropping. It is not possible to fit all the proportions of the world into a horizontal rectangle. It hurts my soul that I have to leave something out at the sides as well as above and below. We solved some questions by inventing 'punctuality'. In this week of negotiations in Brest-Litovsk, our team learnt to record the individual, that is, General Hoffmann's right eye (with monocle). His back with the seven gold buttons of a cavalry officer, in contrast to another cavalry officer's coat that had only one silver button where the spine ends. But the latter was higher in rank. That seemed important to us. We filmed the prince's stenographer, and the prince himself, who was presiding on the German-Austrian side; for a long time, this prince said nothing at all and hardly moved, making him a grateful object to us as he did not disturb filming. A particularly interesting series of snapshots: the German officers' so-called sidearms, hunting knives, which they carry at their sides instead of sabres. The Turkish participants in the negotiations do not possess such things. From these 'experiments', which the camera captured with patience and at close proximity, we were then able to create something like 'film flavouring': i.e. surprises that create astonishment. Later we realized that we had just invented 'montage'. The more we tried and the more we succeeded with our cameras, the more the delegation leadership had to use and respect us, and the more we became comrades. A patriot is someone who sees themselves as useful for something. We were neither supporters of the tsar, nor of the enemy, nor of our own government, but patriots of our equipment.

A highlight of our footage (we were still practising that week) was the departure of the Russian delegation. Comrade Trotsky had broken off negotiations. He had declared (which we were later able to reproduce only by means of written tablets) that Russia would unilaterally establish peace, by force, as it were, and against the will of the allies, whose exorbitant demands for his country he could only reject. After that (two cameras of ours were already set up at the exit of the negotiating barracks when the threatening speech began), he rushed out, followed by the other Russian negotiators. The Russian delegation's train was already arriving at the makeshift station nearby. Here, too, we had posted a camera. They boarded the wagons. Officers of Austria-Hungary and the German Reich hurrying here and there to stop the Russians went unnoticed. No salutations. Departure. That was powerful.

FIGURE 130. Participants of the armistice delegations in Brest-Litovsk. The German officer on the right is wearing a 'bayonet' on his coat, the one on the left a single button at the height of his buttocks, the one on the right seven of them. Leon Trotsky is at the far right. Filmed by our Soviet collective.

FIGURES 131 (ABOVE) AND 132 (BELOW)

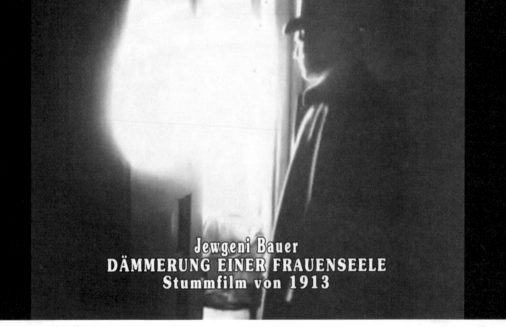

Jewgeni Bauer
DÄMMERUNG EINER FRAUENSEELE
Stummfilm von 1913

FIGURE 133 (ABOVE). Yevgeni Bauer, TWILIGHT OF A WOMAN'S SOUL (silent film from 1913)
FIGURE 134 (BELOW)

**Jewgeni Bauer
(1865 - 1917)**

FIGURE 135

FILM NEGATIVES FROM 1919

The quality of film negatives depends on the amount of silver, which determines the brightness of the chemical substance that will be exposed. Silver would never again be used as extravagantly as in negatives from the year 1919. A 1919 negative produced in Moscow displayed an exceptional amount of grey tones in between precise white and precise black. The 'grey values blossom' in a way that colours cannot in the colour-films yet to come. Colours strike the light dead; they 'replace' light and conceal the world of grey tones.

LIGHT AS A WEAPON
(Report from 1945)

The Red Army leadership had made a special spotlight technique available. Large calibre searchlights were installed in rows along artillery positions as well as the front line. This technique had already been used when breaking through the German front at the Weichsel. Now it was ready for the battle that would follow the break-through across the Oder river, which opened the way to Berlin. The attack took place at four in the morning. Within a second, night became day. The enemy was blinded.

But by the following day, the German defenders had learnt to aim their projectiles at the light source's centre. The searchlights' immense glass windows shattered. The use of light as a weapon: short-lived.

ABBREVIATED OUTLINE OF LIGHT No. 2

ICONS

CINEMA—THE DARK PHASE OF 1/48 OF A SECOND WHEN THE FILM IS TRANSPORTED THROUGH THE PROJECTOR AND NO IMAGE IS VISIBLE = THE BLACK LIGHT OF EPIPHANY (IN THE VIEWER'S HEAD, ANIMATED ASSOCIATIONS DURING A BREAK IN THE IMAGES)

MATHEMATICS AND THE STARS OF THE COSMOS

FIGURE 136

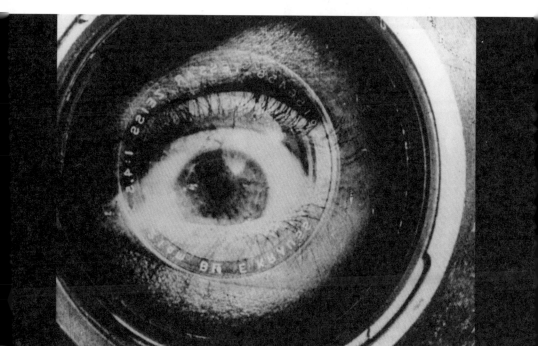

FIGURES 137 (LEFT) AND 138 (RIGHT)

THE DARK PHASE OF 1/48 SECONDS
'IMAGES NOT SEEN IN ANY FILM'

FIGURE 139

FALL OF PEOPLE'S COMMISSAR LITVINOV

On a Monday in May 1939, the entrances to the People's Commissariat in Moscow were occupied by NKVD troops.[2] The secret-service officers moved swiftly through the corridors of the executive floors.

The private telephones of the People's Commissar for Foreign Affairs, Maxim Litvinov, were cut off. Whatever was found on the chief's desk was packed into boxes and taken away. The action contained a THEATRICAL ELEMENT, for Litvinov, who had been warned for weeks, had not turned up at his office at all. He was already sitting around in a wicker chair as the head of an electricity plant in the north of Kursk. Supporters had him transferred there. He was under their protection.

The coup-like ousting in the People's Commissariat was the public version of his overthrow. A Jew and 'internationalist' had been exposed in time and removed from his post. The gesture was intended to favour negotiations with the German Reich. At this time, during the terror of the USSR, there were already abbreviations enough for the public to understand. It wasn't necessary to kill Litvinov to mark him as DECAPITATED.

DEATH IN THE CLASSLESS STRUGGLE

None of the elementary classes—peasant, bourgeois or working—was in power. A sorting out of different classes (which the dictatorship allows) had taken on a short-lived rule always threatened by the elementary forces of the classes that were actually fighting one another.

The train had been stopped. A barricade on the tracks prevented it from continuing onward. At the doors were armed functionaries of the Ministry of the Interior. The marshal of the Red Army and some staff officers got off the train. They were detained. In the carriages, officers accompanying their commander-in-chief

2 Sixteen press photographers were on the scene, as planned.

drew their weapons. Soldiers rushed out of the part of the train coupled directly behind the locomotive, looking for the commander, thinking it was a raid. Everyone was confused.

The marshal was dragged by brute force to a column of parked motor vehicles. His companions were arrested. The motorcade quickly set in motion, while on the train the supporters of the commander-in-chief of the Armed Forces, who was apparently now removed from office, and the representatives of the hated secret police faced off. A rainy day in central Russia.

The marshal, a former tsarist officer. A Jewish general. Chief of the Red Army during the civil war. More committed than Stalin, if that was even possible, in the advance on Warsaw, Berlin, Paris. Decisive during the phase of cooperation with the *Reichswehr*. With his subordinate troops in a position to carry out a coup, the dreaded 'Thermidor'. In this respect, Marshal Tukhachevsky was in danger. If anyone thought he was a Bonaparte, he was a goner. He'd been warned. The office he held was not made for a man, at best, an automaton.

Had he not travelled: no one would have been able to arrest him from out of the middle of the Red Army. Any sensible ruler would have advised against such an attempt, since, if it failed, it would have necessarily triggered the putsch, which in turn should have prevented the arrest. Only while he was travelling would they be able to intercept him.

The security authorities thoroughly demonstrated the overthrow. All the details were laid down in instructions dictated by the general secretary. In this zone of power, no subordinate organ was prepared to commit independent acts.

Hence, the execution of the powerful Red General was particularly cruel. On one of the following nights, standing in the prison cellar, naked, he was hosed with cold water. Then he was made to wait. An impromptu interrogation took place, only to be broken off a short time later, as if news had arrived from headquarters. At one o'clock in the morning, the general, hero of the Soviet Union, was shot in the neck against the whitewashed cellar wall. The same thing happened to seven of his officers in a neighbouring room. No avenger was around. No one heard a thing about what was happening in real time. Nothing but that the USSR had been saved from possible danger, as well as from one of its most experienced defenders in the event it was invaded.

'For there is no existence more chimerical than
the existence between class fronts
at the moment they are about
to collide.'

'LIFE WITHOUT "HOUSING" AND "ARMOUR" IS THE PAINFUL WAY.' *MELANCHOLIA I*

'WHILE, ON THE OTHER HAND, HE HAS RIGHT ON HIS SIDE WHO KNEW HOW TO APPREHEND THE OTHER MERELY AS AN ISOLATED INDIVIDUAL, DETACHED FROM THE COMMUNITY'

—G. W. F. Hegel, *Phenomenology of the Spirit*
(A. V. Miller trans.) (Oxford: Oxford University Press, 1977)

Karl Marx had pencilled seven marks in green next to this sentence in his personal copy of Hegel's PHENOMENOLOGY OF THE SPIRIT and underlined it as well. For what reason is not known. Another note of Marx's, however, suggests that this statement has nothing to do with 'law' or 'right', but with the 'violence conferred by the legal order', which is to say, terror. Marx speaks in this context of the 'outrageous principle of individualism'. He assumed, his daughter Tussy reported, that the 'tyrannization of the individual, his murder, committed by the power of the state, necessitates its overthrow, albeit at a time which the individual will not live to see.'

Comrades Bukharin and Rykov belonged to the so-called right, so-called because they were afraid of the putschist, forward-driving collectivization of the Russian peasant class, and they were correct.

At that time, this portion of the party would have been able to deprive Stalin's faction of power. Out of party discipline and doubts as to how they could replace the energetic general secretary, they refrained from this solution. A little later, the situation was reversed. The Stalinist centre, which had previously disempowered the so-called left and decimated its own centre, put Bukharin and Rykov on trial. FROM BEING COMRADES, THEY WERE TURNED BACK INTO INDIVIDUALS. As a result, they were isolated before the Central Committee. The wild speeches, laughing, interruptions from the masses of the party conference caused their objections to stick in their throats. It seems that committees of more than 200 people develop a negative kind of hive intelligence, a tendency towards hacking away at others.

In the same way as Bukharin and Rykov were condemned and killed, their executioner Yeshov died two years later.

FIGURE 140. Rykov and Bukharin (at the centre of the image, referred to in Lenin's will as 'the Party favourite') being led to execution. Passion rewarded with a shot to the head.

THE PRETEXT FOR YESHOV'S REMOVAL FROM POWER

Yeshov, head of the NKVD, had ordered two of the USSR's best foreign spies to Moscow to arrest and kill them. Genrich Lyushkov, one of the two, defected to the Japanese on 12 July 1938. He published blunt accounts of Stalin's crimes. The second of the clever agents was Alexander Orlov. He surrendered to the Americans on 14 July. Through a middleman he met in a New York coffee shop, he offered Yeshov and Stalin a deal: he would not say a word about NKVD atrocities in exchange for his relatives' lives. If, however, he or they were to disappear, he would have deposited enough material in a bank safe through his lawyer—above all, information about what the NKVD had done in Spain—which would negatively affect the reputation of the Fatherland. Yeshov's final mistake (in the Soviet Union, mistakes were not subjectively counted according to negligence, but objectively according to failed results) was the faked suicide and the escape of Alexander Uspenski. Yeshov had all his subordinates who could have testified against him shot, but he did not use any of the means of power available to him to avert his fate. A coup d'état was alien to him. In the office of the hitherto omnipotent Yeshov, the NKVD discovered six bottles of vodka, three full, two empty, one half-empty, hidden behind books. In addition, four revolver bullets, wrapped in paper, marked 'Kamenev', 'Zinoviev', 'Smirnov', 'Bukharin'. The nature of the record of these 'finds' showed that Yeshov was lost.

Shortly thereafter, in January 1940, he nearly died of pneumonia and a purulent kidney disease. Abrupt cure. Promise that his life would be spared if he confessed unreservedly. He knew that such promises were not kept. The charge of committing sodomy with his lover was dropped. In the end, he was dragged into a special room with a sloping concrete floor and a wall to which he was tied with ropes. He was shot by the head enforcer Vasily Blokhin. Just weeks before he had been the pursuer, with a party and the people of the Soviet Union at his back. At the hour of his death, he was an individual.

STRIPPED OF ALL POWER

On New Year's Day 1939, Yeshov, nominally not yet deprived of his power, was too drunk to hand over NKVD headquarters at Lubyanka to his successor, Beriya. He also left the dossiers he had compiled on Politburo members in his office, unable to take this important collateral out of the building and hide it. On 21 January 1939, Yeshov's picture appeared in *Pravda* for the last time. As commissar for water-transport routes, he was no longer mentioned in official overviews. A pencilled request for a conversation with Stalin was ignored. What conversation could he have had in his condition? His arrest on 10 April was not mentioned in the press. The town of Yeshovo-Cherkessk, named after the all-powerful functionary just a year prior, was renamed Cherkessk on 11 April 1939.

Even into 1940, the man was embarrassingly interrogated. Boris Rodos, an indolent and spiteful man, conducted the interview and was admonished not to kill the fragile, tubercular alcoholic Yeshov. Rodos tended towards beatings. Yeshov confessed to espionage, conspiracy against the government, murder and sodomy. Essaulov, a gentler interrogator, replaced Rodos. Yeshov limited his confessions to espionage. On 3 February 1940, the trial took place with Judge Ulrich presiding. As recently as a year ago, this judge had brought the NKVD chief flowers and brandy. For half an hour the judges pretended to deliberate. After the death sentence, a scribbled plea for clemency. Read out to the Kremlin by telephone. Overruled.

The procedure of removing him from power was staged in such a way that, after the shock of the arrest and the first night in April 1939, escalations and then their alleviation took place. Finally, the ousted man was given an unusually long time to speak immediately before the sentence. 'Shoot me peacefully, without any long struggle,' Yeshov said at the end of his speech. 346 of Yeshov's companions were shot: 60 NKVD personnel, 50 sexual partners and relatives.

FIGURE 141 (ABOVE, LEFT). Yeshov, the executioner, Stalin's intimate.

FIGURE 142 (ABOVE, CENTRE). Yeshov, with his favourite daughter.

FIGURE 143 (ABOVE, RIGHT). Genrikh Yagoda, Veshov's predecessor. After a murderous operation, he too was sentenced to death and shot.

FIGURE 144 (BELOW, LEFT). Molotov with his daughter.

FIGURE 145 (BELOW, RIGHT). Lavrenty Beria, heir of the secret police. Shot in 1953. Insolvency administrator of the cold.

THE UNEVEN NATURE OF ALL PROGRESS IN RUSSIA

All developments in Russia are uneven, notes Leonid Andropov, a sixth-degree nephew of the secretary general (and he bases this on Pushkin). Andropov is an economist of the Nikolai Kondratiev school. And that is why, he explains, ever since Lomonosov, the once fisherboy and researcher, fishing in Russia may be developed in the Barents Sea but completely underdeveloped on the Pacific coast. Russia has the most powerful icebreakers in the world, but no practical type of fishing boat. Since Peter the Great, it has stuck with Dutch blueprints for the construction of small boats. Some large-scale constructions, on the other hand, come too late. That's why in the forties, the time of war, there were abundant stocks of whales within reach of Russian ports. Then, in the sixties, the Soviet Union built the *Sovietskaya Rossiya*, a whaler the size of an aircraft carrier. To pay for it, the barely profitable whaling industry was intensified (and cheated on the quotas). In the meantime, the world's whale stocks had dwindled. Using the ship wasn't worth it. The *Sovietskaya Rossiya* was taken out of service. She's used as a floating slaughter-house for Australian sheep. The necessity of protecting the home crew in antipodean waters swallows up the economic benefits. Statistics have to once again be fudged. That is how unrelated successes, Andropov says, end up bringing the country's economy to a standstill.

FIGURE 146 (LEFT). Leonid Andropov.
FIGURE 147 (RIGHT). Nikolay Kondratiev.

A PROPHET IS MURDERED

Russian economist Nikolay Kondratiev, a Marxist as well as a 'theo-rist above and beyond', founded the LONG-WAVE THEORY OF ECONOMIC CYCLES. Each of these long waves, which have existed since the beginning of the Industrial Revolution, lasts between 51 and 59 years.

1787–1843 / 1843–1898 / 1898–1949 / 1949–2008

(The wave-count continued beyond Kondratiev's death.)

A cycle, according to Kondratiev, can be divided into spring, summer, autumn and winter. In the winter of capitalist develop-ment, there is depression and stagnation. This may be what we are experiencing at the moment. The time of highest dynamics is in the 'spring' and 'autumn of capital'. The late autumn of each cycle is characterized by excessive dynamism and speculative bubbles, as if the vital forces of money were concentrating once more, before the cold comes. Kondratiev's observations did not correspond to the law of the falling rate of profit, according to which the demise of capitalism, not its long-term wave motion, governs the future. Kondratiev was imprisoned by Stalin and sentenced to death on 17 September 1938. He was shot the same day.

FOUR LAST NOTES OF KONDRATIEV

A booklet of Kondratiev's notes appeared posthumously in Paris in January 1939, a message in a bottle. More or less saying:

– A golden age of capital does not exist.
– Most of the organizations in which people can collectively fight back have no production structure of their own. In an emer-gency, they can be blackmailed.
– We have to look for organizations of solidarity that have their own production structure. They exist. In them, people cannot only defend themselves but also offer (without directly attacking a system) autonomous alternatives as well. Not utopia, but het-erotopia.

–   The law of gravity applies to autonomy. Here, according to Kondratiev, it is clear that the cardboard machines of klepto-cracy ultimately exert little gravitational pull on people. There is a stronger gravitational pull in human self-consciousness.

DISCOVERY OF A FORGOTTEN EXHIBITION FROM 1937

In 1987 when all Soviet citizens were looking towards perestroika, that is, to the present and the future, it was not at all easy to prepare a commemorative exhibition for the 70th anniversary of the October Revolution (1917–1987). Vladimir J. Schlomberg, Gorbachev's confidant, had taken on this task. During the research, his people came across a machine hall near Moscow that was unlisted in the directories. Packed in boxes and on large shelves, they found the objects from an exhibition which failed in 1937 because its operators had been caught up by the wave of persecution and were killed.

The billboards, the coloured reproductions of mountainous peaks, the life-size figures of legendary mountain heroes, all revo-lutionary comrades, belonged to the organization *Vsesoiuznoe dobrovol'noe obshchestvo proletarskogo turizma i ekskursii* (All-Union Voluntary Society for Proletarian Tourism and Excursions) = OPTE. One of the heroes and outfitters, Comrade Krylenko, a high-ranking functionary in the People's Commissariat for Justice, had the exhi-bition he initiated packed and stacked in the warehouse (he even arranged for the deletion of the hall from the inventory registers). This is how the treasures had survived. He was arrested the following day and shot a few days thereafter.

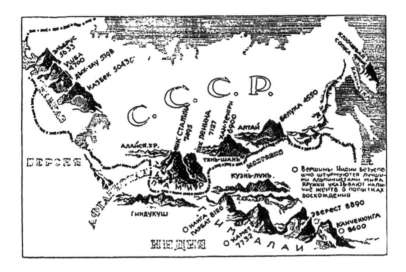

FIGURE 148. Russia's riches include its mountain peaks. To climb them is a comrade's highest virtue. Having said that, Khrushchev maintained that 'our country folk have no particular appetite for climbing'. He meant that they were indolent, that they did not spontaneously strive for party advancement.

CLIMBING THE SOVIET UNION'S HIGHEST MOUNTAINS

Gorky formulated the 'higher and higher' (всё выше и выше) motto for the aspiring Soviet man who overcomes the forces of nature. This was achieved by Soviet aviators, by the numerical peaks of tractor production in the statistics and by MOUNTAIN CLIMBING. For a long time, LENIN PEAK in the Pamirs was regarded as the highest mountain. Then a peak in the Pamirs at 7,495 metres above sea level turned out to be taller; it was named STALIN PEAK. Following Khrushchev's secret speech dethroning Stalin, it was renamed COMMUNISM PEAK. In the years up to 1937, the mountain-climbing members of Komsomol had climbed dozens of mountains in the Altai and Pamirs and given them socialist names.

In July 1937, the first wave of arrests swept the Soviet Alpine clubs. The professional mountaineers had been in contact with mountaineers from other countries, e.g. with Austrian *Schutzbündler* (comrades who had escaped the reactionary upheaval of 1934) and refugees from the Spanish civil war. This exposed them to ubiquitous suspicion.

Vitaly Abalakov, Hans Sauberer, Pyotr Sarichnyak and finally Krylenkov became victims of the accusations. The alpinist mass organizations, including the Alpiniades of 1935 and 1936, ended up being led by important politicians.

Флаг СССР поднят советскими людьми на неприступных пиках гор, на высотах земли, там, где еще не ступала нога человека. Важнейшие горные вершины носят отныне великие имена Ленина и Сталина.

FIGURE 149. A difficult-to-reach mountain peak crowned with the flag of the USSR.

FIGURE 150. Only two ideas became material force because they seized the
masses, Schlomberg argues: electrification and aviation. In this respect,
the Soyuz Orbiter is a continuation of the biplanes of 1923.
The exhibition RUSSIA 1917–1987 was an attraction.

FIGURE 151. 'We were on Mount Elbrus. Now we are going up Mount Kazbek. After that, Stalin Peak.'

BODILY RAGE

There are bodies that, from youth onward, feel completed by blood pressure, circulation, digestion, consistency of skin surface and the NARCISSTIC FEELING OF SELF. One can see by their posture that such bodies require little of that complementary spirit which, according to Andrei Tarkovsky and Rudolf Steiner, comes from the stars and tempers such austere physicality. When such a robust creature seizes power, humanity often has to wait quite a long time before it departs through death. Through its aggressive satisfaction and often sadistic psychology, it is particularly well suited to defending its power. The observation was in reference to Stalin.

IN THE BLINDEST FURY OF DESTRUCTIVENESS, WE CANNOT FAIL TO RECOGNIZE THAT THE SATISFACTION OF THE INSTINCT IS ACCOMPANIED BY AN EXTRA-ORDINARILY HIGH DEGREE OF NARCISSISTIC ENJOY-MENT—Sigmund Freud, *Civilization and Its Discontents* (James Strachey trans.) (New York: Norton, 1961), p. 81.

LACK OF DESTRUCTIVE RAGE IN DEER SPECIES

Having its seedbed in the US, consistent Darwinism was long obscured by Soviet orthodoxy in Russia. Strangely enough, these materialists tended towards Lamarckism. Now Vladimir Sobotkin has created an institute in Akademgorodok (that in the meantime has split into branches) which in its Darwinian renaissance surpasses even the elite US universities. He has specialized in the thesis that there is not one but seven *non*-hierarchically superimposed modes of evolution (that is, seven evolutions).

Among these, the most interesting for him is that of sexual mutation and selection. A Siberian deer in the prime of life, writes Sobotkin, initially moves 'stiltedly' past its rival. He never attacks directly. For a long time, he *demonstrates*. His opponent is given sufficient time to consider whether to withdraw voluntarily. This instinct to begin the fight not with a fury of destruction but in the form of careful deterrence corresponds to the growth of the antlers. Initially it develops as a pointed, deadly horn. A duel between deer with this weapon would be fatal for both rivals, according to Sobotkin. However, no young deer have ever been observed to engage in combat at this early stage. In the meantime, the antlers branch out, so that this horn framework becomes 'entangled' with that of the opponent 'and it is not the deadly point but the stronger pressure that decides the fight'. If the weaker of the two fighters flees, the other does not pursue him further than 7 kilometres. Nor does he undertake a new attack or launch a destructive strike.

According to Sobotkin, it has often been proved that the fate of the previous year's 'top dog' (so to speak) was decided for having spared the previous year's rival. He had grown older while the other had grown to greater skill. The evolution of the cervids, however, has not introduced the kind of duel that was common between knights in medieval tournaments. In ancient times: Themistocles sought tirelessly to defeat Xerxes, the scientific universalist Sobotkin continues, who had retreated after his defeat at Salamis. With the help of the Greek fleet, he wanted to defeat him at the Hellespont to block the way. It was not enough that the Great King of Persia had fled from him. A northern storm, which did not cease to blow, prevented the destructive fury of the Greek leader, whose zeal—in the event of a victory for the retreating Xerxes—could have led to the destruction of Greece.

Following evolutionary biologist Josef Reichholf, Sobotkin explains the origin of the sense of beauty—in other words, the advantage that a large, branched antler brings in terms of a doe's affection (which compensates for the inadequate keeping away of the rival)—from the absence of destructive rage. The ugliness of Themistocles' face, on the other hand (not to mention that of martens'), was painstakingly concealed by artists. According to Greek sources, only in its transmission did the naval commander's repulsive face become 'noble and beautiful'.

'I HAVE MOVED MOUNTAINS, I HAVE ROOTS IN MY MOUTH'

Heiner Müller sucked his whisky glass dry, his cigar was almost nothing but ash. In the early days of the Russian Revolution, he reports, the BIOCOSMIST faction had a majority, without their concerns ever having come to a vote in the Central Committee. Their point of departure: we may not only claim (greedily) justice and liveliness—the two elements of utopia—for just ourselves, the living but, rather, for all our ancestors who created the conditions for our revolution, that is, for the dead as well as for the living. What religion promises for Judgement Day, we, the young revolutionaries, will realize industrially in the foreseeable future. Everything is a question of solidarity.

Laboratories are needed!

Can the cycle of a deer shot by hunters be reactivated? Can the bullet 'disassembled' in the body of the deer be collected there, reunited on the spot to form a cartridge and stored again in the shooter's rifle while—no less importantly—changing the hunter's mind so that he abandons his will to destroy and acquire prey and does not immediately shoot his gun again?

Müller and I agreed, drunk as we were, that the arrangements for such a 'miracle' would require the work of millennia, but—even more than the work of CERN—they would be worth it, since an instant, a timeless and placeless particle, even less than a gramme, would 'balance out' all the efforts for this chance (namely, the 'utopia' of reversing an act of annihilation).

We sang:

'Three hunters went into the forest,
To shoot the white stag . . . '

They wanted to shoot the white stag. They fell asleep. The rare creature appeared unexpectedly, jumped over the hunters and saved itself in the depths of the mountains. The duped marksmen, as depicted in *Sang und Klang für's Kinderherz*, had not yet finished waking up. Perhaps they had not believed that a white stag would come. 'Sleepers of the 1000-year Reich,' Müller added, 'cannot react when the stag jumps at all.' That was a consolation.

Even if the scene seemed unusable for the theatre, it was a good example of history's 'flipped switch'. The heart of the white stag— well supplied with blood, refreshed in forest air, alert—moved away through the fields.

What would such a white stag have been in Russia in December 1991? Müller asked, already taking notes. The sleepers aren't asleep, the stag doesn't jump, there are no albino animals in the tundra, the guns don't fire.

So, neither hope nor miracle was spent. In a hundred years, something else may happen. Is the revolution like a corpse in cold storage? 'I hope competently,' Müller replied. Old men often have samples of their no-longer-intact seed frozen. You never know what will come of such stock in the future.

A vague tenderness seized us (and I refuse to attribute it to the drug). At least once in our lives, we wanted to transform a deadly bullet back into the waiting cartridge in the hunter's rifle. 'And the arm into a plough,' Müller insisted. What do you want with a plough? I asked. The ore belongs back in the veins of the mountains.

'There is still a small institute for Marxist-biocosmist alchemy,' Müller replied. Founded in December 1918. It survives near Astana in Kazakhstan. It's rather networked, especially in Latin America. It's settled into rental space in a new building constructed in 1991.

'MAGGI' STARS WHIRL / GUILLOTINE / 'DRINK VAN HOUTEN COCOA!'

FIGURES 152 (ABOVE) AND 153 (BELOW)

FIGURES 154 (ABOVE) AND 155 (BELOW)

FIGURES 156 (ABOVE) AND 157 (BELOW)

THE RENEWAL OF FILM HISTORY FROM TASHKENT

- You say that film history was almost renewed from Tashkent?
- By a hair.
- Where did you and your group fail?
- An investor, here we call them 'oligarchs'.
- How can an oligarch hinder you? Isn't that just an excuse for why your project was ultimately unsuccessful?
- How were we supposed to know whether we might indeed have succeeded when we only had a year? The oligarch would not have been a threat to us. What was dangerous was his support through the militia and the ministries.
- One hears that the cinema hall you had at your disposal, designed for an audience of up to 5,000 souls, was too large for a single person to have been able to rewrite film history within it.
- Sure, regardless of what we showed. At best, we had 13 viewers, not 5,000.
- Because during all the upheaval, times were just too hectic for people to concentrate on cinema?
- They found that what we were doing, the hall itself, the cultural centre, was cinema.

For many years, the Tashkent International Film Festival had been dedicated to the films of Africa, Asia and Latin America. Most of the republics of the USSR had such festivals. The 1991 summer festival in Tashkent had still been a great success. The large hall of the Palace of Culture—as mentioned above, designed for an audience of 5,000 with red wallpaper and gold-covered chairs, illuminated by huge chandeliers—was crowded with organizers and invitees. Loud-speakers and projectors worked flawlessly. The moment when the centrally controlled dimmer lights slowly shifted from 'extremely bright' to 'completely dark' was evidence enough of great cinematic art. We owed such effects to the experts in Moscow.

This headquarters was now cut off from us. The officials and organizers of the Tashkent festival, all of them Russians, had returned to their heartland before having to accept deportation by the Republic of Uzbekistan. They handed over the documents and facilities of the festival, including the Palace of Culture, to us, the local Komsomol representatives, which had a film group at its disposal. At the beginning, we tried to fill the large hall. We screened Bondarchuk's *War and Peace*, all the stock left over from the empire's central warehouses in the local film studios, including rarities from China, Japan and Latin America. Nothing proved to be an attraction to locals. Despite only asking 50 cents entry (converted into European currency). We retreated to the side rooms of the Palace of Culture. We established production facilities. With the use of the lush electrical installation that surrounded us like a canopy of stars, we set up a fire tent in the great hall (originally developed by the authorities as an emergency hospital for 30 people): within such spatial limitation, we were able to communicate with the festival's target groups in Asia, Africa and Latin America. We were connected to the empire's public communication network which was still functioning due to inertia (we did not have to pay for telephone calls or electricity). Our idea was to distribute around the world the rich stock of technical equipment that had been stored in the film studio in Tashkent and which had been given to us together with the Palace of Culture, and to inspire widespread autonomous film production. We, for our part, shot domestic films like devils, which, together with the 'world film' we had planned, would allow us in five years' time to grow into the 5,000-seat cinema.

SEMANTIC FIELDS FOR REASON, HOPE, FUTURE

'NATURE, ENERGY, AND METAL SPOILS PEOPLE [. . .] PEOPLE WILL CORRODE FROM THEIR DOUBTFUL SUCCESSES, UNTIL THEY WILL HAVE TO BE CRUSHED BY EFFICIENT ENGINES, GIVING THE MACHINES THEIR FREEDOM'

'THE LOCOMOTIVE STOOD MAGNANIMOUS, ENORMOUS, AND WARM IN THE HARMO-NIOUS SWALES OF ITS HIGH MAJESTIC BODY'

'HE SAW THAT TIME WAS THE MOVEMENT OF WOE, AND AS TANGIBLE A THING AS ANY SUBSTANCE, THOUGH NOT FITTING TO BE WORKED'

'BEFORE THE RYE IS RIPE, SOCIALISM WILL BE DONE!'

FIGURE 158

'. . . FOR THE SAKE OF BEING UNMISTAKEN, HE REJECTED THE REVOLUTION'

'AT HOME HE SAT AT THE LITTLE CORNER TABLE . . . AND BEGAN TO READ ALGEBRA . . . UNDERSTANDING NOTHING, BUT FINDING FOR HIMSELF A GRADUAL COMFORT.'

FIGURE 159

'OUR HOPE STANDS ON AN ANCHOR AT THE SEA'S BOTTOM'

' . . . USED TO HUNGER, AND ALL THE SAME HAPPY IN THEIR CHILDHOOD'

'SOMEWHERE FAITHFUL DOGS POINTED THEIR MUZZLES INTO THE INK OF THE STEPPE AND BARKED.'

FIGURE 160

PROTEGO ERGO SUM
SAYS THE COMMUNITY TO WHICH I BELONG

How old and how young are the dangers from which one is to be protected?

UTOPIA

I am able to protect.

I am able to find emergency exits.

I am able to repair.

I am able to calm the souls who are 'out of their minds',

to calm. I cause them to

to fly around calmly . . .

I postpone the Last Judgement, yes, I believe

that the next war can be prevented.

In each of these sentences, a different subject speaks.

Across the rules of grammar.

CLEAR MOSCOW EVENINGS, WHEN THE NORTHWEST WIND BLOWS

During the brief period at the turn of the year 1923/1924 when it was uncertain whether the working class or Stalin's bureaucracy would take over the party, Dr Kleve, a private scholar who was a regular at a health resort in the Harz mountains and enjoyed the beneficial physical effects of the Life Reform[3] movement (it now breathed within him), took the train to the capital of the Revolution: Moscow. He'd been recommended to the organizational leaders of an international socialist circle as a good tip and was to give a lecture. He was received at the Belorussian railway station, given noble lodgings, equipped with food coupons. One of the scurrying women

---

3 The same Institute for Life Reform in the Harz that Franz Kafka had visited.

who kept the grand hotel brought the newcomer a bowl of cherries. After that, Kleve was forgotten. The presentation was cancelled for organizational reasons; no new date was given. And so Dr Kleve settled into his room, 'making use of the time' as if sitting in a room at the foot of the Harz Mountains. As long as he had pencils and paper and access to a selection of food that did not require him to eat pork, his behaviour was the same.

Dr Kleve had a theory that was objectively suitable for solving the problems of the Soviet Union in 1924. Problems, that is, with respect to the labour opposition.[4] But Kleve did not speak Russian, and German-speaking comrades in those days were always in a hurry. He found no one to whom he could have explained the elaborate core of his theory. Hence, he had a problem: 'In the opinion of the Socialist congresses, a theory becomes reality when it grips the masses.' In other words, if a theory is correct, the masses will take it up. The fact that they 'take it up', that they come to it of their own accord, verifies the theory. But no masses made their way to Dr Kleve's hotel room.[5]

Were the theories of the 'magician', all alone in the grand hotel waiting for someone to question him, thus disproved? Why doesn't

4 At the centre of Kleve's theory was a combination of Alexander Bogdanov's *Proletkult*, Abilev's *Political Economy of Labour Power* and selected rules from Welliglott's project, *Lebensquell*, to which the mountain institute in the Harz was also oriented. Thus equipped, in three years the labour opposition would be unbeatable.

5 Perhaps Leningrad would have been the place for Kleve where he would have had more luck. A detail of his theory was that under socialism the concept of a nation's capital had to be modified. The capital is not in any central place (since, after all, the patriots carry it around in their hearts and all central points are in the labour process, that is, in the machinery itself). But since the TRUE SOCIAL RELATIONSHIP needs a corresponding place that can be grasped by the senses, the METROPOLE OF THE WORKERS is in Leningrad, with an enclave for the south in Odessa, for the centre in Omsk, for the East in Vladivostok, for the orthodox in Moscow and for the lonely North in Arkhangelsk. All these components are the equivalent of 'capital city'.

a poor system—a stockpiling failure which doesn't require any quick success—ask the only one in the city that knows the answers? A 37°-warm MESSAGE IN A BOTTLE, straight from the Harz?

After six weeks of patiently adapting to NOTHING HAPPENING, Dr Kleve took the train across the two borders back to Germany.

THE CHOIR OF SINGING CONCEPTS

'Under the government of reason, our cognitions cannot at all constitute a rhapsody but must constitute a system. [. . .] The whole is thus articulated (*articulatio*) and not heaped together (*coaservatio*). [. . .] The mathematician, the naturalist, the logician are only artists of reason. [. . .] The legislation of human reason has two objects, nature and freedom.

'Reason is driven by a propensity of its nature to go beyond its use in experience . . . to the outermost bounds of all cognition by means of mere ideas [. . .].

'Thus if wax that was previously firm melts, I can cognize *a priori* that something must have preceded (e.g. the warmth of the sun) [. . .] That the sunlight that illuminates the wax also melts it, though it hardens clay, understanding could not discover let alone lawfully infer from the concepts [. . .]. However, there is also no permissible skeptical use of pure reason, which one could call the principle of its neutrality in all controversies.'

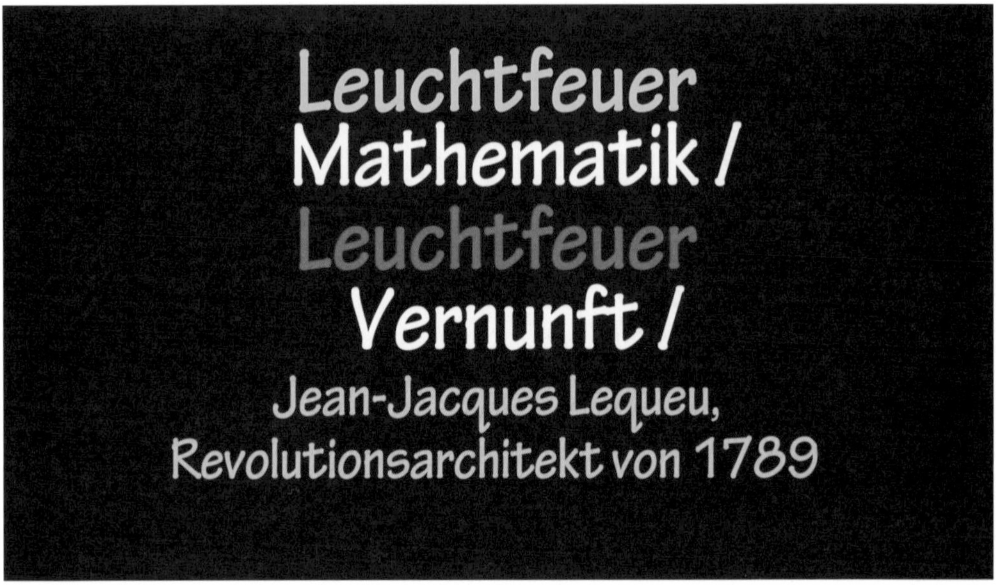

Leuchtfeuer Mathematik / Leuchtfeuer Vernunft / Jean-Jacques Lequeu, Revolutionsarchitekt von 1789

FIGURE 161 (ABOVE). Beacon of Mathematics / Beacon of Reason, Jean-Jacques Lequeu, Revolutionary architect of 1789.

FIGURE 162 (BELOW)

FIGURE 163 (ABOVE). Lequeu built a lighthouse for wanderers in Africa's deserts.

FIGURE 164 (BELOW)

$$\frac{1}{\pi} \int_{-\infty}^{+\infty} \frac{\cos az}{b^2 + z^2}\, dz, \quad a, b > 0$$

FIGURE 165 (ABOVE)

FIGURE 166 (BELOW). Only ONE copy of the work exists, in Paris /
Untested in Africa's praxis.

Das Werk existiert
in *einem* Exemplar in Paris /
In der Praxis Afrikas
nicht erprobt ...

A PLAN OF EISENSTEIN'S AND DZIGA VERTOV'S NEPHEW

Vertov's nephew, who bore his family's name, Kaufman, was a brilliant cameraman who drafted a fleeting sketch for a film in a Moscow cafe that was supposed to lead to a film version of Marx's *Das Kapital*. The characters, he noted, were the classes. So far so good, as far as party conformity was concerned. But Kaufman intended to 'document' affectionately all classes, even those that preceded capitalism, even 'superfluous' ones or those 'formations' that were not called classes in their thousand-year struggle.

Twenty years later, he would have been killed by the German occupiers because of his ancestry. Now, in the summer of 1921, just 12 kilometres away from the city where he was sitting, surrounded by stone, there was an abundance of plants and herbs making up Russia. That a man could endlessly traverse the distances of the continent on the back of the Behemoth did not enliven the soul. The soul needs narrow spaces, quick routes to the Other on which to lean or from which to push off. For nervous city dwellers, the wide horizons around Moscow were not unhelpful.

'CROSS-METAMORPHOSES'

For the screening, Kaufman called for an orchestra of four players: an accordion, trumpet, two pianos. In district towns a violin is added. A musical accompaniment to the film scenes just as in the melodramas which dominated the screen until 1917.

First, sequences of 'metamorphoses': brains, muscle, nerves, hands or feet are in action. This leads to: clothes, weaving, electric lights, grain, a butcher's wares, even money. For each of these productions, the way back is shown. FOR EXAMPLE: the monument to the cow slaughtered 20 minutes ago. Now we put the offal back into the animal in the slaughterhouse. The separated body parts of the cow fold in on one another. The skin is pulled over it. In reverse, the cow leaves the slaughterhouse (as an individual or in a herd?). She wanders along the country roads to her village, the pasture. Happy cows.

With a piece of gold or a thaler from a murderer's haul, this backwards time lapse, Kaufman notes, is much more complex.

What follows are 'cross-metamorphoses': one commodity value transformed into another. Grain into shoes, shoes into gold, gold into dinner or services. This is how Kaufman intended to turn the first line of the first book, first section, first chapter of *Das Kapital* into film, if possible, in several variants for the same 'plot'. The accompanying text: 'The wealth of the societies in which the capitalist mode of production prevails, appears as an "immense collection of commodities", the individual commodity as its elementary form.'

EISENSTEIN'S PROJECT:
TO 'CINEMATIZE' MARX'S *DAS KAPITAL*

Seven years after preparing Kaufman's sketch, Sergei Eisenstein (he had just released the film *October*) is planning to film *Das Kapital*. Running parallel to that project is his plan to create a film version of James Joyce's *Ulysses*.

–   How do you imagine such a film, Mr Eisenstein? You would need a full-length format for four pages of *Ulysses*, for example, for the 'Sirens' chapter. The outer plot could be filmed in seven minutes. But the 'sensual richness of the texts' requires infinite length. The 'imagery of surplus value' is no different. It encompasses all of modern life.
–   I am in the process of making a sketch and adding a shooting schedule.

In fact, Eisenstein had compiled a convolute of buzz words from *Kapital*. Collaborators had scouted locations. Beginning with electrification, Eisenstein wanted to narrate backwards to the terms 'immense collection of goods', 'social wealth', 'alienation', 'commodity fetish', 'circulation', 'world money', 'rate of surplus value', 'working day', 'cooperation', 'division of labour', 'big industry', 'so-called original accumulation' all the way up to the 'modern theory of colonization'.

FIGURE 167

Dramaturgically, he points out, it lacked a 'conclusion'. Concluding with the seizure of power by the revolutionary government was not enough. A vision of the future seemed impermissible to him because it had to take place in reality not in the cinema. The great director felt a 'hunger for a dramaturgy of the people'. The restless man (thereafter he travelled abroad, shot films in Mexico) had an exposé written for him by Academy member V. I. Smirnov on how to introduce the figures of the 'collective worker' and 'collective capitalist' into the film. Answer: in the form of a cinematic commentary. Eisenstein translated this in such a way that in the manner of the choruses in ancient drama, broad family chronicles (over several generations), a history of tools (over and beyond their generations) and a history of wealth in world history (from Egypt's 'Axial Age' until today) were to interrupt the sequences of the film. He noted 'misappropriation of wealth'. This made for stories that could be told on film. A lot of his notes (plus hand-drawn sketches for scenes; essentially, he wanted to shoot the film in the studio) reminded him of Richard Wagner's *Rheingold*. The economist from the Workers' and Collective Farmers' Control Commission responsible for trying to estimate the costs of the project came to the conclusion that the project could not be realized in the cinema under a length of 16 hours.

THE HISTORY OF FILM AS RELAY RACE

In Kaufman's sketches, an octavo notebook, there is an underlined section in red: in documentary film, as in a relay race, one filmmaker must pass on their experience to a filmmaker of the next generation, and the next generation to a following generation. Social change requires periods of up to 600 years; the documentary observer's interest must be oriented to this. Documenting the development of the human species is necessary, Kaufman writes. In music, he continues, knowledge of notes and artistic qualities are passed down from generation to generation, why not in the 'only authentic science there is, film'?

ABBREVIATED OUTLINE OF LIGHT
No. 3

ICONS

THE SPOTLIGHTS OF GREAT WORLD FAIRS

THE LIGHTS OF GUM DEPARTMENT STORE

WILL-O'-THE-WISPS IN THE SWAMP

THE LIGHT IN THE SOUL OF THINGS

THE COMMODITY FETISH—ALL COMMODITIES ARE ENCHANTED PEOPLE

COMMODITY FETISH VS THE LIGHT OF THE ICON

Ever since people began to sell the best of what they make, they have—enigmatically intertwined with one another in such doing—carved invisible marks into the things they produce: COMMODI-TIES. This occurs in a spiritual cuneiform. 'Electrified' from the beginning. In this respect, a spiritual fire glows within all commodities. And within that, in turn, the living and the dead burn—all those whose lifetimes are built into these things. In commodities of great beauty, in objects of unusual use value, in things for sale that we love dearly, next to the light of the soul the voice of a demon can be heard: 'Made by a maker'. The more reserved the light of the soul, the quieter the occasionally PERSUASIVE VOICE, the more irrefutable the pull that things exert.

A piece of jewellery made in Paris by the ingenious goldsmith Cardillac—considered a sensation on the breast of a duchess—did not bring happiness to the wearer. The artist's avarice of soul drove him to retrieve the BEAUTIFUL THING he'd made. He killed the duchess and carried the jewel to a hiding place. He could not do anything with the jewel, because if he showed it, he would be convicted as a murderer. Buried and hidden away, the masterpiece's

FIGURE 168

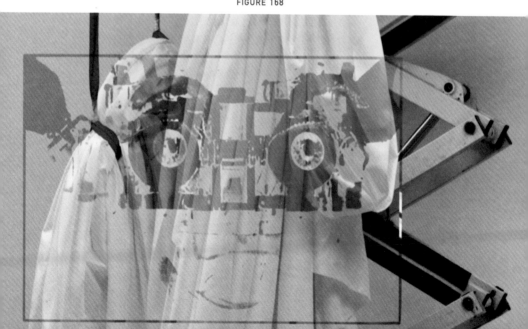

luminosity was quickly extinguished. Cardillac liked to look at the miracle with wide eyes, but it would not brighten. The individual piece, the 'valuable object', must be flooded with the imagination of many, potentially of all people, to be able to account for the COMMODITY FETISH, the 'LIGHT OF THE SOUL'. The evil spirit which speaks incessantly in both good as well as bad commodities and praises its thing—in this respect, it is a mistake of Marx when he says the commodity fetish shows itself only as an image— expressed in summary and abbreviated form: 'I will be yours and will not be taken back by my author'. It signals a promise of security with which the planned economy is unfamiliar.

Throughout great Russia of the nineteenth and the beginning of the twentieth centuries, however, the lights of the commodity fetish initially moved only in the cities. In the villages, they were in open competition with the icons. These 'WINDOWS OF THE WORLD SOUL' fundamentally reject the principle of merit buzzing about inside commodities: goods, the icons say, are windows of the SOUL OF WORTH. The difference lies in *two* letters: the LD or the TH, but can be the cause of fatal disputes, indeed, of bankruptcies and civil wars. Police violence is of no use at all in settling the conflict.

A LATE PROOF OF MARX'S
MONETARY THEORY OF VALUE

Recently three young Russian physicists and a German teacher founded a start-up engaged in REINSURANCING a new novel digital currency, a successor to Bitcoin. The project was begun by an interest group in Portugal with gold hoarded from Angola. Reaching the company's objective required complex mathematics. The company was to provide centuries of stability and to receive black money from Russia and Cyprus. The formulas the young entrepreneurs arrived at were easier to derive from Marx's theory of value and money than from the plethora of phenomena gained from practise. In essence, money is invisible.

Already in the heyday of the Frankfurt School, right after its protagonists returned from their emigration to the US, it became difficult to translate what could be observed in society—sociology, into Marxist form. It was easier not to name central Marxist concepts such as DEAD LABOUR, ENTFREMDUNG, COMMODITY FETISH, but to recognize them within realities and to transform them directly into narration. As a result, many scholars stayed with simple description.

THE COMMODITY-LIKE CHARACTER OF LOVE, THEORY AND REVOLUTION
(Report from 1923)

It is improbable that, in the PERIOD OF CAPITALISM, love of all things, which regulates intimacy (the most important thing we have), will not be affected by capitalism. So spoke the Western visitor to People's Commissar Trotsky. The latter shook his head. The problem was not an item on the Politburo's agenda. The subject requires quiet time long enough for discussion.

The Western visitor had taken a seat in a wicker chair in the kitchen. The kitchen butts up against the telephone exchange. The Kremlin's thick masonry did not permit any alterations. Capitalism did not necessarily have to do with money, the Western visitor continued. Being an author, he had rank, so Trotsky was forced to listen to him. Trotsky's seven assistants listened too. The elementary form is known to be the commodity, the visitor continued. It displays a quasi-theological mutability. In the sack of grain, I see a sliver of the diamond I exchange for it, part of a house, a school, a piece of forest or gold, I see the eyes of a beggar, etc. Why is this any different for love relationships? In advanced industrial societies, the exchange of commodities is fed by the search for happiness. With commodities of love and hate, however, this is linked to the condition that commodities can only be traded under cover, as if under a black cloth (or under the table). In 15 minutes, the People's Commissars' meeting would be beginning downstairs, on the floor below the kitchen.

Trotsky replied that he'd often noticed the latter condition, 'as if under a black cloth', in Russia. Nothing at all is openly exchanged between the sexes. They coexisted hostilely and suspiciously; this was the continent's problem.

Such a question cannot be treated dilatorily, the Western visitor continued. He'd made the long journey here and, having grown accustomed, he was used to waiting. This led him to believe that here, too, at the centre of power, leisure reigned, namely, the time to present and weigh thoughts in a calm manner. This unresolved blockade between the sexes, he believed, had been preventing Russia's progress for 400 years. Soviet power had the problem, and it would be negligent not to address it analytically when the theory was indeed available.

–   Marxist theory?
–   That's the one.
–   In its psychoanalytic interpretation?
–   That's where it's going. In their elementary form, even theories have the character of commodities: metamorphosis.
–   Under black cloths?

No, this does not apply to theory at all. No hidden exchange. On the contrary, theory is not ashamed. The exchangeability of theory, its permanent change of shape, its social (chameleon-like) character is much easier to handle than PERMANENT REVOLUTION. THIS TURNS THEORY INTO PUBLIC AMUSEMENT. Now Trotsky and his seven-man throng of helpers really had to get downstairs to the meeting.

PETERSBURG CULTURE IN ALASKA
(Report from 1872)

Even after Alaska was sold to the US, Russian brothels—St Petersburg–style establishments—lingered around the goldfields. They delivered a piece of civilization into the wild. What a difference: finding 'satisfaction' on a tree trunk while remembering some trace of sensation from the homeland with a lot of rubbing (like a bad ceasefire) *vs* lying down on the linen of well-kept beds and, depending on rank, being assigned a 'countess', a 'native', a 'Neapolitan' or some other kind of seeker. Oftentimes, ejaculation was no longer possible out of sheer happiness.

'Russian countess', 'Greek strumpet', 'Indian chief's daughter', 'Italian nightingale' (a prostitute who pretended to be a singer, and in fact could accompany her voice for a short time on the piano), the 'nun', the 'learned lady': all were studied roles, detached from the wild spirit of nature outside, which also shaped the customers' tendencies. The fifth madam in a row had put a lot of emphasis on IDEAL IMAGES ('so the customer, in his solitude, takes something marvellous back outside'). This proved to be an impediment to the brothel's ongoing praxis. In the end, the guests paid for everything to last as long as possible, not just 'success'.

PHANTASMAGORIA CONCERNING THE DEVIL'S RIVER
(Report from 1964)

One of the first measures taken by General Secretary Khrushchev immediately after his assumption of power was the rededication of the 'construction site above Devil's River'; the construction site was named after a subterranean body of water which had flowed into the Moskva for centuries and had a cathedral built over it by the tsars in the nineteenth century. It belongs to the peculiarity of such waters that buildings erected over them remain unfinished.

And so, after the revolutionaries demolished the cathedral, the gigantic monument to Lenin planned since 1928 containing a restaurant in his head remained just a torso. Khrushchev had the remains of the 'torso over Devil's River' removed. His envisioned an open-air swimming pool on the site instead. In the cold of the Moscow winter, the USSR's trade unionists were supposed to be able to sink their necks into the warming broth. Above their noses, a mist of water arose spontaneously from the difference between the water's temperature and cold air, the most diffuse and finest kind of tiny fountain, a Versailles of the people, so to speak. As it turned out, ice crystals formed on the comrades' eyebrows while their ribs remained in the 37° water. The general secretary was almost omnipotent in those early days. Nevertheless, he did not manage to hire any documentary filmmakers to capture the final phase of construction. In the Moscow studios at the time, only feature-film directors were available.

FIGURE 169

FIGURE 170

FIGURE 171

FIGURE 172 (FACING PAGE, LEFT). Hotel Excelsior on the Lido.
Photograph by Gerhard Richter.

FIGURE 173 (FACING PAGE, RIGHT). An editor from CAHIERS DU CINEMA visited and took photographs of my family and me in our beach cabin at the Hotel Excelsior in late autumn, 1983.

'THE MOST DANGEROUS MOMENT OF THE COLD WAR'

'THE MOST DANGEROUS MOMENT OF THE COLD WAR'

From the Adriatic Sea, yellow-edged clouds pushed towards the Lido. They could have been mistaken for poisonous. In fact, however, there was no danger. Their colour was caused by light reflected off the water in surprising ways. I believed that summer belonged to my happier times.

Perhaps our daughter, born only 21 weeks earlier, was still a bit young for a trip to Venice. We were worried that she might get caught in a draught and catch a cold. My film THE POWER OF FEELING had to do with war and pre-war in five sequences, that is, the ability to foresee when war will break out.

IDYLL AT THE EDGE

We drove to Venice in a used Mercedes. At Franzensfeste, we turned off the Brenner Autobahn and took the road through the mountains. Our daughter Sophie, born in March 1983 and 21 weeks old, was lying in her basket in the back seat. We stopped at a mountain pass. We laid the baby in the sun on a blanket we'd spread over the car's radiator and gave her a bottle. It was quiet. Our girl, quite vivacious, stirred her limbs, sucked rapidly. How secure and together our familial bond made us feel! We saw no reason to hurry.

The Mostra Internazionale d'Arte Cinematografica is one of the most celebratory events of my life. I had been here in 1966 with *Yesterday Girl*, in 1968 with *Artists Under the Big Top: Perplexed*, in 1971 with *The Big Mess* (with Fassbinder). In 1982, at the age of 50 (I am the same age as the festival), I received the Golden Lion for lifetime achievement alongside several other directors. Now, a year later, my film team was waiting for me to shoot on location. And my film *The Power of Feeling* was to be screened at the Sala Volpi. A cosy view. The wind off the mountains was warm. We put our child back in her basket and went on our way.

THE POWER OF A BOLD IDEA

When the ice storms and fogs still prevailed in the North Sea, that is, at the start of 1983, the US naval leadership had the idea of sending a nuclear-armed fleet of stealth-camouflaged aircraft carriers and cruisers in the direction of Murmansk and Arkhangelsk. Just short of the border of Russian territory, all of a sudden the fleet appeared to the Soviet naval stations off Russia's coast. From out of their camouflage and the fog. In case of conflict: a deadly proximity.

This idea was to give a 'show of strength'. The after-effect of such BRINKMANSHIP continued to be devastating in the late summer of 1983. The immediate result had been a wave of dismissals within the Soviet Admiralty. Many inexperienced, sloppy people were suddenly new to the service.

A PHYSICAL FEELING OF FEAR AND
MISUNDERSTANDINGS MEET BY CHANCE

In the autumn of 1983, the Politburo of the CPSU consisted pre-dominantly of old men. The thoughtful and forward-looking General Secretary Yuri Andropov—who is said to have laid the seed for perestroika—was unsettled because he distrusted his body. He could probably sense his death, which came to him in February 1984. Factions had formed among the leadership, who were waiting for the succession, if only the old man would die soon!

People know that, then as now, the various departments of the Pentagon outside Washington, DC, are constantly coming up with papers and plans. It was no different at NATO. Many of these plans are forgotten, others are stored in archives. Some are actually executed. But what will happen on the basis of the plans, neither outsiders nor insiders can say.

In one of these plans the scenario of a DECAPITATION STRIKE was sketched out. In 14 individual analyses with illustrations, the aim was to use a new, sophisticated target-acquisition technique to concentrate an atomic explosive force over Moscow. It was assumed that, after dropping the bombs, the ideological enemy would momentarily be without leadership. Then, provided that the period of paralysis was sufficient and the chaos could still be untangled, one would only have to take over the 'evil empire'. This plan had been announced to the KGB by one of the USSR's spies, a mole at the Pentagon, and was now available to the Politburo. What they did not know was that, thanks to simulations by the Pentagon's computers, the plan had already been abandoned.

IN FACT, NUCLEAR WAR ARISES DECENTRALLY

In name and intent, decisions about war and peace in nuclear terms are *centralized*. It forms the modern core of the monopoly of force. At all control points, the four-eyes principle. In fact, however, the decision makers form a choir of many voices. A single suitcase containing a code number is never the trigger. The moment of decision, as Major Alfi Windischrätz of the Austrian Secret Service never tires of explaining, is not the launch of the first intercontinental missile, but can be the takeoff of an airplane, the accidental exchange of tanks or the penetration of a nuclear submarine into a foreign port of war.

One night in early September, sitting in one of the bunkers east of the Elbe, the pilots of Russian fighter-bombers carrying tactical nuclear weapons were already in their planes. The penultimate stage before takeoff had been announced. Any misunderstanding, any additional misinformation, any reaction according to the pattern of swarm behaviour would have caused the planes to roll out of cover and take off. The targets were predetermined. After takeoff, the planes could not be called back since the enemy was expected to try and do just that electronically. As soon as they were airborne, the pilots were uncoupled from their superiors.

THE DARK SIDE OF PROBABILITY

In the harried days of September 1983, before a subcommittee of the Central Committee that had a little more time to listen than the people in the Politburo, the military psychologist I. V. Smirnov gave a lecture. He pointed to the 'sediment' of mentally unstable suicides and paranoiacs (in the latter case, fanatical patriots with obsessive ideas), who—in possession of a dangerous weapon—would not hesitate to use it. He estimated such a danger of war with a 0.3 per cent probability, while he estimated an attack by Western Allies (given that their command centres would have half an hour of survival time after an attack on the Soviet Union until they were wiped out by the counterattack) at 0.001 per cent. And the four-eyes principle? It will not prevent someone who is determined, and who suffers from self-aggression, from doing anything because they will kill their comrades before being stopped.

IN 1926, ADVANCED RUSSIANS DEVELOP EVACUATION PLANS FOR LARGE CITIES THEY DO NOT YET EVEN HAVE

The guest speaker from the USSR addressing select German police chiefs and disaster control officers at the Adlon Hotel, Dr Vladimir Vilenski, was considered in 1926 one of the best students of the Moscow-based work-shift and disaster manager Gastev. Just that year, the working group sponsored by the party had designed bold, futuristic cities for Russia's vast expanses. And examinations on how to bring the masses to the factories, entertainment venues and sports stadiums—and, in the event of a catastrophe, quickly out again—had been ordered.

The movement at bottlenecks (узкие места) has not yet been sufficiently researched, the speaker said. My job is to examine openings which will be used by fewer visitors or fugitives (бегущие) than can actually pass through them: here there is no difference between an OPENING AS A BOTTLENECK and an OPENING AS A FREE SPACE. But should a dense crowd approach during a dangerous situation, their carrying capacity (пропускная спо-собность) decreases. It is as if people's fear, their shock, manifests as a kind of baggage. My teacher Gastev says that fleeing people turn out to be wider than the space through which they are trying to fight their way through; thanks to their egos, they blow up like balloons (телоаэростат), become more voluminous, so that in the end nothing at all moves through the opening, though, according to our calculations, the space is large enough to accommodate the flow. We experts call this a TANGLE (клубок).

– But any non-expert would call it the same thing.
– Yes, but people only believe the expression when it comes from an expert.

And thus, Gastev's disciple continued, a PLUG (пробка) is formed. Wherever a plug has formed, accidents and death are sure to follow. The opening is closed when the people in front of it cause an 'arch' (дуга) whose fighters are battling the 'doorframes' (дверная коробка), the arch being opposite to the direction of movement.

The young expert gave his lecture in Russian, while the two women next to him took turns translating, as the flow of Vilenski's speech was eruptive and fast. Occasionally, they debated how to translate one of the expressions into adequate German. It isn't easy understanding the movement of an onrushing crowd in relation to the door, wall and centre of an opening. For example, to Russian ears the term 'doorframe' sounded plausible, while in German they had to search for the word to describe such a limiter to experts. 'Door post' (дверной косяк) would have been the wrong word to describe a long corridor beginning from a door and ending with a staircase. The arch's stable position, Vilenski continued, will be destroyed immediately after its creation. In a panic, everything is movement. A stable arch is therefore a rare phenomenon. But the arch is always formed anew in a matter of seconds. That is why it looks as if the crowd of people, anxious to be rescued quickly, is 'paused' at the bottleneck.

Under favourable conditions in a stadium (namely, the arrival of latecomers), the guest speaker explained, I saw a particularly beautiful arch, which I also photographed. He also passed around other photographs which documented a blockage of all escape routes.

Probabilities in the formation of arches (образование дуги) are so difficult to judge because this phenomenon cannot be observed in everyday life. When catastrophe strikes, there are no observers. We know only its statistics, the average result. Therein the realities are melted away, which are always extreme. There are two opinions about the formation of the arch. Some say that the key lies in the creation of a so-called PSEUDO-OPENING (псевдопроем) formed by those who, coming from the side, join the flow of people. After they have wedged themselves in (вклиниться), they form a partition to the opening. This is the effect of the pseudo or sham opening. These alternately emerging and decaying 'pseudo-openings' cause the pulsating character of the process, which we Red Army soldiers experienced in a simulation we were able to film. It has to do with a passage not of bodies but the will's effect on the bottleneck.

Others assume that it is the radial compression of people moving in parallel formation up until then—because each one in the middle, supposedly the 'most open' place, wants to overcome the bottleneck, but not by getting close to a wall—in other words, COLLECTIVE DETERMINATION (коллективная целеустремленность), that triggers crowding. According to this, the plug does not 'think' from its edges but from its centre.

'If at this moment of general purposefulness
the masses coincidentally come together in the form
of a continuously bent chain
which covers the opening,
wedged into the passage
they thus form the arch.'

JUDGEMENT DAY'S HEARTLAND

The sun and everything that moves around it because of its gravity takes 225 million years to orbit the centre of the Milky Way MORE OR LESS HORIZONTALLY. Like a bouncing ball, the solar system periodically crosses the zero plane of the galaxy. It shoots rapidly, once every 32 million years, through the gravitational field that is at its densest precisely at this zero plane. But what remained unknown to Soviet science and became clear only in the conversation between astronomer Karina Sedova and astrophysicist Lisa Randall: while on this VERTICAL BOUNCING TRACK, our globe and therewith almost one-fifth of the earth, 'our Russia' crosses through a narrow slice of highly concentrated DARK MATTER.

What's the result? The sudden gravitational shock during the sun's passage through the disk 'combs' Oort cloud, where the primordial rocks, the comets from primeval times, all residual matter that did not become moons and planets, move chaotically and stationary around the sun. As a result of the irritation, larger masses of this matter shoot towards the sun and beyond into the solar system. The probability is great, Ms Sedova reports. In fact, it is an absolute certainty that these FLYING BODIES, pushed by the gravity cloud of dark matter, will bring collective death in their wake.

– 64 or 65 million years ago, everything turned out OK with the Yucatan catastrophe. Why won't it work out this time?
– It turned out OK for the frogs and the turtles. Our civilization won't survive it.

At the time of Sedova's report to the Leningrad Academy, however, in many former and now abandoned industrial cities in Russia (as well as in some industrial wastelands on the US East Coast) there was a yearning to strip away civilization, to eliminate the torment of the present, to demand a new beginning: if the Revolution failed, then better an end with horror. A tail of longing like comets often have.

Members of the academy's astrophysical department judged that just one of the celestial bodies, irritated by the dark matter hitting our moon, would be enough. The side effect would be devastating for the Blue Planet. What's to be done?

That was difficult to answer because the time period of 'the self-assured apocalypse' was only determinable to within a hundred years. It could happen next week, or our country could be in for a long wait. To be informed about the catastrophe in time, we'd have to develop extremely fast fibre optic cables. On the other hand, one of the participants said, capturing enormous amount of data would be useless in the event of an emergency.

ADJUSTMENT OF A CHILD'S SOUL
(Report of the author from 2020)

I don't know anything for sure. But I'm still restless and was considered hysterical when young. I was the firstborn. For a while, my parents were infatuated with having a son. Every day I was weighed. A strange person, a usurper from Schlanstedt in our house, a so-called maid, came between me and my parents. She served my parents but, as far as I was concerned, was indolent, frivolous and malicious. When I screamed, she put me in the 'broom closet', a dark dungeon. I know this not from my own memory, but because it was later uncovered and told. If this person had not also taken money from the kitchen treasury, she would not have been dismissed.

The young couple, my parents, were still breathless after three years of marriage. They were busy with themselves and their appearances in town. My mother was considered a positive addition to the mood at every event. On off days, she had to rest up and get ready for her next performance. As a doctor with patients to see, my father took pride in showing off his firstborn to guests; initially he showed interest but later had no time to take care of me. I threw up a lot, cried piteously, complained about the bad treatment by the maid, whose name was Leni, who thanks to that lost all credit with my parents. It was my weight loss on the scales rather than my whining that alerted them to the deterioration of my person. They were worried.

As I said, the tyrannical Leni was dismissed for reaching into the cash box. In her place came THE NEW one, Magda Stolzheise from Westendorf (a suburb of my native Halberstadt). She was determined to make her fortune in my parents' home. Now working in a respectable household, her chances of finding a man to whom she wanted to entrust the rest of her life were increased.

The primary task was to get me, the firstborn, who showed signs of maldevelopment, up to snuff. Magda had nothing but intuition at her disposal. No siblings whom she had already raised, no service experience in other houses. It was her first position. As she later reported, I was 'unbalanced'. When you run around in a draught and then sink back into lethargy without moving an inch, you get caught in the cold wind that blows in from the Harz Mountains and catch a cold. It leads to inflammation of the middle ear. In the periods between illnesses: grumpy, rebellious, pushy. Meanwhile protest in my intestinal tract deepened and skin rashes that were not subject to will flared up. Magda, as she later said, came to the impression that my devastating condition was not due to any present cause. My unruly performances (performances that had already exhausted Leni's patience) weren't at the root, but a fundamental inner confusion. She made sure that I stayed close to her. She did not invade my space. She sought to instil habits. She talked a lot while she worked in the kitchen or repaired curtains. She was interested in feeding my curiosity, so that I would develop interests that would make me forget my confusions. Through the fiddling and telling, she turned a whiny spirit into a child at play. That was a matter of about three months.

Magda gave me new, privileged access to my parents. Nothing could attract my mother's attention in the long run if it was opposed to her household of pleasures. A crying child and bad news made her nervous. But now there was some positive news. With every presentation to my parents. We—my parents and I—became closer again. Just like in the halcyon days when the crown prince was still a new thing.

After a year I was in working order ('repaired') thanks to Magda's natural talent. At one with myself, the inner civil war that had already broken out inside me was immobilized. As if in some kind of endemic disease, however, the basic cause of strife smouldered. It can still break out today and throw me into chaos. The new girl, Magda Stolzheise, was one of the women to whom I owe my ability to exert control.

MY RUSSIAN BROTHER

Once again, Magda was able to use her 'art of repair' which she'd developed on me as a training object. She had accompanied a Russian commander, of whose household she was in charge, when he was transferred to the garrison of Burg near Magdeburg. A beautiful and large villa on the outskirts of the city. In the sluggish days of the occupation after 1945, there was a lot of luxurious time. Not because it would have been rewarded by the colonel or his wife or even noticed, nor because she was more partial to the Russian child than to children in general. From the pure surplus of her presence, she raised the child in a way that made it possible for him to eventually become a Russian minister of engineering in one of the ministries in Moscow. By then Magda was long dead. The career made the young man an oligarch at last. Magda spoke Russian so well that the stories she told him made his mind go round and round.

She turned the Russian child—the family came from the southern slopes of the Urals; the parents were unaccustomed to caring for their young satellites all that much—into a curious 'Western soul'. I got to know this foster brother, physically unrelated to me, in St Moritz. I recognized him by his gestures. A piece of Magda Bügelsack, nee Stolzheise's soul had coagulated in him. The Swiss found the man to be un-Russian, which seems to match R. Smetz's thesis; namely, that rather than being shaped by social class, some genes are shaped by differently elaborated characters to fit a particular class instead. These are dimensional relationships, Smetz maintains, transmitted from person to person, as in the case of a contagion, and they create that universal desire which characterizes 'city dwellers'. Smetz calls this particular character QUICKSILVER. Though stunned to immediately recognize my brother among countless strangers in the 'Palace' bar, I find Smetz's theses exaggerated. There are hardly any sources in his book at all. There are probably none that exist for such matters.

FIGURE 174. An anatomical picture from Persia, fourteenth century.

FIGURE 175. Medea. The woman from Kolchis, today, Abkhazia.
To the northwest, the Crimea.

CORKING AND UNCORKING
(Report from a specialist in 2019)

Formerly serving the border troops of the GDR, I was picked up as a female specialist by the successful secret services of our brother nation, the Soviet Union, and enticed away (as a trade-off) from my father republic even before the fall of the Wall. True experts of border areas are rare, and I see today, 30 years later, that my services would be worth their weight in gold on the precarious border between Mexico and the US. The experts there: perplexed. The mechanical erection of walls and fences isn't the way to stop border crossings. My name is Ludmila Herold and I come from the village of Sorge in the Harz Mountains. At the age of 21, I had already mastered all the relevant military examinations. I was promoted out of the ranks. Later, I was recruited as a spy by the Ministry of State Security. I was an agent. I had more than enough medals. Now I am a Russian citizen. My rank in the apparatus is secret and therefore cannot be disclosed here.

Once I was a specialist for 'corking' escape routes in the Harz Mountains. This mountain range has a lot of obscure terrain. Because of my successes in this area of the globe, I was appointed to urgently seal some border zones of the Pamir. If you can seal the Harz, you can seal any border on the roof of the world. The skills that were temporarily concentrated in my home republic, the GDR, were never tapped by the world because my republic lacked an opening to the world. Socialist blossoming in one country alone will not succeed. Trees and plants, when growing skyward, need unimpeded light and unobstructed roots.

All joking aside, my task in Russia was to block the trade routes for poppies and heroin across the mountain paths of the Pamir. And highly toxic, predominantly Islamic, terrorist groups. These groups sought to infiltrate and strengthen the rebellious forces in Chechnya. Yes, attacks in the subways and in large cinemas, concert halls and sports arenas came into consideration.

It goes without saying that, considering the driving force and intelligence of this opponent (at least as far as the movement in the terrain is concerned), corking paths and high mountain trails without taking into account the subjective factor on the other side would be a futile labour of love. A NEW KIND OF THINKING was necessary here, one which we call the 'rhizomatic imagination'. The term comes from our experts. Our mission as border guards begins before the 'border violators' start moving. That is, we've got to anticipate their intentions, which—similar to mushrooms advancing their colonies underground—advance tunnel-like into our country long before the border is ever crossed. We analyse the STRUCTURE, the MOTIVE, and stand ready with our machine guns for when the invaders come up the trail. Our weapons are our reputation. The rumour that we will reliably strike closes the border more than it would be possible to do by setting up posts or building an obstacle. The corking of the border, says the textbook I prepared for internal use—I teach courses and training sessions—the so-called interdiction, takes place on the subjective side, in the opponent's head. All this fits in with my original training in the dialectical-materialist method, to which my heart is still attached. The heart is often attached to what it's learnt first. Just as grey geese follow the mother or person that raised them for life. Not all that much of Marx has remained in my new Russia, yet I remain a patriot. But this does not apply to my courses and the subjective-objective methodology. The subjective side—that is, the human side and not that of the GREAT APPARATUS OF THE WORLD—is what protects my country.

All the same, I often wish that with my more than 40 years of experience (I am approaching 70, but am still in the service, an exception due to my indispensability) I would be given the opposite assignment: to bring migrants, people with a thirst for life, professionals, *into* the country. Just like a planter or a plantation engineer, I would—together with my brothers and comrades—lead our great Russia to repopulation. My trained instinct would glow (I would prove myself the disguised Trotskyist that I am!). In a consistent succession from Tsarina Catherine the Great—who, like me, comes from central Germany—Russia would become a true paradise of immigration. And Khrushchev's slogan would become reality: 'overtake the US without imitating it'. With a fair amount of input from the reservoir of 7.2 billion inhabitants, that is, the MASSES, who populate the Blue Planet's largest expanse of earth! Before and beyond the Urals! We could already choose the immigrants as they made their decisions by means of the emphatic-rhizomatic method. This requires fine control. When fine-tuned control takes hold of the masses, a pioneering spirit is born. This would be the optimization of my special knowledge and its application to 'uncorking'.

'*Sensuousness is the basis of all science.*'

A CHANGE OF PROFESSION INTO THE NEW COUNTRY

I entered the service of Russia as a Brandenburger, that is to say, a Prussian. That was in 2013, just like Baron vom Stein entered Russian service in 1812. Faced with the alternative of expressing my dissatisfaction with the 'Anschluss' (as the French say, alluding to Austria's annexation in 1938) of my republic, the GDR—my country's symbolic DECAPITATION was reflected in the demolition of the Palace of the Republic and the construction of a baroque palace in its place—by joining the AfD or choosing a new fatherland: I skirted the issue and went East. Becoming naturalized was a difficult process. Why can't you take my professional potential into account and my loyalty to my newly elected fatherland by looking into my eyes and shaking my hands instead of by having me fill out questionnaires?

In any case, I have prevailed, and serve—as did Freiherr von Stein—the country of my choice. I have founded a Moscow-Zurich-Paris marriage bureau. It's a success and quite a big seller. I make people happy by connecting and replanting them. Even as a child, I was fascinated by my father's rock garden, where he liked to go after work. That was in the old house. To plant moss and flowers in the desolate rock which will grow up through the cracks. In this disruptive, rocky time, I run one of the most successful start-ups there is, with branches in three metropolitan areas. I also use the Internet; competing with the dating site Parship is my specialty. I do not develop hardware; rather, I deal with the softest commodity on the planet: the search for happiness. In the beginning, my matchmaking business only worked in an East–West direction. As of late, I can also show marriages in the direction of West–East. My father, a physician and socialist, would be proud of me, the matchmaking genius, if he knew about it.

AN INCIDENT JUST EAST OF SPITSBERGEN

In July 2019, Lithuanian fishing boats attacked Russian fishing vessels east of Spitsbergen to drive them away from the fishing grounds. There is a sea area here that does not belong to either the economic zones of Norway or Russia, as established by the Spitsbergen Treaty of 1920. It is a disputed maritime territory. The Lithuanians invoked a fishing license from the EU. These seabeds that travels up to the Arctic are a dangerous area for interstate conflicts. In this specific case, Russian warships appeared the next day, which displaced the Lithuanian fishing fleet. The verdict of the International Tribunal for the Law of the Sea is still pending. The reason for the fierce

dispute between the fleets is the settlement on this part of the
Spitsbergen Group's continental block by snow crabs. They settle on
the seabed and are not subject to fishing agreements. Snow crab
meat is as expensive as lobster meat. The snow crabs migrated from
the West Atlantic to this particular seabed just a few years ago
and have multiplied rapidly. Companies from Norway, Poland,
Lithuania, Estonia and other EU countries have established bases in
northern Norway, industrially equipped for the mass harvesting and
processing of these valuable resources.

As luck would have it, thanks to this 'gold of the sea'—the cool
flesh of the prolific snow crab—the old idea of a central GDR banker
from the year 1990 obtained a real foundation in 2019. He had pro-
posed to build on the trade and communication routes of the
Comecon, the economic system of the Eastern bloc, which had just
been disarmed and destroyed, but whose lineage (personnel knowledge, common celebrations and successes, gifts, bribery and hence
relationships of trust) was still intact, to organize a new kind of
ORIGINAL EXCHANGE COMPANY. The shipyards in Rostock
would build ships to be delivered free of charge to Murmansk and
Arkhangelsk. These ships would then harvest the White and the
North Seas. The spoils would eventually get back to Rostock and be
canned in factories there—in the process, new jobs would be created—for export. The profits would be divided between the Russians
and their partners in the new states of Germany.

The '2019 Gold Rush', the snow-crab windfall, would make such
exchanges now, in 2019, marketable and sensually representable.
The shipyards, however, no longer exist. Sanctions have interrupted
the potential supply chain and all the lobbying and media forces,
already up in arms over the Nord-Stream 2 pipeline project, would
oppose the revitalization of this beautiful project.

I WAS A TRANSLATOR IN MINSK
(Report from 2015)

I was a witness to the legendary evening session that led only to a sham peace that was nevertheless a (hole-filled) cease-fire. I noticed the chancellor watching the Russian president closely. It was in the fourth hour of the night. Aside from her, no one else in the room was wide awake. Later, I questioned the chancellor on the plane. She had checked, she said, to see whether, in the sitting posture and the president's facial muscles, she could observe a sudden stiffening, a 'craziness', which could spell the failure of negotiations. She could read them; although Putin sought to maintain a poker face, a mask, the movements of the facial muscles are not subject to willpower. Just as experienced foresters in the forests of Mecklenburg-Western Pomerania can tell from the posture and flews of foxes running towards them whether it is an 'accidental attack', a case of rabies or the *crazy fox* syndrome. For forester Heinz Ullman, whom the chancellor knew, assumption alone is no reason to shoot an animal. You have to examine closely their muzzles, dentition, saliva secretions, posture of the lights and body. In a figurative sense, the Chancellor had acted as a forest guardian. To the chancellor, the Russian president seemed to be 'trapped in a communicative cage'. According to what she said on the return flight, she did not think he was making decisions alone. Rather, she opined, his decisions seemed to come about as if from someone caught in the middle of a raging school class at recess. Was he reliable? She didn't know but sure hoped he would turn out to be on a case-by-case basis.

INCIDENT DURING A RECENT NATO MANOEUVRE

Through the oblique axis of the earth's body up here in the north, the sun turned the sea and the green-grey coast of Norway transparent. Far away but perceptible on the computers yet invisible to the naked eye: the US aircraft carrier, the 'backbone' of the manoeuvre. Set off from the fjord, on high ground, marching columns practicing predefined targets. Referees with watches check the times. Unlike earlier manoeuvres in northern Norway, this time it's with real troop movements. Referees decree a 'disruption'. A column must stop and wait for the referees to give the go-ahead before they move on. The delay must be compensated at the end of the day.

Unscheduled at five o'clock in the morning: Russia announces a missile manoeuvre. In the immediate vicinity of the target areas of NATO's manoeuvre. Missile firings were to be practised all the way up to the movements of the 'enemy' fleet. A contractual announcement 15 minutes before the start of the exercise. How can one divert attention on the NATO side, focused on fulfilling the manoeuvre objectives, to avoiding an accident between two rival manoeuvres under emergency conditions? The face of the NATO spokesman at the impromptu press conference is stoic. In 14 languages (some technical terms are standardized), the NATO sub-units of the manoeuvre discuss their redeployment.

This was punishment for having humiliated the Russian armed forces back in 1991. The commander of the Russian manoeuvre at that time had been a young man of 26. He had taken an oath. He had learnt and learnt at the academies, and in the meantime had found companions.

He always placed the impact of his missiles so close to NATO's frigates and salvage ships that their targets could no longer be reached that day. Negative assessments entered into NATO officers' personnel files. At the end of the morning, the NATO ships fled south.

Directing this nearly colliding double-manoeuvre presupposed *skill* on the side of the Russians. Such a thing exists only with a high degree of motivation.

FIGURE 176. Launch of a stealth bomber from a US aircraft carrier on the high
seas. The 'damaged house wall' aesthetic comes from an elephant skin
being placed by Anselm Kiefer in front of the camera lens.

'A WORLDWIDE CRASH CAN TAKE PLACE
IN ANY WORLD-FORGOTTEN PLACE'

In 1989, I was 30. Now I am 60. In the summer of 1990 (at the time
the Berlin Wall came down), I found myself working abroad as a spy
for the GDR). I was adopted by my brother comrades in the Russian
intelligence services. I didn't even go back to the capital of the GDR.
My skills were too valuable for my brother comrades to have fed
me to the lions of the Western services. I was given nice quarters
in Moscow and a dacha in the surrounding countryside, but I seldom
lived there because I was deployed in Syria. There I was responsible
for Yemen, and I still am. My former employers had a large department for Yemen. For a while it seemed that we might take over in
South Yemen before it was disastrously united with the North. We
had seeped into all the positions of control. Our work was appreci-
ated on the ground. This now stood me in good stead in my role as
an observer and agent of influence for Russia. Keyword Syria: One
often chooses the expression 'civil war' for the doom that befell
that country, whose traditions go back to antiquity. War, yes, but I
did not find any 'citizens' there. The category citizen entails the
bourgeois mode of production. The beginnings of industrialization—none of that is to be found here. A trained spy can see that
immediately, just as a doctor can draw the correct conclusions from
their patient's blood count.

For my new compatriots in the Russian intelligence services,
it is often difficult to see the scars, the ramifications and the con-
spiracies in the 'war' that has been going on for more than 30 years.
Neither the 'Great Patriotic War' nor 'War on the Agents and
Infiltrators of the West' give a clue to the 'amorphous war' that prevails here. A Saxon like me sees that more quickly than many a
Russian. It's not for nothing that we count the poet Karl May as one
of our native sons. The art of storytelling may be more important
here in the Orient than the compilation of data. A man from Perm
will see it differently. I must make an exception with regard to
my direct superior, Colonel Yevgeny Shuvalov. He runs the services centrally from the port city of Tartus. He's in charge of my
working group. Although he never travels anywhere, nothing of the

subversive movements between the Euphrates and the Red Sea escape him. He often laughs at the naive interpretations of the US or the Saudis. The prejudice still holds that weapons, tanks, drones and aircraft carriers will decide the battle in the Middle East. In fact, the advantage lies in KNOWLEDGE. In the past, such a statement would have been considered an 'idealistic deviation'. But experience says: true power lies in empathy.

At this point, I must make a comment on the character and type of 'modern war'. This war is neither modern nor old. It's a chameleon. The range lies somewhere between the cleaver and the long-range nuclear warhead. This war is taking place between masks. A specialist from Akademgorodok who had travelled here pointed out to me that this war was a primitive repetition of the Thirty Years' War that once raged through Central Europe. When a hotspot goes out in one place, the flame, linked underground, breaks out in another. Seventeen parties are influencing this particular network from the side lines. In such a box of snakes, we spies operate on the downlow. I do not believe that war can be tamed.

FIGURE 177. Russian graffiti in the basement of the Reichstag. Today the seat of the German Parliament. Fought over in 1945. The basement is full of graffiti and is under historic preservation. It has been built over.

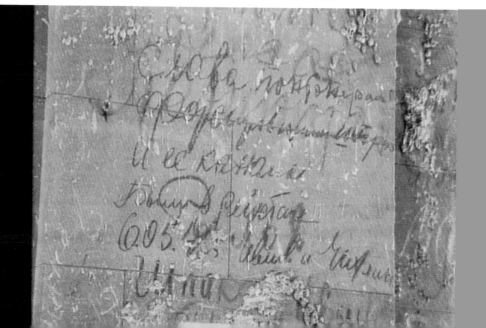

END OF LIFE

Staying at the Brandenburger Hof Hotel in Berlin at the age of 91, a young Russian born in 1929, who had lost both of his parents in 1937, went for a late-night walk through the streets of the Scheunenviertel, which he had last seen as a soldier in 1945. The pavement stones, irregular because of the war, were still as desolate as they had been back then, but with fresh grass sprouting up in-between. In the meantime, the entire area was surrounded by new buildings, buildings to which he no longer had any connection at all.

NOTES AND
SOURCES

[Unless otherwise specified, translations are from the German by the current translator. Special thanks to Thomas J. Kitson for help with transliteration from the Russian and German, and for explanations.—Trans.]

FIGURES 178–181. Sketches of the Melnikov House by Thomas Demand. Konstantin Stepanovich Melnikov, architect (1890–1974). Architecture in one's mind and architecture as converted space: both SPACE.

P. 9: 'Utopia = "nowhere"'

FIGURE 182

'STROLLS THROUGH RUSSIAN SEMANTIC FIELDS'
(by Rosemarie Tietze)

SEMANTIC FIELD 'SPACE' 1
ПРОСТРАНСТВО / PROSTRANSTVO

As a translation of *prostranstvo*, dictionaries suggest 'space', a variant (in German) that is as accurate as it is unsatisfactory. Certainly, the lexical fields partly overlap: in philosophical or existential meaning, in 'space and time', for example (quite literally, *vremia i prostranstvo*); or in the dimensions of the universe, 'air space' or 'outer space', there the languages agree. (*vozdushnoe* or *kosmicheskoe prostranstvo*). As well as in the small, everyday life, when an 'in-between space' is meant, for example—that there is still enough space between the table and the wall to put a sofa. The same applies to the figurative use of 'play space' or 'area'; in Russian too, there is such a thing as a 'cultural space'.

But as soon as it comes to a three-dimensional, closed space, the languages drift apart. With *prostranstvo*, 'space' cannot be a synonym for 'room' [cfr. 'Raum' in German]. The Russian word 'room' is more open, has more surface area and expanse and tends towards the boundless.

No wonder, one might say, just have a look at Russia on the map. The association imposes itself but leads perhaps to trivial conclusions, even if certain connections between the size of the country and the mentality of its inhabitants cannot be dismissed out of hand. Based on Russian geography and history, the philosopher Nikolai Berdyaev developed thoughts on the 'power of spaces over the Russian soul'. Before we indulge in speculation—which could become tricky from an external perspective—let us return to the term *prostranstvo* and simply continue to sound out the way of thinking that lies within the word.

In *prostranstvo*, space extends in all directions. Boundaries may exist, but one does not see them—perhaps they must be sought out. In the Steppe, or within snow-covered, endlessly stretching fields. 'Empty' or 'enormous' or 'immeasurable' are adjectives that like to combine with *prostranstvo*. It is true that man can sometimes feel lost in the *prostranstvo*, but mostly the Russian attitude to the word is friendly and positive; one appreciates the possibilities that open up before one, one feels cramped, less comfortable elsewhere. Apart from that, *prostranstvo* is a calm, objective term.

Russian, however, has another word etymologically related to *prostranstvo* but that is, at the same time, more strongly charged with feeling:

SEMANTIC FIELD 'SPACE' 2
ПРОСТОР / PROSTOR

Again, a survey of the dictionary: 'vastness' is the meaning that all dictionaries can agree on, yet all of them feel slightly inadequate, for they cite other nuances in German; from talk of 'spaciousness', 'expansiveness', 'unrestrictedness', 'unboundedness' and even 'freedom'. *Prostor* is vast space, time without limit or end, adorned with epithets such as 'boundless' or 'unfathomable' or poetic ones like 'alluring' or 'blue' or even 'proud'. This *prostor* stimulates the imagination, and romance and pathos are not too far away. The spirit loves *prostor*, the proverb says; 'spirit' can also be replaced by 'genius' or 'soul'. As a character by playwright Alexander Ostrovsky exclaims: 'Oh, give the soul *prostor*, it would like to let off steam!' Ilya Repin has captured such emotional exuberance in his painting *What a Freedom [prostor]!* (1903): A young couple, both dressed in dark jaunty blue, stand up to their knees in the midst of foaming, green-black ocean waves, but they are not frightened and, despite the storm, are holding each other's hands, laughing happily.

The fact that *prostranstvo* and *prostor* are key words for the view of the world condensed in the Russian language is also shown by the impressive series of synonyms: *dal, shir, razdole, privole* . . . These can only be described, no longer translated individually. Their meaning is based each time on the idea of 'vastness' or 'distance', and it resonates in 'unbound, free, carefree life'.

Finally, I would like to talk briefly about a riddle that the Russian mentality still poses for me. I cannot solve it, even though I've been dealing with Russia all my life. A Moscow friend, the textbook definition of an intellectual, who knows her way around Russian intellectual life and in the outside world, who has been in the Caucasus and the Himalayas, says frankly and cheerfully, almost a little proudly, about herself: 'Topographically speaking, I'm a cretin.' Well, she's not alone in that. A scouting spirit doesn't seem to be all that desirable to Russians.

Whenever I walk through Moscow, I am asked for directions almost once or twice a day; in Munich, this almost never happens. In Russia, it is generally accepted that people will ask rather than orient themselves with the help of a city map or what-have-you. A popular proverb dating back to Russia's state beginnings is: *Iazyk do Kieva dovedet* = 'Your tongue will get you all the way to Kiev.'

What is wrong with the Russian sense of direction? Shouldn't it be particularly sharp in a country with these kinds of distances? Well, this shows trust in one's fellow human beings; or is it rather mistrust of official signposts—which were often lacking in the countryside in the past? Or does it simply show a love of adventure, coupled with trust in God? Man will certainly arrive somewhere? What's going on there?

АВОСЬ / AVOS
AND THE MANY SHADES OF THE APPROXIMATE

A succinct two syllables, unassuming, in its simple everydayness it seems innocent, almost ingenuous. At the same time, it sets clear accents, usually at the beginning of a sentence. *Avos, oboidetsia*: 'It will be all right.' Or *Avos, ne opozdaem*: 'Hopefully we won't be too late.' Or *Avos, nichego*: 'Never mind.' Or *Avos, proneset*: 'Won't hit us for sure.'

The wordy, different translations reveal a dilemma. In German, it has to be paraphrased, there *avos* does not exist. The dictionaries offer 'perhaps' or 'possibly', the former of which points in the semantic direction but does not shed any light on the meaning or aura. On the one hand, *avos* always looks to the future, to what will or could happen, it does not serve an open time horizon like 'perhaps'. Moreover, unlike 'perhaps', it is by no means neutral. The things that resonate there! A wide range of moods and feelings: hope for chance, for a happy outcome, no matter how muddled the situation may be; daring, plus a measure of recklessness and wishful thinking—the world belongs to confidence! While this care-free *avos* often appears with a smile, the more common, distressed or gloomy variety prefers to warn of life's imponderables with a raised forefinger: 'Don't expect anything good from *avos*; 'Don't believe *avos*— *avos* is deceptive, it disappears in the forest.'

The word thus acts as a tint in many ways. And just as it eludes exact semantic delimitation, so too it eludes exact grammatical classification. Linguists argue about whether it belongs to the group of particles or adverbs; 'modal word' may serve as a compromise. What is indisputable is that the native speakers are very fond of it. The many derivations bear witness to this. It occurs as a verb, *avoskat* or *avosnichat*, = 'who often says *avos* or 'relies on it' and the next proverb pops up: *Kto avosnichaet, tot i postnichaet*, i.e. he who trusts in such illusions 'also suffers hunger'. It is also common with prepositions, *na avos*, for example, means 'on the off chance, at random': '*Na avos* the farmer also sows the grain'; or even existentially: 'The Russian has grown up *na avos*.' With so much intimate closeness, the diminutive form of the noun popular in Russian, *avoska*, materialized during the Soviet era: In the pre-plastic era, *avoska* was the net or folding bag that one always had in the economy of scarcity, just in case, after all, you passed a queue where there was a shortage of oranges being thrown onto the market, who knows . . .

The appreciation of *avos* goes further. The word is accepted as a characteristic of the Russian mentality, and not from a critical outside point of view but by Russians themselves, since time immemorial! In the *The Tale of the Priest and His Workman Balda*, Pushkin has the priests place all their hopes 'in the Russian *avos*'. It goes without saying that the hope is unfounded, that no saving act of fate intervenes. In the unfinished tenth chapter of *Yevgeny Onegin*, Pushkin even elevates the word to a national code: *Avos*, O national shibboleth . . .

Incidentally, the expressive *avos* does not stand alone on a wide field. The proverb says it has a brother: *nebos* or *neboska*. As *avos* is stressed on the second syllable, *nebos* gives very similar shades, namely, probabilities and speculations, albeit even more colloquially, familiarly and often in the form of tag questions: *Nebos, golova bolit?* — 'You've got a headache, right?' A good half-century ago, the successful author Nikolay Nosov introduced the two rhyming dwarfs *Avoska* and *Neboska* to literature and there they still frolic today, showing Russian children what the characteristics of the two names are all about. Adults, on the other hand, use the pair of siblings as a warning against too much exuberance: '*Avoska* twists the rope, *Neboska* throws the noose.'

The next proverb takes us a step further: '*Avos, nebos, da kak-nibud.*' This time, the third component can be translated without a doubt: *Avoska*. *Avos, nebos* and 'somehow'. Of course, it would be to cross the bridge of 'somehow' and go even deeper into the realms of the uncertain and approximate. Especially since the brittle category of indefinite pronouns ('someone' or 'anyone') in Russian already offers more nuances than in German. Not to mention adding partial comparisons which successfully blur contours as well! Alone for the harmless *vrode* (= 'like, something like, in the manner of, similar to') the Russian dictionary of synonyms lists 89 variants. No, that would cause our heads to spin.

Let's confine ourselves to the just quoted *Avos, nebos* and somehow. The Siberian-wide Russian landscape of the vague, the random and longed-for is succinctly summed up by this trio sums up the Russian landscape of vagueness, coincidence, fantasy and longing. Russian, they say, stands 'firmly on these three stakes' (caution, irony!). Well, but what can you do? All that land mass doesn't prevent a Russian existence from being on shaky ground, you never know what's coming—how can one take care, let alone take precautions, or even make provisions?—and perhaps God or fate, without any intervention on our part, may take a happy turn, *avos* . . .

SEMANTIC FIELD 'FREEDOM'
СВОБОДА/SVOBODA AND ВОЛЯ/VOLIA

Whoever thinks of 'freedom' in Russian has *svoboda* in mind. Whoever is sitting in prison or in a camp, however, longs for *volia*. So does the choice of the Russian word depend on whether the person thinking or speaking is in freedom or bondage? No, it's not that simple. To explain why there are two words for 'freedom' in Russian, the terrain of the two semantic fields would have to be surveyed in more detail.

First, *svoboda*. Here we are in familiar territory. The Russian nuances of meaning are largely the same as ours. Doing what you want, as long as other people's freedoms are not infringed upon or laws violated. And thoughts, of course, are free. The ideal of 'liberté', philosophically and politically, concretized in terms such as 'freedom of will' (*svoboda voli*), 'freedom of the press' (*svoboda pechati*) or 'freedom of speech' (*svoboda rechi*). Perhaps *svoboda* emphasizes a little more strongly than the German word that there should be no restrictions whatsoever. Furthermore, *svoboda* is often attributed to the forces of nature, as when Pushkin sings of his farewell to the sea: 'Farewell to you, unharnessed Ocean!' At the same time, there is the Russian expression, 'City air makes you free'; today an older variant of the word, namely, *sloboda*, means 'suburb'.

And so now *volia*. A complex term with diffuse boundaries, so let us begin carefully with the etymology. In *volia*, there is a widespread Indo-European root, the word is related to 'will', 'choice', 'want'. Even today 'will' or 'wish' or 'aspiration' underlie the spectrum of meanings from which 'free will' and finally 'freedom' are derived. But what kind of freedom? Unlike in *svoboda*, rules or laws do not play a role; *volia* does not recognize such categories—*volia* is freedom from any pressure or coercion, freedom paired with carefreeness and bravado. Therefore, *volia* pushes out into the free, the open; as the cultural historian Dmitri Likhachev explains: 'It is *svoboda*, associated with vastness (*prostor*), with unlimited space (*prostranstvo*).' And so *volia* is a basic trait of the Russian mentality. The people were so fascinated by the unbridled urge for freedom that even an ostentatious double with an adjective, *volia vol'naya* (of which 'free freedom' is only a poor representation, of course), became established. Apart from countless other derivations, there is also the abstract *volnost*, for which dictionaries offer 'freedom' yet a third time; what is meant is the state of being free.

The centuries of totalitarian rule in Russia have certainly contributed to the development of this ideal of freedom in all its diversity. In the tsarist empire, it was the Cossacks who knew early on how to evade any kind of supervision; even today, *volnyi kazak* is a metaphor for 'free man'. And the immigrant German colonists of the time were *volnye liudi*, 'free people', who enjoyed privileges over the native peasants. The latter were, for the most part, serfs and thus tied to their village (even in the Soviet era, the freedom of movement of the rural population was partly restricted). When the serfs were freed in 1861, *volia* gained another level of meaning. From the peasant's point of view, it became shorthand for the abolition of serf-dom. However, not everyone yearned for such *volia*—it also brought new fears to the people in the countryside: who will 'take care of us' if not our master? Even 40 years later, Firs, the old household factotum in Chekhov's *Cherry Orchard*, speaks of *volia* as 'misfortune'. In the Soviet Union, the use of the word changes yet again: from the perspective of the prisoners in the GULAG, it now stands for the whole world outside, beyond the camp gates.

Few Russian terms are as charged with the history of culture and mentality as *volia*. Compared to *svoboda*, the word lost a bit of its gravity over the twentieth century, but the sense of independence continues to stir people's minds. There are still those who rebel, who break away from the usual routine and go underground, vagabonding through the prover-bial Russian expanses, at least for a while. The view of Russia from the outside often sees only the authoritarian state structure, but not what lies beneath this layer. But thanks to *volia* an attractive anarchy in everyday life prevails. Even in the regimented Soviet times, Germans could learn to walk on the forbidden lawn or to cross the street against the red . . .

We should not, however, let our walk through the semantic fields end in everyday life, as this would not do justice to the highly tense pair of terms *svoboda-volia*. Once again Pushkin helps us out of this jam, for he introduces us to yet another shade. Most of the time, *volia* comes across as impetuous, with emphasis and passion, in a famous line of poetry. However, Pushkin surprisingly relates it with *pokoi*, 'calm':

Na svete schastia net, no est pokoi i volia.

Literally: 'There is no happiness in the world, but there is tranquillity and *volia*.' And in the next line, he rhymes it with *dolia*, 'Go, Fate.' What Pushkin longs for in a moment of the summer's dejection of 1834 is a retreat from the world to a peaceful hermitage in the countryside, where he can devote himself to his poetic labours within the comfort of his family circle—quiet, undisturbed and unrestricted.

BACKGROUND MATERIAL FOR THE THREE ESSAYS INCLUDED IN THIS PART

Anna A. Zaliznjak, I. B. Levontina and A. D. Šmelëv, *Ključevye idei russkoj jazykovoj kartiny mira* (Key Ideas of the Russian Linguistic Image of the World) (Moscow, 2005).

Aleksej Šmelëv, 'Russkie avos i nebos Revisited', *Die Welt der Slaven* 62(2) (2017): 276–303.

Anna Wierzbicka, *Semantics, Culture, and Cognition: Universal Human Concepts in Culture-Specific Configurations* (New York: Oxford University Press, 1992).

*

FIGURES 3–4 | Contact sheets for *All of Russia's Souls Point to Heaven With Their Roots*, film triptych. From the exhibition *Georg Baselitz*, Fondation Beyeler, Basel, April 2018. The images of the triptych are from Eisenstein's *Ivan the Terrible*, from Mussorgsky's opera *Khovantschina*, in the production by Andrea Moses, Stuttgart State Opera; in addition to stills from Mussorgsky, *The Sorochinzy Fair*, production Barrie Kosky, Komische Oper Berlin.

'All of Russia's Souls . . .': Russian Opera—Halberstädter Sammlung

PAGE 16 | 'The souls of the fallen trees grow too / Along with the moon and its beloved stars'. From Else Lasker-Schüler's poem 'Aus der Ferne'.

FIGURES 6–11 | Contact sheets and film stills from 'Architecture for Space Travel. Philipp Meuser: "Between Constructivism and Cosmonautics"', *News & Stories*, 9.12.2015, Sat.1.

→ 'Space Design. Interior Design in Outer Space', *10 vor 11*, 9.2.2015, with Regina Peldszus.

FIGURE 7, IMAGE 0042 | Film still from *Emotionality and Hard Photos*. 'Photo Series by Ludwig Rauch: Baikonur, Right-wing Extremist Poison, Everyday Life in Moscow', *10 vor 11*, 11.4.1994.

PAGE 25 | 'And any submarine that found itself in the area where this waterfall . . .': In fact, German submarines in the straits of Iceland and Greenland sent to interrupt the British fleet's barricade ended up being pulled 1,000 metres into the depths. Only one of the boats returned to its home port. The crew reported the unusual natural phenomenon. Research showed that the underwater waterfall had existed for 1,000 years.

FIGURE 12 | Still from the *Circus* (1936) by Grigori Alexandrov.

PAGE 46 | 'My soul is already sloughing off its skin': From Friederike Mayröcker, *études* (Donna Stonecipher trans.) (London: Seagull Books, 2019).

PAGE 47 | 'Nothing Between the Body and Head but Music': In addition to ' "Rather Dead than Alive without Love": *ANTIGONA* by Tommaso Traetta: A Model Opera of the Enlightenment', *News & Stories*, 18.9.2011, Sat. 1.

PAGE 51 | 'Ernst May': As a city councillor for building in Frankfurt am Main, Ernst May founded a school oriented towards constructivism and functionalism. In 1930, he travelled to the Soviet Union along with his co-workers. There he turned to the planning of modern industrial cities in Siberia.

FIGURE 183. Ernst May.

PAGE 59 | 'map [. . .] contained all of the country's particularities.' See also:

My grandfather used to say: 'Life is astoundingly short.' To me, looking back over it, life seems so foreshortened that I scarcely understand, for instance, how a young man can decide to ride over to the next village without being afraid that—not to mention accidents—even the span of a normal happy life may fall far short of the time needed for such a journey.

—Franz Kafka, 'The Next Village' in *The Penal Colony: Stories and Short Pieces* (Willa and Edwin Muir trans) (New York: Schocken, 1948).

FIGURES 28–9 | From Island 6 of the film installation for the exhibition *The New Alphabet*, Haus der Kulturen der Welt, Berlin, 10.1.2019.

PAGE 69 | 'Words, Sentences and Semantic Fields from the Fatherland of Particularities'. Quotation-montage from Andrei Platonov's novel *Chevengur* (Anthony Olcott trans.) (Ann Arbor: Ardis, 1978).

PAGES 78–82 | For information on the Ket language, see Ernst Kausen, *Die Sprachfamilien der Welt. Teil 1: Europa und Asien* (Hamburg: Helmut Buske, 2013).

PAGES 91–5 | 'And further, Zakhar Pavlovich had observed . . . ' and 'ah, my comrade in arms . . . ' Quotation-montage from Platonov, *Chevengur*.

PAGES 97–8 | In protest against the fact that the Kurdish armed forces were abandoned by the US, US Secretary of Defence Mattis resigns from his post.

FIGURE 44 | Marianne Van den Lemmer Collection / FUEL Design Publishing. London. From: Olesya Turkina, *Soviet Space Dogs* (London: FUEL Publishing, 2014), p. 31.

PAGE 105 | 'Coughing blood into a handkerchief in Russia.' Based on a line by Ben Lerner in *Mean Free Path* (Port Townsend: Copper Canyon Press, 2010).

PAGE 109, PAGE 249 | 'When Samael, the angel of punishment . . . ' and 'Black fire (strong in colour) . . . '. Gershom Scholem: *Die Geheimnisse der Schöpfung. Ein Kapitel aus dem Sohar* (Berlin: Schocken Verlag, 1935).

FIGURES 48–54 | Contact sheets and film stills from the film *26.–28. November 1812*, about Napoleon's crossing of the Berezina. Film stills using glass plates by Kerstin Brätsch. First shown at the Vincent van Gogh Foundation, Arles, 2019.

PAGE 132 | 'A buzzard sets off from the grid map': From Helmut Heißenbüttel, *Textbuch 8* (Stuttgart: Klett-Cotta 1985), p. 85.

PAGE 147 | 'SILENTLY AND HOPELESSLY I LOVED YOU . . .', quotation after Pushkin from the poem 'I Loved You' (Babette Deutsch trans.). Available at: https://allpoetry.com/I-Loved-You

FIGURE 60 | 'Winter protection for German soldiers in Russia'.

Guidelines for Winter War II, 25:

Newspaper in several layers provides very good protection against the cold. Therefore, always carry sufficient supplies.

As a makeshift protection against the cold, the units are also provided
with the following in sufficient quantity:

Paper head hoods

Paper vests

Paper leggings

Paper foot rags   To be worn between underwear
and outer clothing

Paper sleeping bags

Paper pads

PAGE 149 | 'And what by night had been terrifying lay pale and illumi-
nated in simple expanses': From Platonov, *Chevengur*.

FIGURES 64–8 | In Treptower Park, Berlin, a Soviet memorial was erected
in the post-war period. The Western Group of the Red Army's last
parade before being shipped back to Russia took place in 1994, in
the vicinity of this memorial. Non-military groups from Russia and
Belarus gathered on 9 May 2019 (the commemoration of the victory
over the Third Reich isn't based on the surrender of 8 May 1945 but,
rather, on its repetition on 9 May 1945 in Berlin-Karlshorst).

PAGE 166 | 'Bushwhackers from Minsk': On 7 December 1991, Presidents
Boris Yeltsin and Leonid Kravchuk (Ukraine) and Stanislav Shush-
kevich, Speaker of the Belarusian Parliament, met in a hunting lodge
for state guests near Viskuli. The next day, they signed the Belovezha
Accords, in which the secession of Ukraine, Belarus and Russia from
the Soviet Union was agreed. The term 'Bushwhackers of Minsk' was
coined by Gorbachev.

FIGURES 69–73: 'The Bushwhackers' Raid: James A. Baker III and Mikhail
S. Gorbachev on the Final Days of the Soviet Union', *Primetime*,
16.6.1996, RTL.

→'20th Century Fiction: Star Wars: How Political Opportunism in
Reykjavik Paused for One Moment', *News & Stories*, 30.1.1995, Sat.
1, with Valentin Falin and Mikhail Gorbachev.

→ 'Gorbachev in Reykjavik', *10 vor 11*, 29.3.1993, RTL.

→ 'Gorbachev in Bayreuth', *Primetime*, 17.10.1993, RTL, with Heiner
Müller.

→ '1440 Seconds with Gorbachev in Munich / The Gold Chain: "A Long Day's Journey into Night"', *10 vor 11*, 27.4.1992, RTL.

PAGE 186 | 'The Modest Great Russian Sky . . .' Quotation montage from Platonov, *Chevengur*.

PAGE 189 | 'Don't fall, star, my star, stay / there, send the cold, send the light': Paul Celan's version of a line by Sergei Yesenin. Translated here from Celan's German.

FIGURES 77–81 | 'The Coup in Moscow: On the 2nd Anniversary of the Event', *News & Stories*, 16.8.1993, Sat. 1, by Christel Buschmann.

→ 'Mozart and the Coup', Primetime, 1.12.1991, RTL, with Frank Michael Beyer.

FIGURE 78 | On the second day, gunmen show up at the White House, the seat of parliament defended by President Yeltsin's supporters, dressed as Belarusian officers or Cossacks.

FIGURES 80–81 | The dismantling of the monument to Felix Dzerzhinsky on the evening of the third day of the coup. Dzerzhinski, a confidant of Rosa Luxemburg's, was the first chief of the GPU, the Soviet secret and security police.

PAGE 196 | 'Falling in love with tanks under your windows': Quotation montage from Svetlana Alexievich, *Secondhand Time* (Bela Shayevich trans.) (New York: Random House, 2016).

PAGE 196 | 'Semantic Fields of Intimacy': Quotation montage from Platonov, *Chevengur*.

FIGURES 82–3 | 'Workers' Paradise as Dream Factory: Boris Groys on the Mass Culture of Utopia', *News & Stories*, 15.2.2004, Sat. 1. The conversation and the images in the film refer to an exhibition at the Schirn Museum, Frankfurt.

The sensational and much-visited exhibition DREAM FACTORY COMMUNISM at the Schirn in Frankfurt showed testimonies to Soviet artistic propaganda as well as its echoes in contemporary SOZ ART, which takes up the traditions of the thirties and criticizes, caricatures and transforms. A closer examination of the images reveals that they do not merely obey purposes, nor that the conscious intentions of the artists alone have shaped them. Rather, feelings go into the pictorial representations, and utopias of the addressees of this 'advertising without commercial content'. This gives the pictures warmth. This collective unconsciousness is what makes the exhibition so appealing: Mass Culture of Utopia.

The media theorist, art critic and exhibition organiser Boris Groys, involved in this exhibition, reports.

→ 'Art as Power's Ape. Boris Groys on Deconstruction, Nature and Gruesome Images,' *News & Stories*, 21.11.2004, Sat. 1.

In connection with the filming of Alexander Kluge and his team in Moscow, see, in addition to the conversation with Primakov ('The Man for All Seasons. Meeting Russian politician Yevgeny Primakov', *News & Stories*, 17.10.2004, Sat 1.), the following programmes:

'A Woman Who Knows What She Is Talking About: Russia's Internationally Most Popular Crime Novelist Alexandra Marinina', *10 vor 11*, 16.2.2004, RTL.

' "I Am Your Voice": The Russian Presidential Candidate Irina Chakamada', *10 vor 11*, 25.10.2004, RTL.

'The Rarest Object that Fell From the Sky: Dr Andrei Ivanov on a Meteorite Called Kaidun', *Primetime*, 31.10.2004, RTL.

'A Man of the First Hour in Chernobyl: Dr Vladimir Shikalov in Action during the Nuclear Catastrophe', *News & Stories*, 7.11.2004, Sat. 1.

'Fine-Tuning the Universe: Prof Dr Abhay Ashtekar on the Mysterious World of Quantum Gravitational Loops', *10 vor 11*, 8.11.2004, RTL.

'Fathers and Sons: Viktor Erofeyev on his Documentary Novel GOOD STALIN', *10 vor 11*, 15.11.2004, RTL.

'Melnikov's House: A Son Defends the Famous Cylinder Construction of His Genius Father', *Primetime*, 5.12.2004, RTL.

'The Battle on Ice: Sergei Prokofiev's Film Music for Eisenstein's Classic *Alexander Nevsky*', *10 vor 11*, 13.12.2004, RTL.

'A Biologist in Russia's North: Dr. Mikhail Glazov on a Sparse but Sensitive Ecology', *10 vor 11*, 20.12.2004, RTL.

FIGURES 84–5 | Contact sheet and film still from 'The Man for All Seasons: Meeting Russian Politician Yevgeny Primakov', *News & Stories*, 17.10.2004, Sat. 1.

FIGURES 86–8 | 'The Rainmakers of Moscow: Ensuring Favourable Weather Conditions at the Victory Celebration on the 9th of May', *10 vor 11*, 3.7.1995, RTL, camera: Stefan Zimmer.

FIGURES 91–6 | 'Russia's Diana: Farewell to the Popular Representative of the People, Galina Starovoitova, Shot by Commandos in St Petersburg', *News & Stories*, 11.1.1999, Sat. 1.

FIGURES 98–101 | √-1. Imaginary numbers.

Imaginary numbers cannot be 'counted'. The operations with complex numbers do not correspond to objective quantities in the external world. But they are 'imaginable'. In French, to imagine is called *imaginer*. This is why Descartes called such operations with complex numbers imaginary = i.

For Velimir Khlebnikov, the mathematical world of signs is autonomous. It is independent of the extra-mathematical and extra-poetic environment. He is concerned with the music of things. √-1 is for him the 'summit of all knowledge'. This root means freedom. Freedom for rebellious words. He and Daniil Charms compare imaginary numbers to trees and their roots to rhizomes. Polyphony can best be expressed by imaginary numbers. i does not denote a single line on the surface or in space, but always something geometrically multiple. i = 'two-faced root'. Heinrich von Kleist points out that mermaids appear 'as the result of a root-counting process'. An interpreter or expert in the White House, in order to understand Russian phenomena, would have to know not only the Russian language but also learn non-Euclidean geometry.

→ Anke Niederbudde, *Mathematische Konzeptionen in der russischen Moderne: Florenskij-Chlebnikov-Charms* (Munich: Verlag Otto Sagner 2006).

→ Detlef Laugwitz, *Bernhard Riemann 1826–1866: Wendepunkte in der Auffassung der Mathematik* (Basel: Birkhäuser, 1995).

'Language of the stars' is an expression of Khlebnikov's. See also:

→ 'Language of the Stars: "Algebra of Words" in the Russian Avantgarde', *10 vor 11*, 27.6.2016, RTL, with Dr Anke Niederbudde.

FIGURE 101 | In the circle of a children's-book publishing house that had published children's books from England and Russia during the tsarist era—*The Annotated Mother Goose*, for example—a group of poets including Kornei Ivanovich Chukovsky and Osip Mandelstam gathered after 1917. We have the latter to thank for the poem about

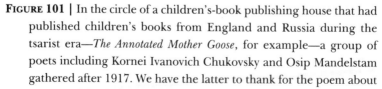

the tram that has lost its child, the little tram. Fortunately, the little tram is found again. '"Hello, This is the Crocodile!" Dr. Gertraud Marinelli-König about Children's Books in the Russian Revolution (1920–1930)', *News & Stories*, 3.2.2016, Sat. 1.

FIGURES 108–10 | '140 Years of Russian Light. Dr Natasha Drubek: "From Icons to Russian Silent Film"', *News & Stories*, 21.3.2017, Sat. 1.

FIGURES 108 | The inventor's name is reproduced in the caption, in the spelling adopted in Germany in 1890.

PAGE 283 | 'The dark phase of 1/48 of a Second [. . .] no image is visible': In the classic film cameras developed by the Lumière brothers and Edison, the film negative has perforated strips. The celluloid (Italian: *la pellicola*, the skin) is guided along the camera's optics by this perforation. The transport phase lasts 1/48 of a second. During this time, the film remains unexposed. The technology of the projection devices corresponds to that of the cameras. Here, the perforation of the print is guided along the light source. During this transport phase, it is dark in the cinema for 1/48 of a second. This is how cinema is created with 24 frames per second. One-and-a-half-hours of film offers the viewer's brain a 45-minute break for independent activity.

Due to its inertia, the eye 'sees' a flowing, uninterrupted image. 'The eye sees' is a figure of speech here. It is a vigilant, numerically strong community of synapses, in heavy traffic and counter-traffic among themselves, a republic behind the mound of vision, way back in the mind, which creates the images. We are completely unaware of the dark phase. The synapses, however, in their work far below consciousness, enjoy the break. The dark phase encourages them to indulge in 'dreamy freedom'. In the course of history, however, the DARK PHASE is something horrible. It contains all that the heart does not want to talk about. The reflex is to remain silent. The dark phase and light phase take place simultaneously, unlike in film. In 1937: marriages, births, advancements, inventions, happy repairs, progress of projects. At the same time, the 'flash of the revolver in the convict's neck'. Here nothing can separate the light and dark phases. Hans Magnus Enzensberger refers to political measures that nevertheless try to do so as an act of 'surgery like Russian roulette'.

The Cinema in the Viewer's Head

A smell of mud and fish protein mixed with salt water. A strong breeze from the Adriatic's opposite coast. From the Cinema Palace, in the shade past all the boutiques, you reach the Excelsior Hotel Palace. I am sitting on the terrace, opposite me the Nobel Prize–winner Prof. Dr Kandel. He seems ageless.

– Professor, you say that the groups of brain cells that 'spark' billions of times every second, like in a concert, they speak a language that we do not understand and cannot speak. How do they speak?

– In the length of a fraction of a second. They can make this like a syllable or like the very short sounds of birdcalls.

– And between these apparently very rapid processes and the environment, nothing but misunderstandings?

– Which have coordinated with each other in evolution. Only the misunderstandings remained.

– And how do the impressions in cinema relate to this?

– For 48 fractions of a second it is dark, for 48 fractions of a second an image is exposed. For the brain, this is an interesting kind of movement.

– Which of these does the brain 'see'? Does it see the black between the images?

– Like being drugged. It 'sees' the black continuously, while the same brain sees the 'image' as continuous, albeit 'flickering'. A polyphonic impression.

– Unconscious?

– Non-conscious. Does the stimulus that makes the brain dream lie in the rapid change?

– But with a film lasting two hours, one whole hour of darkness (the brain works autonomously) and a whole hour of images (the brain responds to stimuli).

– And that is better than reality.

The Nobel Prize–winner had developed his elementary research on the nervous system of a sea snail the size of a rabbit. Two streams of information related to the cinema, he said, would not be something that this intelligent animal with its large but not numerous nerves could respond to. Only the human head is set up as a cinema (and has been since the Stone Age). Personally, Kandel said, he did not consider the pleasure he derives from going to the cinema from time to time as inferior to his scientific activity from which he, however, derives his income.

PAGE 279 | 'How the Soul Nourishes Itself on Light and Dark': Werner Nekes on "What Is Time in Film?"', *Primetime*, 16.1.2000. RTL.

FIGURES 154–5 | 'It's good when / On the gibbet, in the face of terror, / You shout: / "Drink Cocoa — Van Houten!"'—Triptych Mayakovski, 2018. From Vladimir Mayakovski's poem 'A Cloud in Trousers', first published in 1915. Translated by Andrey Kneller. Available at https://www.unlikely stories.org/old/archives/cloudintrousers.html

PAGES 308–09 | 'Semantic Fields on Reason, Hope, Future'. Quotation montage from Platanov, *Chevengur*.

PAGE 311 | 'Protego ergo sum.' According to Carl Schmitt, based on Thomas Hobbes, the monarch's classic motto 'I protect, therefore I am.' The sovereign's authority is founded on this promise, and this authority dissolves when the sovereign cannot follow through.

FIGURES 161–6 | 'Beacon of Mathematics / Beacon of Reason.' From the installation of 20 July 2019 at the Grand Palais, Paris, on the occasion of the 50th anniversary of the lunar landing in 1969.

PAGE 317 | 'A Plan of Eisenstein's [. . .]':

In the month of 1929 following Black Friday (a Thursday in Russia)—a major stock-market crash which triggered a recession that did not end until 1934—the Russian Sergei Eisenstein visited Dublin's James Joyce in Paris. I am moved to see the two of them together in the dark flat. Perhaps it only seems dark to me because the great poet is almost blind. A strange mixture of languages between the two. Joyce has pulled out a gramophone record. On it, a reading from *Ulysses*. He wants to play it for his guest. That day they do not get the chance. Eisenstein, for his part, had brought with him a script of hundreds of pages as well as some stills from a number of screen tests. In a leather carrier bag, far from Russia, dangling heavily off his arm, lugging it up the five flights of stairs. Joyce was unable to read anything. Among great misunderstandings, the two geniuses buried themselves in the project.

In the manner of *Ulysses*, Eisenstein thought, the film plot was limited to a single day. A household and a day's work in socialist Russia. A proletarian couple. Eisenstein thought that all the categories of the Marxian conceptual cosmos would be touched on throughout such a day of work and life.

My publisher Ulla Berkéwicz was the one who made me aware of my two idols' Parisian encounter. With my collaborators and friends, directors like Tom Tykwer, we produced a collection of attempts to recreate at least some scenes of the Eisenstein project that never came to fruition.

For readers of the *Container* who've made it this far, the adjoining link is available →

DVD I: Marx and Eisenstein in the Same House

What did Eisenstein want to film? It's about his notations on the 'cinematization' of *Capital*. What do texts written by Marx almost 150 years ago sound like in 2008? It has to do with an approach via the ear. Where is the boundary between antiquity and modernity when it comes to ideology? In 1929? In 1872? Earlier? How would money, if it could think, explain itself? Can capital say 'I'? Dietmar Dath on the core content of Marx's famous book. Sophie Rois on money, love and Medea.

DVD II: All Things Are Enchanted People

What does 'commodity fetish' mean? Which sorceries, according to Marx and Eisenstein, cause capital's gentle and stormy violence? Why are people not the masters of what they create? What does 'association of free producers' mean? Do revolutions fail for lack of time or on principle? What does 'all things are enchanted people' mean? With a film by Tom Tykwer on the richness of details in a film image as soon as you're interested in the production process of the things that can be seen.

DVD III: Paradoxes of the Exchange Society

We live in SECOND NATURE. This is what Marx is about. This 'social nature', like the biological one Darwin explored, is aware of evolution (and Marx would have liked to become Darwin's cousin for the economy and society). But in this 'social change', most things behave differently than in original nature: dogs do not exchange bones. Humans, who live in a modern society, obey the principle of exchange. How do you read *Das Kapital*? What does exchange value mean? Should Marx have written more books, e.g. on the political economy of use-value, the political economy of revolution or the political economy of labour power?

More recently, on the diaries of Eisenstein's project: Elena Vogman, *Dance of Values: Sergei Eisenstein's Capital Project* (Zurich: Think Art Diaphanes, 2019).

From the contact sheets to Alexander Kluge: *News from Ideological Antiquity. Marx-Eisenstein-Capital.*

nadia venedig 09

nadia venedig 10

nadia venedig 11

nadia venedig 12

nadia venedig 13

nadia venedig 14

nadia venedig 15

nadia venedig 16

FIGURE 184

FIGURE 184_09 | From *The Eifel Tower*: *King Kong and the White Woman*, film from 26.12.1988, *10 vor 11*, RTL. 'Utopia's Getting Better All the Time While We're Waiting For It'.

FIGURE 184_10 | From *News from Ideological Antiquity*: *Marx-Eisenstein-Capital*. Marx teaching an early human.

FIGURE 184_11 | *From News from Ideological Antiquity*: *Marx-Eisenstein-Capital* (DVD II, Nr. 9). Oskar Negt and Aleander Kluge debating the line 'Revolutions are the locomotives of history'.

FIGURES 184_13 AND 14 | From *News from Ideological Antiquity*: *Marx-Eisenstein-Capital* (DVD III, Nr. 5). Two pianists studying the score of the only opera to ever take place in a factory: Max Brand's *Maschinist Hopkins* (1929).

FIGURE 184_16 | From *News from Ideological Antiquity*: *Marx-Eisenstein-Capital* (DVD II, Nr. 1). Director Tom Tykwer's sequence.

FIGURE 185

FIGURE 185_06 | From 'The Rebirth of *Tristan* from the Spirit of the Battleship Potemkin. With Werner Schroeter' in *News from Ideological Antiquity. Marx-Eisenstein-Capital* (DVD I, Nr. 20).

Richard Wagner's musical drama TRISTAN UND ISOLDE is about the utopia of love and is considered a major work of musical modernism. The filmmaker and opera director Werner Schroeter has staged Wagner's musical drama in Duisburg in such a way that, at the last moment of their lives, the utopia of the revolution so-to-speak, the doomed sailors of the Battleship Potemkin (following the battle-ship's escape from Bulgaria, they've been delivered to the tsar) have this utopia of love played for them, or rather, they invent it. TRISTAN AND ISOLDE on the Battleship Potemkin. 'The rebirth of TRISTAN From the Spirit of the Revolution: Werner Schroeter Stages Richard Wagner in Duisburg', *10 vor 11*, 2.11.1998, RTL.

nadia venedig 17

nadia venedig 18

nadia venedig 19

nadia venedig 20

nadia venedig 21

nadia venedig 22

nadia venedig 23

panzerkreuzer

FIGURE 186

Figure 185_18 and 19 | From 'The Collective Worker of Verdun. With Helge Schneider', in *News from Ideological Antiquity. Marx–Eisenstein–Capital* (DVD II, Extras, Nr. 6). About German miners digging blast tunnels. In competition with their French colleagues who, in terms of blast-tunnel expertise, are by no means their inferiors. Whoever digs deeper and detonates first, blows up the other one. For a visitor from Sirius, the film suggests, it would look like cooperation.

Figure 186_20 | The concierges of Paris. Scene based on Eisenstein's script sketch for his Karl Marx Project. The concierges, who have been supervising the Parisian apartment buildings since the Great French Revolution, have invested their savings in shares of the Siberian Railway. Now the Soviet government is not paying them back. As a result, the concierges make sure that Communists in Paris do not win a majority in elections. This, Eisenstein says, is one of the challenges to which my film must respond. How do we win back the concierges of Paris without dividend warrants? With Ute Hannig. *News from Ideological Antiquity*: *Marx–Eisenstein–Capital* (DVD III, Extras, Nr. 3).

Figure 186_23 | Closing sequence to *News from Ideological Antiquity*: *Marx–Eisenstein–Capital*. It concerns Marx's 'real' grave in London. A simple ledger-stone in the Jewish section of the graveyard in no way identical to the monument erected by the International.

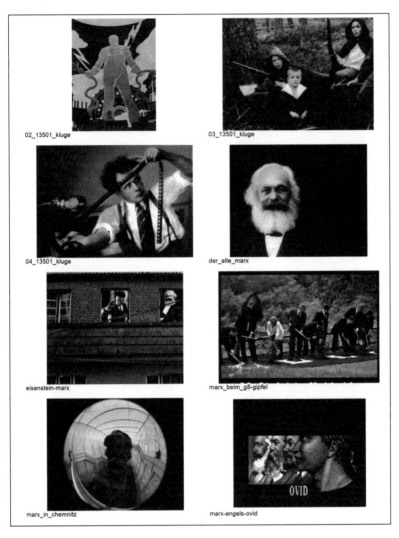

FIGURE 187

FIGURE 187_02_13501 | The collective worker of Chicago. Poster at the World's Fair in New York in 1939: 'Best Years of Our Lives'.

FIGURE 187_03_13501 | To the right of the image, Sergei Eisenstein.

FIGURE 187_*marx-engels-ovide*: 'Eisenstein and Marx in the same house.'

PAGE 321 | 'Ever since people began to sell the best of what they make, they have—enigmatically intertwined with one another in such doing—carved invisible marks into the things they produce: COM-MODITIES. This occurs in a spiritual cuneiform. 'Electrified' from the beginning. In this respect, a spiritual fire glows within all commodities. And within that, in turn, the living and the dead burn—all those whose lifetimes are built into these things.'

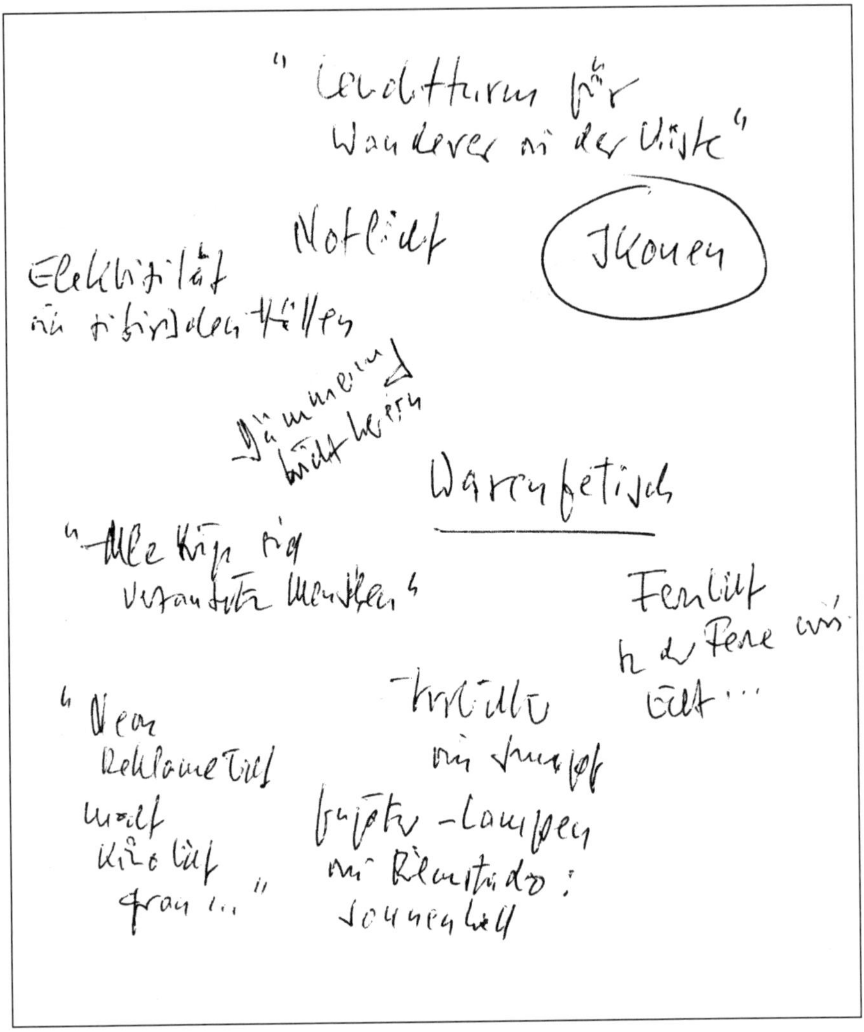

FIGURE 188

Karl Marx, *Capital*, VOL. 1., SECTION r, 1887: 'The fetish-like character of commodities and the secret thereof. A commodity appears, at first sight, a very trivial thing, and easily understood. Its analysis shows that it is, in reality, a very queer thing, abounding in metaphysical subtleties . . . ' (Samuel Moore and Edward Aveling trans.)

Torch of freedom
What is a commodity fetish?

What in the festive events of the great French Revolution, equipped by the stage designer David, is called the TORCH OF FREEDOM appears (and has for centuries) inside the real people of Western Europe as an incandescent light or smouldering bit of wood; one can also say: a rebelliousness that lends itself to various uses.

The new INNER LIGHT—is it a RELIGIOUS FOUNTAIN OF YOUTH? It is the seat of saving, of diligence, of the accumulation of wealth. Necessity and oppression never extinguish this light, rather it is *fanned* by external compulsion. No human community has experience with how a people could survive as TORCHES OF FREEDOM. The torch of freedom as shown at public events or carried in a monument's hand are only allegories.

Suddenly, 200 years after the 'invention of freedom', it turns out that all the objects that people exchange with each other have an illumination from within. The exchange value shines as an image or plan, just like consciousness once did in the past.

With this reference, Antonio Gutierrez-Fernandez, chairman of the Academy in Havana, will open his lecture to the Central Committee. The small circle of defenders of the Republic meets once a week for educational lectures. The root of revolutionary change in Cuba was immediate outrage against the dictator Batista's regime: flaming. But to create the 'passionate perseverance' required by the defence of the Republic of Cuba, a second spark had to be discovered, an expectation of salvation, a glow independent of a tyrant's presence. The Spaniards, Gutierrez-Fernandez says in his lecture, bring EUROPEAN STRUCTURE to the island, but in a pre-industrial form. It does not carry any light within. Some thoughts of possessiveness and revenge, yes. They import slaves, they exterminate natives.

Examples from Marx will not explain how the Cuban light of the soul works. But such an INNER LIGHT has been demonstrably measured. Otherwise, Cuba could not exist as the only socialist country in the world at present (apart from the PRC). Gutierrez-Fernandez contradicts the thesis that the Cubans are an EASILY INFLAMMABLE PEOPLE. Rather, an incandescent light or light of the soul glows in every human being (at a short distance from the skin, the aura shines all around). These appearances of light, what Gutierrez-Fernandez calls ORIENTATION LIGHTS, will, however, be masked by the billions of sparks in the commodities that also flood Cuba as soon as republican defences fail. The lights, apparently lit by people, which indicate the use value of commodities like GRAVE LIGHTS OF DEAD LABOUR as it were, cover up the INNER LIGHT; that is the reason why it is more often visible in years of shortage and times of need.

PAGE 350 | Thanks to having been burned in 1933, the Reichstag building, which had been fought over in the last days of April 1945, stood empty. The stone ashlar was built at the time of the founding. The deputies of the Reich were never reallyable to govern the political colossus, the 'German Reich' erected in 1871. In the cellars of the burnt ruins (the ruin-like character concerns the interior, not the imposing exterior of the stone building with its four corner towers), rooms for children and women in childbirth were erected and used between 1943 and 1945. Now, in September 2019, the president of the Bundestag, Schäuble, received 11 children who had been born there, among them Walter Waligora and Mareile Van der Wyst. The 'children' were over 70 years old.

FIGURE 171 | 'Column of Progress'. After a motif of James Ensor, projected on Stage Nr 3, 'Profiterol', by Katharina Grosse. From the exhibition *The Power of Music. The Opera: Temple of Seriousness,* kunsthalle weishaupt, Ulm. Printed on aluminium, 2019.

FIGURE 177 | Graffiti in the Reichstag, *10 vor 11*, 8.5.1995. RTL.

ILLUSTRATION CREDITS

Figures 1–2: Matthias Ziegler, Munich

Figure 14: Gerald Zörner (gezett), Berlin

Figure 23: Archiv Klaus Wagenbach (01_0240_B)

Figure 44: Marianne Van den Lemmer collection / FUEL Design & Publishing, Londong. From Olesya Turkina, *Soviet Space Dogs* (London: FUEL Publishing, 2014), p.31.

Figure 45: luliiawhite / Adobe Stock

Figure 47: picture alliance / ullstein bild

Figure 56: Shutterstock

Figure 57: Detail of a drawing by Sir William Rothenstein, 1933, Collection of the London School of Economics and Political Science. Photo: J. R. Freeman & Co Ltd. Reproduced with kind permission of the London School of Economics.

Figure 62: From Horst Scheibert, *Die 6. Panzerdivision*, Eggolsheim: Edition Dörfler im Nebel Verlag, no year given.

Figure 103: From Michael J. Benton, *Paläontologie der Wirbeltiere* (H.-U. Pfretschner trans.) (Munich: Verlag Dr Friedrich Pfeil, 2007), p. 358 (middle image).

Figure 104: Benton, *Paläontologie der Wirbeltiere*, p. 25.

Figure 105: Benton, *Paläontologie der Wirbeltiere*, p. 379.

Figures 148–51: From Eva Maurer, *Wege zum Pik Stalin. Sowjetische Alpinisten, 1928-1953* (Zurich: Chronos, 2010).

Figure 172: © Gerhard Richter, 2020 (04022020)

Figure 176: Using a piece of elephant skin from Anselm Kiefer. Reproduced with kind permission of Anselm Kiefer.

Figures 178–81: Thomas Demand, from the *Melnikov Project*, 2010 © VG Bild-Kunst, Bonn, 2020.

Figure 183: Germanisches National Museum Nuremberg, Deutsches Kunstarchiv, DKA_NL May, Ernst_IB2-0062a

All other images are from the author's archive.

ACKNOWLEDGEMENTS

As with my previous books, I owe a great debt of gratitude to my editor Wolfgang Kaußen. I thank Thomas Demand and Katya Inozemtseva of the Garage Museum of Contemporary Art for the inspiration for this book. My assistants Barbara Barnak, Beata Wiggen and Gülsen Döhr were indispensable. I would like to thank Ute Fahlenbock for the imaginative production of the texts and pictures that often deviate from the usual.

LIST OF STORIES